D1539286

DARK

OBSESSION

A True Story
of
Incest and Justice

SHELLEY SESSIONS
with PETER MEYER

G. P. PUTNAM'S SONS/NEW YORK

G. P. Putnam's Sons
Publishers Since 1838
200 Madison Avenue
New York, NY 10016

Library of Congress Cataloging-in-Publication Data

Sessions, Shelley.
    Dark obsession : a true story of incest and justice / Shelley
Sessions with Peter Meyer.—1st American ed.
        p.   cm.
    ISBN 0-399-13497-2
    1. Incest—Texas—Case studies.   2. Child molesting—Texas—Case
studies.   3. Sessions, Shelley.   I. Meyer, Peter, date.
II. Title.
HQ72.U53S37   1989   89-36591 CIP
362.7'6—dc20

Printed in the United States of America
1   2   3   4   5   6   7   8   9   10

This book has been printed on acid-free paper.

CONTENTS

This book is dedicated to all the children out there who are suffering from child abuse and to the people who have made me what I am today.

The Layfields, who went out on a limb for me, took me into their home and loved me as one of their own.

Williams, Pattillo & Squires, my lawyers, my friends, my "fathers," who believed in me and made it possible.

My brother, Michael, who will one day understand all this and know how much I love him.

And most of all, my husband, Rob, whose undying love and understanding have made me complete and given us the joy of our new baby boy, Brandon.

I love you all.

—Shelley Sessions

No one really knows how involved it all was. The details of it. They just think that it happened a couple of times—or once.

They don't know about him taking pictures of me. They don't know how really sick it was. They just think, "Oh, he made a little mistake and everything is okay now." That's how they think. They don't think of all the obsession. . . .

PROLOGUE

A REASON FOR BEING

Everyone calls it the last taboo—except those for whom it becomes a daily duty to terror. For them, the children, the centuries of forbidding mean little. They feel only tiny bits of time and the slow murder of their souls. Even when incest occurs between two consenting adults, it is, in almost every culture, a sinful and illegal act with unhealthy consequences. But when children have their innocence plucked from them by the center of their universe, there is mostly hell to pay.

The story told in these pages is about one young girl's hell. Shelley Sessions lived for eight years as the victim of her father's sexual perversions. From the time that she was eight years old, until she was sixteen, he molested her. A big man who should have been her first and last protector became her tormentor. She became a hostage.

To know something about incest is to begin to appreciate a special brand of terror inflicted on many young children. We begin to understand why James B. Twitchell, in his *Dreadful Pleasures: An Anatomy of Modern Horror,* says that "The fear of incest underlies all horror myths in our culture."

But despite unanimous agreement about its evils, the last taboo lives on. In 1976 there were 6,000 reports of child sexual abuse in America, most of them incestuous. By 1986, according to the National Committee for the Prevention of Child Abuse, there were 250,000 reported cases, over 72 percent of them perpetrated by a father or stepfather. Because of the shame and secrecy that pervade the incestuous relationship, those numbers are considered by most experts to be just the tip of an iceberg—as many as 90 percent of incest cases aren't reported.

Periodically, we get glimpses of the mass beneath the surface of public reports. In 1984, for example, after ABC aired a television movie about incest and displayed telephone numbers of special "hot lines" for victims, social agencies in thirty-five cities reported 2,000 calls.

Most estimates put the number of victims in the millions. Some say that as many as 12 percent of American girls between the ages of five and seventeen are sexually victimized. The American Psychological Association estimates that 12 to 15 million American women have experienced abuse by a relative, in degrees of seriousness ranging from fondling to intercourse.

One reason incest is so pervasive is that it has no social-class boundaries to contain it. Stereotypes about victim and victimizer often don't work.

"The man next door who goes to church and gives to charity is sometimes a perpetrator of incest," said Dr. Stan J. Katz, a Beverly Hills psychologist and frequent expert witness for the Los Angeles superior court.

"He was chief of staff at a hospital and we belonged to the Cadillac and country club set," one incest victim said about her father. It is not an atypical situation.

Shelley Sessions' father was rich and respected in the small Texas community where the family lived. Shelley had nice clothes and expensive horses, plenty of toys, her own room—everything a girl could want. But affluence is not an inoculation against incest. Money and community respect don't stop fathers from sneaking into their daughters' bedrooms at night.

Nor does money and class stop the pain.

Incest victims report a kind of emotional numbness that sets in as their fathers or stepfathers begin to molest them. It is an instinctive, protective trick, a form of denial, not of the incest, but of the feeling of overwhelming confusion and revulsion that accompanies it. "The feelings literally die inside and what you have left is a shell," said Dr. Kathleen Oitzinger, a therapist for incest victim Cheryl Pierson, a New York girl charged with killing her father in 1986.

Victims can't feel good about anything, including themselves. Their sense of shame is total. And it can last for years after the abuse has ceased.

Why this is so, according to psychiatrists and sex-abuse victims, has to do with the special relationship that child and parent have. Children are completely dependent on their parents. They are built to trust in the parents' prowess as protectors. And when a protector becomes a violator, a mirror is shattered. The act robs the child of the ability to trust anyone, including herself.

"Trust is the foundation of a child's life," wrote incest victim Lana Lawrence in *The Washington Post.* "My father exploited that trust through incest. Without the ability to trust, it is impossible to develop loving relationships."

Another reason incest continues is because children are such easy marks. They don't seek help *against* their parents because they seek help *from* their parents. Incest is a cruel blow precisely because it robs children of their only place of refuge. In this way sexual abuse by a father or stepfather often goes on for years. Few other crimes can be so successfully committed for such long periods of time.

Incest is also an invisible violation to all but those directly involved. Unlike physical abuse—the burns, bruises and broken bones that kill more than 2,000 American children every year—the effects of sexual abuse are not so easily observed. Worse, the child often doesn't understand what is happening; and when she does understand, she is often so burdened by shame, frequently conditioned to feel that shame by her abuser, that she says nothing. There are no broken ribs or skulls in this process, but the emotional and psychological blows are nonetheless severe.

Victims blame themselves for what is happening, yet continue to look to parents for approval. A silence descends over the child's emotional life; a terrible paralysis of feeling. The great taboo is characterized by a great silence—one of the most insidious lock-steps known.

"It's difficult to believe it even if you think it," said Karla Digirolamo, executive director of the New York Governor's Commission on Domestic Violence. "Incest is a taboo issue. It is an ugly issue. We as a society don't want to talk about it. Some can't listen to it."

The secret—referred to as "the secret trauma," "the common secret," a "conspiracy of silence" or simply The Secret—is so well-kept by the victim that no one even suspects the abuse. And the abuser, supported by a culture which believes in the sanctity of the home and the authority of parents over children, is safe, doubly protected.

So it was that in the case of Cheryl Pierson, who paid a classmate $1,000 to kill her father, neighbors and friends recalled seeing Cheryl in bed with her father watching television. As a friend said, "I thought I was the sick one to presume that it was anything but innocent."

Most victims learn ways to cope with the double-bind of fear of their abuser and dependence on him; they develop ways of living with revulsion over the act and powerlessness to do anything about it. They block feeling. They look the other way. They numb themselves psychologically.

The abuse becomes a pattern; and that pattern is part of the family unit—which is the child's sole source of comfort. And added to the burden of shame and guilt is a fear that in revealing the abuse, the child will break the family apart. That becomes yet another reason for not speaking out.

"Protecting the parent is the child's way of maintaining hope," said Dr. Alvin Rosenfeld, director of psychiatry for the Jewish Child Care Association of New York. "Abused children bend themselves and do whatever they have to do to keep a family together."

Dr. Ruth Cohen, a psychiatrist and assistant clinical professor at Cornell University Medical College, said that "There's a collusion of silence that often exists to keep this quiet at a tremendous emotional expense." But there are also "many reasons to deny that the abuse is going on," she continued. "Children rely heavily on their parents for security. An intact family is very important to them. They fear foster care and they are embarrassed about what has happened."

The mothers of girls abused by fathers and stepfathers are often given an excuse for looking the other way. Daughters don't want to hurt them or precipitate a fight that would break the family apart.

In some cases mothers go even further. "My mother pushed me into those roles" of substitute wife and mom, one victim reports, "because it made life easier for her. She would say, 'Your father's coming home—you can make him feel better.' I understood somehow that I was a big little girl and that if I did what I was told, no one in the house would get hit, and if I didn't, everyone would get hit."

Damned if she does and damned if she doesn't, the victim is also being given a perverse kind of power: thus a little girl can control the mood of the household.

But most incest victims simply suffer in silence until old enough to leave home—then they carry the pain with them and bear the scars of the abuse for years. Those that don't speak out, often act out. They beat and abuse their own children. They shunt friends and lovers. Sometimes they kill their abusers to escape.

But always the oppressive, coercive silence is only a mask. It hides its opposite: rage. Hate. Anger. The cycle of abuse is a difficult one to break. We will see in this story how that cycle is created and perpetuated. Abuse creates anger; anger, abuse.

One girl, after years of being sexually abused by her father, took an ax to him while he slept on the living room couch. She was exonerated by a jury.

After her celebrated 1987 trial, Cheryl Pierson was sentenced to six months in jail for her role in her father's murder. The judge in the case said he received more than 100 letters expressing sympathy for what she had been through. But he still couldn't understand, he told the girl, why she couldn't have said anything.

Lana Lawrence, ten years after a thirteen-year incestuous ordeal ended, put it this way, in describing why coming forward was such a frightening act. "The thought of testifying against my father in court was horrifying. I was breaking the silence that he demanded I keep—I was betraying him. I felt ashamed, as if I were to blame for the abuse and should have been able to stop him. As I testified, I could see the hate in his eyes. My mother sat next to him; I had been abandoned. Her support of my father strengthened my belief that I was a very bad person."

The terrible tragic irony of incest is that many of the child's worst fears—about being blamed for the abuse, about tearing the family apart, about not being believed—are frequently born out. "I've seen some families go wild," said Joyce N. Thomas, director of Children's Hospital's Division of Child Protection in Washington. "It can be dangerous. . . . They often blame the daughter."

Even if a child manages the courage to spill the beans, she has to face intense public scrutiny if the case goes to court. And many children crack under the pressure. They can make terrible witnesses.

Prosecutors in the Seattle area's King County report that they get conviction rates of 80 to 90 percent on their felony cases—only 60 percent on molestation cases.

On the other side of the country, Elizabeth Holtzman, New York City's Kings County District Attorney, complained that a 19th-century state law prevents conviction of a child molester without evidence corroborating the child's testimony. "The problem is that sexual abuse of children hardly ever occurs in public," said Holtzman. "The state trusts a child to tell the truth when a bicycle is stolen, but not if she has been raped, or if her father has sexual relations with her, or if her stepfather or a stranger sexually abuses her." One study of 145 cases of sexual abuse in New York showed that only two convictions could be obtained.

"The child has to endure the shame of being interviewed by police, testifying in court and being told she's a liar by many people," adds Dr. Katz. "The father may go to jail, and the parents may get divorced. That makes the child a victim twice over—once by being molested and now by being blamed for the family breakup."

Few children threatened with the responsibility of destroying their family will lightly traipse into the act of revelation.

A fragile young psyche, barely formed, is terrorized by a physical and emotional giant. Incest victims are put in such a bind that escape becomes a lifelong challenge.

Lana Lawrence's father was sentenced to two years' probation and fined $750 for his criminal sexual conduct. "My sentence was the emotional aftermath of the abuse," Lawrence wrote. "Healing the wounds of my childhood has required more than the passage of time."

Another incest victim told *New York Times* reporter Nadine Brozan that "We spend most of our adult lives being overwhelmed. We are distrustful of everyone, especially people with whom we are supposed to be close, even spouses. We tend to have extreme emotional mood swings. We are overwhelmed by a sense of worthlessness, by absolute dependency on secrecy to maintain our identity."

Salvation can come only when the cycle is broken and the secret released. For the victim the incest must move from being one's identity to being one's experience.

Says Lana Lawrence: "Over and over, I needed to recount memories of the abuse in order to accept and let them go. For all of my life, the memories controlled and haunted me. Now I had control over them."

Shelley Sessions has wrestled with the same memories. And she has recounted them, painfully, for this book. In doing so, she seeks not simply control over her own memories, but also to give control to others.

Child abuse is an insidious violation. It is a betrayal of the weakest and least protected members of society. This story is told in the hopes that the horror of such violations can be known—and stopped. Anger, abuse and distrust must be replaced by love.

"The essence of incest is secrecy," said Dr. Judith L. Herman of Harvard. "Anything that breaks the silence—breaks the taboo on talking about it—makes it more possible for victims and others to speak out."

That is Shelley's hope. She knows that incest is a crippler. But to refuse to face it is to fail oneself, as well as the tens of thousands of young people now desperately trying to escape their own hells. Shelley Sessions spoke out—not because it was easy—but because it was necessary. The last taboo should not be the last secret.

I

KIDNAP

Shelley staggered up the carpeted steps of the ranch house. The booze helped to loosen her hold on the banister and reality at the same time. It was past midnight, her mother's usual bedtime.

At the top of the stairs, a wobbling Shelley hesitated a moment, then decided to say good night to her mom.

The last couple of weeks, in more sober states, Shelley felt as though her mother were coming to understand her. After all these years, it seemed, Linda was finally on her side. They still had their fights, but with Bobby gone, Shelley felt closer to her mother than she had in all of her sixteen years. Shelley padded down the hall to what used to be her mom and dad's bedroom, the master bedroom, which was now just her mother's.

It was a hot July night, but the cool air that circulated constantly through the Circle S Ranch's house was invigorating. Shelley felt steadier than when Ricky dropped her off at the front door.

That night Shelley had had more to drink than was sensible, but much less than what she had been known to consume on recent occasions. Not that she saw anything wrong in her sprees. She was celebrating, and with good reason. The authorities had taken her millionaire father away. At last she was free. If her partying period seemed a bit extended, why shouldn't it be? After so many years of living according to her father's various whims, Shelley felt she was due for some celebration. She was more than relieved that he was finally gone. She was happier. She would have been happier if he were dead.

A slight crevice of light outlined the bottom of her mother's bedroom door. Shelley pushed it open and slowly peeked around the corner. She hadn't expected to find Linda up at this hour, but there she was, wide awake, sitting in bed with Shelley's seven-year-old brother Michael. It came as even more of a surprise finding him awake. It was well past his bedtime.

The events of the last two months had completely flipped Michael, Shelley knew. Her bright-eyed blond waif of a little brother was too confused and angry to be happy. To cheer him once Shelley and Ricky had given him a roadrunner that Ricky had caught. Michael dearly loved animals. But Michael killed it.

Linda had been begging Shelley to spend more time with him. So Shelley had spent most of that day with Michael. She took him to the mall in Corsicana, eight miles up the road, and bought him shirts and then went to the movies. Michael had had a great time. Despite all that had happened, he adored his sister. But when Shelley entered the bedroom, Michael said nothing. He seemed unusually shy, averting his eyes from Shelley's questioning if slightly unfocused gaze.

Shelley was too inebriated to notice the odd fact that although it was so late, both her mother and brother were fully clothed under the covers.

Lately, ever since her public revelations about her dad and the consequent uproar, his suicide attempt only a month before, nothing surprised Shelley. Her mom had been behaving strangely for some time, always grappling to find an anchor. Now, with Bobby gone, she was completely adrift. Money wasn't a problem, but money wasn't enough. Linda, Shelley's mother, thought her daughter was wild. Her son was depressed. She knew nothing about the businesses. Only God, it seemed, was the answer. She looked up at Shelley with her wide, dark eyes and smiled wanly. Michael said nothing.

"Good night, Mom," Shelley said perfunctorily, weaving in the doorway. "Good night, Michael."

" 'Night, Shelley," the little boy squeaked.

Shelley didn't ask what her mom and little brother were doing up at that hour. She hardly wondered. Nothing seemed odd to her anymore. For the last two months all she knew or cared about was that her father-tormentor was gone.

"Shelley," her mother called out, "I love you."

Shelley hesitated a moment, as if it had occurred to her that something *wasn't* right. But she chose not to ask. "Good night," she said again.

Linda was an emotional woman, a native Texan, mother of two. She loved Shelley, but the girl was putting her through hell. Linda felt she could no longer deny it: Shelley had the devil in her. Her church friends had convinced her. "I loved her so much," Linda would later say, "that I knew that if she hated me the rest of her life—I'd rather have her hate me than destroy herself on the streets, like she was doing."

In Linda's opinion Shelley was growing wilder by the day. Linda had heard reports that Shelley had been in Kerens, the little central Texas town, a few miles down the road, taking her blouse off in the middle of the street. Linda fretted with each new report. "Shelley was drinking and I didn't know what all she was doing. I suspected that she was doing some drugs, I don't know, but she was acting really strange." It made Linda very nervous and doubtful. Her religious friends and counselors told her that Shelley was running the show. That wasn't right. And that made Linda nervous too. She wanted to do God's will, but she wasn't sure what He wanted. So she found herself relying with increasing regularity on the words of her pastors and preachers. And they told her that Shelley should be put in her place.

After Shelley left her room that night, Linda turned her light off and waited.

In her own room, Shelley quickly undressed, slipped into her

nightgown, then collapsed onto the bed. In the adjoining bathroom, lying folded and neat on the sink, was a piece of paper that
she hadn't noticed. It was another unnoticed clue. And had she
paid more attention, had less to drink, she might have guessed
that something was wrong. "Thank you for spending time with
Michael," the note read. "Thank you for trying. I'm glad and I
love you."

Shelley Sessions, at sixteen, had been the envy of her Kerens High
School classmates. She lived on a big ranch, drove a brand-new
Silverado pickup and traveled the state with her rich dad, showing
prize cattle that she raised and cared for, getting her picture in
the newspaper. She was popular and sought after by the boys. She
was her father's darling, everyone knew. And he was a local boy
made good. Still young, handsome, and rich from his wheeling
and dealing in the volatile oil-trading business, Bobby Sessions
had a suave, honey-coated drawl that made him a dashing and
popular figure in Navarro County. His ranch stretched for a
thousand acres across the central Texas landscape just sixty miles
southeast of Dallas. His family had better than the good life.

*People often looked at me as though they were saying, "You got
it all." And we did live in a luxurious, five-bedroom house with
pool and game room, weight room—even a wine cellar. But I'd
always be thinking, "You don't know what you're talking about.
I don't have anything."*

They hadn't guessed Shelley's secret. Her emptiness was visible
only after a careful search of her eyes. And even now, with the
secret spread over the front page of the paper, many people
accused Shelley of causing the trouble. The burden of the secret
had made her tough beyond her years, but shedding it had made
her more vulnerable than she could have suspected. She was just
beginning to appreciate the complicated machinations of the
adult world, a world more precarious than she had ever imagined.
Shelley fell asleep that hot July night without seeing what was
coming—without ever guessing.

*   *   *

Shelley wasn't sure how long she had been out, but the phone must have been ringing for a long time when she finally rolled over to bump the receiver off the cradle. Why hadn't her mother answered? Shelley wondered groggily.

"Hello?" she sighed.

"Shelley, this is Talulah!" It was her mom's best friend, and she sounded hysterical. "Where's your mom?"

"I don't know," Shelley groaned.

"Well, go get her!" Talulah ordered. "Go get her!"

Shelley threw back the covers and slowly slid out of bed. She was still woozy as she stepped along the wide hall in the dark. Her mother's bedroom door was open—but Linda was not inside. Michael was gone as well. "Mom?" Shelley said. She went to the top of the stairs and called again. But there was no answer. She went back to her bedroom.

"She's not here," Shelley told Talulah.

"Okay, thank you, Shelley. 'Bye." She hung up quickly.

I got back in bed and didn't think anything of it. I mean, I was so stupid.

Less than an hour later the lights went on in Shelley's bedroom. It was still dark outside. Shelley had never heard the doorbell, but two people, a woman and man, were at her bedroom door, then walking quickly to her bedside. The woman bent over and jostled Shelley gently but firmly. Shelley covered her head with a pillow and groaned. "You have to go, Shelley," the woman whispered.

Shelley moaned, pulling the pillow down tighter.

"Hurry, Shelley," the woman kept saying as she prodded her to get up. "We're friends of your mom. We gotta go. We can't waste any time. We're here to help you."

Finally Shelley turned over and blinked groggily. Through her tired eyes she thought she recognized the lady, but wasn't sure. She didn't think she knew the man. What were they doing in her bedroom? Then she suddenly realized that something wasn't right. She sat bolt upright.

"Who are you? What do you want?"

"We're friends of your mother," said the woman, "and we've come to help you. You have to get up now."

"He must have escaped," Shelley thought. She remembered what the sheriff had told her: "If your father gets out, I'll send somebody to pick you up. Go with them." They said Bobby had been hallucinating in the hospital and that he'd threatened to kill her. She had heard death threats from Bobby himself—he called from his hospital bed. He was still obsessed with her, said the psychiatrists. "I'll get dressed," Shelley said, her mind racing.

"No, no," said the woman. "There's no time! Just hurry. We've got to go *now*."

Wearing only her nightgown and a few pieces of jewelry she still had on from her night out, dragging a blanket and pillow behind her, Shelley let herself be hustled off to a van that had been snuggled up to the front door of the house. She now recognized the woman as Sarah Conn, her mom's friend and religious counselor. A lanky boy was at the wheel—Conn's son, whom Shelley had brushed off once despite her mom's request to be nice to him. The man who'd come to her room must be Conn's husband, or so Shelley thought.

The night was still warm and clear as Shelley bolted through the big front door and into the back of the vehicle.

She was sure that her dad was now making his way home from Dallas to get her. He could do anything. And this was exactly what she'd been afraid of. She felt reassured when the van sped out of Corsicana and headed south.

"Where are we going?" Shelley asked from the back of the van as the road straightened and she began to waken.

The strangers—Shelley wished now that she had talked to them when they'd first been introduced—smiled calmly, their features lit only by the dim dashboard glow. "Someplace safe," Sarah said, repeating the same mantra of assurance: "We're friends of your mom." Shelley did feel safe—until she began asking questions. "Where did my mom go?"

Sarah Conn didn't answer.

What *did* happen to her mom? Why hadn't she taken Shelley

away herself? Shelley's questions multiplied as the distance from home increased. And, as they multiplied, Shelley began to feel less safe.

Sarah had taken the wheel. The boy sat next to her, and the husband sat in the back, next to Shelley. The miles stretched on, the road stretched on. No one said much anymore. The radio played spiritual songs and Shelley began to realize that they couldn't be taking her to any safe house for her protection. She could have gone to Ricky's for that, right down the road. Her boyfriend and his family would have protected her. Shelley glared at the big silent man next to her and knew he wasn't there to protect her but to *guard* her in case she tried to make a break.

That's when Shelley went for the door, once she knew she was being kidnapped. She got the door open in one swift move. She could hear the wind whizzing past. But the man smothered her like a blanket. He slammed the door shut.

"Where are we going?" Shelley screamed as he pushed her hard into the seat against the far side of the van. No one answered.

"Where are we going?" she asked again as the vehicle sped past Austin, one hundred fifty miles southwest of her home, and kept going.

"We are taking you to get help, Shelley," said Sarah.

Shelley screamed, "Who are you? You don't know if I need help. Who are you? Why are you doing this!"

Sarah calmly guided the truck on, but her husband, next to Shelley, looked tense. "You do need help, Shelley," said Sarah.

If I'd only paid attention to the clues, I could have gotten away. My mom had taken my truck so I couldn't leave the house. She hid it somewhere. But I had a horse I could have taken off on. I could have hid in the woods. I could have swam across the lake. I could have taken my three-wheeler. I could have done some-thing—if I had some kind of warning. I could have gotten away. I could have had somebody pick me up or something. But I just wasn't expecting it.

"I have to go to the bathroom," Shelley said.

The Conns didn't believe her and the van continued on.

One thing Shelley had learned from her father was the art of survival. And when the van finally stopped for gas near San Antonio, she went for the door again. This time she made it.

Still in her nightgown and wearing no shoes, Shelley dashed across the station's lot and onto the street, where cars braked and swerved to avoid her. The commotion, however, slowed Shelley only enough for the man and boy to catch her and drag her back to the van. It happened so quickly that none of the early-morning passersby noticed.

This time her mother's friends—her captors—threatened to tie Shelley up. They drove for what seemed like hours more, and as the sun was coming up, Shelley saw the sign announcing entry to Corpus Christi—over three hundred miles from home.

Shelley sensed the van slowing to a pace that suggested arrival. She was sore, cold and tired; but still hoped, vaguely, that, wherever they were, she was there for her safety.

The van came to a stop at a shabby guardhouse occupied by a gatekeeper. Shelley could see that they were at the entrance of some institution. A sign hung on a post: REBEKAH HOME FOR GIRLS. It was the preferred euphemism—the place was a "school" for girls with serious drug and discipline problems, founded by preacher Lester Roloff. The home was under fire from Texas education authorities for questionable discipline methods, including the use of corporal punishment.

"Oh, no," Shelley sighed. She didn't know all the details, but she had heard enough to know about the place. She could see some of the features that helped make it infamous: a Cyclone fence fanning out in either direction, topped by barbed wire the entire distance. The guard waved them through. Shelley tried to reassure herself: "No problem. I can talk my mom out of anything."

She was relieved to see other people. "There's been some mistake," she told the stern woman at the admitting desk. "My mother doesn't know what kind of place this is. She will come down here to pick me up."

There was even less sympathy from the new strangers than from the old ones.

"And while you're waiting for your mom," one of the custodians said, "you can take that off and put these on—" The woman shoved a red and white dress and shirt at Shelley. "And learn the rules. No jewelry, no makeup, no jeans, no hairspray. Dresses only." Shelley barely heard. Mechanically, she donned the new clothes. She was sure she wouldn't be staying long.

I just kept saying, "Now let me talk to my mom. Where's my mom? I want to talk to my mom." "Well, you will see your mom later." And I kept saying, "I want my mom now." And she took all my jewelry off. She said, "You can't wear jewelry here, and you don't wear makeup here, and we wear dresses and you don't wear jeans." And I was going, "Oh my God. Oh, man." I was freaking out.

Another stone-faced woman directed Shelley to a small anteroom beside the front office and told her to sit down. Shelley couldn't believe what was happening to her. Just a few hours before, she had been saying good night to Ricky, the boy she loved. Now this. As good as a million miles away and weird people all around. All she could do was hold on until her mom got there. She waited until almost noon.

"Shelley?" Shelley looked up, her eyes red with tears.

Linda was at the door, a shy smile on her pretty face. She wore a sundress and small jacket. "I flew down," she said nervously.

Shelley leaped up, tears of relief now flowing, and ran to her. "I'm so glad you came," she sobbed. "Please take me home now."

Linda seemed like Shelley's last and only ally in this strange place. She clung to her mother, overjoyed and frightened at the same time.

But Linda couldn't look her daughter in the eyes. Instead she sat down on the edge of a hard chair and motioned for Shelley to sit next to her. The sandy-haired girl slowly obeyed, incredulous. What was going on? Why did her mother seem so jumpy?

"You're not going home, Shelley," Linda finally blurted. "You have to stay here."

For a few moments Shelley just stared. Then she told her mom that she couldn't leave her. She promised to be good. But Linda started to rise.

"No!" Shelley screamed. She grabbed her mother. Linda struggled, but the girl, now in a full fit of rage and panic, proved stronger. She was holding on for dear life. Linda's jacket ripped as she pulled away.

When two burly men appeared, Shelley swung at them. Her father had once felt the same blows and laughed. Her father was the one responsible for this. Even as the guards pulled Shelley away, she kept telling herself, *My mother won't let this happen.*

"Why are you doing this to me?" Shelley sobbed.

Linda turned. "So that you can learn to be a good wife to Ricky."

Shelley was led away to a small room upstairs and dumped on a bed. She heard the lock fall into place as the "room captain" shut the door behind her. What had she done? Hadn't her father pleaded guilty? Why was *she* being locked up?

She cried fiercely. From the bed next to Shelley's, another girl tried to comfort her.

"My mom will be back," Shelley sobbed. All day she said the same thing. She waited that day, and the next. She would wait for almost a year among the prostitutes and drug pushers and juvenile delinquents before any move was made to release her.

I was sitting there, you know, just waiting for my mom to come back and get me, but she never showed up. So it was weird. I cried for the whole year.

Through her tears Shelley would gradually gain the resolve to reclaim her life.

II

A MOTEL ROOM

Shelley's journey to the Rebekah Home for Girls began five years earlier with another journey: her family's move from New Jersey to Texas.

Texas was Shelley's native state, but New Jersey was the first real home that she remembered. Houston, her birthplace, she recalled only vaguely.

But when she was eleven years old, her father changed jobs, giving up nearly fourteen years with Amerada Hess, the giant oil company, to take up with a small, aggressive new oil-trading partnership in Houston called Tampimex. And for some reason, Shelley didn't really know why, he had decided to drive instead of fly back to his native Texas. He said it was so that the kids could see the country, but Shelley didn't care to see it. But she didn't protest; even then she was afraid of her father, a big man with dark hair and a loud voice and hands that could talk to her, usually via a belt.

My father was very strict and I'd get in trouble for anything and my mom would try to take up for me and then they would get into fights and then there would be a big argument.

They drove and drove for all of one day, in the big new station wagon, her mom and dad in the front seat, her dad driving. It was the summer of 1978. Shelley and Michael, her two-year-old brother, sat in the backseat, looking out the window at the wide green spaces streaming by, all day, all day long.

When night came, Bobby pulled off the road to a place with neon lights shining in the dark. The foreboding that Shelley felt was in the strangeness of the place, and it would remain dim for years to come. The motel room was small and crowded. There were two beds. In Shelley's house all the bedrooms had just one bed, even her mom and dad's. Shelley's mom took her into the small bathroom and helped her off with her clothes and then into one of the beds. Michael was already under the covers, squirming, reluctant to go to sleep.

When Shelley slid under the covers, he kicked at her; she kicked back. They squealed. The fresh sheets and fresh room were like new toys that made them giddy. But Bobby wouldn't stand for any nonsense. He didn't want his two children fiddling, so he separated them. He put Michael with Linda and he climbed into bed with Shelley, who felt his weight as if a boulder had rolled up next to her. Her dad settled hard on the mattress, which creaked noisily. Pretending to sleep, Shelley eventually drifted off.

But then she woke with a start and realized that her dad was touching her. The room was dark and she felt her dad's big hand in her underpants. Shelley screamed. She didn't know what else to do because it frightened her so, since she didn't *think* about what to do. She was scared, in the dark, with her dad touching her like that.

Linda flipped on a light. "Shelley, what's wrong?" she said in a half-whisper.

Bobby too seemed to be waking, rubbing his eyes in the light. "What's wrong?" He looked over at Shelley, who was scrambling out of bed, rushing to her mom's side. She almost pulled Linda out of bed and into the bathroom.

"He touched me," Shelley told her. "He put his hand in my pants."

Linda was quiet. "Bob, did you touch Shelley?" she asked sternly.

Her husband was incredulous. "What?"

"You put your hands in my pants," Shelley insisted. She sobbed, frightened to death. Bobby, looking hurt, began sobbing too. Linda wasn't sure what to do.

"I must have thought it was you," Bobby told Linda.

Much later, he would remember: "I started crying; Shelley was crying. I apologized. I didn't know anything about it; I was asleep. Shelley said, 'That's okay.' We hugged each other, loved on each other and that's all there was to it."

But as Shelley would soon learn, that's not all there was to it at all.

BOBBY AND LINDA

Bobby Sessions and Linda Brotherton were ready for each other when they met at a Houston party in 1969. Bobby had just come out of a marriage that was over before it began, and Linda had escaped a marriage that had gone on far too long.

He was handsome, twenty-eight, had a good job and was hankering for some stability in his life. She was very pretty, petite, only twenty-two, and wanted a daddy for her little girl. Shelley was then just two: a cute, pixie-eyed bundle of energy who clung to her mother as often as she fought her.

Linda knew immediately that Bobby was very different from her former husband, Charles Brotherton. Bobby was a flirt, a ham, a brassy young man who seemed to know exactly what he wanted out of life. He had the steely, intense blue eyes that made people feel they were somebody when he looked at them. His first wife, he told Linda, had run away with another man just six months after they married. Linda wished that a runaway spouse had been her problem. Her husband had regularly beaten her for the last two years of their marriage. Now she needed the promise of kindness. With Bobby Sessions she seemed to find the man she felt she deserved.

They were surely in the right place for starting over. That year, 1969, was boom time in Houston, a city that boasted prosperity without zoning, a wide-open mother lode of possibility and promise.

Houston had surpassed Dallas as Texas's number-one city during the sixties. And it had come to take a place among the major metropolises of America. Ten major natural-gas pipeline companies had plopped their headquarters in the city. Oil, shipping and manufacturing industries thrived. The young and ambitious flocked to Houston from all over the country. Even the federal government, no small thanks to a Texas favorite son who had become President, contributed to Houston's growth. When the National Aeronautics and Space Administration built its manned spacecraft center just twenty-two miles away, it made Houston a name synonymous with the space age. And this was one of the greatest years of space history: 1969, the year a man first walked on the moon.

For what he wanted to do—which was make money—Bobby Sessions couldn't have been in a better place at a better time. He was working for one of the world's biggest oil companies, Amerada Hess. He had started with Hess in 1964 as a trainee in the accounting department and had gradually worked his way up, demonstrating an agile mind and a flair for sales. Bobby loved burning the midnight oil, of which there was plenty in Houston in the sixties. His first wife had worked for an oil company.

Bobby had been toiling in Hess's crude-oil department as a salesman, on his way to managing the department, when he met Diane Vittum in 1968. They lived in the same apartment complex, Cotswald Village, off Houston's Gulf Freeway, near Hobby Airport. One night she found herself at one of his parties.

"There were lots of parties," recalled Diane, "and I didn't go to very many of them, but I do remember going to that one. I don't know who I knew over there, or if my roommate knew someone over there. I met Bobby that night.

"He took me out on the balcony of the apartment and started singing this song to me, 'More,' and I thought, 'God that's fast.' "

It was fast enough for Diane to fall for him. They began dating and Bobby proved the perfect gentleman. "He would light my mother's cigarettes, and he would not let me get out of the car unless he went around and opened the door for me," she recalled.

"Even in high school, all the girls were just crazy about him," remembered Bobby's younger sister, Betty Duvall. "All the girls wanted to date Bob. He just had a way with women. And I can't put my finger on it because I was always scared of him. But he is a very gentlemanly person around women and makes them feel important."

Bobby seemed to have lots of friends. He had a good job. And he worked hard on his appearance. "His hair had to be sprayed and not one hair out of place," Diane recalled. "He had a very suave personality and I guess didn't want that image broken."

The image seemed to hold through the couple's wedding, on June 1, 1968, at the Methodist Temple in Port Arthur, Diane's hometown on the Gulf Coast, east of Houston. The ceremony cost several thousand dollars, included five groomsmen, five bridesmaids, and was, according to Bobby's sister Betty, "a very elaborate wedding, done just according to Diane's specifications. There were brunches and teas and lunches. I mean it was a big, big thing."

Diane was just twenty-two. The newlywed couple flew off to Acapulco for their honeymoon. It all seemed perfect—except for a little secret that had almost bubbled forth before the wedding. Diane had been in love with another man, a Vietnam veteran who drank too much and was hated by her parents. Bobby knew about him, but had convinced Diane that he could make her love him. Diane agreed to let him try, but as the wedding date approached, she had doubts. And Bobby seemed to be getting jealous about her every contact with other people. "We already had the invitations printed," she recalled. "And my dad came in and said, 'Look, it might be embarrassing and you would have to give people's presents back. But it's better for you not to get married now than to go through a divorce later.' And I said, 'Okay, let's not.' But Bob just started crying and pitching a fit. So I don't know if it was pity or what, but we went through with the marriage."

Then, on the honeymoon in Acapulco, she dropped a bomb: she wouldn't sleep with him. Amazingly, Bobby didn't object. "He was very patient about it," Diane recalled, "and did not force me at all. In fact, he said, 'If you'll just give us six months, I'll never force you to have sex or anything. Then, if you want to, we'll get an annulment. But just please try'—and I did."

Almost immediately, however, the gremlins burst forth. There were odd ones, like Bobby's insatiable appetite for money. Though both of them had decent jobs—Diane was a secretary for the purchasing manager of Tenneco Oil—Bobby got a paper route to supplement their income.

"He used to get up at four in the morning to throw the *Post* or the *Chronicle* on people's doorsteps," she recalled. "He mostly did it. I wasn't about to get up at four, work to six, then go to more work at seven or eight."

He also became an instant "family man"—without family. Once married, he dropped his friendships. He and Diane rarely invited people over. They both worked, they came home, had dinner together and stayed home. He was compulsive about his home life. "He never went out," remembered Diane. "In fact, if he was going to be like five minutes late coming home, he'd call me."

And he became ever more demanding of Diane. Suddenly he wanted to know where she was at almost every moment of the day. He'd call her at work, asking whom she had had lunch with. It was jealousy of a kind she hadn't seen before. "I guess when you are dating someone, it's different," she recalled. "Everything is romantic, and if someone's jealous, you think, 'They really care for me.' You don't realize it might be a sickness or it might be an obsession or it might be something wrong with that person."

Bobby began to time her trips to the grocery store—sometimes following her there, sometimes quizzing her about a five-minute delay in her return. A drive up the beach with her parents once had Bobby making frantic calls to the police and friends after she had been gone just ten minutes' time. "It was embarrassing," Diane recalled. "It was a phobia. But then the sex—I couldn't believe it because he was so patient with me. He never forced me, never forced himself on me at all."

Bobby once said to Diane's father, "I just wanted somebody to love me."

But as his possessiveness increased, the last straw for Diane came rapidly. On a Sunday night, just after Christmas, her patience had run out. After a horrible fight, she called her dad in Port Arthur and begged him to come get her. "I just thought, 'I'm becoming an animal here.' We didn't fight about money or sex, just about jealousy. I felt like a bird in a cage. I just couldn't live with it." Diane started packing her bags, throwing things into boxes. Bobby, she recalled, "was sitting there moping, with his head down, crying."

It was over before anyone could get to know the married couple, their quirks or peccadillos. Betty Duvall, who lived in Houston during her brother's first marriage, recalled visiting the newlyweds with her sister Pat. "They were having a big fight inside when we got to the apartment, and we just had to stand like outside until they finally came to the door. But he never told us what it was about. See, Bob's not the one to talk much about himself like that."

And when the marriage ended, he didn't say much about that either. "He said that he went home one day and she had moved everything out of the apartment and run off with another guy," Betty recalled.

Bobby closed the books on the incident, telling friends and family that Diane left him for another man. Who would know any differently? Who would care?

Linda, his new sweetheart, surely wouldn't. She was a dream, and much dreamier than Diane. "Real naïve," was Betty's first impression, "uneducated, very unaware of things. But other than that she was real sweet."

Young, pretty, fun-loving—and in love with and loyal to him. With Linda, Bobby found someone over whom he could exercise his compulsive need to control. They found stability in each other. Linda needed it. She was married at age sixteen—to Charles Brotherton, a drifter who always seemed to be in trouble.

For a year and a half the young couple struggled—mostly against each other. Linda bounced around as a receptionist and typist at the County Tax Office, processing license plates and researching property taxes. Her husband became an alcoholic and bounced around Linda. He beat her and acted as if he didn't like his new daughter very much either—born Shelley Rene Brotherton in Houston on May 5, 1967. The marriage was over a year after Shelley was born. At age nineteen, when most girls were just leaving their senior proms, Linda Brotherton was a divorced mother.

Bobby Sessions appeared just in time to save Linda and Shelley from a hardscrabble life. Linda was working hard at a low-paying job—a typist, receptionist and mail clerk for a Houston law firm—trying to raise a child and get her former husband to contribute something to support them. Bobby seemed everything that Charles Brotherton wasn't: stable, kind, sensitive. And industrious.

Born in the small town of Kerens, 180 miles due north of Houston, he was a country boy made good. Just before meeting Linda, he was made a manager of Amerada Hess's crude-oil department. Less than a year after Diane left him, Bobby and Linda tied the knot. Bobby would later joke that at the time he thought his financial condition was "poor." But Linda's "was worse than mine." He promised to accept young Shelley, then two and a half, as if she were his own daughter. And, in fact, he soon made it legal.

"At the time of the marriage," Bobby recalled, "I made the decision that Shelley had to be my daughter. So I adopted her."

In order to complete the adoption, Bobby negotiated Charles Brotherton out of the picture. He wanted absolutely no interference from Shelley's natural father. "I knew that before we got married I couldn't have another father coming around part-time or [with] visitation rights," he would explain.

So, after marrying Linda, and within a year of adopting Shelley, he met with Charles Brotherton three times to work out the

arrangement to keep his stepdaughter's real father out of her—
and his—life. He promised Brotherton that he would never again
have to worry about child support. As Brotherton relinquished all
rights, Bobby inherited them.

Bobby Sessions was the only father Shelley would ever know.
And he seemed the ideal one. With Bobby the good provider and
Linda the attentive mother, the three of them made a perfect
little family.

"Bob and Shelley seemed as close as a stepchild with a man who
never had a child could ever be," recalled Bobby's sister Pat, who
visited the couple in Houston frequently. "And Bob and Linda
were very much in love. They had a very happy home."

But at the same time Bobby wasn't able to do much about a
little girl who, whether because of temperament or abandonment,
was rebellious, aggressive and stubborn. "She was a darling," her
mother remembered, "but she was very hardheaded. She gets that
from us, because we, too, are very strong-willed. As an example,
I used to work when she was small and we would argue. She would
give me a hard time over what socks she was going to wear, what
petticoat she was going to wear, what dress she was going to wear,
what barrette she was going to have in her hair, which part we
were going to have; if we were going to have ponytails or—you
know, it was just a hassle every morning trying to get her dressed
because she was so set—as a little tiny, tiny girl—set how she
wanted things.

"I remember one morning, I just—I just couldn't stand it. She
was halfway dressed and I put her outside the front door for a
minute—then brought her back in and got her dressed. . . . She's
always been strong-willed."

Bobby couldn't seem to break through the belligerence of his
newly inherited daughter.

"Shelley had a shell around her; she doesn't want anyone to
touch the inside of her and never has," recalled Pat. "Even as a
baby, when you would love her—most children respond to love
and affection. Shelley was unresponsive. It was like, 'Okay, I'll let
you like me, but don't get too close. I'm not going to love you in
return.' "

"We'd get toe to toe," Linda recalled. "But at that age I could win. But it was growing, it was getting more intense."

Intensity was a word right out of Bobby's book. He knew that adopting Shelley made a big difference to his own family life because, he recalled, "Shelley was someone else's child. My personality could not accept that, and Shelley had to become my child. She had to be my daughter one hundred and ten percent. And because I tried so hard, I thought that I had to to have the same thing back from Shelley."

Bobby got a big career break in 1975 when he was offered a job in New York City as a vice president of Amerada Hess, heading up the company's International Crude-Oil Division. He jumped at the opportunity and moved his young family east, when Shelley was just eight. Once they moved, he then proceeded to work even harder than he had in Houston.

Bobby found a home for the family in the suburban New Jersey community of Bridgewater. He commuted to Manhattan, by car, one hundred miles each day. He regularly worked eighteen and twenty hours a day—always figuring out how to make more money in the intensely competitive but lucrative spot oil market. It was like playing the stock market, and Bobby developed an uncanny ability to know when to buy and sell the oil in the huge tankers floating across the world's oceans.

This was the fast lane. Still in his early thirties, Bobby already had eleven years' experience in all phases of the oil business for Amerada. He had come up through the company's training program and now was joining top management in the Manhattan headquarters. And Leon Hess, the founder and chairman of Amerada as well as owner of the New York Jets football franchise, rewarded loyalty in his company. It was a principle of his business, as a newspaper reporter put it, "to stick with someone you already have and know."

Back in Bobby's home state, the government and industry leaders lobbied for increases in production and less regulation. Texas was among the first to lift regulations and push major exploration and drilling for oil. Bobby was prepared for the Arab boycott of 1973 and for what the oil-industry response should be: aggressive.

Initially, the prices of oil and natural gas went up. The headlines read: "ENERGY PINCH ALTERING FAMILIES' LIFE-STYLES IN CITY AND SUBURBS."

And while many American families were belt-tightening because of the energy crunch, Bobby Sessions' family was prospering. Bobby was an oil executive with a lovely large home, swimming pool, friends, free box-seat tickets to Jets games, a fast car, a lovely wife and two beautiful children—Michael was born in 1976, the family's first year in the east.

Bobby had it all—or almost all. He kept in touch with his family in Houston, flew his mother and sister to visit him in New Jersey and took his wife on weekend vacations to Paris.

"At that particular time in the crude-oil business everybody was just making money hand over fist," Bobby recalled. The family led the good life: a two-story colonial on a tree-lined street in a quiet town. There was a big backyard and a swimming pool. Shelley learned to ski and had pool parties with her friends.

But Bobby's driving personality began to spill over into home life as it hadn't quite done before. He became more demanding of Linda and Shelley, more needy. He started squeezing the life out of his all-American family.

The squeeze was perhaps to make up for something missing from his own life. He himself was reared by a strict father, and Bobby had rewarded him by refusing to visit him during the elder Sessions' fatal bout with brain cancer in 1967.

His youthful search for support from his father became an adult drive for approval from his employers and love from his family. He smoked continuously, gulped Dr Pepper continuously, worked continuously. And with his children he worked continuously for affection—and demanded it.

From Shelley especially, since he felt he had gone out on a limb on her behalf, he required obeisance.

He had immediately taken charge of rearing Shelley, even

throwing the little girl's baby bottle away soon after he and Linda were married.

"She's too old for that," he told his new wife.

That was the first minor skirmish in a battle that would continue for many years. Linda had developed a special attachment to her little girl because of the abusive environment that the two had survived together. She told herself, she wasn't going to let anybody hurt Shelley again. But Bobby was determined to have the warm and affectionate relationship with Shelley that he hadn't been given by his father.

He began to crave Shelley's attention in a way that he had craved Diane Vittum's. But the little girl, already abandoned and bruised by a man, wasn't easily going to let down her guard.

He was always real strict and I'd rebel against him. . . . I got whipped a lot and grounded a lot. I was always in trouble. I mean, in front of people or when anyone was over, if I did the littlest thing, he would just blow it way out of proportion—you know, take me up to my room and whip me. I could accidentally spill a glass of milk and he would say that I was being rambunctious, you know, too rowdy, and just scream and yell at me, in front of anybody, it didn't matter.

One Christmas, Bobby flew his family from New Jersey to his mother's house on West Collins in Corsicana, Texas, for the holiday meal. Shelley and her cousins, Michelle and Gary, Missy, Amy and Kyle, and her brother, Michael, were at the children's table in the kitchen when Bobby came in and told Shelley to eat more of her green beans.

"Shelley looked at me and I looked at her and when he turned around and walked out I ate all of her food for her," recalled her Aunt Betty.

Shelley found an ally in Betty, who, from the beginning thought Bobby was unreasonable with his daughter.

"At family get-togethers he would make her sit at the table after all the other children were through eating until she ate everything on her plate. And I would sit there and eat her food when he wasn't looking so she wouldn't get in trouble," said Betty.

During these same visits the cousins and aunts and uncles often watched as Shelley was reined in by Bobby. Once, Shelley spilled a glass of milk. Bobby screamed, "Shelley!" and everyone in the room froze. "What are you doing! I told you to be careful!" Shelley tried to say she hadn't meant to spill it, but he cut her off. "You need to settle down. Go to your room!"

I would understand more him yelling at me like that if I had been running around in circles in the kitchen and spilled something. But just casually knocking something over. Kids are going to knock stuff over.

Bobby and Linda had contrary views about raising children. "I was lenient," Linda recalled, "and he liked to go by guidelines or rules. I fluctuated every day." The differences in child-rearing theories led to differences in child-rearing styles.

To hear Linda tell it, the only source of trouble in the marriage was the parenting styles—which meant, as Linda could have known only vaguely, that *Shelley* was the source of trouble.

"He was a disciplinarian," Linda would later say about her husband, "and I was a real humanist. I just thought you talked with kids. You reasoned with them and swatted them every now and then. So I was always bucking his going strictly by the rules, following a real tight line. I was real flexible. We bucked on our ideas a lot."

Bobby believed that Linda overreacted. "My wife's first husband was very abusive to her and to Shelley," Bobby would later explain. "Because of that my wife has always been very defensive anytime I tried to discipline Shelley."

The severe outbursts from Bobby brought angry backlashes from Linda. "I always tried to protect her against her dad because I just—she was so important to me," Linda said later. "It's just like she was me, almost, and she is very precious to me."

Soon the arguments about Shelley's behavior became a regular event at the Sessions house. Teachers noticed Shelley's grades falling at school and spoke to Linda about it. But the fighting continued at home. And Shelley's problems in school continued.

Shelley became the source of friction in the house—or so Bobby and Linda believed. Bobby wanted strict obedience from his daughter; Linda couldn't discipline her. Linda even called a social worker to set up an appointment for her daughter.

"I didn't think there was a problem," Linda recalled. "And I just thought, you know, we were like any other family. And I heard someone on the radio talking and it just hit me that it sounded like my family was needing counseling bad."

Linda called a counseling service and made an appointment. But the counselor wanted Shelley to come too.

"And when I was calling to make the appointment and Shelley was there and she started yelling that she was not going to go, there was no way she was going, and I told the lady, 'I'm sorry, but I've changed my mind.' And the lady said, 'Honey, you've got a worse problem than you think,' and hung up."

Shelley was running the house, the counselor told Linda. "Your daughter is telling you what she is and isn't going to do," the woman said.

Unable to cope with their own problems, Linda and Bobby made Shelley the reason for their fights—and the counselor had further incriminated the little girl. It became, despite their loud fights, an unspoken understanding between Bobby and Linda: Shelley was the problem. But it would start a pattern of denial and projection that would make of Shelley a permanent and ideal victim.

In Shelley Bobby had met someone who didn't succumb to his charm or his demands. And he needed her affection and love as much, more, than other things he desired. And one day he touched his eight-year-old daughter and felt something quieting in the touch. Like a cigarette or a cola, it soothed a raw nerve.

That's when he sat down next to her and touched her shoulder, running his hand quickly and lightly down her arm. He talked to her, asking her about her friends at school, and felt, for the first time, the kind of intimacy he had been seeking.

He would massage my legs and my back and then he would get closer to other parts of me.

Shelley had always called Bobby Sessions "Dad." She had been too young to know about Charles Brotherton when he was around. Now Shelley was eight and Bobby, the only father she had ever known, was doing something "weird." She didn't know why, but she knew she didn't like it. She tried to push him away, but somehow that made Dad more anxious to "massage" her. It was a new word and it didn't make sense. Her dad said it was something for tired muscles—but she didn't have tired muscles.

Usually every day after school all the neighborhood kids would meet and we'd play, you know, sports and stuff and then when I'd come home at night and get ready for bed, then he'd come up there and massage my legs and tell me how tense I was.

The big hill at the end of the street was perfect for after-school play, softball and kickball and tag.

I can remember him coming up to my room and start massaging my legs, you know. That's how it all started. I can remember thinking, you know: "Well, my legs don't hurt. Why is he massaging my legs?"

Shelley had felt the same violation when her first father bolted. Always wondering what would happen next, she built a wall around her real feelings—a fortress that kept even her from knowing what she felt.

Bobby increased her pain by violating the dearest part of a relationship with his daughter. He began touching her—to pull her back, he believed, from the brink that his rigid discipline had sent her. Almost as if countering the violence of his discipline, he dove into intimacy. But for the little girl, it was like being pushed into the abyss: no light, no bottom, nothing to hold on to.

For both violations, Shelley hated him. And she now had no one to trust.

My mom and I were close, but we weren't. I don't know how to explain it. We were close, but then we weren't close, you know; we weren't close enough for me to tell her what was wrong. She is very naïve and very dependent on him. I don't know—she's not a real secure person. She's like the frail type.

Her mother wasn't there one summer day in 1978 when Bobby

came to Shelley while she was swimming. She was just eleven then.

"Shelley, I want to talk to you."

Shelley climbed out of the pool reluctantly. Dripping, she grabbed a towel and came to him.

"Sit down, Shelley," he said, pointing to the picnic table. "I need to tell you something."

When she did, Bobby gave a short preamble of solicitation, about how he loved her and how she was old enough to hear this, then said he had to tell her something that she might not want to hear.

"Shelley, I am not your real father," he said. "You are adopted."

Shelley was stunned. And confused. She ran into the house, crying, into her bedroom, and locked the door.

I hated him more after that. Because you find out that you've been adopted. And at first I thought they had both adopted me. I didn't know that he meant just him. I didn't know that my mom was my real mom.

Shelley was glad when her mom told her that the family would be moving back to Texas. Not that she knew the difference between the two states, but she knew she didn't like New Jersey—although her aversion didn't have much to do with the state. It was her family life that was the problem. Maybe if they made the right move things would change.

If life was memory, then Shelley was losing hers. Her father's massages were gradually squeezing from her the ability to be open to the world; they focused her. Her playmates, her teachers, her little brother, her town, the trees on the street, the snowmen in winter, even her favorite monkey, with diaper and no hair, passed down to her from uncle Ricky and cousin Michelle and cousin Gary—they were dim images even as they appeared.

Maybe if they moved to Texas, her dad, who wasn't really her dad, would stop massaging her. But then, in a strange motel room, somewhere on a road, somewhere between New Jersey and Texas, sometime between June and September—he touched her again.

We were moving back to Houston and we were in a hotel room and I woke up in the middle of the night, and he had put his hand in my underwear and I woke my mom and told her and she confronted him about it and he said that he thought it was her.

IV

HAPPY BIRTHDAY

I had wanted a horse since I was little. I always loved horses and I always checked out books about them and learned all I could about them so that I could learn to care for one.

Bobby finally gave in to one of Shelley's insistent requests. As a thirteenth birthday present, he announced, Bobby and Shelley would select a horse.

Shelley was overjoyed. For years she had been dreaming of having her own horse. It was one dream she hadn't kept to herself. She asked her mom and dad repeatedly if she could have one. When they were still in New Jersey, she would bring home books from the school library on horses and spend hours reading, and idling over the pretty pictures. In Houston she had friends who actually owned horses. She loved to visit them just to wander the stables and, whenever she could, jump on the bare back of one of the beautifully sleek animals. Shelley had prepared for a horse with the diligence of a rodeo queen.

Even while indulging her fancy for horses, Shelley could not keep domestic tension at bay. There seemed to be more and more fights now; her dad always ordering her to do things or not to do things. Shelley didn't like him, and frequently balked. He screamed at her and Shelley screamed back. Then Linda sailed in, scolding both father and daughter, usually ending in a verbal fight with Bobby.

Bobby wanted a monopoly on control over every facet of family life. He asserted himself into everyone's activities with a dictator's zeal. Shelley felt powerless—except, it seemed, in her ability to trigger these screaming matches.

Always fighting. We never got along as most families do.

Her father didn't disagree about the frequency of fights, but he was quick to see them as battles between good and bad, right and wrong. "I think the fact that from day one Linda was so protective of Shelley, and the fact that Shelley could do no wrong—there was always a problem," he recalled. "The majority of the time most of our arguments were over Shelley one way or another."

One thing Bobby had no control over was Shelley's growing up. Her brown hair was long and silky, and her mom helped her comb it out—and told her about what was happening to her body—not to worry. Her breasts were growing. It was an odd sensation, but she accepted the beginning of her menstrual period with a certain degree of pride as well. And she continued to guard her intensely private, intensely personal feelings.

Or so she thought. One night as she lay in bed, starting to turn the lights out, her dad came in. He stood just inside the room, looking quietly down at his daughter. She asked him what he wanted, but he just stood there. "You're weird," she mumbled, but he didn't hear.

"Now you're a woman," he finally blurted out.

Shelley felt a tingle of terror run along her spine. She didn't know exactly what he meant, but the blank expression in his eyes and the way he said it made her uncomfortable.

The Sessions moved into a rented house in a Houston subdivision on September 1, 1978, while their home was being built. Shelley liked school and her friends and got along well.

When Bobby left Amerada Hess he was making $78,000. He and Linda had sold their house in Bridgewater for about $150,-000, and had invested some money in resort property on the Gulf Coast.

Bobby had come back to Houston to trade crude oil for Tampimex, a company owned by two brothers from New Orleans. The brothers were looking for someone who knew the worldwide markets and who could also give them entry to Houston's oil industry. After fourteen years with Amerada, Bobby relished the chance to operate outside the corporate culture. He was ready to stretch his entrepreneurial instincts. Bobby was joining the network of oil traders who could, as he later described it, make "fifty, sixty or a hundred million dollars a year. There were lots of small companies that had been founded making those kinds of dollars." Bobby worked with two other men in the Houston office of Tampimex. There were no layers of corporate bureaucracy in this operation. The three split the costs of their salaries and overhead, and then each took 10 percent of the profits they generated. A six-figure income was not hard to come by under these arrangements.

The financial step up was reflected in the price of the new house that Bobby moved his family into in May 1979: $250,000. The location was equally impressive for a farm boy from Kerens: Spring, an opulent suburb fifteen miles north of Houston on Route 45.

It was the nicest house on the block, and had a swimming pool, which not all of the homes on the tree-lined cul-de-sac boasted in a subdivision called Southern Oaks. The Sessions joined in block cook-outs and swimming parties and weekend jaunts to Cancún.

Bobby and Linda occasionally threw backyard parties with catered Mexican food, sometimes rowdy enough that guests doused each other with beer. Weekends the family spent playing tennis at the nearby Old Oaks Racquetball Club.

Having started in Houston as a single parent, Linda was now returning as a full-time housewife with two happy children and a husband who could make a dollar. There was a certain sweetness in coming back to your hometown in such style. Her daughter could have a horse, and her son, just now three, a quiet yard. Linda's only worry seemed that young Michael not wander too close to the pool.

Though Shelley didn't give much more thought to her adoption, she still *felt* abandoned. She had sorted out with her mother her role in the family. And for her real father she kept only a black hole in her heart: *He doesn't care about me, why should I care about him? That's how I feel. I mean, I don't care who he is or where he is. I don't care.*

Only once more would Shelley hear the name of Charles Brotherton, her real father, mentioned. She was almost thirteen, in the seventh grade, at her mother's parents' house, Grandma and Grandpa Bellard, in Houston for Christmas. At one point cousin Michelle pulled her into the spare bedroom.

"Look at this," said Michelle, thrusting a small piece of newspaper toward Shelley.

Shelley peered at the newsprint. She read a story about a man being arrested: Charles Brotherton.

"That's your real dad," Michelle whispered.

"How do you know?" Shelley shot back, defensively.

"My mom told me."

Shelley was crushed.

The day finally came, Thursday, May 5, 1980, Shelley's birthday. She turned thirteen, a teenager, was up early and, not having to go to school, she and her Dad hitched a horse trailer to the pickup and headed north. It was a long drive, more than three hours, to the small town of Corsicana. The north-central Texas town was the birthplace of the first oil well west of the Mississippi—and Bobby Sessions.

In 1894 Corsicana's town fathers had brought a drilling company from Kansas to sink another water well for this growing merchants' hub in farm country. Instead of water, the drillers found oil. It took almost a year for Corsicanans to realize the potential of the failed water well that they had sealed off. But two years later Corsicana became the site of the first commercial oil field in the Southwest, and began to ship the commodity to the Northeast.

The potential for mineral riches began the tradition of property owners in Navarro County setting up drilling rigs in their backyards.

Bobby had grown up with oil machinery all around him—watching big, woodpecker-like devices bobbing up and down across the landscape. He knew the area well, and his mother and other relatives still lived there. His mother, Lottie Caskey, who had remarried, welcomed Bobby and Shelley to her house that morning. They didn't stay long, however. Instead, they went right to work looking for a horse.

Before the oil boom, Corsicana had been primarily an agricultural seat, once the leading producer of Texas cotton. But it was easier to let cattle and horses graze around the oil derricks than it was to plow around them. Ranching, not farming, became the leading agricultural industry.

With that heritage, Bobby nourished his dream of being a horse breeder. In looking for a horse for Shelley, he was realizing his own fantasies too.

By the afternoon, Shelley and Bobby had found two horses that they liked. Bobby told the owner that they would be back the next morning to pick one of them up. Then they both went back to Bobby's mother's house.

It was late by the time dinner was finished, and Bobby and Shelley went to their separate rooms. After putting on her nightgown and crawling under the sheets, Shelley sensed a presence. She looked up from her bed to see her father at the door. This time he came in and sat on the bed.

"Excited about the horse?" he asked her.

Shelley hesitated. "Yeah," she said. "Sure."

But then Shelley pulled back abruptly—she felt her dad sliding his hand up and down her legs. "You're a woman now," he said. His eyes were round, unblinking. Shelley didn't know what to do.

Emotionally, Bobby was now letting Shelley become more an equal than a daughter. Bobby reasoned—he had an explanation for everything—that he had finally found a way to his daughter's heart. "Shelley was being stubborn about a lot of things," he later recalled, "and I just wanted to see a love in her for me for a lot of things." The problem was that that love, according to Bobby, "just didn't seem to be there."

In Bobby's mind, he was seeking "an avenue of approach to show some attention, some affection," as he put it. "And I started to massage her legs around her vagina area."

"Having a horse will be a lot of fun," he said as he rubbed her.

Shelley was silent, her unbelieving eyes focused on her father's wandering hands.

"I'll bet you can't wait to get it home," he continued, continuing his rubbing.

Shelley remained mute, petrified. She closed her eyes as Bobby moved his hands all the way up her legs.

"How bad do you want that horse?" he asked. A glint of lechery revealed his goal: control. In his voice was anger. A threat.

The hint dropped heavily. Shelley understood. She still said nothing, but was thankful when her grandmother came into the room.

I didn't know what he was doing and then my grandmother came in to tuck me in and she just kind of looked at him and then walked out. He stayed in there. And he just kept feeling me everywhere and putting his hand in my underwear. And then she came back in there and asked him what he was doing and then after she left, he went back to his room.

Did Lottie have an intimation of what was going on?

Perhaps she was recalling a scene that had played out with Bobby and her youngest daughter when they were children; a scene in which she had found Bobby lying on top of Betty. Lottie sent Bobby to his room, drove with her daughter to the Chevrolet dealer where her husband, Clarence, worked, told him what she had found, and returned with him to witness a sound thrashing of her son.

One thing that had remained with Betty ever since was the curious fact that her father "didn't seemed shocked."

What was Bobby doing lying on his daughter's bed? "Just talking," he told his mother.

Did she know? Shelley couldn't sleep for a long time that night. Her dad had said nothing about what it meant, what he wanted, what was going on. He told her only not to say anything about "What we have between us."

But that meant nothing to the thirteen-year-old. Shelley lay there, scared to death. Confused. What was he doing? Why? It felt terrible.

They stayed only one night in Corsicana. Shelley named her horse Misbehavin'.

V

HOUSTON HORROR

The next morning Bobby was in a fine mood. Shelley wasn't, but it was hard not to feel excited as she helped walk Misbehavin', her proud Appaloosa, up the gate ramp of the trailer.

On the long drive south, however, Shelley couldn't think about her horse. Bobby had other surprises in store for his daughter. Next to her, in the driver's seat, he was unzipping his pants.

"Shelley, look over here," he said over the whine of the engine.

Shelley scooted closer to her door. She stole a glance out of the corner of her eye, but stayed as far from her dad as she could without climbing right out into the air, trying to shut out his drooling voice.

"Look, Shelley," he said again. "C'mon—look over here."

Frightened, curious, ashamed, she finally looked. That made Bobby smile. "Just watch it," he said. "See how it changes."

Bobby continued to play with himself. Every time Shelley tried to look away, he ordered her to look. "Watch it grow," he kept saying as the truck and trailer kept moving along the straight Texas highway.

The white lines of the highway sped by, and the spring wildflowers were in full bloom along the north-central Texas inter-state. But Shelley saw none of it.

One hand on the wheel, Bobby Sessions fondled himself.

The next day Shelley was alone at home, staying away from school—sick. She was more confused than ill, but she really didn't feel well. Linda had gone on an errand. Shelley didn't tell her mom because, Shelley believed, Linda should have known. She just wanted her mom to do something. When she heard her bedroom door swing open, she sighed, "Mom?"

"No. It's me, honey."

Shelley froze. In an instant Bob was at her bed. "How y'all doing?" he asked solicitiously, running his hands up and down his teenaged daughter's legs and torso.

"Get away!" Shelley pleaded, trying to hide under the covers. But Bobby kept it up.

I don't know how to explain it. He's your dad, your parent. And you're supposed to obey your parents. A kid's supposed to know to obey his parents. And that's what you think about. They're my parents, they're my guardians. Obey your parents.

It was the beginning of Bobby Sessions' precipitous descent to obsession. The new house, sprawling along a tree-lined street in the plush suburb of Houston, the booming oil city, became Bobby's small and secret bordello. Shelley, now thirteen, was his mistress.

Now he came into Shelley's bedroom all the time. Every chance he got, when no one was around, he touched her. What if he got caught? He pushed on, defying the odds, invigorated by the risk, keeping his daughter under his wing.

And Shelley was there, close, budding, easy. That was the word: easy. Bob's urges were strong and his nerves strung tight. Shelley was easy and dangerous. The combination was an intoxicant too powerful for Bobby to resist. Night after night he was drawn to his daughter.

I was afraid of him. I didn't even know what he was doing when he did something, you know. I mean, I didn't know anything about the law or anything. I didn't know what was going to happen to me. I just didn't know.

At first he used the effects of horseback riding as the excuse to molest Shelley, reminiscent of a tactic he had used in New Jersey.

Shelley was stiff from the exertion. "You must be sore from the riding," he said to her as she got ready for bed.

Shelley said that she wasn't.

"Let me give you a massage," he said as he slid onto his daughter's bed.

Shelley backed away. "No, Dad, my legs aren't sore!" she protested.

He only smiled, pulled the covers back and began kneading Shelley's legs. He moved up the leg higher and higher—one thing always seemed to lead to another.

He would start coming into my bedroom at night and just start feeling me. He just fondled me for several months.

Bobby knew what he was doing was wrong. But he sold himself on the idea of this being a way to his daughter's affections. It sounded good to him. And that was enough.

"I loved Shelley very much and I enjoyed what we had together," he later claimed, "because for me that was the first time we had ever had love shown between us."

Shelley had a different idea of the encounter. She didn't know what sex was—she didn't know "wrong" from "right" or "normal" from "abnormal." She didn't know the law. She didn't know fathers could do such things. Her world was the world of her father and mother, her providers, her supports, her definers of words and scenes. And when her father came into her bedroom, Shelley saw a large part of her existence come into the room as well.

Shelley resisted. And Bobby thought of the sexual interaction as "a problem and a hassle." But it didn't stop him. If anything, it excited him to more daring indiscretions. Ignoring Shelley's resistance, he raised his demands. And, within a few months of his daughter's birthday, he had moved from fondling to sodomy to intercourse.

Bobby knew it was wrong. He knew that sleeping with Shelley's mother while molesting her daughter was wrong. But he failed to recognize it for the unspeakable violation it was.

He started performing oral sex on me. He told me how much he loved me and that this was the way that he could feel love between us as a father and daughter. . . . I thought it was gross. While molesting his daughter day and night, Bobby was also planning a major move. At thirty-eight he had made enough money to go back home and live a life that he had always dreamed of. He was finalizing the deal to buy a ranch near Corsicana.

On the surface, he would move back a rich man, local boy made good. But it was the broken surface on a well-churned pond; parts shined, parts altogether dark. Because of what he was risking with Shelley, he worried more and more, smoked even more than his usual four packs of Winstons a day, drank even more than his usual forty Dr Peppers. A conqueror returns home—a nervous conqueror.

He didn't have to worry about money anymore. In 1980, his last year with Tampimex, he reported wages and bonuses of over three million dollars. He had left Tampimex for a job with another small oil company, which promised $2 million to sign and a $1 million guarantee.

As a going-away present, his colleagues at Tampimex give him a picture of a three-masted ship under full sail in battle—a symbol of the oil industry's warlike edge. It was an appropriate emblem of the battle he would quickly join at his new job.

Before he signed on, Bobby had his lawyer add a rider to his employment contract stipulating that he wouldn't be expected to do anything illegal or unethical in order to earn his sizable keep. "At the time there were three different prices in the oil business, especially on domestic crude," Bobby later explained. "There was an old oil price, and a new oil price, and a stripper oil price. And there was like a $35 to $38 a barrel difference in those prices. And a lot of guys were just very simply buying old oil and reclassifying it as new and turning around and selling it and making thirty-eight bucks a barrel—all of which was illegal. So we made a stipulation in the contract that if there were any illegalities in the company or if he asked me to do anything that was unethical, especially illegal, that I would simply take my bonus and the monies I had earned to date and I would leave."

Ten days after starting his new job, Bobby would later claim, his boss asked him "to use my influence to call AMOCO, Shell, Gulf, Texaco, all of the majors, and try to work out some kind of scheme where you could buy old oil and turn around and reclassify it as new oil." Bobby said no and left, taking with him the $2 million stipulated in the contract.

With the $3 million he made in 1980, Bobby decided to go into business for himself. He started Circle S Energy Company to broker crude oil for himself. He also established trust funds for Michael and Shelley and lent the trusts' money to buy a 10-percent interest in Circle S Energy. He split the rest of the stock between himself and Linda. Bobby, of course, remained the boss.

At the same time he finalized a deal on the purchase of almost 400 acres of valuable ranchland, with buildings, in Powell, a one-store town on Route 31, six miles east of Corsicana, the Navarro County seat. Planning for the move was burning Bobby up. He smoked more and more, gulped soda and, first to calm him, then to agitate him, he had Shelley. During the four months between Shelley's thirteenth birthday and the move to Powell, he instigated a crescendo of illicit sexual activity.

Shelley froze as he tiptoed in and slid onto her bed. She froze. She wanted to scream, vomit, cry—she did cry, quietly—but this was her father—and whom do you scream to? He was on top of her now. Bobby pushed on, emboldened by the ease with which he could give in to his lust—by the fact that it satisfied a need, felt good.

Bobby could not control himself. He told no one. And he rationalized: "I knew it was wrong, but I enjoyed it and Shelley loved me and she enjoyed it when it was happening. I just never really thought about the consequences or anything else."

Bobby took what he wanted from the child.

Then one Saturday afternoon he called Shelley into *his* bedroom. His and *Linda's*. Linda was shopping, and there was Bobby, in his terrycloth robe.

He laid me down on the bed and he started and I just can remember how much it hurt.

The pain of his penetration was immediate. Shelley had no point of reference by which to judge it. But she began to comprehend just how wrong it was. It was a not-right-with-the-world wrong, a not-as-things-should-be wrong. Children know good and bad, even if only as they know hot and cold. Shelley knew it was bad for a father to hurt his daughter this way, especially when she hadn't done anything wrong. Why would he punish her if she'd done nothing wrong? The evil of Bobby's assaults on her only made the pain worse.

Shelley felt she had no one to turn to. She tried to resist Bobby, using grown-up logic. "What if you make me pregnant?" she asked.

"Don't worry about it. I've had a vasectomy." It was as if Bobby had planned it all out.

For Shelley, Houston was not spacecraft or oil booms or ponytails or even horseback riding—it was four months of horror. From then on, when she thought about Houston, Texas, her home, she would see a big, hulking man slinking out of the shadows.

Shelley got some respite in front of the television set: a passive, hospitable and entertaining friend. Early Saturday mornings she snuggled up on the living room sofa and watched her favorite cartoon characters. But that last small shelter quickly disappeared one morning when she looked up from the set to see the shadow of her dad stepping down to the living room. He was in his bathrobe, a sign, Shelley was beginning to discern, of trouble.

He would sit beside me and then he'd fondle me and then every few seconds he would jump up and go and look around the house to see if anybody was awake yet.

Linda and Michael were still asleep upstairs.

"Are you crazy?" Shelley yelled.

Bobby Sessions was nothing if not bold with his daughter; willfully blind to the pitfalls of his obsession.

His sexual desire was a perverse obsession. In a few short

months Bobby went from touching to penetrating, changing forever his daughter's life. Shelley had become a sex object, pure and
simple.

Bobby believed they were "having an affair."

But Shelley didn't. And she begged him to stop.

He told her to imagine that he was a sexy television star.

"Tell me that you love me," her dad would whisper, half
demanding, half pleading. "I love you, Shelley. Love me back."

Shelley would say nothing, but her silence didn't dissuade her
father from his assaults.

On the increasingly frequent drives to Powell, Bobby would
make sure that Shelley came along, despite her protests. And on
the long drive he would order his daughter to undress. If she
hesitated, he "helped." Cars and trucks streamed by as Bobby
Sessions ogled his naked daughter, who was trying to huddle
against the cold door of the passenger seat or to the floorboard.

Shelley tried to thwart him by inviting friends along. But only
once was she allowed to bring a friend—and even that didn't stop
Bobby Sessions.

*It was late at night and she lay down on the floorboard and went
to sleep. I laid down in the seat and went to sleep and he started
fondling me and put his finger inside me.*

For the record Bobby continued to tell himself and Linda that
Shelley was a stubborn child, "beginning to run with the bad
crowd." They needed to protect her. Part of the reason for moving to Corsicana, he told Linda, was to get Shelley to a healthier
environment.

Linda sensed that something else was wrong. For months she
had watched Shelley grow more morose and Bobby more moody
and demanding. She watched Shelley and Bobby argue over everything. Shelley couldn't make a move without her dad telling
her how to do it—or not do it. And, invariably, the fights between
father and daughter resulted in pitched battles between Linda
and Bobby. Linda suffered through the fights. She hated every
minute of it. She didn't understand Bobby's intense need to
control everything. There was no escape—except when he himself stormed out in anger. And as the move to Powell loomed

imminent, Linda actually suggested to Shelley that they leave him.

"This is the time to make the break," Linda told Shelley during one of Bobby's runaways. "We'll stay in Houston and let him go to Corsicana."

It was the happiest news that Shelley had yet heard. Deliverance. She had waited for her mother to *see* what was happening to her.

But Linda's resolve to leave Bobby lasted only as long as her husband stayed away. When he returned, Linda was quickly in his camp again. To Shelley, Linda had denied her the one real chance of escape.

VI

HELL ON THE RANGE

It was the last day of her eighth-grade year. But Shelley didn't show up at school. Her dad had chosen that day as moving day. And the Sessions family was heading north, to Powell, population 130.

"The reason that I understood that he moved back," Betty Duvall later explained, "was that he wanted his children to grow up in a smaller town and have the liberty that you didn't have in a larger city. Such as living on a ranch and having horses and dogs and cats and all that kind of stuff. But I really don't think that was his primary reason. This is just my opinion. I think he came back to show everybody how well he had done."

Bobby told some people that the reason the family was moving to Powell, Navarro County, Texas, was the difficulty in managing the ranch properly from such a distance; other people heard that he was seeking a "more wholesome environment" for his children. He had always wanted to get into the horse and cattle business. And besides, he would later say, "We wanted to get our kids out of the Houston schools. Seemed like a better place to bring up a family."

Shelley didn't appreciate the irony—but neither did Bobby.

For him, the return was a bittersweet though triumphant journey back to his wholesome roots.

But Bobby also knew that the Houston boom wouldn't last. He felt that the oil business was on the verge of going kaput. Now was as good a time as any to go raise horses and cows.

They moved into a small brick house on the property while Bobby began construction of his mansion—a five-bedroom, 13,000-square-foot brick house on the shores of the 45,000-acre Lake Corsicana. Bobby would be a rancher and oilman. He quickly bought another 600 acres, on two tracts five miles from his homestead.

The new ranch had grown to nearly 1,000 acres of rolling, rough-and-rugged Texas cattle and oil land, and ran along Highway 31 for miles—miles more than anything Bobby could have imagined when he was growing up there.

He paid for it in cash. No mortgage. He was so flush that that year he also paid nearly a million dollars in income taxes. His former employer of less than two weeks, Minro, had filed for bankruptcy and demanded the $2 million bonus back. Bobby settled by returning $1,050,000. It didn't seem to make a dent in his plans. The son of a laborer, he had left town in his early twenties. Now he was back, paying cash for a million-dollar ranch.

And so he did come back to Navarro County as something of a conquering hero. And if it was so remarkable, it was in large part because his early life had been so undistinguished. His grandfather had been a sharecropper. His daddy was an auto mechanic at a Chevy dealership.

Clarence Sessions had also been a tough taskmaster, a "minister of music" at the First Baptist Church of Kerens, before moving to Corsicana to play at the Central Baptist, then Westside Baptist, then, when he was sick, at Emmanuel Baptist. He was responsible for the songs on Sunday mornings and nights, special services on Wednesday nights, Thursday visitations, and all rehearsals.

Bobby was born on March 3, 1942, an unplanned but wanted child, at home, in Kerens. He was the second of four children born to Clarence and Lottie Sessions, and the only boy in the family. He got good grades in school but never distinguished

himself as a scholar. He had an athletic build and good coordina-
tion, but didn't do well in sports. The arts were more his game.

He had a good voice and the desire to use it, showcasing with
a group of fellow students from Kerens High. They sang popular
music and called themselves the Octones. There were seven of
them, with Bobby as vocalist. There were no dances back then,
in the early sixties in this Bible Belt Baptist bastion. So the
Octones sang at talent shows at the high school and at Navarro
Junior College's annual talent show for elementary, high school
and college students. The group traveled to the Adolphus Hotel
in Dallas to audition for the "Interscholastic Starmakers" spon-
sored by KLIF radio. They won a trip to the statewide elimination
round but failed to make the final cut.

Bobby's favorite tunes: "Blue Velvet," "Put Your Head on My
Shoulder," "Sixteen Candles," "Mr. Blue" and "Puppy Love."

In his senior year Bobby landed a leading role in the class
production of *My Little Oscar*. He played Webster Piper, "a
hardworking businessman who appears irritable."

And he wrote sports stories about the Bobcats, the high school
basketball team, for the *Kerens Tribune*.

He would often tell people that he had been accepted to the
United States Naval Academy at Annapolis, but no one was ever
sure what happened. Other relatives recalled his saying it was
West Point that turned him down. He went to neither one.
Instead, he attended the local Navarro Junior College for five
semesters.

Bobby had a hard life at home. His father was known as a rigid
disciplinarian when it came to his son if not his daughters.

"My dad never screamed, he never screamed," recalled Betty.
"Now he gave Bob spankings. You know, back then you used a
big leather strap. I'm not talking humongous, I'm talking about
just a normal leather belt. My sisters tried to tell me I didn't know
the things that went on. I didn't know a side of my dad that was
mean. . . . But I remember getting two spankings but for something I had done wrong. And as far as strictness, he didn't want
us to dance, drink or smoke or go to parties."

Bobby never understood why, but Clarence Sessions never

expressed any warmth or love for him. He felt exceedingly lonely, estranged from his own family.

"He made Bobby work for everything he ever got and he never gave him anything," Betty recalled. Trying to put the money together for his first car, a 1960 green Chevrolet Impala, Bobby mowed lawns to get enough money for a down payment. He learned that he had to work for everything he got—except for what he could borrow from his sister Pat, who was working at the Dairy Queen. That money Bobby would spend on pool games in Corsicana. He would rely on his mother's tempering his father's strict treatment of him. "I know my mother was always taking up for Bob," recalled Betty. "She took him to Dallas for the talent show. I mean, she was doing things like that all the time for him."

Clarence, on the other hand, favored his daughters, while not allowing Bobby to differ with him on any matter. Bobby resented this and turned his anger on his sisters. During junior and senior high school, Bobby made a point of refusing to speak to his sister Pat, who was three years younger and overweight. At the same time he was molesting his youngest sister, Betty.

"I can remember times that [my parents] would be going out and I would be crying and begging them not to leave me," Betty remembered about the times that she had to face Bobby. "And they'd say, well, your sisters are going to be here with you. But I never felt safe when my dad wasn't there."

Betty's first recollection of Bobby molesting her was when she was six years old. "He had me in the barn," she recalled. "Another boy was there who was visiting his grandparents who lived right behind us. And [Bobby] did molest me.

"[My mother] knew what happened," Betty continued. "My dad was working for that Chevrolet place and the day she found Bob on top of me, she put me in the car, sent Bob in the house and she said we were going to see my dad. So we did. And when we drove into the Chevrolet place he came out and it was like it wasn't a big shock to him. She just looked at him and she said, 'Buddy, Bobby had Betty down.' And it was like it was no big deal, it happened before. That was how I felt. Now I could be wrong. And so he just went back inside and took his paint mask off and came out and went home. And Bob was waiting in the house and he proceeded just to tear him up with a belt.

"And then Dad started toward me and grabbed me by the arm and Bob screamed and hollered and said, 'Don't strike her, don't strike her, Dad. It's not her fault, it's all my fault.' So it was like I really felt sorry for him, yet I didn't understand.

"I was only about six years old so I don't really remember a whole lot except my mother made me feel really guilty. She just told me that I had better pray to God for Him to forgive my sins. And she took me in the bathroom and started stripping me down, took my clothes off and said that I had to get in the bathtub and get clean. It was a real guilt trip she put on me at an early age."

But, despite the beating, Bobby continued to molest Betty through high school, threatening physical violence if she didn't go along with his fondling or told on him. During family gatherings Bobby would sometimes order Betty to come into a bedroom and hold up her dress while he masturbated. Or when her friends visited, he asked them into the barn, where he engaged in the same self-sex.

"He ejaculated in front of me. And we had a houseful of guests eating," remembered Bobby's sister. "He was in his bedroom and called me in there and said, 'Hold your dress up.' And I said, 'Why?' and he said, 'Do what I say.' And I did, and he stood there right in front of me." The guests, according to Betty, were probably from the church. "We were always having people over. For the tea parties. My parents had sets of friends, they played dominoes with them all the time and would have dinners and things like that."

Betty took a lot of abuse from Bobby. "I remember a time that there was no one at home except he and I, and my mom had her own shop and she had gone to Dallas to buy things for the store and she came home and he had me in his bedroom. He was doing the actual act of intercourse. And another time we were at my aunt's house in the country and she had horses and everything and he had me down in the barn there too.

"It was before I ever started school. I tried to erase it all out of my mind because nobody ever wanted to talk about it. It was like this happened and forget it. See, even after I was a teenager and, you know, started developing and things like that. Well, he would make accusations at me like if I came through the house and had a robe on he'd say, 'What do you have on under that robe?' You know, just different things like that. And I remember one time I was setting the table for dinner and he said you know you're really beginning to blossom out. It was stuff like that all the time. And I remember those two very distinctly because it's a frightening thing. And anything you've ever been scared of you remember." Pat and Betty saw their older brother as driven, even then; as controlling, manipulative and very demanding.

He was twenty-four and living in Houston when he heard that their father, then fifty-four, had developed brain cancer. But Bobby rarely visited. And not until Clarence was breathing his last breaths did Bobby show concern—he jumped in his car and drove ninety miles an hour to Corsicana. He arrived too late. His daddy had died. And the young man wept openly and unconsolably.

Perhaps it was the love denied him that pushed Bobby to his intense desire to be somebody—and to control.

No one could miss Bobby Sessions' *new* place, driving the needle-straight divided highway between Corsicana and Kerens. And most of the locals knew, or had heard, that Bobby had paid cash for it.

It was big ranch for a man with a big appetite for power and money. Sessions named it the Circle S—and he formed Circle S Energy and Circle S Construction. He hired Richard Ruiz, who later became ranch foreman. "When I first went to work there I worked part-time for him," recalled Ruiz. "I was with the city and I overlooked his cattle. And I went full-time in the construction end of it, running the bulldozer. And then he had an opening to take it over and I took over the whole thing after eight or nine months."

Bobby ended up with a complex of buildings on his property. A few hundred yards south of where the mansion was going up, Ruiz and his crew built an office for Bobby's various businesses. "We had an old barn and we attached the office to the barn," recalled Ruiz. "We built it ourselves. The barn was tin. It was a dirt floor on the inside until we went in there and put concrete in places where we stored our equipment and stuff.

"We stored our tractors and put our bigger equipment inside. It was a huge barn.

"We built the office next to that. It was nice. He had a real big office and I had a big one and a big reception area. My office and his office was carpeted. But the reception area wasn't. We had a full bathroom with shower and everything in it and we had a break room with your microwaves and coffeepot and all that stuff in there. Bobby had beautiful furniture and bookcases and a desk and TV and all that stuff in there.

"He had pictures of Shelley on the wall, and the cattle. You know, when we got to showing cattle he put the pictures of them and me and the cattle up there on the wall."

For Ruiz, Bobby had built a four-bedroom house behind the office. And to the left of that was yet another barn. The original house, where Bobby and his family stayed the first year at the ranch, was another few hundred yards south of that. Another half mile down the road was a cattle barn. It could hold up to three hundred head. "It was a magnificent barn," recalled Ruiz, "and we added on to what was there. It was all enclosed and heated."

Besides being a move for the kids, coming to Powell was a nice tax dodge for the cash-rich Sessions. He set up a network of companies and tax shelters to distribute and hide some of the cash he had accumulated in his years of wheeling and dealing in crude oil. He started the Sessions Family Partnership, which included himself, Linda, the Michael Bryant Sessions Trust and the Shelley Rene Sessions Trust. The Sessions Family Partnership in turn owned the Circle S Energy Company, which owned the Circle S Ranch Corporation, Circle S Construction and an oil-brokerage business called LAB Interests.

Though Bobby Sessions acted like a rancher, his forte was seeing business opportunities and building on them. That was the art of the oil deal that he now applied to ranching.

"When I came up here, we were looking for somebody with

a bulldozer to clear some of our land for us, and we couldn't find anybody," Bobby recalled. "And everybody we asked told us if we did find somebody to let them know because they needed this, that and the other done. It finally dawned on me that if so many people needed so much work done, maybe I should buy a bulldozer and do their work and do my own work when I wasn't busy."

So Circle S Construction was born, and it immediately set to work building roads, contracting out to the county, hauling gravel, demolishing old houses for the city of Corsicana, putting in septic tanks and a little bit of everything else. "We cleared about seven or eight hundred acres of timber for a big ranch down there in the bottom," recalled Ruiz.

Bobby didn't know much about ranching either. But he quickly decided that raising horses would be too expensive and that his prime 375 acres would be better used for commercial cattle breeding.

One thing that Bobby knew very early on was that the ranch was a much better place for sexual assaults on his daughter.

He had an insatiable appetite for sex. And Shelley bore the brunt of his desire. There was no escaping it.

The house that the Sessions family moved into that fall was a ranch house—low and long, with a pitched and gabled roof that seemed to sling the sky further outward. By Bobby's standards and tastes, it was old and small and he immediately set to work building his mansion down the gravel road and on the edge of the lake.

For a different reason Shelley too hated the house. Across the hall from her bedroom was her parents' bedroom—and that, for Shelley, meant her father and tormentor was close at hand.

Every night he would come into my room and just fondle me and my mom would come to the door and ask him what he was doing and he'd say, "We're talking about the horses," or something like that.

As soon as he left her room, she ran to the bathroom and scrubbed and scrubbed.

* * *

"We just thought he was a poor country boy made good," recalled Cherry Layfield, who grew up with the Sessions family in Kerens.

The poor boy had gone off to the big city, made it big and come back to enjoy the fruits of his labor.

Those fruits included the thousand-acre cattle ranch, a construction firm and plans for a mortgage-free mansion. For the grandson of a sharecropper, this was heady stuff. And Bobby was more than happy to spread his good fortune around—to the best effect.

He took care of his family first. He bought two of his sisters and mother a house in Corsicana. When Bobby and Linda moved into the mansion, he gave Linda's parents the smaller house and then paid the utilities. They arrived from Houston. He bought Linda's parents other things as well—a new van for Mr. Bellard. "You know, how can you not get along with somebody that does all that for you?" wondered Betty Duvall.

Bobby hadn't mixed that much with the rest of the family—and hadn't allowed Shelley to stay over at her cousins' house—until he moved into the ranch. Then he entertained them. At holidays, everyone from both sides of the family came to the Circle S. Bobby and Linda supplied the Thanksgiving dinner. They always gave the best gifts for Christmas.

Shelley enjoyed being surrounded by all this family.

I was always close with my uncles on both sides. And my aunts. We always had fun, everyone together. There were swimming parties and volleyball or badminton games.

But Bobby watched over these family get-togethers with a demanding eye. Even his nieces and nephews fell under his jurisdiction.

"Don't yell at my daughter!" Betty snapped after Bobby had upbraided her child for running through the house.

"She needs some discipline, Betty," he retorted sternly.

But most of Bobby's attention was reserved for Shelley—whom he seemed to hound with relish during these family bashes. No one quite understood why. Bobby would shoo Shelley away from them. He would tell his daughter to quit bothering Uncle James,

Betty's new husband, when Uncle James didn't feel at all bothered by his niece. Bobby even told James not to get too close to Shelley.

I have always been real ticklish and my Uncle Ricky used to always tickle me and I would scream and laugh and throw a fit—and I'd get in trouble.

"Shelley, you need to settle down," Bobby yelled. "You don't play in the house."

"Shelley, you drink too fast."

"Shelley, you put your fork down too loud."

Bobby didn't want anyone to have anything to do with me. It was just so evident how well I got along with everybody—and didn't get along with him. They could discipline me and I would do what they asked. It was just so clear that I loved everyone to death and would obey them. But when it came to him—you know, if he'd be over here, I would be at the other end of the room. If he came over here, I'd go there. Wherever he was in the house, I'd go the other way. Always. I'm sure they had to notice it.

Everyone made allowances for Shelley, walked around Bobby on tiptoes, without understanding exactly what Shelley had done or why she was so singled out. But Bobby kept providing, hosting, controlling. And his control of the family holidays and affairs didn't come without a price.

He was like the boss of the family. And he controlled everybody because when they were poor or when they needed some money, they'd come running to Bob. . . . He would organize everything. Tell everybody what to do and when to do it and how to do it. I just wanted to say, "Shut up!" At holidays you went to whoever could afford to feed everybody—which was always us. Everybody came and we had five bedrooms. Everybody stayed. So it got to the point that whatever Bob said, everyone jumps.

After his mother remarried, Bobby bought the newlyweds a house.

He more or less supported everybody and that's how you get them to where they worship you. He had them live at the ranch. They worked for him. They owed him. So he controlled them.

Shelley felt like a tiny speck in the face of all this influence. Her father was godlike. She couldn't even *think* about challenging him.

He gave Betty's husband, James Duvall, a job at the ranch. Shelley's uncle Ricky worked there; a distant cousin, on her father's side of the family, Uncle Don, worked there. Bobby was the man with open arms. Marriage problems in the family brought people to Bobby. He was rich, he was there.

"I helped him build the ranch," recalled James Duvall. "Driving bulldozers, dump trucks and working cattle, building fence, you name it."

But he knew the price of working for his brother-in-law. "He made my job extremely miserable. He done everything that he could to degrade me all the time I worked for him."

All of the family were always jealous of me and Michael. What we got for Christmas, for instance. We didn't just get a few presents. We'd get Honda three-wheelers and everything. It was like Toyland. Tons of clothes, toys, stereos, anything. They just went all-out. And everyone in the family expected them to go all-out for them. We were the money in the family.

And it got to where my mom just hated holidays because she felt like—she couldn't go shopping and get something that she really wanted to get for them because there was so much pressure on her. They expected so much. They expected great gifts. We were the money in the family. She got to hate Christmas—she said it was just like a job and not joyful. Everyone only cared about "Hey, I can't wait to see what Bob and Linda give us for Christmas."

He spread some of the same magnanimity around town.

He bought the prize cow at the local county fair—and paid $5,000 for it, knowing that the money would go to charity. That philanthropic act earned him a front-page story and picture in the next day's *Corsicana Daily Sun.*

Bobby stayed out of clubs like Kiwanis or Rotary, gaining his influence by single acts of largesse. "The only thing he really became involved in was the livestock area," said Betty. "Such as the children's expos, and he would spend large sums of money on that."

Or he would give a gift to a local children's sports team and bask in the praises from parents and kids alike.

Bobby was such a good sport and booster that Joey Ray Layfield, a Kerens native and president of the county's Little League Baseball program, handed the reins over to Sessions. It proved a wise move—for the Little League.

"The first thing he said was, 'There's not a kid in town who's going to have to pay anymore,' " recalled Joey Ray's wife, Cherry, who also grew up in Kerens and knew Bobby's sisters. "And they didn't. He got out and got sponsors for what he didn't put up himself. Nobody paid that year. Nobody paid nothin'. And I'm talking four full teams, uniforms, equipment, everything."

"Man, he throwed money away," was how it looked to Cherry. "And people around here ate it up."

Betty saw how wide a cash wake Bobby left behind. "He started an account at the bank where I worked, Corsicana National, and he put lots of money in there," Betty recalled. "And the president of the bank came over one day and he had never ever done this to me before and it kind of shocked me, but he reached down and kissed me on the forehead. And I said, 'Mr. Stiles, what is that for?' And he said, 'Well your brother just deposited two hundred fifty thousand dollars.' And I went, 'Oh, now I get it.' Everybody was really impressed because he had money."

The kisses by Mr. Zane Stites, president of Corsicana National Bank, may not have been a regular thing for Betty, but the bank tellers saw Bobby frequently. "Everybody just thought he was wonderful."

On Saturday mornings Bobby seemed to have a coffee klatch for the local police and county officials who dropped by his office to chat.

He had hired several employees from the local police department to work part-time at the ranch. Ruiz, his ranch manager, had been a Corsicana city employee, and as he remembered it, "I was friends with all of them. Another foreman that worked there, Leslie Cotton, was a police officer and we knew all the policemen down there.

"Bob went to school with Cotton," said James Duvall. "He

talked Leslie into quitting his job with the sheriff's department
and going to work for him."

"I introduced Bobby to everybody that I knew down there,"
said Ruiz. "And people would come to him for donations and
stuff. He helped anything to do with kids. He'd donate anything.
He put up a good image."

Bobby kept his ranch hands and visitors well fed. Though he
didn't drink, he loved Dr Peppers, and had a delivery truck stop
every week. "He was a Dr Pepper freak," recalled Ruiz. "But you
got to understand that he bought the drinks for the ranch hands
and everybody that worked there. You could go to his house
probably right now and I'll bet there's six, seven, eight cases of
Dr Pepper in the garage. He just loved Dr Pepper."

The Baptist church in town got a van from Bobby—and then
it got a sermon. As if he had the right, he marched to the front
of the congregation and issued a warning. The kids of Kerens were
going down the path of sin. And the parents were letting them
go. Too many children drinking and fornicating, Bobby told
them. Fifteen-year-old girls will be getting pregnant if mothers
and fathers don't start paying attention and get their children off
the streets.

Everyone knew Bobby Sessions had his girl off the streets. But
despite this flair for the grand gesture, Bobby remained a shad-
owy, brooding, unpredictable character to his family and the
townsfolk. Unlike other rich members of the community, Bobby
didn't become an establishment member of the local elite, and he
didn't serve on bank boards or community committees.

Bobby was an enigma. All that most people knew about him
was that he had two years of community college, left town—a
very small town at that—to become an accountant and came back
with a couple of kids and a couple of million dollars. No one really
understood how it all happened. And the mystery added to his
aura as his flamboyant gifts, domineering personality and
unorthodox style contributed to a reputation for deeds done and
undone.

"Bobby was a nervous guy," Ruiz recalled. "He chain-smoked,
bit his fingernails."

One story had it that Bobby slept with a gun on each side of him. Another said that he used to blackmail girls in college to get sex. Bobby Sessions could do just about anything. And with his office now at the ranch, he was always home and always protecting his property—including his daughter.

We had just moved here and these boys from school came to see me and everything. And he just run 'em off. I mean, when anybody come down that dirt road, he was out that door and in that pickup. He wanted to know who it was, anyone that came down that dirt road—nobody came down that dirt road unless he knew and talked to him. Nobody.

The first episode passed quickly into local teenage lore. Ricky Layfield, Cherry's son and a classmate of Shelley's at Kerens High School, remembered it with gusto: "Brad Tarking and Danny Kilcrease, they came down in front of his house when Shelley first moved over there. And they honked the horn or something, and shit! Bobby jumped in that Renegade and zoom, zoom, tore it down and pulled a gun on 'em, jumped all over 'em, told 'em not to do that ever again, and all this. There was a big uproar over it. I mean, shoot, yes, they'd blow that story up so big, it was like they was getting shot at and stuff, the way they told it. Everybody was totally petrified of that man."

"He put the fear of God in people that even spoke to Shelley," recalled Cherry Layfield. "Coach's boy went over there to see Shelley and he run him off to a fare-ye-well. His daddy said there was something wrong with that man."

Bobby Sessions had a powerful need to petrify. But his domestic rages were always worse than those outside the family circle. During one of the many domestic battles with Linda over disciplining Shelley, Bobby stormed away. And before he left, he locked up the gas tanks, changed the locks on all the doors and turned the electricity off. Three huge freezers full of meat spoiled. Days went by. No one heard from him.

Shelley thought—hoped—that this was it. Her mom was talking—yelling—divorce. Shelley prayed for such a salvation. Some spoiled steaks would be a small price to pay for his timely riddance.

VII

SHAME

Bobby Sessions had a loveless childhood thanks to his father. And he was now making sure that his daughter, in the same county, would have the same. A small girl, she was being treated—by her father at least—as both daughter and wife. Shelley didn't understand that role, much less know what to do with it.

No one knew what Bobby was doing to her, or could have suspected that he had told her not to tell. At times he dangled a carrot in front of Shelley: he would stop, he promised. Each time, Shelley believed him; she wanted so much to believe. Each time Bobby ran away, she hoped it was the end. Each time her mother threatened divorce, Shelley hoped she would make good on the threat.

But Bobby always returned. Linda always reneged. This time he said he had gone to Oklahoma. He apologized and was quickly back in the saddle. For Shelley the pattern was a form of psychological terrorism that the young girl, now a freshman in high school, little understood.

Her father couldn't seem to get enough sex. And with his office at the ranch, he could indulge himself almost whenever he wanted. When Shelley came home from school, Bobby would go to her room or order her to his office. When Linda went grocery shopping or ran errands, which she frequently did, Bobby forbade Shelley to go along. Then he would search her out.

Or, not wanting to wait for Linda to leave the house, Bobby made up errands to send her on. Knowing what would come when Linda left, whenever she could, Shelley ran out and jumped in the car with her mother.

When this happened, Bobby would later storm into Shelley's room—"You knew you were supposed to stay here," he would scold. At night, instead of reading her bedtime stories, Bobby Sessions made love to his daughter.

Sometimes in the winter, if the ranch hands didn't come to feed the cattle, then he'd take me down there to help him feed them and he'd take me down to the bottom of the pasture. Or, one time, I was in the barn working my cattle and a Mexican was in there working too; and he sent the Mexican back to the office so he could have intercourse with me in the barn.

During the first year on the ranch, while the family lived in the old brick ranch house, Shelley was so harassed by Bobby that she began locking her bedroom door. He told her not to, but she did it anyway.

The tactic didn't work. It was an affront to parental authority, Bobby told Linda, and shouldn't be tolerated. Since there was a reality on two levels, often locked together, Shelley couldn't escape the one with the sexual abuse. Her angry outbursts were entreaties against the sexual abuse. But they looked to Linda as Bobby described them: rebellion.

"Shelley had a real good anger," Linda would later say, "and she is strong, physically, and she used to—whenever she would get mad, she would go storming off and slam doors or cabinets or whatever, and it got to the point where the slamming of the doors was so bad that we took the door off her room so she couldn't go storming off and slam the door in our face."

To the outside world—and Linda seemed part of the outside world—Shelley was belligerent and difficult to discipline. And Bobby used that perception to bend Shelley to his secret sexual will.

Shelley thought that the missing door might even be a safe-guard in disguise—a door open on the secret. But even without a door on her bedroom, just across the hall from her parents' bedroom, her father came in to touch her.

My mom would come by and say, "Bob, are you coming to bed?" and he'd say, "Just a minute." Then he'd tell me that if I ever heard her coming down the hall, to start talking about the cows; start asking questions about 'em, or about the next cattle show.

Shelley heard her mother coming—but she was silent. It was the quiet rebellion against the jailkeeper. Startled, Bobby had to improvise. "Well, yeah, we'll talk about that tomorrow," he said. Shelley put on her most expressionless face to reinforce the image of Bobby talking to himself.

I was thinking, "My God, my mom coming in here during this and all she would say is, 'You've been in there awhile, Bob. Aren't you ready to come to bed?'" So ignorant.

Oral sex. Intercourse. Fondling. In the living room of the big house, Shelley didn't hear him approach. She just felt his hand on her shoulder.

"Don't mess with me," she said. She was gradually getting braver with Bobby. But it was a bravery conditioned solely on familiarity. And Bobby didn't pay any attention. He continued massaging her shoulders and fondling her breasts.

Most often Bobby wouldn't even sit down on the couch. He'd remain standing so he could walk away fast should anyone come. He couldn't even wait any longer for his wife to leave the house: he took his daughter even when Linda was just in a different part of the house.

He was always sneaking around here and sneaking around there. He was just so brave about what he was doing. I mean . . . like he . . . in the morning when I would get up and be watching cartoons in the living room, my mom and Michael would still be asleep, he'd come down there and try to do something. I'd be throwing a fit. Are you crazy? Like he was so obsessed, he could not, you know, he could not stop.

How many ways can a man fantasize his sexual desires? And
have them so easily met? How many times a day? It was summer
now and Shelley was home. Bobby made his daughter perform sex
with him everywhere, at any time. In her bedroom, in his office,
in the barn, in the pickup truck, even in his and his wife's bedroom. He ordered her to wear short, cut-off jeans around the
ranch.

On the weekends, when Linda went shopping, Bobby found
Shelley and brought her to a bedroom. His boldness included
going to Shelley's bedroom when his wife was in the shower.

*You'd think that he'd be tippy-toeing around, you know, and not
be causing waves. But he was very arrogant, very powerful. And I
was afraid of him.*

Bob leavened his abuse with worldly rewards. He tried to bribe
Shelley, which fed her confusion. Shelley could have almost anything she asked for—and more. Diamond rings and Rolex
watches were unsolicited gifts. He provided well for his family—
Shelley especially.

*I used to get an allowance of like $5 or $10. Then, when all this
started, he'd come in and throw some money on the dresser.
"Here's your allowance." It would be $40 or $50. It was almost like
he was paying for having sex with me, you know, but it was my
allowance. It got to be where I'd have a bunch of money and go
shopping with my mom. And she'd say, "Where are you getting
all this money?" And I would say, "I've been saving my allowance."*

Bob fixed it so Shelley didn't have to lie. The big secret was
easier kept if Shelley could tell the truth about all the small things.

That was a mixed blessing her first year at school. Shelley was
the newcomer—a "rich bitch" at that. Her daddy had already cut
a wide swath in the county, gaining a reputation for wealth that
his daughter carried with her to Kerens High.

*When we first moved there, everybody called me a little miss rich
bitch from Houston. Because they're all country girls and I came
wearing tight jeans and makeup and having my hair done. And
they didn't wear makeup and didn't care how they dressed. And*

all of a sudden, here I come from the big city. And for a long time I'd have to prove myself to make friends. I'd walk down the hall and they'd say, "Rich bitch." And I was thinking, "Look, give me a chance, you know. I'm not a rich bitch."

"Naturally, she just stuck out everywhere," recalled Ricky Layfield. "She was a different face and it's kind of a hick school and everybody knows everybody. So you notice a new face, especially one that looks good. All the guys were just talking about her right away. And the girls were just jealous. Shoot, mine was in on it too. She talked trash about Shelley. Shoot, they all did, they talked trash. But we couldn't really figure out nothing about her, because she was always to herself."

But Shelley soon began to prove to her schoolmates that she was no rich bitch—in fact, the other girls started dressing better, getting their hair done. Shelley made friends, became popular.

"Right away, when you met her, you liked her," said Ricky. "So she got popular. She was pretty cool."

Bobby meanwhile was turning up the heat on Shelley at home. As quickly as she made new friends, Bobby chased them away. Slumber-party invitations had to be turned down. She wasn't allowed to attend football, baseball or basketball games.

What Shelley was allowed to do was pursue her interest in animals—which kept her home, on the ranch, close to him. Her dad bought three more horses and Shelley rode every day. She rode for fun, through the fields and pastures, jumping and training her charges in the ranch's corral.

In the spring of her freshman year Bobby suggested that she enroll in an animal show school. She thought that was a terrific idea. Then he revealed the hitch: he was going too.

They traveled together to the LaRue show school in Georgetown, about 120 miles southwest of Corsicana, the seat of Williamson County, an agribusiness center and home of Southwestern University.

Just the two of us went down there and we stayed in the hotel and we just went from morning until afternoon learning everything about cattle and how to raise them and how to show them and how to groom them and how to take care of them. And then every—

*whenever the class was over we would go back to the hotel and he
just wanted to have intercourse every time I turned around.*

The school lasted a week. Shelley learned too little about cattle—and too much about sex.

Weekday mornings in Powell were usually a safe time for Shelley.
She, Michael and her mother were up early, six-thirty, to get ready
for school. Shelley loved Apple Jacks or Pop-Tarts for breakfast.
Linda would then pile the kids in her white Cadillac and drive
off by eight.

Shelley's first class was Future Farmers of America; her second
was English, then typing, lunch, biology, algebra and history.
Linda fetched Shelley after school. She came home, changed
clothes, did her chores—work the cows, feed them, clean them,
whatever needed to be done that day.

Shelley's dinner was rarely with the rest of the family—at least
not with Bobby. Arguments at the table had become so frequent
that Linda sent Shelley to the laundry room to eat, to stay out of
her dad's way.

Bobby made weekends hard on Shelley, who would volunteer
to go grocery shopping with her mother to get out of the house
and away from her father. But he forbade that, telling Linda he
needed Shelley to help with the cattle.

Sundays were important days for Linda. She had become more
and more religious as she sought answers to the family's turmoil.
The evangelical Baptist faith promised a way of patching the
seemingly unbridgeable rifts. One day she announced that she
wanted everyone to go to church.

"Make up an excuse," Bobby told Shelley. "Tell her you're
sick." And Shelley did as she was commanded.

Another week, Bobby had another excuse for Shelley. "I have
to ride the horse this morning," Shelley told Linda.

Bobby made his own excuses; usually work. And Linda went to
church with Michael.

A few times, however, Shelley managed to sneak off to church
with her mom and Michael without telling Bobby. She appreciated the brief escape, even though the service offered her

nothing. Trapped in the mad grip of a man who told the world he was her father, Shelley at first had high expectations about church, but she soon changed her mind.

I never heard the preacher talk about being saved or being a child of God. I mean, if you go to church that long and don't know. They go just to say they go.

On top of that, she was berated by Bobby when she got back. "You know better," he scolded in his angry whisper. "You know you're supposed to stay here anytime there is a time." Anytime there was a time was every time there was a time. He had made his daughter his daughter-mistress. And he had made of himself a lovesick father-suitor.

He had convinced himself that it wasn't his daughter he was having sex with. At the times when the truth of his perversity could not be denied, he told himself, "I was looking for love from Shelley. That's what I wanted from Shelley was her love." Bobby then just ignored the shame, embarrassment and its consequences for his young daughter's life. "I might have thought about it occasionally . . . that if somebody knew it might embarrass her or do whatever, but it really was not forefront."

The summer months, when school was out, were very different. Shelley loved to ride her horses in the morning, goof off, watch soap operas, ride her three-wheeler to various parts of the ranch to watch the ranch hands work. She swam in the lake, worked the cows three and four hours a day. At least once a week Shelley and her mom went on a shopping expedition to one of Dallas's first-class department stores. Neiman-Marcus was a favorite. Linda indulged her love of clothes and jewelry and taught her daughter to do the same.

It was easy to buy, since Linda's closet in the new house was the size of a small bedroom: fifteen feet square, with an adjoining, hidden closet for furs and a strongbox for jewelry. Bobby and Linda had a sauna, shower and Jacuzzi in their master bathroom. And next to that was a weight room, with mats and mirrors.

And he brought his daughter there, so he could look at himself and her as he violated her.

"You're just lying there," he complained, "doing nothing."
And Shelley would continue to lie there, doing nothing.

"You're gross," she muttered. She meant it. That's all she
thought about him.

*I'd lay there stiff as a board and look at the ceiling and not blink,
not move, not nothin'. And that pissed him off bad. I was so
terrified, so ashamed at what was happening.*

At the other end of the house, far away, was Shelley's room,
complete with her own bathroom and walk-in closet. At first she
was glad for the distance from her father, but she soon learned
that the distance was as much a bane as boon. It didn't matter.
Nothing mattered with Bobby. He always figured out a way of
getting what he wanted.

*I always had this weird feeling that every time I took a shower
he was watching me. Because it seemed like every time I got in my
shower, he would go to the attic. I went up into the attic one day
to see if I could see anything, but I couldn't. But it was so weird
to me because every time I got in the shower he would go to the
attic.*

Bobby Sessions was smart. He seemed to have covered most of
the bases, covered his tracks to the bases, and still hit home runs
every time up. He could see Shelley everywhere. He had thought
of everything.

The "affair," as Bobby thought of the relationship, had become
familiar. It had developed its own rules and rituals. Shelley could
smell him coming—his Winston 100s were like a cloud of con-
tamination—and going. And when he wore his terrycloth robe
around the house, Shelley closed her eyes. "Look at me," he said
to Shelley as he swung it open. "Look at it."

*I knew every time I saw him with that terrycloth robe that he was
fixin' to come to my room. And it just got to the point where every
time I saw that robe, I would just—blaaaah—I felt like throwing
up. But I would never look.*

*Like, I'd be in my room and didn't know my mom was going
somewhere. And I could hear someone coming down that long,
long hallway. Like in the morning, when I was eating my Apple*

Jacks and watching my cartoons and I'd see him coming down with that robe, I knew something—he always tried to get me to touch him or always wanted me to look. And I would never look. I would never touch. He always wanted me to kiss him and I never would— ugh! He always wanted me to touch him. And I would not. I mean, I don't even know what he looks like. I would not look. I would not! I didn't care if he tied me up, I just would not look.

He never did tie her up, but Bobby had his share of kinky tricks. He gave Shelley crude pornographic books, ones that he had kept since high school—an odd bequest. But he urged her to read them, to learn from their explicit sexual detail. She didn't.

He had Shelley take her clothes off and lie on her bed as he snapped Polaroid pictures. She didn't know what he did with the pictures or why he took them. She didn't care.

Bobby didn't even know what he was going to do with the pictures. "At the time I thought it was so I could look at her, because I didn't know that this would go on forever," he recalled later.

There would be an end to this. Even Bobby admitted that. He just didn't see an end.

Shelley cried, "Why are you doing this?"

"Because I can't get any love from you any other way."

He owned her. He could do with Shelley what he wanted and she was powerless—she *felt* powerless. And that was all that mattered to him.

I was so terrified, so ashamed at what was happening. He had me convinced that it was my fault, that I did it, I was the guilty one. Like, so much shame! I loved my mother and everything, you know, and he had me so convinced that I would hurt my mother if she found out. That it would be me that hurt her.

Bobby would stroke Shelley while threatening her. "You went to bed with me," he told her, "and I'm your mother's husband."

I felt like I was hurting my mother. I could never figure out why he would want to have sex with me when he had my mother, cause my mom was pretty and everything. I don't know.

Bobby left Shelley in her confusion. He counted on it as an engine of guilt, to keep Shelley quiet. He had made Shelley an unwitting participant—she didn't choose to become her father's lover, of course, but she didn't act not to be. For Bobby, that was acquiescence enough. "I knew it was wrong, but I enjoyed it, and Shelley loved me and she enjoyed it when it was happening," he later rationalized. "I just never really thought about consequences or anything else."

What Linda saw was a deteriorating domestic situation. The family continued to fight—with Shelley at the center of things—and Linda continued to try to do something about it. In Houston she had tried to arrange for counseling but couldn't get Bobby to go.

Now, in Powell, Linda put her foot down. "I just demanded that we were going to get counseling," she recalled.

Together Bobby, Linda and Shelley drove to Dallas. Over the course of a few months they saw a counselor five times. But never did the subject of incest come up.

VIII

DON'T KISS THE BOYS

In the middle of her conversation, Shelley heard it. A slight click on the line somewhere meant someone was on an extension.

"I'm on the phone," she said. Nothing. She yelled again into the mouthpiece. "I'm on the phone!" Still there was no response. She told her friend she had to get off now, and hung up.

At the same instant Bobby Sessions dropped a phone receiver into its cradle in his office. It was a special phone he kept to the side of his desk, used only for what he had just used it for: monitoring Shelley. Ranch foreman Richard Ruiz had picked it up once, by mistake. "At first I didn't know what it was," he recalled. "But it was a phone in his office where if it rang up in the house he could pick it up and listen to phone calls without them knowing it. He could go in there and hear all the phone calls. . . . It was a weird situation."

The other phones at the ranch were connected as well, though not with this specific purpose in mind. Nonetheless, Bobby could monitor Shelley's phone calls from any phone on the property. They were set up to ring at the house and in the office. He had already directed Linda not to answer the phone unless it rang more than three times—which meant that Bobby's secretary or any ranch employee who was at the office would answer it. If it was a weekend, Bobby could take his calls at the house.

And Bobby had a more sinister gimmick as well. In the attic above his office he had installed a reel-to-reel tape recorder. "When the phones rang at the office, they also rang at the house," recalled James Duvall. "And anytime that he was gone from the office, he could switch this switch and it would record everything that was said while he was gone from the office. If the secretary answered the phone, it would record everything that was said. If somebody called the house, which was all on the same line, and asked for Shelley, this machine would record everything. He would come back and he would play these recordings back."

James had built the platform in the attic to bolt the device on. According to James, "On his bookcase he had this recorder reel behind doors, Japanese-style trim, in brass. And behind these two sliding doors he had this reel thing. And every once in a while, when he'd be playing the reels, you couldn't go in his office."

The move to the mansion didn't do anything for Shelley's chances against her father's dogged advances.

It was more frequent. Sometimes it would be several times a day. Just any time he got a chance.

But Shelley was now fifteen and spreading her wings. And Bobby could feel his grip on her harder to hold. Shelley was outgoing, popular and very active.

Bobby was scared. He tried to tell himself he was doing this out of love for his daughter; that she would love him more. But he knew better. And he acted as if he knew better—not by quitting, but by tightening the reins.

Just as he monitored Shelley's phone calls, he routinely went through her dresser.

Once he found notes that a couple of us girls had passed back and forth. You know, such and such a boy is so cute. And he got all mad. I wasn't really doing anything out of the ordinary. Girls like boys.

Everywhere that Shelley went, someone, usually Bobby, was sure to follow. He didn't want to let her out of his sight because he thought, as she got older and wiser, she might figure a way out.

And as a jealous and suspicious lover, Bobby was rarely disappointed.

As Shelley entered her sophomore year in high school, Bobby had every reason to be worried about his hold on his daughter.

But he had to become more inventive to follow what was fast becoming the hurly-burly life of an energetic and popular teenager. Shelley's world now far exceeded the boundaries of her home—and that posed a double threat: she could leave him; she could tell on him. The possibility of either made Bobby crazy with jealousy and fear that surpassed anything even his first wife could have imagined.

At home he was in almost complete control. He would, for example, allow Shelley to drink—even to get drunk if she wished. But she never did.

Outside, Bobby tried everything to maintain his vigilant control. He constantly warned his daughter he didn't want her getting mixed up with the wrong crowd at school. He preached to Shelley the evils of the world, as he had to the church crowd that Sunday. And he maintained the fiction, even to her, that he was worried about her getting mixed up with the wrong people.

Henry Edgington, a self-described "ex-hippie" turned Protestant minister, worked a lot with the students in Kerens and the surrounding towns. He knew Shelley from youth gatherings at The Yellow House, the former parsonage of Kerens' Church of Christ, which he and other members of the church had turned into a place for the teenagers to gather, and which became a popular alternative to cruising Main Street. And, though not a member of his nondenominational Church of Christ, Shelley sometimes came to services with his regular congregants.

They were not at all fast times in Kerens for young people, one reason that Edgington's modest affairs became so popular. "Our regular services for young people would start at six, Sunday evenings, and they'd be finished by seven. Then we opened up our little Yellow House and started having a meal and what we would call a devotional, every Sunday night. And sometimes it would be an actual devotion and we would sit and talk about things, sometimes we'd sing devotional songs, campfire-type songs that the kids would like and the adults would hate. Because it would seem too fast for the old folks," Edgington remembered.

"We started out with something like five or six teenagers then and ended up with thirty-two one Sunday night."

Shelley got out whenever she could—but it wasn't often, for Bobby issued new rules as fast as there were new opportunities. He forbade her to leave the school campus at lunchtime, while everyone else rode off to the barbecue store or home. Bobby seemed to always find out about those times that Shelley ventured off to town from school. It seemed to Shelley that her dad had spies everywhere: a ranch hand would be there, telling Shelley that her father wanted her back at school.

Bobby often followed her personally, for he had amazingly little to do at the ranch and plenty of free time. As the quintessential gentleman farmer, his businesses were almost as playthings. His ranch managers and workers ran the cattle and construction businesses and oversaw details. Sometimes Shelley would look out a window at school and see her father, parked across the street, sitting in his Jeep Renegade, watching.

In spite of his persecutions, Bobby would complain to Richard Ruiz, who had a daughter Shelley's age, that Shelley didn't appreciate anything he had done for her.

"I knew he was having problems with her," said Ruiz later. "He'd ask me what I would do. I didn't know what to do. They couldn't talk to each other in public. You could see that she either had a chip on her shoulder or he had a chip on his. And he would buy her something and then something would happen and he would take it away. It's just like the horses—the horses and the cattle. One time he would say, 'Go down there and take care of Shelley's stuff for her.' And they'd have a blowout or something and the next day he'd come in and say, 'Don't go down there and feed so and so, that's Shelley's job. If she wants the goddamn thing,' or something like that, 'let her go do it.' You know, things like that. He had a temper and she had a temper."

Shelley, meanwhile, was beginning to subvert her father's orders and advances in a manner that matched her coming of age.

In the small window of outside activity allowed her—at school—
she began to blossom.

*My plan was to get involved in stuff to get away from him, so
the more I did, the better everybody would like me, the more they
would vote for me, and the more I would get to stay away from
home.*

*Normally, I wouldn't have done that because, you know, I would
never be the person that would get in front of the class to talk or
make a speech. I'd get embarrassed or leave.*

Shelley joined the Riding Club and Future Farmers of America, was an FFA Secretary and was elected cheerleader and the
Sophomore Class representative to the Student Council. She
became the manager of the girls' basketball team. She kept her
grades up. In the spring she signed up for the track team and ran
the half mile. She overcame the rich bitch image and, despite her
father's best efforts and worst fears, she became popular.

She did all this to escape her father. Anything that would get
her out of the house, away from him.

And, as though Bobby understood this, Shelley was made to
regret her social successes. Bobby did everything he could to
thwart her forays into the outside world.

Shelley had earned a job as manager of the girls' basketball
team during her freshman year. But before she could celebrate her
good fortune, her father told her she wouldn't be traveling with
them.

*He would try to get me out of it where I didn't have to go to the
out-of-town games. He didn't want me going anywhere, and the
coach would jump over my case about it because those were my
responsibilities.*

Even during home games Shelley was subject to embarrassing
parental rules. Bobby forbade her to leave the gym without him.
After the games, while her friends filed outside to jaw, Shelley,
the team's manager, had to wait on the court for her father or
mother to come get her.

From the ordinary world, the one that her friends at school
lived in, Shelley appeared to be radically sheltered. Friends sym-

pathized. Some fathers were strict; few as protective as Bobby. And no one suspected the obscene reasons for his rules.

My friends got to do pretty much what they wanted to do. And nobody was going home to what I was. Every time I went home, I'd think, "My God, he'll be coming in my room." You think about it. That's why I stayed away as much as I could. Or tried to stay around my mom as much as I could.

That's why I always tried to have a girlfriend spend the night on the weekend. Because I thought this time I'd be safe, if someone was sleeping with me in my bed. You know, if I had a friend with me, I was safe.

So I always used to beg my mom, call her from school or something, ask before he got home. And I'd hurry up and get the girl over there, before he said, "No."

It usually did protect Shelley, but she paid a price. "You knew you weren't supposed to have anyone over," he scolded when he pulled Shelley aside. His voice was low and harsh. "You can't get away from me, you know."

It frightened Shelley. Everything she seemed to do was Bobby's concern. He was more powerful than anyone she knew—he was more concerned about the details of her life than anyone she knew. He knew everything.

Bobby's obsession with his daughter brought him perilously close at various times to drawing attention to the relationship.

He cautioned her not to let *anyone* touch her. Those times that he would allow her out on her own—to visit a friend or go shopping—he would follow her to make sure she was going where she said she was, to make sure she wasn't cheating on him; and if he couldn't follow, he'd send a ranch hand to do it.

As a cheerleader that year, Shelley was driven to football games by Bobby, who then made sure that she didn't wander from his gaze. In the stands, cheering with other parents and adults, Bobby was honored as the school's most prominent benefactor, sought after by the principal and others. From her sidelines position, Shelley knew that Bobby was leering from the bleachers, his casual demeanor an affront to her.

"I can remember being at ball games," Linda recalled, "and we are sitting there watching the game, and on their break the girls would run back behind us where the cars were. And Bob said, 'Linda, Shelley doesn't need to be back there. Somebody needs to be watching.' And one of us tried to keep an eye on what all those kids were doing because the parents don't go check on them. They just all sit there and visit."

If Linda wasn't along and he had to leave his seat, Bobby asked someone to keep an eye on Shelley. It was an odd request, but willingly fulfilled by Bobby's friends—his concern seemed like such pride in his daughter. Other parents envied the Sessions for their confidence, their beauty, their money, and thought Shelley was so well-behaved.

Shelley was disgusted. And to add to her pain, Bobby wouldn't let her go to after-game parties. Although there were plenty of invitations, there were no parties for Shelley. No dates. No movies.

It was terrible. I got involved in everything at school, figuring that I would get to get out more. I finally had an excuse to go out. But it didn't matter. So it was worse being popular and being in everything. It would have been better if I hadn't tried out for anything.

In a sense Bobby's "paranoia" was justified: Shelley *was* searching for an escape—but the immediate route she chose could hardly be called wayward. She became a cheerleader, FFA sweetheart, rodeo queen, manager of the girls' basketball team. She got good grades. She fought off her father by focusing on school activities that he couldn't touch.

Ironically, Bobby was also being socially active—for different reasons, of course. He preached in church and sang in the choir. At high-school social events, he would participate. And he cultivated his reputation as a local boy made good by continuing to donate lavishly. His picture was frequently in the newspaper for his generous gifts.

Bobby had become the "best" father in order to cover his dark secret. In this way, his divided life began. He talked publicly about his concern for wholesomeness while leaving stacks of *Playboy* lying around his office and study. In fact, he collected *Playboy* for eighteen years, was a member of the Playboy Club and carried a club card.

He preached against the sinfulness of the county's youth; against drugs and sex. And he believed that Shelley was "a wild young girl."

It was such a double standard. Like when he got up in church and told those parents about what they let their kids do. Meanwhile, at home he's doing this to his daughter. It was just such a double standard.

But Bobby didn't shy away from the public. He invited Henry Edgington to come out to the ranch and see him after he heard Edgington sing and play his guitar at a talent show at the National Guard Armory. "He heard me talking to another fellow about wishing I had somebody to back me to put out a record," recalled Edgington. "You know, we always talked like that, hoping somebody would hear it."

Edgington did visit, some weeks later, and played with Bobby, who sang a song or two. Edgington also got to know Linda. He already knew Shelley from his substitute teaching at the high school and her occasional appearances at The Yellow House.

"I was getting to know them pretty well," said Edgington. But the preacher also knew of the control Bobby exercised over his daughter, showing up at the schoolyard at lunchtime to check up on Shelley and her friends. "Bob was so protective all the time," he recalled.

The small-town living that Bobby announced was what he was after when he moved to Powell did not serve secrets well. Shelley was conspicuous often by her absence.

"The town wasn't that big," said Edgington, "and Shelley would have known all the kids there."

In Kerens, if you didn't meet at school or the athletic events, you'd cruise the old brick road.

"We have a drag up here called Main Street," Ricky Layfield later said. "You go up here to the blinking light, take a right there, go across the railroad tracks and you'll see a button in the middle of the road. You go down it, there'll be a middle street, and then there's a dip, where that dip is you make a U-turn, you come back up, go around that button, go back and they'd sit along the sides.

"Well, sometimes they just cruise around and don't do nothing, just cruise around and talk and listen to the radio. Pull people over and talk—you know."

Main Street might have one or two cars on it, sometimes two dozen. Everybody had cars because most kids worked at least part-time and could pay for them. Shelley was no different: she wanted a car, and a stereo in it.

But Shelley rarely made the scene. "She might have every now and then, but it was no everyday thing, and she never did cruise around," Ricky remembered. "She'd make a drag with somebody, one loop; zoom, she had to go."

Bobby had to reach deeper for the anchors. She couldn't date. She couldn't go to parties or to friends' houses for the night. Bobby not only wanted her all; he wanted her quiet.

"How bad do you want to go out?" he would ask her. How badly does any teenage girl want to go out?

Then he introduced a new word into his lexicon of pathology. "You'll have to do a turn if you want to."

Shelley didn't have to ask what he meant. His new threat: "More turns." The term was an apt one: a prostitute's word for a sexual act. Bobby made it into a sort of double-edged sword. Violation of a rule would merit a punishment of ten more turns; a privilege requested would require a payment of ten more turns.

He really couldn't do anything to punish me, you know, if I didn't do anything wrong. Like, he couldn't spank me if I went to church with my mom, because she would say, "What did she do wrong?" So he would just add turns. It got to where he would add just for anything. Like, if he came into my room one night and I said leave me alone, I'm tired, I need to go to sleep. Well, you know, that's ten more turns.

Bobby got his turns no matter what. His sexual assaults on his young daughter were almost daily occurrences no matter how many turns she "owed" him.

As Shelley became more interested in her peers, Bobby played adroitly on her social desires and anxieties. He liked to make an elaborate show of bartering sex for privileges, thereby making it seem as though she were involved in the decision.

Incredibly, by demanding sexual favors from his daughter as currency for his permission to do something, Bobby further convinced himself that it was the only way to maintain his parental authority. "Shelley would want certain things or want to do certain things which normally I wouldn't have let her, and she had this over my head," Bobby would later explain. "So, in order to give her the things she wanted, sometimes I would say, Okay, for ten turns, or whatever, I will let you do that." In his mind, Bobby wanted to believe that Shelley was blackmailing *him*—using "this," the secret, to get what she wanted.

"When it got to a real crux of a situation, either I would give in and let her do what she wanted or I would add more turns," he claimed later, still trying to shift the burden of responsibility.

But if he felt like he was always being had by his daughter, what kept him playing the game? "I was always afraid if I held the line too hard, then Shelley would say, 'Mom, this is what's happening.' And then everything would go down the tubes."

So, in another perversion of reason, Bobby assigned turns in order to keep a lid on his crime—as though this were part of being a father. Shelley came home late from school: "That'll be twenty turns."

To get other normal teenage privileges, Shelley had to pay: pay her dad with her body. Of course, she would have had to pay anyway; Bobby would have pressed his demands even if she had wanted nothing from him. He created the illusion of exchange to fulfill his fantasy of a willing partnership between his daughter and himself; and to reinforce Shelley's guilty belief that she was somehow selling herself.

Did Shelley *know* anymore what was normal? Did she *feel* she was a prostitute? "You want that horse?" He smiled. "How bad?" Bobby had the best little whorehouse in Texas—or so he wanted Shelley to feel.

"When is this going to end?" Shelley asked her dad. "When are you going to stop doing this to me?"

This was the real world Bobby knew. "Probably whenever you graduate and leave home."

Shelley didn't believe it. It already seemed like forever.

"I didn't think that I could stop it," Bobby recalled. "I thought the only way to stop it is to say, hey, this is what has been happening and then suffer the consequences. So I didn't see any way out."

Bobby's no-exit was a convenient way of feeding his obsession. But Shelley was moving in another direction.

A popular girl, Shelley was invited to many parties. Gradually, she began to threaten Bobby with exposure if he didn't let her go. Bobby was confused, worried. Was Shelley's belligerence a sign of things to come? How long could he hold out?

Bobby faced two equally unappetizing prospects: if Shelley dated, he would have to share her with other "men"; he would have to confront his own jealousy. And there was mounting fear of another prospect: the more she mixed with others, the more tenuous his hold on her became.

Bobby knew that Shelley was popular—he had paid close attention through the FFA, the girls' basketball games and the cheerleading. He had chased away any young man who spent too much time with her. He imagined that "she was quasi-going with this young boy. I had said some things to her about the way things looked. The way they stood and held each other and this, that and the other. And then she wanted to go to a party."

He finally gave in. "You can go," he said. "Just back off the boys."

Shelley laughed derisively: she understood the bind that Bobby now found himself in.

"Just don't kiss the boys," her dad said. "Go dance, do whatever, just don't kiss the boys."

Sessions wanted a deal, hoping to surmount this new challenge to his domination of his daughter. He told her that they had to trust each other, each give a little, and that this would be a time to start. Shelley could go to the party—that was Bobby's part of the deal—and Shelley wouldn't kiss the boys—that was hers. Shelley agreed.

When Bobby picked Shelley up later that evening, the first thing he asked was, "Did you do what you were supposed to do?"

Shelley laughed. "No!" she snarled, feeling her new powers over her father.

Bobby exploded. He slammed on the brakes. "Okay!" he shouted, "let's just go back in there and tell everybody! Let's tell them what you've been doing with me for all this time!"

Shelley cringed. "No!" she said. "No." Her ocean of confidence evaporated. She felt the quick pain of doubt and shame. She wanted desperately for someone to know what her father was doing, but she was too ashamed to tell. She felt dirty. Would others think she was, once they knew? And that was the irony: Shelley's popularity became Bobby's best guarantee of secrecy.

Bobby's preoccupations looked odd to Shelley's classmates; but their awe of Mr. Sessions' money and power kept darker suspicions at bay. "Maybe if we hadn't been blinded by her appearance," remembered classmate Ricky Layfield, "we could have read it. But, you know, everybody was saying, this is a rich girl, she's got no worries in the world. And all the time she had more than anybody could imagine. She didn't ever show it."

Only Shelley knew the perverse truth about her father's "protection."

If I had been sleeping around with all the boys in school, that would give him reason to think, "Well, she wants it or something." But I wasn't. I never got to go anywhere. Everyone in school used to make fun of me about it.

"When we were in high school," recalled Ricky, "you couldn't take her out or nothing. That was just out of the question. It was like nobody I ever seen in my life. Everybody was tripping out on the guy because he was so overprotective. Everybody was saying, 'Man, you can't hardly talk to her alone if he's around.' He'd come up to the school and she'd be talking to somebody and, boy, he'd stomp them feet, you know, 'Let's go,' he'd say. Forget it. He was just a trip. . . . But everybody kind of overlooked that because he was a rich man and he helped the school and was going to help everybody."

But there was an inevitability to Shelley's growth that kept pushing her into conflict with her father's obsession and her own fears.

One part of that inevitability was boys—they liked her. Shelley liked them. They called her. And at school, Shelley had boyfriends despite Bobby's best efforts.

Everyone at school thought I was a virgin, and that's one of the reasons why all the boys, you know, wanted to be with me, someone that's never been to bed with anybody. And I was sitting there all along thinking, "If you only knew."

But Bobby, wittingly or not, had squeezed Shelley into a psychological corner, an emotional no-exit.

You think about it, you know, think about later, when this is all over, and you go to bed with one of these boys from high school or something and they find out you're not a virgin. They're going to ask you, "Well, who have you been sleeping with all this time?" What are you supposed to say?

And that's exactly the vulnerability that Bobby played upon. He was a man of such sales acumen that he could make millions of dollars in a risky international game of oil trading—a modern horse-trader's gamble—and succeed in the world's power capital, New York, hobnobbing with the best in the business. He was a wheeler-dealer, master of the trade of reading human strengths and weaknesses. He knew when, where and how to strike.

A fifteen-year-old girl was hardly a match for his genius. And his own daughter. . . .

He'd laugh, just like this Jack Nicholson laugh.

"Do you actually think somebody's going to have you?" He had the eyes and smile of the devil. "You actually think somebody could love you after what I've done to you?"

And it starts to sink in and you start to believe it. What's the use? What can you do?

* * *

Shelley was popular almost in spite of herself, but her boyfriends were school-hour only. She wasn't allowed to date, or go out at night even with her girlfriends.

Most people in high school, when you say you have a boy-friend, you have a boyfriend, you go to the movies, whatever. Well, I had a boyfriend, but it was just school. It wasn't like he could call me or he could come over—it's just like going together, but in school.

Shelley's hours at school were the only ones that even approximated time that was her own. And into those she squeezed a social life. Without going on a single date, she met and broke up with a half-dozen boyfriends.

Jay Colvin and Shelley went steady for a while—an "at-school" steady, which meant that she didn't talk to other boys. "You looked at Shelley for very long and Jay'd get hot," recalled Ricky Layfield. "We'd sit over and do it just to make him mad. And she'd eat it up. Her head swelled big time."

Jay paid a visit to the ranch to see Shelley—but he didn't get far. Bobby chased him off with a shotgun.

This was exactly why Shelley had started signing up for all the activities.

Everyone was terrified of him. All the guys were afraid to speak to me because they didn't want to get shot.

Shelley waited for her dad to leave town, then asked Linda if she could go to the movies with Jay and some girlfriends. Though more understanding than her husband, Linda increasingly backed up Bobby on rules in the interests of what she believed was family harmony. She told Shelley, "No movie."

Shelley didn't sulk. Instead, she changed into her jeans, called her friends, then told Linda she was going to the barn to work the cows. She jumped on her three-wheeler and sped off to the barn, a quarter mile away. Once there, she waited a few minutes for her friends to pull up to the back of the building.

It was the first time Shelley had tried to sneak out. She was worried, thinking that her dad had spies everywhere. But it was worth the risk. She liked Jay. She had let him peck at her cheek in the hall at school. But nothing else. It hadn't bothered her. Her father's acts hadn't made her detest boys—nor had it diminished the excitement of these innocent liaisons.

Now, she and Jay were sitting together, holding hands in the dark in front of the big-screen showing of *An Officer and a Gentleman.*

"Shelley!" The loud whisper was unmistakable. And Shelley wanted to sink through the floor when she heard her mother's hiss to the left. Linda bent low, not wanting to make a scene. And Shelley was thankful for that. "Shelley," Linda said, "I think we better go."

Shelley popped up immediately. " 'Bye," she said, waving bravely to Jay and her friends.

It was pretty embarrassing.

These incidents didn't seem to hurt her popularity. As fate would have it, they made her even more the object of attention— as well as causing a few heated squabbles among the boys.

There were rituals only the students could understand.

It's just known. Like, this is my territory, so don't try to flirt with her. That's being steady. Between classes he picks you up at your room and walks with you to your other class.

All-state football quarterback Russell Anderson, son of the coach, had talked to Shelley a few times while she was going steady with rancher's son Barry Choate. Barry was good-looking, but Russell was a charmer. He opened doors for girls "like a gentleman." And when the quarterback asked her to go steady, Shelley said yes. Shelley told Barry the next day before school began.

But Barry didn't take the morning's news so well and immediately challenged the football player.

I don't know how they started it because I had my back turned, talking to somebody, when Barry came up.

Other kids were beginning to gather around. "Barry was real jealous and he just fronted Russell out," recalled Ricky Layfield. "And Russell called his bluff and they just went at it." But just as quickly Ricky, a bystander, was on top of both of them.

"I broke it up," he recalled, "and got hit in the process. I was joking around with 'em, though. I said, 'Yeah, you're all fightin' over her and she'll be mine.' She never did hear none of it. I was talking trash, you know, because both of them were my friends, because Barry had been my friend from the time we started first grade. Russell moved in when he was a freshman and me and him kicked it right off. We were about the same size and did about the same things."

The bell for first class rang just as the boys were brushing the dust and dirt off. They ran in to their agriculture class, held in a room with long tables arranged in a U, and took their seats.

Barry sat on one side of me and Russell sat on the other. And they had just finished fighting and I was sitting there, like, uhhh, it was embarrassing.

The ag teacher came in with a slight smile. He immediately called on Shelley, the only girl in the class, and always one of his favorite respondents.

"Shelley," he said, "would you like to tell us what happened this morning?"

Russell and Barry stared at the tabletop. Their hair was mussed, clothes ruffled and knuckles bruised.

Shelley giggled. "No, I would not."

Excited by the events, Shelley decided to risk going off-campus to lunch with Russell and some friends. But she was stopped by a teacher—enforcing one of Bobby's rules, not a school regulation.

I was told before that Bobby had been seen across the street with binoculars. Watching to make sure I hadn't left. That is pathetic. I thought, "Well, he runs three businesses and all he can think of is coming over here to see if I leave school or not for lunch."

The only people who didn't go off-campus for lunch were "the nerds."

I was stuck with the nerds. It wasn't like you were going to park or something at lunch. You'd just go uptown and there was a little store that made barbecue sandwiches. And everyone used to go up there and get barbecue sandwiches, eat them and come back. It was so stupid. And he would make it a big thing.

Shelley's activities were making Bobby increasingly nervous. He began turning up the heat.

IX

GUNS

Toward the end of Shelley's sophomore year, she lost a sure bid for another year on the cheerleading squad. No one understood how it happened. But she and her friends guessed.

"Shelley won it hands down," recalled Cherry Layfield, Ricky's mother. "There was no way she could have lost that cheerleader election, but she did. There was a freshman that got her place on the squad. You tell me that wasn't fixed."

Shelley saw it as another sign of Bobby's far-flung and flailing attempts to regain control.

He knew that I wanted to be a cheerleader in order to get away from him.

A friend of Shelley's went to the principal right after the results were announced—and was told that the ballots had already been thrown away. Without even knowing it, Shelley was preparing the way for a showdown. Her grades started dropping—instead of As and Bs, she was getting Cs and Ds.

I didn't care as much. It was getting harder and harder to keep up the front at school. The more popular I got, the more everyone expected of me. But he wouldn't let me do anything. I had speeches to make for rodeo or something and he was always saying, "You're

*not going if you don't do this." I would always get invited to parties
and I couldn't go. I was in track but my coach started getting real
mad at—she was going to kick me off the team because I could
never go to the meets.*

Bobby was trying to withdraw privileges he had already given.
But it was too late. The fights between daughter and father—over
freedom and privileges—got more bitter. Shelley was no longer
afraid to stand up to him; in part because she could feel a world
of her own coming into reach, in part because she had become
the guardian of the big secret. And as she fought with Bobby, he
became more desperate.

Betty Duvall witnessed one fight, over whether Shelley could
go to a ball game. Linda took Shelley's side for once. "And there
was a big argument that started because of that and he was going
to shoot them all," recalled Betty. "Because Shelley and Linda
turned against him."

It was a sign of Bobby's desperation. Guns. No way out.

Not long afterward, following another heated argument with
Shelley, Bobby stalked off. When she saw him climb into his truck
with a pistol in hand, she raced after him. By the time she caught
up, Bobby was sitting on the ground in the pasture, gun to his
chest.

"Bobby!" Shelley yelled, lunging for the gun. She was hysterical, not understanding exactly what was happening. The gun
moved in every direction, one moment pointed at Shelley, another time at Bobby.

They struggled, Shelley kicking and screaming, until Bobby
finally relented. He released the gun to Shelley.

She could have ended it then; she could have ended it many
times. But it was too late for that. Her anger at him was only
partially submerged, but her shame was buried right alongside it.
She would be blamed. She was sure that Bobby would have
arranged for that.

What wasn't so sure was where Bobby might direct his anger.
A few weeks later, Bobby and Shelley were sitting in the backyard,
arguing. Linda was on an errand. Suddenly Bobby pulled out his
pistol.

*He stood there with the gun pointed to my head. And it seemed
like forever. He just stood there, pointing it at me and I was just
sitting there waiting to die.*

What was there to lose? Shelley was becoming as bold as
Bobby. It was a subtle transference of control. But more and more
Bobby would storm off after a fight; drive down to the field in the
jeep.

*He would just be sitting there with the gun and shaking. And
I am going, "Oh, my God!" One time I said, "If you don't come
back to the house in five minutes, I'm calling the police." And he
would just sit there, wouldn't say nothing. And I just freaked out.
I would go home, wait a few minutes and make him think I was
calling somebody.*

*And I would go back down there to see if he was dead or alive
or whatever. It was just weird. It happened all the time.*

Shelley was now turning up the heat on Bobby, making threats,
not wanting to reveal the secret, but always holding it over his
head.

One night they were eating in the family room, watching
television. Linda was in the kitchen, almost a signal to Bobby to
make a move. He slid over to Shelley's side and touched her leg.

"Don't mess with me!" Shelley snapped.

But Bobby persisted.

"Don't mess with me!" Shelley raised her voice even more now.
"If you don't leave me alone, I'm going to tell Mom everything."
She said it loudly enough to bring Linda out of the kitchen.

"What's the matter with y'all!" she screamed. "What's the
deal? What are you talking about?"

Shelley said nothing to her mother. Instead, she turned toward
Bobby and glared. "Why don't you tell her!"

Bobby looked confused and hurt at the same time. But he
didn't speak.

"I want to know what's going on!" Linda screamed again.
"What's wrong! Y'all crazy!"

"Ask *him!*"

"Nothing," Bobby finally said.

"Tell her, Dad," Shelley shouted. "Tell her. Tell her everything!"

"Tell me what?" Linda screamed.

But Bobby stonewalled. And Linda finally gave up in frustration and marched back to the kitchen. "It was like they were not going to tell me what was wrong with them," Linda later recalled. "Both of them were bad off that day."

"You better leave me alone or I'll tell her," Shelley whispered loudly to Bobby after her mom left the room.

Bobby flew into a silent rage, his eyes registering fear and anger at the same time. "If you tell, nobody will believe you. They won't ever love you. Nobody will ever want you. Nobody will even believe you—you'll be the laughingstock of the town. You tell and you'll be the fool, not me. Even if anyone believed you, nobody would ever want to marry someone molested by their dad. They'll say, 'You're a slut. You're a tramp.' "

He had me thinking, you know, that I did it. I caused it. Everyone is going to hate me. So I might as well shut up. So that's what I did.

Shelley's adrenaline slowed. Once again he seemed to know just what to say—and Shelley believed him. Bobby made her feel dirty and ugly and unwanted. And if anyone ever found out the truth about them, Bobby convinced her, the rest of her life would be ruined as well as his.

Shelley couldn't tell. But she wanted somebody to know. She wanted desperately for her mother to rescue her. Her mom must have known. So why didn't she do something?

She had to have known. I mean, normal kids, you know—I could have seen reactions like that if I was on drugs or something. But normal kids don't act like that to their parents unless there is something wrong.

X

LINDA

We weren't close enough for me to tell her what was wrong. She's very naïve and very dependent on him.

Linda Sessions was a puzzle. Why did she live on a cattle ranch if she was allergic to cows? Drive a white Cadillac on dusty roads where mostly pickups drove? Wear high heels and flowered dresses in a town where cowboy boots and jeans were almost a uniform? And she shopped at Neiman-Marcus in Dallas as often as the K Mart next door.

"Linda, she wasn't around much," recalled ranch manager Richard Ruiz.

All the boys at school used to say, "Take me to your house so I can see your mother." Or, "I wish I was older so I could date your mother." And I always used to get jealous because they said my mom was so pretty. When we'd go shopping, you know, they would say, "Are you going to pay for it or is your sister?" And I'd say, "She's not my sister, she's my mother." She looks young for her age.

"Linda, oh man, that lady's fine," was Ricky Layfield's description of Shelley's mother. "That Bobby's a stupid boy. I mean, shoot, you can look at Shelley and think about twenty years older than that. Man, she's fine, she's a good-looking woman, I ain't lyin'."

There were many excuses and rationalizations—those tricks the mind plays to justify its heart's obsessions. For Bobby it was that his daughter didn't love him, and he needed her love. He told himself that that was why he raped her; and he believed it only because he told himself to believe it. He desired to have his daughter's love and respect—isn't that a normal fatherly yearning? But that drove him toward his pathological equation. He contorted love as though it were part of a circus act. And even when he admitted that what he was doing was wrong, whom did he blame? His wife had prevented him from getting close to Shelley. "Well, my marriage was always kind of up and down. Linda was very defensive of Shelley almost from the word go," Bobby said later. "Shelley could do no wrong. Shelley could not make a mistake. Most of the time our arguments were over Shelley, one way or another."

For Linda, the mind games were dazzlingly complex. For over three years she somehow avoided *knowing* what was happening to her daughter. Somehow she didn't see the writing on the wall; didn't, at least, admit that her husband was molesting her daughter.

She did know that *something* was wrong. Family members don't chase each other, screaming, around the house for nothing; don't have pushing matches in the living room. Husbands don't walk out for days at a time, month after month; don't shut off the electricity. Daughters don't slam doors and shout at their fathers because they like it.

She knew *something* was wrong, and she looked for counselors and preachers to help. In 1981 she accepted Jesus into her life as a personal, living, touchable savior. She began going to church, speaking in tongues, praying for solutions. "The fighting was getting so severe in my home," she said later, "and I couldn't figure out what it was."

"Linda couldn't understand why Shelley was so bitter," recalled Henry Edgington. "Right in the middle of this she was in another big search in her life. It was a hard time for her. You can have all the money in the world and still not be happy, obviously."

After meeting Edgington at the ranch when he came out to talk to Bobby, Linda began visiting the preacher with questions about her Bible study: she was trying to sort out some extreme interpretations of Scripture.

"There was a religious group around—I could only call them Lester Roloff worshipers," Edgington later recounted. "I'm not trying to be too critical, but this group was really radical." Roloff had been a Corpus Christi evangelist who had made a name for himself as a strident fundamentalist and radio preacher. He had operated in the Corpus Christi area for forty years, and his weekly radio show was picked up by religious radio stations around the country.

"They kept telling her that Shelley had a demon in her. They believed in demon possession, evil spirits—that it was Satan within her," Edgington said.

Edgington was wary. He had grown up in Corpus Christi and knew about Roloff: "Lester Roloff was one of the biggest hypocrites I've ever known in all my life."

Linda came to Edgington now, wondering if Roloff's followers were right. Could her daughter be possessed? The two spent several visits puzzling out what the Bible had to offer about the work of God and the devil. Then she stopped coming. "The Roloff people finally got through to her," Edgington concluded. "She was very susceptible at the time."

Linda had remarked on certain changes in Bobby during the last couple of years. For one, he had become much less sexually demanding. She told James and Betty that she had moved into a separate bedroom. She wondered if Bobby had become impotent. In fact, she and Bobby were having very few sexual liaisons—a dramatic change from his previous aggressiveness. But, instead of becoming suspicious, Linda was relieved.

And she had an explanation. "We were fighting and I just thought it was the turmoil in our marriage and just the fighting, and the whole stress is not conducive to intimacy."

But perhaps Linda secretly appreciated Bobby's turning his

tions elsewhere. She didn't really want to know where—she enjoyed the vacation from his intense and constant ministrations.

Aside from Shelley's increasingly violent behavior around Bobby, Linda remarked on other changes in her daughter. "Her grades were dropping," she recalled, "and the teachers had said that she was capable of a lot more than she was putting out. She wasn't trying."

Perhaps too the allure of financial security and the feel of riches helped immunize her against the signals. If she didn't look, then she wouldn't see. Bobby's deviance was blatant, and Linda was as near to being a witness as she could be without participating.

But that witness, Linda thought, was as mediator between Bobby and Shelley. "I was always defending him," said Linda later, "telling Shelley, 'You don't understand your dad.' And I was always telling Bob, 'You don't understand where she's coming from.' I was like a peacemaker and that's what divided the family." No matter how often she stood up to Bobby, she always relented.

The screaming between Bobby and Shelley was driving her mad. And they would never tell her what they were fighting about.

But there *were* issues. The more Linda, Bobby, and even Shelley denied their existence, the more distorted their world became. Following fights, Bobby frequently packed his bags and left for a day or two days at a time.

There were arguments that would have been almost normal in other households: over permissions and privileges, driving the car, going out on dates, raising children, disciplining children. But the intensity made them different. And there were arguments that were normal only in abnormal households: struggles over guns.

"Brother," Linda would later say heatedly, "I make big deals about things. I have chased my husband with a Weed Eater swirling above my head, wanting the truth from him, wanting an answer. When I want an answer, I go after the answer."

No one was going to deliver answers—even under threat of a Weed Eater—because two people reserved a dark corner of denial for incest.

Shelley didn't think she should have to tell—which made the lack of a rescue all the more damnable. She often came close to shouting the truth. But her shame stopped her. She wanted her mother to know without having to tell her. If her mother didn't know, she *should* know; if she didn't, she had to be blind. "If you only knew what was really going on around here!" Shelley angrily shouted. And in the contradictory logic that enveloped all their lives, she would, by not telling, punish her mother for not knowing.

I kinda thought that I was her blood, I would have figured that she'd stand with me. You know, he wasn't—he was just her husband; you can get another husband, you know. She had life so easy. She hadn't worked since I was like five years old. She was too used to, you know, having her maid and having it all.

But everyone, in his and her own way, did know. And everyone had a "reason" for not making an issue of it. Like a jigsaw puzzle, the family fit together. But it was locked together in weakness: Bobby, with his unquenchable thirst and dark obsession; Linda, with her complete lack of recognition and her blind devotion to Bobby; and Shelley, with her youth and rage. Bobby had his own thoughts about why Linda could ignore what was going on. "I was very sneaky," he recalled bluntly.

But his other reasons were ones that he depended on when Linda raged at him: "I don't think Linda—even if she suspected it those times, she didn't want to believe, number one, that Shelley would do anything like that. And, number two, it was just too awful to think about."

Could Linda believe that it was something that her husband of fourteen years could perpetrate? Bobby didn't trouble himself to consider it, he knew that "The few times she did bring up something about what was going on . . . , I would usually talk her out of it."

One night, looking for her husband, Linda walked into Shelley's bedroom. Bobby was lying on their daughter's bed, holding her hand.

"What's going on?" she demanded.

"I felt bad about our argument," Bobby said.

"Leave her alone," Linda ordered.

But Linda didn't see Bobby's concern as sexual. "They had been fighting all day, you know, all afternoon, all evening, and they were both very upset," was how she explained it. "He was in there holding her hand and she was mad as blazes at him. She was trying to go to sleep."

Linda accepted. Part of her new religion called for subservience to her husband. That part of the solution to the family's trials—submission. No more Weed Eater runs. But Linda also firmly believed that she had to get the rest of her family to God. And if not to God, to some good Christian counseling.

She put her foot down and said, "We're going to counseling!" So we went and it was a joke. All of us. They'd pick me up from school and we'd go to Dallas. Go to this Christian counseling, a free clinic or something. A real dump. It was my mom's idea. So we'd just sit there—no one would talk but my mom. And I'm sitting there thinking, "This is so stupid." Why don't we get along? Ha. A joke.

These hesitant attempts at finding mental health faltered within a few weeks, never to be tried again. The secret had been preserved.

Another time, Linda came home and found Shelley in bed, with Bobby lying next to her. Without a direct challenge on the merits, Linda exploded. She had suspicions. But she wouldn't announce them. In the ensuing argument, Bobby threatened to shoot himself. And Linda, frightened to death, picked up Shelley and Michael and hightailed it to Bobby's sister's house in Corsicana.

They got to Betty and James's late, arriving in a chilly spring night, fog choking the roads and fields.

"James, will you go see if you can find Bobby?" she said. "I'm scared."

Betty and Linda took Michael and Shelley upstairs—in a house that was owned by Bobby. Linda told Betty and James that Bobby had come into the house threatening to go to the pasture and shoot himself. "He told Michael he loved him no matter what happened," said Linda. "Then he told Shelley that he had to do what he had to do.

"Maybe he went to the pasture, James. I don't know. He's driving the pickup. See if you can find him."

Linda described the fight to her sister-in-law, and it wasn't unfamiliar to Betty. Bobby was always yelling about how to raise the children. Having Linda show up this time of night was unusual, however. Linda was scared.

"Linda—I know what's wrong between Bob and Shelley," Betty said.

"You do? What is it?"

"I'm going to tell you the truth—Bob molested me when I was a little girl. I believe he's molesting Shelley now."

The kids were settled upstairs. James was looking for her husband, and now Linda was hearing this.

"No, no, that's not true! I don't believe this."

Betty explained. She told Linda of the first time, when she was six years old, her mother found Bobby on top of her and the thrashing Bobby had received. She told Linda of the bath her mother had given her and the pronouncement that Betty needed to ask for forgiveness. She told Linda about the guilt she felt even now. She told about her fear of Bobby.

"I'm telling you he molested me and I know that's what's going on between him and Shelley. I know it.

"Have you ever asked Shelley whether she's been molested by Bob?" Betty continued. "Linda, ask her—don't leave in the morning until you ask her."

Meanwhile, James had found Bobby in a room at the Holiday Inn out on Highway 287 and Interstate 45. He had one of his pistols, a Smith and Wesson .357. But he seemed to have cooled off. James eventually left him alone. And the next morning, Bobby returned to the ranch.

Betty left Linda and the kids at her house and went to her job at the Corsicana National Bank. She got a call from Linda mid-morning.

"She said no, Betty," Linda said.

"How did you ask her?"

"I went to Shelley and asked, 'Is anything going on between you and your dad that you want to tell me about?' "

"Linda, please, don't go home," Betty said. "Wait until I get there and talk to Shelley. I'm coming home now."

Betty thought: *You just don't hit kids like that with a question like that.*

"Betty, my mind's made up—we're going home," Linda said.

Shelley had said "No." She couldn't bring herself to admit it. She didn't want to hurt her mom with the news; neither did she trust her with it. She still wanted *Linda* to do something—rescue her instead of talk to her.

What Betty had told her rankled Linda—and she wondered. She asked Bobby about Betty's accusation.

"This thing has gotten all blown out of proportion," Bobby said. "That's just something that's built and fed in her mind over the years."

Linda didn't press any further. She didn't pursue her suspicions.

More evidence, as far as Shelley was concerned, that she didn't want to know.

Shelley's suspicions proved justified when Linda quickly reconciled with Bobby. And again Shelley was home, fending off her father's hands, trying to avoid his bathrobe.

My mom's mind works however he wants it to work.

"I could never find out the truth," Linda would later protest. "I suspected it. But I could never—I would question them, I could demand, I could never find any proof, and so, it's always like I'm thinking something that's off the wall. And it was always in the back of my mind. I'm thinking something that's off the wall, you know, and so it was always in the back of my mind. And that's why I would be questioning that and shaking my head. . . . I spent all that time . . . trying to find counsel, all that time trying to find an answer with all my might. Somebody had to help us because I could not find anyone to help us or an answer to what's going on with my family.

"I mean, we were a perfectly normal family. We had lots of fun together, but there was this horrible fighting going on between my husband and my daughter and I couldn't figure it out and it wasn't until I called out to God that anything started changing."

But she didn't want to make an issue of It, the big question— those were her words. As she would later say, "Making an issue with Bob is a real tough deal."

Both Bobby and Linda used Shelley as cover to mask their weaknesses.

"I know it's awful," Linda later said. "I know it's horrible. But I don't want to know the details."

She probably didn't want to believe it, so she didn't want to hear it.

XI

ON THE ROAD

Bobby and Shelley sat at the swank French restaurant table in Houston almost as husband and wife. They had been on the road together for a few days now, and Bobby was trying to sell the Houston Rockets' owner some cattle and franchises.

It was the way Bobby did it. "He could sell ice cubes to the Eskimos," recalled Richard Ruiz. Ruiz and his wife were also at the table. The Rockets' owner and his wife were there with another married couple.

Bobby talked cattle as if he were the world's expert. "He could buy or sell you anything. He knew how to relate to people," Ruiz continued. "He could get on your level no matter what your level was. You could be a dirt farmer or you could be the President of the United States—it didn't make no difference. . . . You couldn't help but like the guy." But Ruiz was surprised that Bobby was even out tonight. On the road for the cattle shows his boss would always head straight back to his hotel after the day's business.

"After the shows there would always be places to go and parties," recalled Ruiz. "And Bob, being the owner, should have gone to them. But he never did go anywhere." Only one other time did Bobby go out to the bar and relax with the boys—when they had won the grand champion award at Fort Worth. "He stayed out for a couple of hours," said Ruiz, "and then he said he had to get back to Shelley. Back to the hotel. . . . He always said he had to get back to the hotel to take care of Shelley and make sure Shelley was okay. And he wouldn't let Shelley participate in any extra activities."

Tonight he came to dinner, but still left early. "Have to get this little girl to bed," he said to his friends at the table. "Big day tomorrow."

Shelley smiled politely—it was nothing more—as she said goodnight. But when Bobby put a fatherly hand on her shoulder, she twisted away. She cared little anymore about these public appearances on her father's behalf.

Bobby learned, and made few attempts to act like a father; when he did, he was pointedly rebuffed by Shelley, who looked the ingrate for her effrontery.

Whenever we were anywhere, if I had won something and he'd come over to hug me, I'd pull away, and you know, everybody would think, "God, you little brat."

The ranch manager just couldn't figure me out because I had all these expensive cattle and expensive show clothes and everything, and he'd say, "Why are you acting like this?" He was thinking like I was a spoiled brat. But I wasn't.

Ruiz noticed. "I always got the impression at the shows that she resented being there," he recalled. "Like she wanted to be there but then she didn't. If it were just me and her, it was okay; but when Bob would come up she was a completely different person."

Shelley got along well with Ruiz—and used that fact to further irritate Bobby. Because the ranch manager had a daughter about Shelley's age, he seemed to understand her.

Richard would always go to all the shows and he was really nice looking. All my girlfriends used to always ask, "Can I come over to watch Richard work?"

He did interesting things at the ranch and I used to ride my three-wheeler around and watch him do things. Knocking trees down, whatever. It was just neat to watch. Or like in FFA, when

I was learning how to do welding, I went up there and he was showing me how to weld. My dad couldn't stand it.

But Bobby never let on to Ruiz that he was angry about Shelley hanging out with him—he merely complained about how difficult a child Shelley was.

Richard was always real sweet and we got along real good. And my dad would always hate it because Richard and I would sit there at the show and cut up and talk and I'd walk around with him. Bob couldn't stand it. I mean, he would say, "Why are you paying so much attention to Richard?" He was jealous of anyone I paid attention to because I didn't pay attention to him at all.

Bobby whisked his daughter back to their suite at the Astro Village Hotel, the swank accommodations across the street from cattle-show headquarters at the Astrodome. He always traveled first class. They elevatored up to their spacious, $300-a-night, two-bedroom suite.

"We always stayed in suites in topnotch places," recalled Ruiz. "I had an unlimited expense account. Bobby never went anywhere second class. He always went first class."

Bobby didn't miss a night with his daughter on the road. Linda was home in Powell, 190 miles away. Bobby was now free. No more whispering, no sneaking. He had his way with his daughter.

Bobby Sessions had his way with just about everything. And in the cattle business, especially, he seemed to have the Midas touch.

"He didn't know anything about cattle when he started," recalled Ruiz. "But he is a very quick learner." In his inimitable way, with Ruiz's help, Bobby soon owned a national Grand Champion bull worth hundreds of thousands of dollars.

He started with commercial Herefords, the meat-givers, but changed to the more flamboyant and lucrative business of raising elite, purebred, registered show cattle, buying and selling beasts worth $100,000 and up. Bobby's kind of money.

His first bull investment was half-interest in a six-month-old, for which he paid $50,000. "We paid a lot of money for it," recalled Ruiz, "but the offspring that came out of that bull sold anywhere from $5,000 to $10,000 each." A single ampule of semen from a prizewinning bull would sell for as much as $500.

In a couple of years Ruiz had helped Bobby acquire 50 head of registered Brahmans, more than 60 head of registered Herefords and 150 commercial cattle. Bobby formed a partnership with a cattleman down the road to mate Brahmans and Herefords: "a Braford." Since buyers looked for good bloodlines, and good bloodlines were determined by the prestige of show points, being active on the show circuit was critical to the success of the business.

Shelley, meanwhile, was urged by her Ag teacher to enter a statewide livestock-judging contest in Houston in February of her freshman year. She won a calf purchase certificate for $400 and with it bought a Brahman calf, named Miss Primero Grande. Immediately, she began preparing it for the next year's shows. And, as if it were in her blood as a Texan, she quickly began building a herd. Bobby was impressed by Shelley's interest in the cattle and, for his own reasons, began buying her more Brahman heifers.

She loved the animals. It was another way to forget her problems, escape the house and Bobby. Working with these friendly giants gave her a sense of control over life that had been taken away from her by her father.

You have to spend up to four hours every day with them. And many times more; but it better be at least four hours a day with them.

It's the same all year round. In the mornings you feed them, and after school you walk or brush 'em, just stuff like that, run them, wash them, bath them, brush, lots of brushing.

Basically, you just walk 'em a lot, and you trot 'em, develop their leg muscles and everything and really just a lot of pampering and always just messing with 'em. It really doesn't matter what you're doing as long as you're messing with 'em, so they feel comfortable around you and they don't spook around people.

I'd keep a radio in the barn, playing noisy Mexican music to keep 'em used to noise. Then, when you go to a show, they won't spook.

I had one bull drag me all the way across the ring once when this little girl reached her hand out to pet him. He was kind of a skittish bull, and I had my hand wrapped around the lead rope, and he drug me all the way down the arena, in front of everybody. I was very embarrassed.

Another bull, one time, didn't like people coming around his back end, and I was walking past the judge, and the judge went kind of behind him, to look at the rear view, and he kicked him and the judge fell on his rear. I thought, oooooohhhhh.

Shelley worked hard at what quickly became more than just a hobby. She monitored her Brahmans' diets, brushed them, taught them to obey commands of the rope and halter, and walked them, walked them, walked them—miles a day. She expanded on and perfected the rules she had learned at the LaRue Show school the previous year.

Right before the show you really have to brush them a lot to get the sheen in their coat, and you do little tricks—like, with their hooves, you spray-paint them so they look a darker black. You have the horns cut for show, so that their hair grows over it and it's real pretty looking. If it's not like that, a little horn will show and you spray-paint it black.

And you can Vaseline their eyelashes to make them stand out and look darker. There's some stuff that you can spray their tails. Mostly they do that on steers, to make 'em black or white, and just fluff 'em up. And you have to keep a fan on 'em during the summer to keep their coat, to keep 'em cold, so their coat will get real thick.

Shelley loved her animals.

A lot of people are afraid of them, because they are so big and you think they are temperamental, which they are. But they are also very loving. It's like a pet dog. You know, you spend so much time with them, they follow you around and when you stop they stop, you know, each step you take they follow you, and it's cute.

By her sophomore year, Shelley was on the show circuit: A ninety-pound girl escorting 2,000-pound bovines around the state—to Brenham, Fort Worth, the Heart of Texas Fair in Waco, Corsicana, San Antonio, Victoria, Mercedes, Dallas, Houston, Tyler—and even one in Lake Charles, Louisiana. She went to statewide affairs and small county events.

Shelley loved the shows. But that became yet another form of fun twisted into a mockery of itself.

For him it was great because the more I liked it the better for him, because we were on the road.

During the high season, February and March, Shelley was on the road most of the time. She was in Houston until the sixth of March. And being on the road was a real boon to her chaperone, Bobby.

My mother had very bad allergies and she was allergic to cattle or horses or feed or dust or anything and would get real sick. So she couldn't go to the shows. And then sometimes she would want to go and Bobby would just convince her that "You're just going to get sick and you might as well stay here."

Like many mundane events unexpectedly loaded with significance, Linda's allergies proved a terrible tragedy for Shelley. Linda went to only one cattle show, in Lake Charles, Louisiana— but only two days after Bobby and Shelley had been there.

The road shows allowed Bobby a free hand with his daughter. Usually, only the ranch manager, a helper, Bobby and Shelley traveled. Ruiz would make all the arrangements for the animals; Bobby would make them for Shelley.

And Bobby was bold. He would take a private plane to shows like the one in Mercedes, just north of the Mexican border. He always booked Shelley and himself into one room, even if a suite. Back home, townsfolk, well aware of his flamboyance, were quick to notice that he and Shelley were always traveling together— without Linda. It was very quiet, but there was talk, a joke or two.

But even Bobby recognized the look. "Bobby said jokingly that Linda didn't trust him at one time," recalled Ruiz. "And that's when we were talking about the rooms in the hotels."

It was not funny to Shelley. Bobby couldn't concentrate on the shows while he was on the road. And Shelley did her best to stay away from him.

Wherever the show was, you just want to stay at the barn all day, as long as you can. The whole time he's saying, "Let's go back to the hotel, let's go back to the room." And you're making up excuses. "I have to feed 'em, I have to walk 'em, I promised

*so-and-so I would help them walk theirs." I'd make friends and
stuff and get them to buddy with me all day so he couldn't make
me.*

Shelley was wedged solidly between her love for the shows and
her hatred of her father. But her proudest moment was the Grand
Champion victory she earned at the Fort Worth show.

*I had picked a little heifer right out of the herd the year before
and right from the first moment I started working with her, I knew
she was going to be perfect. Me and Richard halter-broke her and
everything. Most of the other ones we'd buy they were already
full-grown and already halter-broke. But she wasn't skitsy; she was
calm. And the very first show, Fort Worth, she won the Grand
Champion. That's the top. And every show after that she won first
place.*

Shelley's Brahmans all had official names and numbers to sig-
nify the fact that they were certified purebred. Bobby named
them. Miss Primero Grande, nicknamed Blue, was her first, number 187, the baby she purchased with the prize money from the
judging contest. Miss Suva, another heifer, was also known as 658.
She belonged to her father, but Shelley showed her. And Miss
Shelley 109 was the little heifer that won Fort Worth.

The Houston show came in the middle of the show season and
was an important one. Shelley had brought a number of her good
Brahmans along, including Blue and a big beast she lovingly called
Freight Train. Freight Train had, by Brahman standards, a problem: she was gangly. And Shelley had to use a few tricks that they
didn't teach at LaRue.

*She was so tall and so long that I had a hard time filling her out.
And you're not supposed to do it, but we decided to drench her with
beer, to fill her up for the show. It's just for real quick fill. They
get hollow, in their hocks, right below their stomachs, and beer'll
fill 'em out real quick.*

Shelley and ranch manager Ruiz escorted Freight Train out to
the parking lot outside the Astrodome and lost themselves among
the big cattle trucks and pickups. "Me and her used to laugh and
cut up and have a good time as long as Bobby wasn't there,"
recalled Ruiz.

Ruiz brought the beer—quart bottles of the best lager. And they started pouring. And pouring. And pouring. Freight Train gurgled and gagged and gulped. Shelley inspected her beast's belly as Ruiz poured.

It took a lot, she was a big cow. She just had so much height and length, she just wouldn't fill out.

But when they had finally poured enough beer down Freight Train's giant gullet, Shelley had second thoughts—and other problems.

It was terrible because she was drunk and she kept slobbering foam and it was getting all over my clothes, and she wanted to lay down.

I just knew the judges were going to say something, because she was foaming at the mouth, boy, slinging it on my back, the whole shirt was wet. I kept telling the boy behind me to hit her with his show stick to keep her walking because she kept trying to lay down.

For all her efforts—good and bad—Shelley earned prizes like Reserve Champion and Grand Champion, trophies and silver platters and exhibitors' ribbons and pictures in the paper. At the smaller events, prizes ranged from ribbons to halters and feed buckets.

But the real value of the victories came later, when the animal was sold or bred. A prizewinner could be sold for hundreds of thousands of dollars. The stakes were high.

And Shelley had, unknowingly, "inherited" some of her daddy's self-confidence and charm.

A lot of it is your attitude when you go in the show ring. You have to know that you're good, know that your cattle are good, you have to smile the whole time at the judges, you have to constantly keep your eye on 'em, you never can turn your back to the judge. Always keep eye contact. Those are the little things that make you a winner—your style.

Most shows had two different competitions: the junior show for kids in school and the highly competitive open category for the ranchers. Shelley entered in junior and helped Richard in the open division competition.

It's a lot of fun. You meet a lot of people that are involved in that stuff and are just real down-to-earth, do anything in the world for you. Like, if you lost something at the show, they'd give you something. Or if somebody stole some of your feed or something and you didn't have any, you know, somebody would give you some. They're just real friendly people.

Shelley missed a lot of school because of the cattle shows. But in Kerens, where cattle and oil were king, she wasn't penalized. It was the schedule *and* Bobby's demands that were taking the toll.

Shelley was finding it harder and harder to manage the schizophrenic life-style. She was abrupt with Bobby, mean to him in public. Shelley was sending a message, as if she were a prisoner of war forced by her captors to parade in front of the world's cameras. How to get the word out? Wouldn't they know back home that there was something wrong here?

To everyone else it looked like I was being just a spoiled little rich brat, you know, because I was so hateful. He could come up to me and say, "You know, you're brushing the cow wrong," or "You're feeding them the wrong thing," and I'd say, "You don't know what you're talking about."

And the ranch manager could come up and say the exact same thing and I'd listen to him and change it. I mean, I got along with all adults. I wasn't disrespectful or anything like that. It was just him, I hated him, I would throw a fit, I would act like a brat, I didn't care. And everybody else would say, "She acts perfectly fine," you know.

"It was okay as long as Bob wasn't there," recalled Ruiz. "But when Bob would come around, she would just change. It was just like, you know, she turned a different leaf."

I don't see how no one picked up on it. Because he could come up and say the exact same thing that somebody else told me and I would just totally, you know, not take his advice or not listen to him. And somebody else could tell me and I would listen and do whatever they said.

People did pick up on it. Shelley believed that they had to have noticed. She was giving off clear signals, she thought. But no one picked up well enough to do anything to help her.

XII

ON THE RUN

It was just three days after Shelley's sixteenth birthday, and Bobby was more nervous than ever. Gradually, the fights with her were taking their toll. She was fighting back now, and fighting hard.

"I don't want you to see Ricky," Bobby ordered as he lay on top of his daughter. They were both naked. Shelley's mother and brother had gone to town and Bobby had immediately ordered Shelley to go to her bedroom. Shelley looked away, saying nothing. It had been her chief response to her dad's sexual assaults.

By Bobby's reckoning, the odds were changing rapidly. He had given her a pickup truck for her birthday, she seemed to have a boyfriend, and now he had to travel to London for a meeting with a former Tampimex partner. What was she going to do? Bobby was scared. It all might bust apart.

"I don't want you to ruin your life," he told her. "Ricky's no good for you."

Bobby missed the irony of his statement. But Shelley didn't.

Toward the end, the very end, I started saying, "Now, you know, look, if you're going to do this to me, I better get something to where I can get away from you." Like the truck. That's what I wanted it for.

I had been trying to get out, but I didn't have a way.

* * *

As her birthday approached, Shelley had increased her lobbying efforts for a pickup. She had been asking for one for a long time. In the big sky, big land country of Texas, almost everyone drove, and drove early. Most of the students at Kerens High drove to school; many had their own vehicles; and the vehicle of choice in this cattle-and-oil country was a pickup. That's what Shelley wanted for a present. It's what she demanded.

I asked for a truck for Christmas one year—a black Silverado pickup—and I went downstairs that Christmas morning and under the tree was a little black Go-kart pickup. So after that I specified the exact size.

Bobby had promised that Shelley's sixteenth birthday would be the day she'd get the pickup she longed for. But there would be a price. He bought the pickup months in advance of her birthday and taunted her by driving it himself. It was a sleek, new, gray and black Chevy Silverado, with air conditioning, electric windows, AM/FM stereo, cassette deck, tinted windows. The crème de la crème of pickup trucks.

"It was loaded to the brim," recalled James Duvall, "very attractive to the young girls that went the rodeo route. He was trying to be this big-shot rancher and cowboy. And he was turning her into a rodeo queen. So everything he done was pointed toward the rodeo atmosphere. And all the young rodeo group was driving these fancy, beautiful pickups. It was so attractive to her it was like dangling a diamond in front of the lady."

Shelley knew that there was a price she had to pay, but she ignored Bobby's demands for "turns" in exchange for the truck. By now, she realized, it mattered not at all if she said yes or no to his sexual barter demands. He took his sex no matter what. Equally, she determined to take the truck. As it turned out, Shelley didn't have to press. She got her truck and then some. When Bobby passed the keys over to her on her birthday, a glinting diamond ring was part of the package as well.

Bobby knew that even in this Bible-thumping region, girls were eventually allowed to flap their wings. Everyone drove at age sixteen. Everyone dated. Soon enough, he knew, his rule over

Shelley would come into question. Soon, in fact, it would be over entirely. Shelley at eighteen, even Bobby knew, would be free and independent, an adult. He could not hold her. So he gave in to Shelley's demand for a pickup truck to save his own skin. He had to try to look like a loving, indulgent father as well as a strict one.

Even with gifts like the truck, intended to keep Shelley quiet if not completely happy, Bobby saw that their arrangement was wearing thin. Shelley was testing the limits, sounding new territory. She was beginning to make a move for the driver's seat, and not just her truck's.

Shelley sensed her increasing power and was learning how to manipulate the relationship—and Bobby knew it, but couldn't now stop himself. Would she reveal the secret? He could never be sure. Would she leave him? But Bobby now was as obsessed with keeping Shelley as with keeping the secret. He didn't want to *lose* her, even though he tried to tell himself—and promised Shelley—that it would happen . . . eventually. Shelley would someday move out of the house, move away, maybe get married. He couldn't hold her indefinitely. But the thought of his daughter spreading her wings and leaving him was making him more and more anxious.

He continued to believe he could manage the situation and control her. As soon as he turned over the keys to the new pickup, he began checking the mileage every time Shelley drove. He knew what time she left and what time she came back.

Friends and family noticed the change in Bobby. He was smoking more—four packs a day—and drinking his sodas like water, by the gallon. His hands shook a lot and he always seemed to be gnawing his fingernails. He was more brusque with people, lost his patience more quickly, rushed around without getting anything done.

He was acting in much the same manic way he did when the family lived in New Jersey—only this time there seemed to be no work excuse. The construction business and the ranch were doing well. There was no need to feel any pressure. But something was bothering Bobby, driving him to near frenzy.

Other family members noticed that he was particularly obsessed with Shelley. They were aware of his fussy protectiveness, and remarked on the way he and Shelley went without Linda to cattle shows.

But only Betty Duvall had voiced dark suspicions of what was really going on.

Except for Betty, no one took Bobby's attachment to Shelley as the symptom of a nefarious liaison.

"All along I was kidding her about being with her dad all the time," recalled Ricky Layfield. "It was looking obvious to me, but I wasn't trying to mean it or anything. I would just make little old sly remarks. And she'd get mad, like a little old kid head game, and slap at me, but she knew I was joking."

But Ricky didn't know that he had become such an object of attention by Bobby.

In fact, Ricky liked Bobby. Like many of the town's youth, he looked up to Sessions as someone who had made it.

Ricky had had his eye on Shelley for more than a year before he finally had the courage to approach her. But he had come to Bobby's attention first. And Bobby would call Ricky frequently, to chat.

Ricky was a star athlete but not a star student. He was in school for fun, and he had it. But he didn't skip classes. He fished and hunted and had many friends. He couldn't afford a car—he played sports instead of keeping an after-school job—so he bummed rides from his buddies until he was a senior. He also had his own mind, and his feet planted in solid soil. He was a boy of unyielding principle and the audacity to act, some thought irrationally, on it.

"I got kicked out of school for ten days for cussing a coach," recalled Ricky. "He was a little wimpy guy and he thought he was going to push me around and I wasn't going to stand for it. I had a pulled hamstring and he pushed me, you know. Shoot! I just got mad and went off. We got into it. 'Fuck you!' I said and pushed him, threatened to kick his ass and that kind of shit."

Bobby found out about Ricky's suspension—in the way he seemed to find out about everything. He called the Layfield house.

"You have a little problem at school?" he asked the sophomore.

"How did you know?" Ricky asked.

Bobby wouldn't say. He sympathized with Ricky. In fact, Bobby had taken a liking to the young Layfield boy that had baffled Ricky. Bobby would often call out to Ricky when he came to school to pick up Shelley. "Just carrying on like a father to me," said Ricky. "I don't know why. Shoot, that would be the farthest thing from anybody's mind. To think this guy in a Mercedes, good-looking guy, big shot, no problems, nothing. And he'd call me just to find out how things were going."

After his suspension was over, Ricky made the walk to the principal's office to get his welcome-back "licks." But this time the paddle stayed in its place.

"Ricky, you're supposed to be an example setter here," the principal said. "I'm not going to give you licks this time."

The man stood up and shook the boy's hand and told him to go back to class.

Was it the power of Bobby Sessions at work again? Ricky was in awe. "I really liked him," he recalled. "He was like a friend. I could talk to him and tell him what the deal was and everything. . . . But he was a big shot and you're trying to stay sharp, stay with him, you know, 'cause you're always behind him."

Perhaps Bobby was simply scouting the competition. It was not long before Ricky and Shelley became attracted to each other. It just happened. In the school parking lot one afternoon at lunchtime. On the spur of the moment Shelley invited Ricky to go for a ride in her new pickup truck. "Silver and black, long bed, cruise tilt, black interior," Ricky enthused. "It was the nicest car on the lot—teachers and all. And it was a pickup.

"When we got back to school we just sort of wiped everything else out. She broke off hers and I did mine. We waited about a day and a half and shwooosh, that's all I could stand—about a day and a half. I wouldn't let nobody know that I liked her or nothing, but she knew it, 'cause—she just knew it, I guess, and then from then on out, it was me and her."

"May the fifth—I won't ever forget it—is when Shelley really came into my life," Cherry Layfield recounted. "On her birthday. Because Ricky came home from school that day and told me that

Shelley walked up to him and said, 'Hey, today's my sixteenth birthday and I can start having dates.' And he came up to me and—he just wanted me to say it out loud—and said, 'Why do you think she said that to me?' 'Well, gol, Rick, I think she wants you to ask her for a date.' 'You really think so?'

"So I don't know what happened, but he went out to Shelley's house that Saturday night and when he got home I asked him, 'What'd y'all do?' And he said, 'Me and Bobby played pool all night. . . . I didn't spend any time with Shelley.' He said he had a pretty good time, but he didn't see much of Shelley."

Immediately, the relationship between Bobby and Ricky changed. There were no more calls from Bobby. No more invitations. He was told that Shelley couldn't date.

Ricky wasn't going to argue. "He was an old friend of the family and everything and shoot, look what I live in here. And look at the mansion out there. It was a big trip. I am a little ol' hick-town man, you know."

Shelley would argue with her father about Ricky, to no avail. Suddenly, Bobby was telling Shelley that Ricky was a wild kid, a bad influence.

His reputation wasn't bad, it was just normal teenage, you know, Mr. Cool and everything.

But Bobby would have nothing of it and forbade Shelley to see Ricky. The two teenagers had to steal away in secret.

Ricky had become a rival in "love" as much as a threat to secrecy. And Bobby was almost hysterical with concern.

By now, Shelley on some level had come to accept her father's sexual assaults as a part of her life. Sexually, she was an adult; emotionally, very much a teenager. She still had to ask Bobby's permission to see a boy, and even promised him that she would change Ricky in order to make him more acceptable to her father.

Shelley saw Ricky despite Bobby's objections. She went out with him when Bobby went to Europe, risking Bobby's wrath in doing it. But she was beginning to think that it was worth it.

My dad was in London, and me and Ricky were starting to like each other. I never really thought about him before because he was

*always wild and I always lectured him, telling him, "You need to
straighten up," and all this. So he'd always come to me for advice.
And all of a sudden we started liking each other.*

Shelley took the opportunity of her dad's trip to ask her mother
if Ricky could come over to play pool or something.

"You ask your dad when he calls," Linda said.

When Bobby called, Shelley asked.

"Just for an hour or so," Bobby said. "But you know the rules."

She knew the rules all too well. But she also knew that the first
rule was that Bobby could change the rules whenever he wanted.

*I don't know what happened. Ricky might have stayed too long
or something. But when Bobby came back, he was furious.*

Bobby received a phone call from a schoolteacher friend who
knew him well enough to knew that he would want the news that
Shelley was spending a lot of time with Ricky Layfield.

Bobby was outraged. He thanked the teacher and rushed to
school, where he found Shelley on her lunch break. He pulled his
daughter aside.

"Are you going with Ricky?"

"Yes."

"What about what we talked about before I left?"

"I'm going with him and that's all there is to it." Shelley threw
down the gauntlet, her first overt challenge to Bobby's sexual
authority since his assaults began.

"No, it's not!" Bobby shouted and stormed off.

Bobby went home, picked up a ranch hand and returned to
school. But he didn't seek out Shelley. He drove through the
parking lot until he spotted her Silverado.

When Shelley got out of class a little later, she walked to the
parking lot, only to find her mother waiting for her in her big
white Cadillac.

"Get in, Shelley," said Linda. "Your dad had the truck picked
up."

Shelley fumed all the way home. Linda tried to defend Bobby,
but Shelley wouldn't hear of it. And she didn't understand how
her mother could continue to defend Bobby.

The anger bubbled over when they got home, Shelley soundly condemning Bobby. Linda grabbed a broom and came after Shelley, swinging wildly but landing blows with only moderate accuracy. Shelley managed to field the swings, finally grabbing the handle and jerking it. Linda shrieked in pain, her wrist sprained, and ran off to her mother's house. From there she called Bobby at the office.

"Shelley has gone bonkers!" she screamed. "I can't control her. Go talk to her."

Bobby went to the house, but he didn't "talk" to Shelley—he met a daughter in full tirade.

"What did you do with my truck?"

"I told you not to see Ricky."

She was going to go out with whomever she wanted, do whatever she wanted. "I'm not going to listen to you anymore!" she shouted. As her fear receded, it seemed that anger in equal parts moved up to take its place.

It had been like that for the last couple of months. The shouting matches had increased in volume. And Shelley no longer hesitated in punching at Bobby if she was mad at him.

During one argument, a shoving match sent Shelley crashing to the floor of the laundry room.

He was standing over me. And I just kicked as hard as I could—right in the right place. He staggered. And I went up to my room and slammed the door and locked it. I just wanted him away from me. I just started where I was going to fight back. I mean, I just had enough.

There was no longer any give for Shelley. She felt that this was the end—no more debate. *"What did you do with my truck?"* she screamed again. "I want the keys to my truck!"

Bobby stared at his daughter icily, then turned and started for the stairs.

"I'm going to tell everyone what you've been doing to me," Shelley called after him.

Bobby only muttered, "I'll put an end to *all* this."

Shelley ran after him, suspecting what would happen next. She found her father in his bedroom, already pulling his pistol from the dresser drawer. He then walked to the big French doors that looked out over the placid lake and endless range and onto the second-floor balcony.

"You won't have to worry about me anymore," he shouted at Shelley, who was already coming out behind him.

This wasn't the first time that Bobby had threatened Shelley with his suicide. "You're not going to do that," she said, grabbing him from behind and trying to wrestle away the gun.

I got panicked, thinking, "If he kills himself, they're gonna blame me. They're gonna think I did it." And I just panicked! So I just ran after him, hitting him, trying to grab him.

Bobby pulled away easily. "How would you like it if I just shot you and then me?" he yelled, gesturing with the gun.

"Go ahead, kill me," Shelley screamed back. "It would be better to be dead!"

She lunged at him again, groping for the gun. The two wrestled each other to the edge of the balcony, then down the circular stairway. Halfway down, Bobby seemed to stumble. He doubled over, clutching at his heart as he pitched forward. Lurching downward, he landing in a heap at the bottom of the stairs, unconscious.

"Get up!" Shelley shouted. She kicked him in the side. "Get up. You are not having a heart attack. Give me the keys!" She kicked again.

I didn't know where I was going to go, but I was going to try to get some money or something and get all my stuff and just get out of there.

Bobby suddenly got up, as if nothing had happened, and stomped off to the front of the house. Shelley followed after, shouting for her keys.

He got into his pickup and was driving off. I grabbed the door and it came open and I was just hanging on. It was a big mess.

"Give me my truck keys!" Shelley kept shouting as Bobby accelerated. She was banging on her father with her free hand. Finally, Bobby pulled the vehicle to a stop. He reached into his pocket and threw a set of keys toward Shelley. They sailed by her and landed on the ground.

Shelley scooped them up, ran to her own truck and backed it up to the door under the breezeway of the house.

I went upstairs and was bringing stuff down and he went upstairs to my room—and started helping me. He got my stereo and was bringing it down the stairs and I grabbed it away from him and I said, "Don't touch any of my stuff. I'll do it myself."

Shelley threw bags of clothes and toiletries into the back of her truck.

As she climbed in the cab, Bobby came out.

"Where you going?" he asked, pleading but angry.

"None of your business!" Shelley shouted, starting the engine.

He came closer and, with the same confused focus on Shelley that he always had, he threw a hundred-dollar bill at her. "Never set foot on this place again!"

"Don't you worry about *that!*" she shouted back, gunning the engine and throwing her Silverado in drive.

The house of cards was beginning to tumble. Bobby was not only losing his free sex, he was losing control over the only witness to the crime. And as quickly as he told her never to return, Bobby pleaded, "Come back!"

I got to Kerens and I didn't know what to do so I picked up one of my friends and she said, "Your dad was just here." And I said, "What?" And she said, "He came to tell my parents that you ran away from home and not to let you live here."

Now that the shock of what she had done was wearing off, Shelley was frantic with fear, sure that her father would be after her with a gun.

Each place I went, he seemed to have been there. I went to my friend Kim's house and got her and just rode around with her. And I guess right after I picked her up, he went there and told her parents that I'd left home and don't let her stay here.

Just as Kim finished telling her about her dad's frantic visit, Shelley saw him. He was driving down another street and didn't see her. She gunned her motor and sped off.

She had finally made the break. But what happened now? She had thought about this moment but hadn't at all planned for it.

And now, it seemed, her father, the Svengali, was everywhere. He would probably kill her.

At that moment Shelley saw her algebra teacher, Dede Scott, pull up.

A few days before that I had told her that we had bad problems at home. And she told me—we were really good friends and every-thing—that "If you need me, come find me." So she pulled over and she saw that I had everything—I had clothes piled up in the truck. She said, "What are you going to do? Where are you going to go?" And I said, "I don't know."

So she gave me the keys to her house and told me to go unpack. And I moved in with her.

But Shelley had only run away from home; not from Kerens. She felt safe enough with Dede to continue to go to school—driving back roads so Bobby wouldn't see her—and bold enough even to go back to the ranch. It was a cautious expedition that she took, with Ricky and a fellow classmate. Hoping to avoid Bobby, they drove the back road to the back side of the lake, to swim and sunbathe. But they hadn't been there long before they spotted a fast-approaching cloud of dust.

The three teens were scrambling to their truck as Bobby skid-ded up in his.

"You better come back home," Bobby told Shelley, who was agreeably surprised that her father didn't pull a gun.

"Never."

"Your mother is going to send you away," Bobby yelled.

"Send me away? Send me where?"

"I don't know, but she's going to have you sent off."

Shelley thought it was a bluff. "I'm not coming home."

The next morning's paper was another shock to Shelley. An ad, full-page, jumped out at her. The unsigned "Ode to My Daugh-ter" almost made her sick. . . .

My daughter left home yesterday
It was like a part of me died.

And yet it spoke a truth, between the lines, that only Shelley could truly understand; despite his assertion.

> She left because of my rules, you see:
> She just never could understand. . . .

Unfortunately, Shelley was alone with her knowledge of the truth. And Bobby's ode was a drippy confessional, complete with references to the meanness and cruelty of his own father and his terrible childhood. Now, the ode implied without much subtlety, Bobby had to suffer his daughter's callous departure. It generated the requisite sympathies.

"Well, after that, people just thought Shelley was terrible," recalled Cherry Layfield, who had defended Shelley's right to run away. "People would knock on our door. 'How dare she do that to her daddy like that? His heart is broken.' People looked down on us like we were dirt in the street."

A few days later, however, Shelley's classmates got a taste of the other side of Bobby's obsession. Shelley was trying to take notes in algebra class when her father burst in.

"Where's your teacher?" he shouted at his daughter, who was stunned by the public spectacle.

"What are you doing here?" she demanded.

Bobby barely looked at her. "I don't want to talk to you," he growled. "I want to talk to Dede Scott."

The other students were deadly silent. Bobby cast an icy glare around the room. But Shelley said nothing and he stormed out.

The students ran to the door and listened to Bobby stomp down the hallway to the principal's office. They could hear him upbraid the principal and demand the resignation of Dede Scott for harboring a runaway.

It was Bobby's sickness: scared to death that Shelley would tell, scared to death that she would leave him, he acted insanely, as if he wanted both, and made scenes the world could see—and guess about.

The school's secretary hustled out of the office right after

Bobby went in and ran up to Shelley. "You better come with me," she said brusquely.

Shelley's face registered alarm. But the woman quickly reassured her, "Don't worry," and tugged her into the girls' restroom. "We'll wait here until your dad's gone."

Bobby finally left the building. But the fireworks weren't over. Shelley came out of her hiding place and back to the classroom, where her friends were gathered at the window. Outside, in the school parking lot, Bobby had maneuvered his pickup truck next to Shelley's.

Everyone watched as Bobby swung out of his truck and ambled to the rear. He began hurling boxes and clothes—Shelley recognized them as hers—from his truck into hers. The classroom was frantic, as much with awe as laughter.

"We're sitting in class and he's out there throwing boxes and boxes of hers in the back of the truck," recalled Ricky Layfield. "It's right there in front of the whole class. Everybody's sitting there and checking it out. The whole school is checking it out. And then we knew it was pretty serious."

I mean, I was just going, Gawd! He's just chunkin' clothes and everything. Just kind of pushing it into mine. It was incredible.

When Sessions finally left, Shelley was summoned to a meeting with the principal. He told her that her father had demanded that Dede Scott be fired.

Shelley started to protest, but the man raised his hand. "Don't worry, she won't lose her job," he assured her. But right afterward he told Shelley she shouldn't be staying with Dede.

Under the circumstances, Shelley thought, it was just as well that she find another place to live. She didn't want to make any more trouble for Dede, and she knew that once Bobby was onto something, he wouldn't rest until he'd finished the job. She was again worried that Bobby was going to kill her.

And the next day, on her way to meet Dede for lunch, Shelley was startled by Bobby pulling up beside her.

He rolled down the window of his truck. "You better not leave that truck alone for one minute," he warned her, "or it will be gone."

Shelley faced two problems now: keeping the truck and finding a place to stay more than a night or two—the time it would take for Bobby to locate her and warn parents that they were illegally harboring a runaway minor. Shelley knew he had an extra set of keys: he could make good on his word.

Bobby found her a number of times. He threatened, he cajoled, he blustered. He promised Shelley that the sex was over—then he reminded her that her mother wasn't going to put up with her running away; that she would send the police out after her. "And I wouldn't want that."

In fact, Bobby had been trying to stall Linda from calling the police because he feared what would happen if Shelley were picked up by them and decided to tell why she had fled.

It only confirmed what Shelley always knew: her father not only had eyes all over town, he practically controlled it. For many people, especially Bobby's friends, Shelley was an ungrateful daughter. She had everything—if anything, Bobby had spoiled her by lavishing on her all these material goods. They were trying to help Bobby get his daughter back; they had read the ode and sympathized.

A couple of nights later, as Shelley and some friends sat in their cars uptown, other friends ran up to her. "Your dad and some men are in town looking for you," they huffed, "and they've got shotguns!"

Shelley was parked on "the drag," the small piece of road on the north side of town that was unofficially earmarked by the local kids as their cruising grounds. On warm weekend nights a procession of cars—ten, fifteen, twenty, twenty-five—would wind its way up and down the street.

"You just cruise around, don't do nothing," Ricky Layfield explained. "Just cruise around and talk and listen to the radio. Pull people over and talk, ride around and drink."

When the Bobby alarm was sounded, a dozen of the cruisers

huddled around Shelley, trying to decide where to go. But they were too late.

He came up there with another man and a shotgun in his truck and he's trying to jerk me through the window of my truck. And I am screaming and cussing at him, trying to hit him through the window.

"You whore!" Bobby shouted. He had the door of Shelley's truck open and grabbed her, jerking his daughter roughly out of the truck. "You slut!"

Shelley pounded at Bobby with her fists, screaming, "If I'm a slut, you made me one!"

But he easily overpowered her and pushed her against the door. Shelley smashed into the side mirror and fell to the ground.

Her friends had been watching in shock, but now a few of the boys took a cautious step toward Bobby. He ignored them. "I've been looking for you all night," he screamed, slapping Shelley across the head. "Where have you been? You've been out on some dirt road with Ricky, haven't you?"

Bobby hit her again, but this time a couple of the boys stepped up. "Better leave her alone, Mr. Sessions."

As if awakening from a trance, Bobby stopped his tirade, turned and left.

Shelley pulled herself up from the dirt, as much embarrassed as hurt. "Let's go home," she said quietly to her friend.

Bobby had completely lost control. He continued to pursue Shelley in every way he could. He focused on Ricky Layfield as well. The boy represented an uncontrollable threat.

"He kept calling up here," remembered Cherry Layfield. "All this time, he kept calling up here, asking if Shelley was here. And I said, 'What would she be doing here?' 'Well, she's run away from home and if she's in your house, I want you to throw her out on the street. You throw her out!' Boy, he got vicious. 'You throw her out and maybe she'll come home.' I said, 'Well, she's not here, but if she comes here I'm not throwing her out. I'll try and talk her into coming home, but I'm not throwing her out in the street. Don't you know if I throw her out, she'll take to the road and hitchhike? She's liable to go to California and you'll never see her again.' 'No. No. No. She'll never do that. You just throw her out.'

"I said, 'You don't know what you're talking about. These teenagers'll hitchhike plum outta the country. I know. I had one to do it.' He said Shelley wouldn't do that. I didn't know what was going on then."

Frustrated, Cherry called Bobby once to try to talk some sense into him. "You couldn't talk to the man," she recalled.

"And I went over there one day and tried," Cherry continued, "to talk to Shelley's mother. But he never let her open her mouth. Never. Every time she'd start to say something, he'd do the talking.

"Well, then Bobby started telling me that he was fixin' to put her away. He was fixin' to put her in some sort of home. He said her mother was going to do it. He said, 'I have nothin to do with it.' And I said, 'Linda, you don't need to do this.' And she said, 'Ah—' And he said real quick, 'This is her decision.' "

Almost two weeks had passed since Shelley had gone on the lam—and it was getting harder and harder to find a place to stay. "Nobody wanted to put Shelley up," recalled Cherry Layfield. "They were scared. They were all scared of what Bobby would do to them if she stayed with 'em.

"Everybody kept saying, 'You can't stay here anymore. You have to keep moving.' We called up Tina and asked if she could stay there. And, no sir, those people wouldn't let her stay there. She stayed at Ruthie's one night and they told her to get her stuff and leave."

The only place left was the Layfield house. Shelley had never even been there and barely knew Cherry Layfield or her husband, Joey Ray, even though he had grown up with her father. The family lived down a gravel road in a tiny two-bedroom house in Kerens, just off Route 31. Cherry and Joey Ray raised five children in this house—one that was not much bigger than Shelley Sessions' bedroom.

Cherry made Ricky give up his bed for Shelley that night. But Shelley didn't sleep well. She had come to the house of the boy that her crazy father had decided was his enemy.

I could never sleep this whole time. I always thought someone was fixin' to come in and get me. I was always hiding. It was terrible.

The next morning, to keep a low profile, Ricky drove Shelley to school in his mother's old Datsun. But Bobby's spies must have been working overtime—and they hadn't been at class long before Shelley heard from Ricky that her dad already knew where she was staying.

They had staked out Ricky's house. And were waiting for me to come back from school. Me and Ricky kind of panicked and we thought, "We can't go back there." So my friend Jackie sent me to her mother's house in Malakoff. So I went there and spent the night. And I couldn't call Ricky or nothing 'cause we thought the phones were tapped and everything.

Ricky arrived the next day with Shelley's clothes and drove her to his sister's house in Roane, six miles north of Powell on county road 1129. By now Shelley was so tired of running she felt like she had "moved a hundred thousand places. . . ."

"It got pretty rough for a while," Ricky recalled. "She'd be flopping here and there and here and there."

Bobby didn't waste a moment. The next day, while Cherry, Ricky and Shelley went to the local Air Show, he walked out in the middle of the funeral of his Aunt Leora in Kerens—a funeral he was paying for. The entire Johnson family, Bobby's mother, was there when he quietly leaned over to Linda and excused himself. "We were burying her that day," recalled Betty, "and he just left."

He fired the big Coupe de Ville back to Powell to pick up one of his ranch hands and then returned to Kerens. But he didn't return to the funeral.

"They parked down the street from us," explained Cherry Layfield. "And he run up our road here—Joey Ray was here, sittin' in the house, and watched him. And he ran up here and got in Shelley's pickup and took off. Pretty cagey."

He took the Silverado back to the ranch, drove into the heavy equipment barn, chained it to a bulldozer, then returned to the funeral home.

"Came back and sat right down next to Linda while the preacher was preaching," recalled James Duvall.

At the cemetery Bobby asked James if he wouldn't mind coming back to the ranch with him.

"He asked if it would be all right if Linda and Michael goes with Betty," recalled James. "And I said sure. He said, 'I'd like for you to go back to the ranch with me.' He said, 'I think Ricky Layfield is going to try to maybe pull something this afternoon.' I said, 'What? Why should he do that!' He said, 'I went and got her pickup.' I said, 'You what?' I said, 'Bobby, you know you gave that—that's her pickup and you went and stole her pickup.' He said, 'I never have changed the title over into her name. It's still my pickup.' And I said, 'Ah, crap.' I said, 'Yeah, I'll go with you.' So we went to the ranch, to the office, and we stayed in the office and sat and talked. And he told me some of the most bizarre mess I ever heard in my life. And he was constantly on the telephone, trying to get a hold of—well, he was talking to different people trying to find out if any of them knew or had seen Shelley anywhere.

"He called one of his buddies, the schoolteacher. And he called, what's her name—the teacher, Dede Scott. And he also called—I can't remember his name—he was a highway patrolman and he bought cattle. He called him and asked him if there was any way that he could get out and look for her. He said, 'I'll pay all your expenses and everything.'

"He'd talk to anybody that would listen to him. And he finally run out of people to talk to on the phone so he started talking to me about these weird sex things down in Houston that one of his good buddies was doing and was making big bucks at it in pornography. And all the time I was sitting there I thought, 'Bobby you're sitting here telling me all this perverted bunch of junk that your buddy done and you're really telling me what *you* done.' Now, during this time he had run back and forth, and I mean he'd literally tore her pickup apart out there trying to find notes, letters, anything in this pickup that might have some kind of evidence of something in it. And I mean he went through it with a fine—about every thirty minutes he'd think of some place he didn't look at and go back out there and he'd look under the hood, he'd get down on the ground and crawl up under it, even underneath the pickup. He was just going wild.

"He wouldn't be saying anything all the time he was digging around but he was just digging frantically, nervously digging and looking. I kept saying to him, 'Bobby, what are you looking for?' He said, 'I'm just looking.' And I thought, 'My God, this guy's losing his mind!' "

All the ranch hands had gone home and there was no one in the office. Just Bobby and James. And all the time Bobby chewed on his fingernails, chain-smoked his Winstons and chain-drank his Dr Peppers. He also kept a loaded pistol on his desk.

"He had a .357 Magnum laying on the desk—this gigantic beautiful executive desk. A .357 Magnum chrome plated laying on the desk. And I was sitting there on the sofa and the barrel of it was pointing at me and I could see every round in the chamber and I said, 'How 'bout moving the muzzle of that thing, Bobby?' Well, he grinned and he takes it up and lays it on the other side.

"He kept saying, 'I can straighten this all out, I can if I can just get her—sit down and talk to her.' He said, 'I can get all this straightened out and everything will be all right.' Well, I made the comment, I said, 'Why don't you just leave her alone?' I said, 'Bobby this Layfield boy—' He said, 'He's just sorry and he's no good. He won't ever amount to anything. They're poor people and they ain't got a dime,' and on and on and on. And I said, 'Well give it time,' I said.

"He was really angry. And he said I'll kill him if he comes out here. This Ricky was wild as an Indian anyway. An old country redneck boy who lived in an old shack you could throw a housecat through! And Bobby was afraid of him. And I really believed if the boy would have come flying out there like some brazen hero Bobby would have killed him. I mean there's no doubt in my mind. He would have killed the kid."

Into the night Bobby talked and phoned and searched Shelley's pickup. James Duvall watched and wondered. He had known Bobby for almost twenty-five years, had worked on the ranch for him from time to time. He listened to Bobby talk, followed him back and forth.

"He just wanted company. He never did like to be alone, period. It's strange but all during the course of this whole thing you've got to understand this guy's brilliant. Let me try to explain it to you with all honesty here. He is an extremely handsome man, he is highly intelligent, he is the type man that has a lot of charisma about him, he can talk to you on any level about any situation and do it extremely intelligently and even more so to the point he will put you in a position in a course of conversation that all of a sudden you thought you knew what you was talking about but all of a sudden this guy knows more. And he is so brilliant. And he had megabucks at the time. So taking all of that into consideration, anybody was willing to listen to him. Because he could almost really convince you that Pope Paul himself was really the monster. And you'd believe it. I mean I've got to give him— he's really a mathematical genius almost to the point, you can't trip him up, you can't outtalk him. I mean he is the most clever one person I've seen in all the course of my life. And I'm also including Warner Brothers and they can pull some of the best stunts in the world. And he is the best of the best. He could teach Warner Brothers a few tricks.

"I mean, he could carry on any conversation. He could go into depth. I'll give you a for instance. If I was fussing about my car insurance, the cost of it. He was kind of a story buster, you know. And it would start off as normal conversation and before the end of it you'd be so confused. You'd almost want to call your insurance company and say, 'Man, I'm glad that you're ripping me off.' He's one of those type characters. It's hard to explain. And I promise you, if you were sitting right here in my living room, and Bobby were sitting over in the chair, and you spent the evening with us just casually talking about anything that popped into our mind, and if Bobby got a telephone call and he had to go, and if Bobby left, you would look at me and say this guy is unbelievable. I mean, he would blast your mind out with his charisma and what he knows. He has a computer-type mind that he does not forget anything and exactly to the 'T' of the event and everything surrounding the event. He has a mind like an elephant. He doesn't forget any word that's been said to him—nothing. He can quote you verbatim. Things that was said to him ten years ago."

This night Bobby did a lot of talking. And James Duvall's mind got blasted more than a few times.

"He would tell me about a college down in Houston and this buddy of his, he said that 'I'll tell you how to make big bucks.' And it was a college—some kind of college down there that the rich people went to. He said what you do is you go down there and you get parked and you watch these girls. And you pick one out that's been standing around out there talking to a boy and he said when she leaves you follow her and find out where she lives. And you buy you a 35mm camera and he said you always find one living in a low-level apartment. Easy access to and not being seen and the whole nine yards and get you a good 35mm camera with a zoom-up lens and, he said, lots of time you can catch them in parking lots having sex acts—and he said if you're really, really good you can photograph them through the windows. He said if it's on the second floor you can rent the apartment across the way and with this camera and tripod and take these pictures and pictures of her and her boyfriends going through this long things—and he said then you present the pictures to her and blackmail her.

"I just sat there listening to all this stuff. He would hide in closets and take photographs. With prostitutes—he would hire this prostitute to play up to this rich guy. And you would stay in the closet while she brought him in there and have all these love affairs there and you'd be taking the pictures with this camera and you would put toilet paper in the trigger mechanism so it would trip silently and all kinds of bizarre stuff. And if I was Bobby sitting over there looking at me I know I must have looked like I was bombed out, spaced out and white as a sheet.

"He said this good friend of his explained all this to him. I said, 'Come on, Bobby. Your good friends don't go around telling you stuff like this.' He said, 'Ah, never mind, you don't understand anyway.' He said, 'You never lived in a big city.' And I thought, 'Oh God—man, this guy. . . .' "

It was midnight before Bobby went to the office refrigerator and grabbed some Twinkies. He continued to talk, drink his soda and smoke and pop Valium from the little aspirin case he always carried with him.

"We just sit there in the office until two o'clock in the morning. It seems like he would trigger out, you know, mentally. And he'd go off the wall telling you all this stuff. And then a little bit later he would think, 'God, I need to call so and so.' It seemed like he'd come back to reality for a minute and he'd call so and so and talk for a minute and then he'd hang up. And then in a few minutes we'd be right back into this same identical conversation. So this went on throughout and until two o'clock in the morning.

"That and along with Shelley. And that's when he told me he'd literally—and he would drop his head like he was crying, weeping, you know, he'd make this little grunting sound and, of course, there'd be no tears fall. And at one point he told me. He said, 'James I literally love Shelley.' He said, 'I cannot stand to even be around or sleep with Linda.' He said, 'I am in love with Shelley.'

"And I said, 'Bobby you know that will never work.' I said, 'Well, what's the matter with you and Linda? You know, I'm an old country boy—if you have problems talk about them. Try to get things straightened out. Or if you can't, you tear the bedsheet in two and each one of you take a half and call it over, you know.'

"He said he stood too much to lose. He did not want to lose his wife even though they had separate bedrooms; they had no marriage. None. Absolutely none! As a matter of fact, she even thought that he was impotent. . . . She told us. He never would have any sex desires for her as man and wife. None. No love relationship whatsoever. It wasn't her fault; she would try. But he would just roll over, play dead. Vomit or something. Whatever.

"He could not leave Linda, leave her broke, he said, 'I don't want to go through the lawsuit,' and he said, 'Shelley might not understand.' He said, 'It's just too complicated.' And I told him, I said, 'Bobby, you got a problem.' I said, 'You got a lot of money.' I said, 'Bobby, you've got the looks.' I said, 'You've got the intelligence.' I said, 'You've got everything in the world going for you. Why do you want to fool around with Shelley? If Linda don't satisfy you—' I said, 'The best thing for you to do is buy yourself a big motor home, one of the finest money can buy, put all the liquor in there you want, all the Dr Pepper in there you want, put you some clothes in there, get you a handful of money and strike out.' And I said, 'On your way out go through Dallas and pick up two or three prostitutes that are really knowledgeable of what your needs are. Y'all hit the highway and have a good merry time. Blow money—you've got it to blow. And when you finally burn yourself out, then you come home and pick up the pieces.'

"I realized right then he was literally obsessed. He is literally perverted. . . . Everything was coming to light for me. This guy is literally perverted. That night I understood and I became very very weary, mentally exhausted and I thought, 'My God, here I been working for this butthole of a man.' "

Finally James suggested that they leave.

"I remember it was very foggy, we drove up to the house and he said, 'You sleep in the guest room.' And I walked with him into the bedroom—I was just following him. And he said, 'You want to watch TV?' And I said, 'No, I don't want to watch TV.' And he said, 'Well, go down the hall right there and you sleep in the guest room and I'll sleep here.'

"And at that time he reached under the bed and pulled out an over-and-under, double-barreled shotgun. And he laid it across the bed. And I said, 'Bobby, you're not going to need that.' He said, 'You don't know.' And I just thought, 'Well, whatever.' So I went on and got in bed, but I didn't sleep.

"And I don't know what time lapsed but I heard him start to snoring so I acted like I had to go to the bathroom and I got up. He was literally laying there, I just peeped inside there as I went past the door, and he was laying there with that shotgun with the muzzle of it upon his pillow with him.

"He was laying on his left side. With the rifle laying there beside him with the barrel, the muzzle of it laid upon the pillow with him and his hand was on the forearm of the rifle. I remember it just like I'm seeing it right now. He was in his underwear laying on top of the cover. And I thought, 'how bizarre.' "

*   *   *

The next day Bobby called Cherry again, asking her where Shelley was. "She's staying with my daughter in Roane, it's perfectly all right," she told him.

"And just how is she getting around?"

"I'm lettin' her use my old blue car."

Cherry still believed that Bobby's concern was a genuine fatherly one. "I really didn't know nothin' was wrong with the man at that time," she recalled. "Up until then we thought he was just strict. I knew him when he was a boy. I used to play the piano for his dad to lead singing' at church revivals. I never knew nothin was wrong with him. He had a good mother and daddy."

But she soon found out otherwise. Alerted to her dad's conversation with Cherry, Shelley immediately moved again.

And again Bobby went to Cherry. "We had a building down on the highway and he called us down there ranting and raving," she said. "He would say stuff that really embarrassed me. He was hooked on sex and I told Joey Ray, 'He's sure obsessed with sex, ain't he?' He would say things like 'I know Ricky's getting in her pants.' And he told me, 'If Shelley has a baby, it's y'all's. Y'all got to raise it.' I said, 'C'mon, we're talking about sixteen-year-old kids here!' I mean, he got pretty rough-talking and I told Joey Ray, 'I can't believe that man's talking to me like that.' "

Bobby was losing his grip on his secret life—he couldn't seem to keep it from coming out anymore.

XIII

FAILED SUICIDE

The bullet from the .38 pistol entered Bobby Sessions' chest just above the nipple, hit a rib, passed by the heart, pierced the diaphragm, shattered the spleen and exited the side of the abdomen.

The next thing Bobby Sessions knew, he was sitting on the ground, thinking that it wasn't supposed to happen this way.

Linda Sessions had been unaware of the stakes. At some level, perhaps, she knew what was going on, but in her innocence she precipitated the end. She wanted to believe that Shelley had simply run away from home. And she wanted to call the police right away—to get her back right away—but Bobby kept convincing her that he would get Shelley back.

So Linda called preacher Henry Edgington—the only link she knew between God and kids.

Meanwhile Shelley finally found refuge with Julie Ragland's mom south of town. Julie was one of Shelley's best friends from Henry Edgington's Church of Christ group; her mom, Jackie Roberts, told Shelley she could stay as long as she wanted. Given the events of the last two weeks, Shelley was somewhat doubtful of that pledge, genuine though it was.

At about the same time, Linda Sessions was knocking on Henry Edgington's door. The preacher knew about Shelley's problems at home, about her attempts to run away. He had heard the kids talk about it, and suspected that Bobby's overprotectiveness had finally gotten to his daughter. Now, Linda was at the door, requesting that Henry accompany her to talk to Shelley.

They went in Linda's Cadillac. "Linda and I had been studying the Bible together," he recalled, "and she had been coming over every so often and we'd sit out in her Cadillac and talk or she'd come inside maybe or whatever. I don't think she wanted anything to be said about it. We'd just sit outside sometimes and talk and she was really searching for truth and what's good and what's bad, you know.

"Anyway, so she came by one afternoon and she said Shelley's run away from home and found out that she was over at the Roberts'. She wanted me to go with her. I don't know . . . she didn't want to go by herself. So I said okay and we jumped in her Cadillac and took off and went to the Roberts' house.

"And we were standing there at the front door knocking and I think Shelley must have known who it was. She didn't come to the door right away. And when she did come to the door, she was just real hard, like, 'What do you want!' And I thought, 'Gosh, that's no way to talk to your mother.' Here I am, just as ignorant as can be of what's going on. Except I knew—you could always look at Shelley's eyes and see a lot of trouble behind them. I just didn't know what it was, and I figured she was just a typical teenager and didn't like being around her family."

Shelley at first wouldn't budge from the doorway—and she didn't invite her mother or Edgington inside. Finally she came out onto the porch. But it didn't help the mood of the conversation.

"And after they had been talking for a few minutes and they were just arguing," Edgington continued, "I said, 'Y'all are not doing any good, you're just arguing with each other. And Linda was saying, 'Please come home' and Shelley was saying, 'I'm not coming home as long as *he's* there,' and this kind of thing. And I spoke up and said a few things and Shelley turned to me and she looked at me and she didn't want to say anything harsh to me, I could tell that, but she said, 'Listen, you don't know what you're talking about, just stay out of it.' I'll never forget that because I thought, 'Golly, this girl is really tough.' "

Edgington noticed a dramatic transformation in Shelley since the last time he had spoken to her. "Her change was from sad to mad. All this sadness I kept seeing in her face and in her eyes. You know, I kept thinking, 'Golly, she's got everything. Her dad's a millionaire, they own this beautiful home and a company or a few companies—Circle S Construction—and Shelley always has nice show horses and a nice pickup,' and just on and on and on. I just kept thinking, 'Boy, she's got everything—why should she be so doggone sad?'

"But I had seen all this sadness in her. When she'd show up it was there, very present in her face all the time. Just as sad as can be. And I never knew what it was and I kept thinking, 'She's really spoiled.' That's terrible, I know. . . . But the big change was made—from when I had been seeing her around school or one of the school functions and there was always sadness, but all of a sudden there was madness. I mean absolute anger."

If Julie and her mother were in the house, Edgington didn't find out. He and Linda and Shelley stood on the front porch of the old house, shaded from the spring afternoon sun. The preacher was perplexed.

"And I mostly listened. When I did speak up, Shelley cut me off pretty quick. I started giving her all my wisdom and my great massive knowledge of life from the Bible, just trying to say you really need to go home with your parents and you really shouldn't talk to your mother that way and boy here I am with a flyswatter when I needed a shotgun."

The nasty confrontation lasted only fifteen minutes. Shelley refused to budge from her hideaway.

Linda and the preacher drove back to Edgington's house. But Linda didn't want to let him go. She wanted to talk. "We sat out front in the car talking for a little while. Linda was in the middle of a lot of things at that moment. She was in what I guess you'd have to call the big search for the truth. That's the only way to say it, about the truth of the Bible; and if there really is a God, what does he want out of me; and the usual things that people search for. . . . And it began occurring to me that there might be something much deeper than just not wanting to do what Mom and Dad want."

But whatever it was, Edgington also guessed that Linda wasn't up to getting at the truth. "She didn't understand it. She wasn't quite sure why Shelley was so mad. . . . And Shelley really wasn't interested in just hurting her feelings to hurt her feelings. She really did want her mom to know something, but I feel like Shelley didn't think it was going to do much good to tell her because she wouldn't believe it. And I don't think the word naïve would be necessarily a good word there. It really seemed like Linda didn't really care to know the truth. She didn't want to believe something like that."

Part of what was blinding Linda, in Edgington's estimation, was her misplaced loyalty to a radical religious group which had distorted her judgment. "They kept telling her that Shelley had a demon in her. And that's why she needed to go to the Rebekah Home. They could take care of it there, you know, their standpoint at the Rebekah Home has always been if you can't get the devil out one way we'll beat the devil out."

Edgington's assessment of Linda: "She was an emotional wreck throughout all of this."

Linda couldn't take it anymore. She told Bobby she was going to call the police.

Shelley had gone to the house of a friend's grandmother after Cherry Layfield told her that she had divulged Shelley's whereabouts to Bobby. But Shelley hadn't been in the new hiding place very long when she saw a police car pulling up to the front of the house. This was a first—her father must have finally given up getting her back on his own and put the police on her trail.

Shelley and her friend ran out the back door as the police

knocked and hightailed it back to Kerens, to Ricky's house. But as they turned into the drive leading to the Layfields', they spotted another police car. Bobby was tightening the noose.

I couldn't go anywhere. We spent the night in the car in a pasture on a dirt road, waiting for all the police to leave so I could go back.

It was Sunday, May 29, when a Navarro County deputy sheriff called county juvenile probation officer Melanie Hyder at home, to alert her. "Runaways are classified under the Family Code as a status offense," Hyder explained, "and he was just making me aware that the parents were wanting to file a runaway report and asked that she be found."

Why the parents had waited so long before going to the police, Hyder didn't know. But early the next morning Bobby was at her Corsicana office in the old dome-topped County Courthouse in the center of town. He wanted his daughter back as soon as possible, he told her. "I explained to him that I had to work through it and I wanted to talk to Shelley and find out what was going on and that it was going to take time," Hyder recalled. "I would do the best that I could to see what was the problem and maybe arrange for some family counseling, find out why she was leaving home, why she was so unhappy."

Low-keyed, Bobby listened politely, agreeing with Hyder's assessment. To Hyder he seemed relieved that the authorities were getting involved, since he thought that the pressure would scare Shelley into coming back home.

But for Hyder, this case had something different about it immediately. Like just about everyone else in the county, she had heard about the Sessions family—and Shelley's runaway didn't fit the usual pattern. "A dysfunctional family is pretty much the norm with the kids I see," Hyder later explained. "In Shelley's situation it was a totally different thing. Her rearing, her home situation, her dad having a good income—the right schools, the right clothes, the right living situation as far as anyone from the outside was concerned."

Shelley was then staying with her friend Julie Ragland, and the two girls were home alone when Shelley saw the deputy sheriff walking up the drive. She bolted for the back door, then stopped. It was no longer any use to run. They knew she was inside—they probably knew everything that her father knew; and he seemed to anticipate her every move.

The deputy drove Shelley to the Corsicana juvenile authorities in the Navarro County Courthouse.

When she first spoke with Melanie Hyder, Shelley made it clear that she wouldn't go home as long as her father was there. And Hyder made it clear that the accepted wisdom in these matters was that of "making up with your parents," as she put it. "Juvenile is not a place for you, Shelley. It is a bad place and you don't want to be there." But Shelley held fast to her secret hatreds. And Hyder again explained the law to Shelley: that since she was a minor, she wasn't completely free to decide where she wanted to live.

"You need to understand that the people you're staying with are not responsible for you," the probation officer told her. "It's nice that they've been allowing you to stay there, but you really need to go back home and try to work things out with your parents."

Hyder seemed sympathetic and explained that her job was to protect her and to find out why she wasn't happy. But she also reminded Shelley that if she didn't go home, she would have to place her somewhere.

"I need some time," Shelley pleaded. "I can't go home. I'm just not ready to go home and deal with it."

Hyder said that wouldn't be a problem. "I could tell that she was a very levelheaded kid," Hyder recalled. "She was not the typical kid that runs off and does terrible things like a lot of the kids that I do work with. You could tell that she was a very bright girl, had a lot of common sense, was sharp as a tack, attractive, a lot of things going for her. I could tell this wasn't a spur-of-the moment thing for her. There was something very wrong, but I assumed it was that she wanted a little bit more freedom and they wouldn't let her have it. That type of thing."

Bobby meanwhile had called Hyder to find out what happened.

He controlled his impatience, but pushed Hyder for a date when Shelley would be brought home. "I told him that we weren't going to just drop her on his doorstep," Hyder explained, "that it would be better if Shelley came willingly."

So far, so good. Bobby was relieved to know the other shoe hadn't dropped. Maybe Shelley would come back. He would have a chance to set things right.

But Cherry Layfield had begun to see an odd pattern about Bobby's incessant phone calls, and was beginning to worry that something else was happening besides a family spat.

She called Jackie Roberts. "Jackie, somethin's goin' on," she told her friend. "All that man can talk about is sex. I'm a stranger—he shouldn't be talking to me like that."

The two women met later and talked about their suspicions. Neither one wanted to believe their fears. "We knew what each other was thinking, but we never did say the word," Cherry recalled.

Cherry also told her husband the same thing. "I think there's something going on here that we don't know about," she said. Then she called Jackie back, suggesting that they have a talk with Shelley.

The two women sat Shelley down in Jackie's kitchen. "Is there something you need to tell us, Shelley?" asked Cherry.

"No," said Shelley. "No, no, no."

"There wasn't no way she was going to tell us," recalled Cherry.

Shelley wrestled with her choices for the next two days. Maybe there was another option, she thought. Maybe she could just leave the county and the state—but she had no money and no transportation. She wrestled with the idea: should she tell somebody? Her father's warnings seemed very real. If she told, she would embarrass herself and her family; she would bring shame on herself; she would be scorned as a slut. But she couldn't go back home, and she didn't deserve to go to a juvenile home. Why should she have to go to jail? She hadn't done anything wrong.

Jackie knew the clock was ticking. "If you have something to say," she warned Shelley, "you better say it now. Because otherwise they're going to take you away."

It was late Thursday morning, June 2, and Henry Edgington was home, still trying to decide how to convince Shelley to return to her family. When the phone rang, he wasn't surprised to hear from Jackie Roberts. Perhaps she had a solution. But he was shocked at what Roberts had to say: "I know why Shelley didn't want to go home. Bob's been molesting her."

Edgington almost dropped the phone.

"She really needs help, Henry."

"Bring her over here," Henry replied, regaining his composure. "I'll take care of it."

The preacher thought that he could be an intermediary in what had suddenly become a terrible tragedy. "My heart was just breaking for Shelley," he recalled. "And everything then made sense all of a sudden. Everything that I had heard from the kids about Bob."

Within a few minutes Edgington saw Shelley and Jackie hurrying up his front steps. As he ushered Shelley inside, she threw her arms around the pastor. Tears streamed down her face.

Everybody loved Henry. He was, like, best friend to everybody. And, you know, he was always there. We all used to hang out with him. So he seemed like the person to tell.

"Don't worry, Shelley," he said. "Nobody's going to touch you again."

Henry ushered Shelley and Jackie into his living room. Shelley felt safe, if not completely comfortable. Part of her was even wondering why she hadn't done this sooner.

Edgington didn't condemn her or call her a slut. Though she trusted him, Shelley fully expected a man of the cloth to be disgusted by her "confession." When he wasn't, she felt washed by a soothing wave.

"All of a sudden I could see all this relief on her," recalled Edgington. "It was finally out in the open and she knew something was going to be done about it and she was going to get out of this stupid mess. She was so different then, when she came in."

Shelley felt amazingly lighthearted, certain now, for the first time in years, that the sexual abuse was at an end. Talking openly about it had lifted an intolerable burden. Those who were hearing the story focused their minds on the events she was relating; for Shelley the horror seemed to dissolve in the telling.

When she had finished, Henry picked up the phone and called the juvenile probation officer. "Melanie, call off the cops. I'm bringing Shelley over," he said. "She has something to tell you."

It was all amazingly clear to him. Shelley's anger and terror now made perfect sense. A few days before, Shelley and Ricky had come to his house, asking if they could hide for a while. The two teens had looked genuinely frightened, and Edgington had ushered them to his attic. "They said that Bob had made a lot of threats," he later explained, "and they believed he was going to try and kill Ricky."

Now that he knew the truth, Edgington wasn't going to take any chances in getting Shelley to Corsicana. It was a straight ten-mile drive, but it went by the ranch. And he was worried that Bobby might now be desperate enough to do something rash.

He called his friends on the Kerens and Powell police departments and told them not to worry if they saw him speeding by—he was taking Shelley Sessions to Corsicana.

Edgington now motored a little four-wheel gem out of his garage: a 1923 T-Bucket Roadster with an incongruous throaty idle that seemed to rattle the entire machine and, as Edgington described it, "this big beautiful chrome Chevrolet engine, the best thing that could have happened to a Ford." The pastor was a car buff—especially hot rods. "We were afraid that Bob was going to be waiting for us," he recalled, "so I wanted to use the Roadster. It had a 327 built-up engine with almost 400 horsepower, and I could blow anything off the road. These Roadsters will do 160."

The pastor and Shelley arrived at the Corsicana courthouse without incident. Shelley was in a much better mood now than when he'd seen her on the porch of the Roberts' house several days before. It was as if a big weight had been lifted.

On the third floor of the courthouse Hyder ushered Shelley and Edgington into her wood-paneled office and told her secretary she didn't want to be disturbed. Shelley felt a little better now, but it wasn't getting any easier. Edgington coaxed her a bit, then kept quiet.

When Shelley finally got it out, that "my father has been molesting me," Hyder didn't know what to think.

"I was just dumbfounded," she recalled. "I didn't have any idea—I mean, it was real overwhelming." She could only listen as Shelley outlined the story of almost eight years of abuse.

There it was. The faster I said it, the better.

Shelley didn't relate any details; Hyder didn't ask for any. She didn't need any at this point. But even as Shelley was stammering around the tale, Hyder's secretary came to the door of the office. "Mr. Sessions is on the line," she said.

"Not now!" Hyder quickly said. "Now, go on, Shelley."

Shelley felt cold again. Her father found her no matter where she went. Maybe there *was* no escape from him. But the probation officer kept reassuring her that she and Henry believed her.

When it seemed that Shelley had finally gotten her story out, Hyder asked, "Shelley, you understand what a serious accusation you are making?"

"Yes, ma'am."

"And you're sure there's nothing you want to change? This is exactly how you feel?"

"Yes, ma'am. It's the truth."

Hyder again assured Shelley that she had nothing to feel guilty about. "I know how you feel," she said. "A lot of mixed feelings right now. But I'm glad you could talk to me. It's a terrible thing for a young woman to have to go through. And I appreciate your being honest with me."

Shelley could hear the phone ring again. And again the secretary came to the door. "It's Mr. Sessions," she said, concern in her voice. "He says it's very urgent." Hyder simply waved her away and turned back to Shelley.

"Shelley, because this is an abuse case, you're going to need to talk to your mother and make her aware of what's going on." Shelley didn't respond. Hyder could see the concern on her face. "She was real scared," the officer later remarked. "This was the worst thing for her, having to tell her mother. It was easier telling me and Henry at that point. She didn't know how she was going to react. She didn't know if she was going to believe her."

"I know I need to tell her," Shelley said. "Will you go with me, Henry?" The preacher nodded, suggesting that they call Linda right away. On the phone, he told Linda that he had to see her, at his house, to talk about Shelley. Shelley came on the line to confirm.

She was all excited, thinking, "Well, she's coming home."

"You will also have to talk to someone further in the sheriff's department and maybe even have to take a lie-detector test," Hyder said. Shelley nodded her assent.

Shelley was being swept along by events over which she had no control. The veil of secrecy had been lifted, and now the consequences—many of them scary—were slowly being revealed. "It was not easy for Shelley to just dump her cards on the table," recalled Melanie Hyder. "It took her some time to get it out and it was very upsetting. It was hard for her to open up to me, someone she didn't really know that well."

But gradually, for the first time, Shelley was beginning to feel she preferred the unknown to the false security of secrecy.

"Melanie Hyder was so good," Edgington later remarked. "She was very concerned about Shelley."

Shelley left Hyder's office feeling much relief. But she was soon reminded that her troubles might be far from over.

"We started getting around Powell," Henry recalled, "and saw a pickup truck come out of this road that went down to the Sessions' house. It kind of came up at an angle by this big lake, which is right out in their backyard there. We just assumed it was Bob so I just, well, blew him off the road as they say. And I probably got up over 130, 140. It was a pretty straight highway right through there."

Linda Sessions arrived at Edgington's home a few minutes after

Shelley and the pastor, just before 6 P.M. She smiled wanly, expressing what might have been a hope that her daughter was coming home now, but asked Edgington why he had summoned her.

In his living room, Edgington directed Linda to a sofa and Shelley to a chair. He had already asked his wife to take his three children down to the neighbor's: this wasn't a conversation he wanted his kids to hear.

But before Edgington could begin, the phone rang. He had to walk through his den and into the kitchen to answer it. "I didn't want to bother them in case it was somebody full of laughter," Henry recalled. But it wasn't somebody full of laughter. It was Bobby Sessions, wanting to know if Shelley and Linda were there. He sounded nervous. Was there any reason he wasn't asked to come? Edgington sidestepped that question, wondering how Bobby even knew that Linda was there. "We're just talking," said the young preacher, "trying to get things straightened out."

Glad to be out of that awkward conversation, Edgington hung up the phone and returned to the living room, where Linda and Shelley sat silently across the room from each other, avoiding each other's eyes.

Slowly, Edgington began. He explained to Linda why he had asked her to come over—why Shelley didn't want to come home. "Bob has been molesting her, Linda," he said bluntly, somberly.

The room was deadly quiet. Outside the house, the air too had a Texas stillness about it; noiseless and clean in the dusk. The chairs of the pastor's parlor creaked with the restlessness of his guests.

At first Linda stared vacantly across the room. Then she slowly turned toward her daughter.

"Shelley," said Linda quietly. "Is it true?"

Shelley nodded.

My mom sat there like she knew it all along. She just kind of sat there for a minute and looked at me.

"Oh, Shelley," Linda cried, coming across the room. "Why didn't you tell me?" She hugged Shelley tightly. "I love you, Shelley. I love you."

Shelley was limp in Linda's arms. "What would you have done if I did?" she sobbed bitterly. "I was afraid to tell anyone because I didn't think anyone would believe me."

Edgington was moved. "I kept thinking, 'Finally there's some understanding.' Everybody was crying."

Linda sat down beside Shelley, listening to her daughter recount, haltingly, some of the times that Bobby had molested her.

Linda still wouldn't let it sink in. "I don't know why I didn't react harder," she later recalled. "All I could think was, *Why didn't you tell me?* There were so many times I stood there going, *Y'all are crazy. Why do y'all fight each other?* They just fought each other all the time. They were forever fighting. They just could not get along."

The phone rang again. And Edgington traced the twenty steps back to the kitchen. "Henry," came the nervous voice, "what are y'all talking about there?" Bobby was wound up very tight.

"Well, right now it just sounds like they're apologizing to each other a lot," he replied. And again he extricated himself from the difficult dialogue. He didn't tell Linda and Shelley that Bobby had called. Nor did he want Bobby to know what his wife and daughter were now discussing.

But no sooner had Henry returned to the living room than the phone rang yet again. It was Bobby again, his voice now a high-pitched whine. "She's making accusations against me, isn't she, Henry?" "Well, Bobby—" "She's saying that I've molested her, isn't she?" Edgington couldn't stop him. "I knew she'd try something like that, Henry. That's what she's always done when she wanted something. She threatens to tell people that I've raped her and molested her. That's how she gets what she wants from me. It's a lie."

But Henry Edgington knew that Bobby was scared. For the first time since he'd met Bobby Sessions, he detected doubt. "This is the richest guy in the county," Henry recalled. "And all the confidence had left his voice."

"Is that what she's accusing me of, Henry?" Sessions continued. "She's saying I molested her, isn't she?"

"Well, Bobby, yes," Edgington finally said. "That's exactly it,

Bobby, she's accusing you of molesting her since she has been a child." He knew that Bobby would probably continue to call if he didn't say yes; besides, he might as well give him a head start on preparing his defense. He'd need a good one.

"It's a lie, Henry."

"Bobby, if I were you I'd find someone to talk to," the preacher coaxed, trying to stay calm. "Because it's obviously going to get worse."

Then there was a long silence. Finally Sessions said, "Well, Henry, I appreciate what you're doing for Shelley. Watch out for her, will you, during this?—Good-bye."

Edgington started back to the living room and felt a shiver in his back. What's going to happen now? he wondered.

Bobby was in his bedroom when he said good-bye to Henry Edgington. He had calmly placed the receiver back in its cradle on the desk and pulled out a college-ruled notepad. Then he wrote on the sheet of legal-sized, white paper, *Henry, Thank you for caring and for being there when Shelley needed you and when we needed you. May God bless you richly. Bobby Sessions.*

The brief message looked tiny and out of place on the large sheet of paper. Bobby then neatly folded the paper in half, slipped ten one-hundred-dollar bills inside and folded it in half again. He wrote similar notes to Linda and Shelley, left them on the desk, then got up.

It was over. He knew it. There were just a few more things to do. He gathered up the Polaroid pictures he'd taken of his naked daughter and the pornographic books that he had tried to get her to read, burned them in the fireplace, then decided "to take myself out of the picture."

The sun was setting behind the lake as Bobby drove the Silverado toward the water.

After leaving Pastor Edgington's house, Linda drove out of Kerens and headed toward Powell. But instead of turning onto the ranch road, she kept her white Coupe de Ville pointed west. She could see the Circle S buildings and the roofline of the house off to the left. She knew that Bobby was there but she was afraid to go home.

Linda drove on to her sister's house and told Sandra that something terrible had happened. "I was just going to gather the family together," Linda recalled. "I wanted people—the family— together to tell them because I didn't know what was going to take place." From Sandra's, Linda drove on to Corsicana to break the news to Bobby's sister and her husband.

"Y'all were right," she told Betty. "Bob is molesting Shelley." Linda looked badly shaken. And she asked Betty if she and James would come to the ranch with her to talk to Bobby—she didn't know what her husband would do.

At the ranch Gary Penney, Linda and Bobby's nephew, was casting a fishing line into the muddy depths of the lake when he heard a shot ring out. Looking in the direction of the sound, he could see Bobby's black pickup truck.

Gary jumped in his truck and bounced across the rocky ground to see what had happened. He found Bobby half-sitting, slumped over on the ground, a pistol by his side. Blood was streaming out of his chest and back.

"I had stuck the gun to my chest," Bobby recalled. "I remember the gun going off. And looking back—although I don't want to make light of any of this at all—it seems kind of funny because I can remember I was laying there on the ground. I looked down and there was this big hole in my shirt and blood was coming out and I thought, 'Something is wrong.' You know, I'm not supposed to be knowing this is here. I reached around behind me and my hand got full of blood. I thought, 'Wow. I've really screwed it up this time. I can't even shoot myself and do it right.' "

The teenager rushed to his uncle, who was pushing himself up from the ground. Bobby leaned heavily on Gary as he guided him into the truck. Bobby was mumbling, but coherent enough to give the youth, who had only recently moved to the area, directions to the hospital.

Henry Edgington had just gotten off the phone with Melanie Hyder, telling her the results of the conversation with Linda, when Larry Green called. Green was a member of his church, who worked security at the Navarro County Memorial Hospital in Corsicana.

"He told me that Bob Sessions was there and he had shot himself," recalled Edgington. "He didn't know if he was going to make it or not, but I should come over because Bob was asking about me."

Within minutes Henry was back in his Roadster, throttling west on Route 31, wondering what more could possibly happen.

Shelley had already bolted out of Henry Edgington's house.

I didn't want to sit there. You know, I thought, "Jesus, I am sitting here and telling my mother her husband did this to me." It was very awkward, so I just got up and left.

Shelley found herself walking back to the Raglands'. There was no longer an urgency to her life. She was neither running away nor contemplating how to get away.

It was over. After all those years, those threats, the many times Shelley had cried herself to sleep, wishing that her mother would somehow rescue her—now Linda knew. But Shelley felt curiously empty inside. The confession was a catharsis, but it left her exhausted and confused, not invigorated.

But at least the need to choose between juvenile detention and home had been lifted. The pastor had made sure Shelley had a place to stay for the night, then told her not to worry; that the matter would now be put in the hands of the authorities and her father wouldn't hurt her anymore.

She didn't know what to think anymore. A voice inside told her that no one could protect her from her father. And at that moment she heard Ricky's voice calling her. No dream. He was there motioning for her to get into the car. Shelley was relieved, but she couldn't tell him what had happened. They drove around, Shelley doing what she had done for so long: keeping her secret.

They drove to the Little League field, then back uptown to Main Street. Parked at the side of the road, Shelley heard Jackie's husband calling her name. "Somebody's looking for you," he said. "Your uncle or something. Down by the Country Supermarket. Something happened to your dad."

Shelley wasn't especially moved by this announcement; none-theless she and Ricky drove to the supermarket. There they saw Bobby's sister, Pat, and Betty's husband, James—very upset. James ran up to them. "Shelley—your dad shot himself! Your mom wants you at the hospital."

"We started hauling ass to Corsicana," recalled Ricky, "and she commenced to telling me. . . . She was hysterical and I was having to pull it out of her—'What you talking about?' You know. I knew, but I wanted to hear her say it. Everything. Everything I've been thinking. Boy. Everything that had been filling into my head, it was all piecing together. I knew she wasn't lying and I started pulling it out of her and she started telling me, you know, he'd hold a gun to her and tell her if she said anything that he would tell her friends that she wanted it and, you know, that they would hate her instead of him."

Ricky didn't take the news well. He was angry, hurt. He also didn't understand why Shelley hadn't told him sooner. He would have gladly taken care of Bobby for her. He would have protected her.

"My worst nightmare started coming true," he remembered. "God, the grudge started building inside. It was just there. There was nothing I could do about it, there wasn't no help. Everybody gave her help, but they didn't think that I done fell in love with her, bad, real deep, then something like that comes up. Whooooosh. And that just wiped my emotions out."

Shelley told Ricky that many times she had been close to telling him but was afraid for him. "If she had told me something like that, there would have been no doubt in my mind that I'd be sitting in prison right now," Ricky later explained. "Because I was about crazy enough to shoot him. I could have nailed him from a long distance. It would have been premeditated. I'm glad he went and shot himself because it saved me that court cost, fine, going to prison and all that stuff."

They drove to the hospital, Ricky wild with confusion, as was Shelley.

"The most conversation we had about that mess was then," he recalled, "on the way to the hospital. From then on, you know,

I never did bring it back up because it hurt her. It hurt me too, my pride, to think somebody else was with my girl, even though it was molestment, you know, it was knocking my ego down. Somebody used to talk to my girl and I'd throw it down: let's fight. And then this come up and that really tripped me out."

Shelley too was "tripping out." They got to the hospital as soon as they could. Why so fast, Shelley wasn't quite sure; maybe it was inclination, or fear, or just numb response—a kind of testimony to the steely strength of patrimony, patrimony at all costs. The bond to her father in her case had become an insidious mockery, but there it was nonetheless. She hated the man. She had wanted, often, to kill him. Was she driving to the hospital this night as a daughter—or as a killer returning to the scene of her crime?

No sooner did Shelley walk into the waiting room than she knew something of the answer. The family had already gathered. Bobby's family. And they stared at Shelley as if she were a Judas— as if they *knew*. What they "knew," however, was what Bobby had used to threaten Shelley. They "knew" that she was a slut: bad, disloyal, disrespectful and responsible for sending their brother, their son, their husband, to his deathbed. Shelley saw that in their faces. Bobby had been right.

Doctors working on Sessions in the emergency room considered the wounded man lucky to be alive. The bullet had missed the heart by just a few centimeters. But Bobby was going to make it. And Shelley was not at all surprised at that. Bobby survived all; he was powerful beyond belief. He had planned it all; to gain sympathy and show Shelley in the shadowed light of slutdom. After all, how was it that cousin Gary was nearby to hear the gunshot? How was it that the bullet only grazed a couple of ribs? Why did a man with Bobby's expertise in firearms not know how to inflict a fatal wound from point-blank range?

Shelley knew the answers: he didn't want to kill himself, only gather sympathy. And the proof was in the result: he was alive and he had the sympathy.

When Linda and Betty rushed into the hospital, Bobby's mother, Lottie Caskey, was already there, her face numb with worry. She ran to Betty and threw her arms around her, sobbing.

A few minutes later Henry Edgington rushed in. In his distraction he thought he recognized one of Bobby's sisters, or perhaps Bobby's mother, as he strode by the chairs in the small waiting room.

He met Linda coming out of the room where Bobby was being held for surgery—lying on his back on a table. His shirt was off, and his chest was wrapped in bandages to stabilize the bleeding while doctors prepared for surgery. His vital signs were stable, but his breathing was weak and heart rate rapid. The initial physical exam revealed a one-centimeter entrance wound just above the left nipple, with surrounding powder burns, and an exit wound in the middle back at the level of the tenth rib. A couple of nurses were huddled over him, adjusting tubes and pillows.

Bobby was conscious. And when Edgington sidled up, the wounded man grabbed the preacher's hand. "I appreciate you taking care of Shelley," he said in a hoarse whisper, squeezing hard. "I appreciate you taking care of Shelley . . ." He was groggy from medications.

Within a few minutes Bobby was wheeled out, toward surgery, under general anesthesia, his prognosis guarded. Dr. E. Scott Middleton performed the surgery to repair the damaged chest. His report read:

An upper midline incision was made through an old previous chole-cystectomy [gallblader removal] incision with some calcification present in the old scar. . . . There were two holes in the diaphragm, one in its midportion left side and one laterally and posteriorly on the left side. Both communicated with the chest, and air could be heard passing through both holes. The spleen had a large wound in it from the passage of the missile along the greater curvature of the spleen. The liver was not injured. The spleen was removed by immobilizing it from laterally and by dissection.

Bobby was in the operating room when Shelley and Ricky arrived. They surveyed the waiting room. Linda, Bobby's mother, Linda's mother and father, Bobby's sister Pat Davidson, Linda's sister Sandra, cousin Gary, and Betty and James Duvall were all there.

The whole family was sitting there, and they were just staring at me like I was the one that did it. It was weird.

Now Bobby's warnings were materializing: "They'll blame *you*, Shelley," he had said over and over whenever she threatened to tell on him. She had believed him then; now, looking around the waiting room, she wondered how she had dared forget his threats.

"I saw Linda," Ricky recalled, "and she was talking to somebody, smiling. And I thought, 'Wow, this family is messed up. Ol' Bobby blowed half his lungs out and his wife standing there smiling, you know. Shoot, this is a trip, like one of those soap operas.' "

And when Shelley found out what had happened, and that Bobby was going to pull through, she muttered to Ricky, "I wish he would have killed himself."

Ricky thought: "If I had been there, I would have cocked the gun and handed the gun back to him and said, 'Finish it.' "

"I felt so sorry for her because I knew that everyone would resent her so bad," recalled Betty Duvall, who walked over and hugged Shelley.

Richard Ruiz, whom Bobby had fired just a few weeks before, came over to Shelley. "What went wrong?" he asked her.

"He shot himself," she replied, still dazed.

When Ruiz asked why, Shelley would only say, "I can't tell you now, but you don't know the whole story."

Shelley thought she would spend the night at Betty and James's house, but when she got there, her brother Michael was throwing a wild fit, flailing about while James Duvall and Linda's sister and mother tried to carry him to his grandparents' car.

He was just going crazy. He didn't understand why his sister ran away from home and why his dad shot himself. And so I tried to comfort him.

"They literally fought Michael bodily to get him in the car," recalled Betty. "He was only six years old and I felt sorry for him.

"One reason he didn't want to go was that they were always forgetting him. Forget to pick him up at school, forget to take his lunch to him. And I was just kind of like always there. He went to the same school as my daughter and I would just kind of hang around until I made sure every day that he was picked up. One day I stayed until five o'clock and no one ever came. He sat in the van with us but no one came. So I brought him home with me. And I called out to the ranch and I didn't get an answer at his house so I called the grandmother and she said, 'Oh I was supposed to pick him up but I forgot.'"

Shelley got so mad watching her little brother being carried kicking and screaming to the car that she walked out. She drove back to Kerens and stayed the night with the Layfields.

"We sat up with her all night," recalled Cherry Layfield. "And Linda came up here the next morning, spouting all this stuff about Bobby being 'saved' on the way to the hospital. And he was a changed man and wanted Shelley to come back home."

Shelley was bitter. Not with the news that her dad would survive, but with the response to his shooting. It was all part of his plan, more proof of his power.

He didn't go down there thinking he really was going to die. He knew my cousin was down there fishing. He knew he'd be rushed to the hospital. He knew where to aim it. He's very smart. He does not do anything without a backup plan. In business or otherwise.

It was pretty risky. But if he would really want to have died, he would have blown his head off. That's how I look at it. If he really didn't want to live, he would have just swiiiiish! And that would've been it.

But he wanted everybody's sympathy. He knew everyone was going to find out what a terrible thing he'd done. He knew he could get back their sympathy just by getting hurt, being laid up in the hospital.

Everyone was just "Oh, Bob. Oh, Bob." And he'd go, "I'm sick. I'm insane. But now I've got God." And everybody loves him again. So he's not stupid.

Betty too believed that Bobby's self-inflicted wound was a kind of cover-up. "You have to understand how manipulative he was," she later explained. "He just tried to get everybody's mind off of what Shelley had said about him and feel sorry for him. Because if he had wanted to kill himself, he would have shot himself in the mouth and not in the abdomen."

XIV

THE DEAL

Linda didn't stay long at the hospital that first night. She was confused. She didn't know what to think. It was all unfolding quickly—too quickly for her to grasp. She was in the emergency room, then seemed to disappear. She called the Layfields to make sure Shelley was there.

"We had a couch over here and she lay on that," recalled Cherry Layfield. "Then she lay on the floor. She didn't want Ricky out of her sight. She was scared, nervous, shook up bad."

I felt protected because Ricky liked to fight a lot and I thought, "Well, here's my knight in shining armor, he's going to save me, he's going to protect me."

But Linda came by the next morning, hysterical.

My mom begged me to come home. She said, "You do whatever you want, whatever, just come home."

Everyone, it seemed, was confused. The community of Kerens, classmates, relatives, officials—no one really wanted to hear about what was done to Shelley. She felt more like a pariah than a victim, stared at everywhere she went.

After a few days she moved back home—and felt safe there for the first time, because her father was in the hospital temporarily incapacitated.

Or so she assumed.

The police told me that he was hallucinating and that I shouldn't answer the phone.

Then her mother called. Shelley could tell that all was not right, because Linda's voice had the trill of nervousness Shelley had come to recognize as a warning of danger.

"Pack a bag and meet me on the back road," she whispered into the phone. "Right away."

The urgency in Linda's voice was enough to scare Shelley to quick action. She did as directed and within a few minutes was blazing a dusty trail to a far corner of the ranch. Her mother's white Cadillac was waiting and Shelley ground to a halt at her side.

"You have to leave," Linda said. "You have to leave now. Here." This time it was Linda who threw money at her. Shelley looked bewildered—even though nothing bewildered her anymore. "Bobby is telling everybody he's going to kill you!" Linda shouted hysterically. "You've got to leave!"

Bobby had what doctors were calling "an unfolding paranoid psychosis." He was extremely agitated and manic, compulsively talking about Shelley, what she might do now, the need to control her.

For Shelley the nightmare continued. Shelley was sure that he had set up the suicide attempt to fail—plotting, she knew, to earn enough sympathy to counteract the damage Shelley's story would inflict. Next, he would rise from the bed, Phoenix-like, and come get her, finish her off.

Shelley took the money and ran. She was so frightened now—believing that after all was said and done no one could protect her—that she spent the night in her truck, in a back road.

The next day she returned to the Layfields. Henry Edgington and Melanie Hyder helped Shelley through the paperwork. The Wednesday following the shooting, they met with Sheriff Ross at Edgington's house so Shelley could make her formal complaint against her dad. Ross asked Shelley to write down the entire history of the abuse and, whenever possible, to note the dates and times.

"The first unusual thing I noticed (took place in New Jersey) was when Bobby Sessions would rub on my back and legs (telling me to relax from tension) and would gradually ease his way up on my breast or my vagina," Shelley wrote. She gave the same brief description of the night Bobby molested her in a motel room on their return drive to Texas and the ensuing incidents of fondling. "He would tell me to want him as he wanted me—I never did." Shelley listed as best she could remember the dates and locations of the cattle shows at which Bobby had abused her. "When I did not cooperate, he began shaking all over, cussing, hitting and threatening me with things or my belongings."

The sheriff had encouraged Shelley to give details of the sexual abuse—so Shelley wrote, "Details: I was to suck on him and visa versa [sic] and to totally devote myself (making love) as he considered it." Shelley was also asked to recall the last time Bobby had sex with her. She wrote, "May 10 or 11th, 2 days before Bobby Sessions left for a trip to London, England."

When she had finished writing, Sheriff Ross had her statement typed on a "Voluntary Statement (Not Under Arrest)" form. Shelley signed it.

Linda then drove Shelley to Fairfield, Texas, thirty-five miles away, for a polygraph test at the International Polygraph Service. It was the first time Linda and Shelley were really together since the day Shelley had told her mother what had happened. But Linda didn't ask about the incest. She didn't seem to want to know.

Melanie Hyder had also met with Linda, who was still Shelley's legal guardian, and thought that Linda was as confused as anyone. If Linda hadn't recognized it before, when Shelley kept trying to give her clues, she now couldn't avoid knowing: her husband had molested her daughter. She had to choose between them. Or did she? How could she?

"Linda was very dazed," recalled Melanie Hyder. "She really didn't know what to do or how to cope with all this." She stayed away from the hospital, tried to take care of Michael and help Shelley.

Shelley was greeted by IPS president J. D. Williams, whose company's motto was, "Probing the past to protect the future." With Shelley attached to the wires of the small machine, Williams questioned her for more than an hour. "She stated their first sex act was in the form of oral sex by him placing his mouth on her vagina," Williams wrote in his report. Shelley described Bobby's attempts to elicit sexual favors by promising gifts and threatening to "tell the whole world that she was nothing but trash."

She described the cattle shows where "they had sex relations on a daily basis." And finally, Williams noted, "Shelley was questioned about seeking revenge against her father and by doing so made up these stories about sex. This she vehemently denies."

Williams ran two separate tests on Shelley, concluding that "she has been truthful throughout her examination and interview with this examiner."

With these results, the road was now cleared for formal charges against Bobby.

Shelley's statement had started the official wheels of justice turning. For each count of sexual abuse of a minor, there were penalties of up to ten years in jail. Since, according to his daughter, Sessions had racked up hundreds of violations, the district attorney had a chance to put him away for a long time.

Bobby's family went into action right away. They wanted the legal proceedings finished as soon as possible, the incident kept quiet. "Everybody was in a stupor," recalled James Duvall. "Nobody wanted to make any waves, nobody wanted to ask any questions, nobody really wanted to know anything." And no one wanted the publicity of a trial. So Lottie dispatched James to the sheriff's.

Since James was a good friend of Sheriff Robert Ross, he went directly to Ross's house. "He invited me in and I said, 'Look, Bobby, it's a bad situation and I know he's been sexually abusing his daughter. But he tried to kill hisself and maybe this will be the end of the whole thing here.' I said the family is tore all to pieces and we don't know what's going on except the man shot himself and we know that Shelley squealed on him and we know all that. And I said the family really wants to know is he going to go to trial or what's going to happen? And Bobby said, 'Are you here in his defense?' And I said, 'Well, Bobby, I'm here as a family member and at the request of the family to keep him from going to the penitentiary.' "

With his donations to charitable causes throughout the county, Bobby Sessions was a big man in the area, but even James had been in the dark about some of his gifts. "I didn't know he had been making extremely big donations to the sheriff's department," he recalled. "He wouldn't give campaign money, but he would donate thousands towards things like drug abuse and child abuse. It wasn't campaign money, it was money that went into the sheriff's department for different programs."

James left with a promise from Ross to call the district attorney to see what he could do. And the next afternoon Ross called James. "The DA told Bobby Ross," James explained, "that they could do a little plea-bargaining there in-house. But he said, 'First of all I want to make sure this is what all the family wants.' "

Anyone could have guessed that a family member who did what Bobby Sessions was said to have done would create some family divisions of opinion. So Pat Batchelor, the DA, wasn't going to take any chances on doing Bobby a favor by plea-bargaining if some members of Bobby's family wanted him in the slammer.

Ross suggested that James gather the family and come to his house for a little meeting. Linda and her parents came, as did Lottie and daughters Betty, Pat and Wanda. Not Shelley. "This child was scared, mixed up, she just didn't know what in the world was going on," recalled James. "Bobby had called once or twice and threatened her. So Shelley just stayed away from all the family, period."

The sheriff explained that there was a chance that a deal could be worked out. Bobby would plead guilty to one charge of sexual assault but wouldn't have to spend any time in prison. "He said that Bobby would appear in front of Buck Douglas, the judge, and the charges would be read," recalled Duvall. "They would have to give him a probated sentence and he would go to a psychiatric hospital, like Timberlawn in Dallas. They singled that out as a very, very elite, red-carpet psychiatric place for the very, very wealthy."

Sheriff Ross explained that the alternative was prolonged court procedures and probably a prison term of ten years.

"But if the family agreed, Douglas would give him ten years' probation and one year in a psychiatric hospital," recalled James. "He would have to pay for his own treatment." Ross went around the room and asked each person if he or she had any questions. But no one did. Everyone knew the deal Bobby was getting. "And everybody said, 'Well, that's great,'" said James. "'We'll talk Bobby into agreeing with that.'"

Bobby Ross called Pat Batchelor right away.

James Duvall went to the hospital. There was an armed security guard outside Bobby's room—just in case he wanted to try anything.

"It's either ten years in the pen or ten years' probation and go to this psychiatric hospital," James told Bobby.

"I don't want that," Bobby said, shaking his head from his bed. "I can straighten this all out if I can just talk to Shelley."

"You're not going to get to talk to Shelley," said James. "And Linda is fixin' to prosecute you—take you for everything you've got."

Bobby seemed not to hear. He was fixated, staring through the walls of his room.

James brought Bobby back on track. "You've got to make a decision or they're going to prosecute you and you'll go nonstop to Huntsville. If you don't take this, Bobby, you're going to the pen."

After a moment, Bobby pushed himself up on an elbow and lit a cigarette. His back was to Duvall. "Are you sure?" he asked, without turning around.

"I'm absolutely sure," said James soberly.

"Okay. I'll go with a probated sentence—but I love her! She'll understand." Bobby dropped his head and cried.

Duvall wasn't convinced by the tears. "She *won't* understand,

Bobby," he shot back. "She's the one that blew the fuse on you. You're exposed. Can't you get that through your head!" For the first time Duvall was getting angry.

"At that point I was about ready to hand him over to the vultures and let him go to the pen," he recalled. "But I had already gone so far to try to help the family and I thought, 'If we can usher him into this psychiatric hospital, it will give enough time to the family to really get things straightened out and see what's going to happen.' I was really thinking, 'God, Linda, this is your great chance now to rip him off. Take everything he's got, you're rightfully doing it. He's abused your daughter ever since she was a baby.' "

When District Attorney Batchelor and Sheriff Ross arrived the next day, Bobby was prepped. Betty Duvall and Lottie waited in the hall outside as the two men stood around Bobby's bed, laying out the alternatives. If Bobby pleaded guilty to one charge of sex abuse, they told him, he might be able to get a suspended sentence that would include a limited stay in a psychiatric hospital. Bobby's lawyers told him to take the deal. Under the circumstances, Bobby had no quarrel with the plan: he didn't want to go to jail.

When the prosecutor and sheriff saw Shelley the next day, it was to say that she could influence the sentence if she chose to. Linda had asked attorney JoAnn Means to advise Shelley at the meeting. And Linda was there, insisting, as she later said, that "I gave her full freedom to choose and do whatever she wanted."

But as the options were explained, Shelley had only a vague understanding of their import. If sentenced to ten years in jail, said the DA, Bobby would stay behind bars for maybe only a couple of years, then get out. But if he were given a probated sentence, the judge could order him sent to a mental institution where he would not be released until he was cured.

He told me that if Bobby went to prison that he would be out on probation and that the only way to keep him away was in Timberlawn. I told him I wanted him away as long as he could be.

Shelley believed she had chosen the maximum possible sentence.

She was up against it now. Everything Bobby predicted. "The attitude was, here's this little sixteen-year-old going on thirty," recalled a courthouse observer. "Like she asked for it. The same thing people say when somebody is raped. *She liked it,* or, *Why didn't she do anything about it if it was so awful?* And add to that that he was a man of standing in the community and you have problems for Shelley."

Shelley had tried to resign herself to what was happening and had even moved back home. "I'm not running from him any-more," she told Linda defiantly. Besides, she reasoned, Bobby was going to the mental institution any day and would be out of the way.

"Well, don't answer the phone, at least," Linda warned. "He's been hallucinating real bad. Sees snakes and stuff."

But Shelley forgot the warning, and when the phone rang, she instinctively answered.

"Shelley?" came the hoarse voice on the other end.

She wanted to hang up. But she waited through a long silence, now curious about what Bobby would say. "Shelley?" he said again.

"What do *you* want!" she sneered into the receiver.

"Shelley. I'm going to kill you!"

Shelley slammed the phone down. "Mom! Mom!" she yelled, hurtling into the kitchen. "It was him. He said he was gonna kill me."

Shelley was shaking. Bobby's voice was so familiar, so stark. And despite herself, she still believed everything he said—now including his promise to do her in.

"I told you not to answer the phone," Linda scolded.

"Some consolation!" Shelley thought. He was out there, want-ing to kill her. She called Sheriff Ross.

He told me not to worry and gave me all these phone num-bers—his home phone and everything. He said, "If anything hap-pens, you call me. I'll do anything. . . . I won't let anything happen to you."

At the hospital Bobby was waxing hallucinatory—he com-plained of the effect of the medication and swore he hadn't done what Shelley had accused him of. "It didn't happen," he would tell his mother.

But when his mother left the hospital room, he would pick up the phone and try to call Shelley again. It was as if, instead of his finding God and remorse, his new lease on life gave him a new lease on love. "When his mother would walk out of the room," recalled James Duvall, "he would say, 'I just can't give it up. I love Shelley. I'm in love with Shelley.' He would say lots of strange and weird things. And he would try to make you think that he was really bombed out on medication and stuff. But he really wasn't. He knew what was going on."

He knew enough to use the phone beside his bed frequently. Since his finding God, he was on the wire with Linda's counselor, Sarah Conn. "He called several times asking me to help Linda and the children," recalled Conn. "He didn't know what was going to happen—but he knew that he wanted his family taken care of. And he called me repeatedly, very urgently, insisting that I come and give help—do whatever I could do to help his family stay together and not be destroyed."

And he kept trying to call Shelley. "Whenever he was saying, 'I love Shelley,' he literally meant what he was saying," James Duvall said. "Not a father/daughter love, but he really meant he literally and indubitably loved her. As a lover, not as a daughter. He was totally and emphatically obsessed with this girl."

Richard Ruiz had come by a couple days after Bobby was admitted. Lottie had asked him to because Bobby wasn't eating right. She was worried about him; perhaps the ranch manager could help. As soon as Ruiz walked in, Bobby asked for a Dr Pepper.

According to what James Duvall saw, there wasn't as much to the hallucinations as Linda and others thought. "He would be talking along and then all of a sudden he'd start talking about parrots being on the wall. Or it would be, 'Who's that standing there in the window?' Stuff like that. Especially when his mom or his sister would walk in. Betty would walk in the room and he would really go acting stupid. Then they would walk out and he would start talking more rational. He was trying to put on this act that he was hallucinating."

This was just one of many reasons Bobby couldn't find an attorney to represent him. His power and influence had fallen by the wayside among those who were not loyal.

One of his previous attorneys, Jimmy Morris, a former Navarro County district attorney, wouldn't take the case. Morris had hired Pat Batchelor as an assistant DA and had been Batchelor's boss. "And basically he handed him the DA job on a silver platter when he decided not to run," according to a Corsicana lawyer. "So you could say that Jimmy probably did have a little more stroke than anybody around here."

James Duvall searched around without success. "Nobody would have him."

Most lawyers complained that their wives would kill them if they touched the case. So Shelley did have some support. Quiet, but there just the same.

"I was beginning to see," recalled James. "I knew Bobby inside and out. I knew him better than his sisters [did]. I knew him better than his wife. I dealt with him every day. I knew every emotion. I knew how he could manipulate. I mean, he is a brilliant, brilliant man. But for some reason—just an old country boy like myself, I heard about sexual child abuse, but not in my time frame. I mean, I just wasn't raised that way. I couldn't believe a man would do something to a young child like this, I just couldn't. Betty had tried to tell me, but I just couldn't believe it."

Bobby was scheduled to appear in court for formal sentencing on June 13, 1983. Despite the fact that doctors had removed his spleen, Bobby was in the hospital for only eleven days with his wound. But when he heard that Linda was no longer in touch with *his* side of the family and had hired her own lawyer, he knew he had other problems. Bobby was not only worried that Linda would leave him; he also suspected that she would want money in the process.

"Linda turned the tides real fast," James recalled. "All of a sudden she just lost her cool and decided she had to have a lawyer and she was going to take Bobby for everything he was worth.

Within a couple of days she just turned her complete thinking capacity over and she was ready to rip Bobby off."

When Linda hired her own attorney, the family thought at that point they would have a battle with Linda on their hands.

But Bobby moved fast. Even from the hospital, he proved he could maneuver around most obstacles. He called James and Betty and asked them to arrange for him to get into the bank first thing in the morning. Betty had worked at Corsicana National until just two months previously, and Bobby was one of the bank's largest depositors.

James cleared things with the sheriff's department. Ross sent two deputies to drive Bobby, Betty and James to the Corsicana National Bank, three blocks from the county courthouse. "He was still awful sore, still in bandages, still under medication," James recalled. "No need to put him in handcuffs, because he couldn't run anywhere. He was doing well in stitches just to walk." But he felt as if he were racing his wife to the bank. They arrived at seven-fifteen in the morning, before the bank had even opened. The president of Corsicana National was already there waiting for him.

Bobby first withdrew $30,699 in cash and a cashier's check and stuffed it into a briefcase. But when he said he had to get into the safe-deposit boxes, even the bank's chief officer couldn't help—the vault was on a time lock and wouldn't open until eight. Bobby had his court date at eight, so he instructed Betty to open the box later and put everything into another box, in her name. "He wanted everything out of his deposit box and put in the new one," Betty recalled.

Eulah Mae Boyd, a bank clerk, accompanied Betty to the vault. They both inserted their respective keys and opened the box. Peering inside, Betty was surprised at what she found: a Rolex watch in a box with Shelley's name on it, an expensive hunting knife with Michael's name on it, a coin collection Betty later discovered was worth a couple of hundred thousand dollars, and sixty thousand dollars in cash.

Betty simply moved everything into the new vault box, in her name. Bobby's valuables were now safe from Linda.

At the courthouse, a few blocks away, Bobby was appearing before Judge Buck Douglas. The courtroom seemed big enough to swallow everyone up. District Attorney Batchelor stood at the prosecutor's table on the left side of the well as Sheriff Ross and his two deputies escorted the limping Bobby Sessions to his table on the right side. He didn't have a lawyer. Behind him sat James Duvall and, sitting over to the far right of the first bench, Melanie Hyder

The DA read the charge—the *single* charge: On May 8, 1983, just the month before, Bobby Rowe Sessions did "intentionally and knowingly have sexual intercourse with Shelley Rene Sessions and at that time of said sexual intercourse, Shelley Rene Sessions was a female younger than seventeen years of age and was not his wife."

Bobby pleaded guilty. Douglas passed the sentence: ten years' probation, confinement at Timberlawn at his own expense and no release without doctor's authorization. Then he ordered him to pay court costs. Douglas banged his gavel. It was over.

More than three years of raping his daughter and he pleaded guilty to one count of sexual assault. For helping the prosecution get everything out of the way so quickly, Bobby was sentenced to ten years of probation and assignment to a private Dallas psychiatric treatment center—until doctors there decided he could be released. He didn't want to go to the hospital, but it was that or jail. And he didn't want the publicity.

I didn't even know they were having a trial. Nobody even told me. I didn't even get to testify or nothing. They sentenced him without me testifying.

The sheriff's deputies drove Bobby and James back to the hospital to pick up Bobby's belongings, checked him out, then climbed into the white police cruiser for the trip to Dallas.

The cruiser sped along, Bobby sitting in the backseat, clutching the money-laden briefcase in his lap. He stared straight ahead most of the hour-long trip. "I will rise up above this, James," he said. He said little else. He didn't talk about Linda or Shelley or his family or the ranch or his business. He looked at James with his piercing blue-green eyes: "I'll rise above this."

"Well, Bobby," said James, "you got to try to get yourself straightened out first."

They arrived at Timberlawn a little after seven that Monday evening. It was still light enough to see that the setting was opulent—spacious lawns, towering trees and low-slung buildings.

In the reception building the deputies wandered around while Bobby checked himself in. The procedure was much closer to a hotel arrival than a prison one. "It's not a bad place," said Bobby.

"Get used to it," said James. "You're going to be here a year."

Bobby looked at him with the same earnest and intense eyes. "No, I won't."

James Duvall was as usual amazed by his brother-in-law's resolute cockiness. But this time he caught something—a whiff of craziness that couldn't be explained. "I thought, 'Ah, crap! This guy! He got caught, he made a major mistake, made one of these major screw-ups, got off easy and is going to straighten himself out. But no, no, he's going to get out.' That's when I first realized his true colors. And I thought, 'Oh, crap, I have done the wrong thing all the way through. And at this point I was extremely disgusted with myself. Because everything that I'd done was mostly because of the family asking me. It wasn't me doing it out of my own true feelings or anything. I was just trying to help. But when he told me that, my whole heart went to the bottom of my feet. I thought, 'This sucker had done pulled another one of his most beautiful snow jobs.' "

On the way back to Dallas James predicted, "He won't be in there six months and he'll be out."

"No, no," said one of the deputies. "He's got to stay in there twelve."

To which James replied, "You don't know Bobby Sessions."

XV

CELEBRATION

"The good Lord has blessed me with just almost a total lapse of memory for about sixteen or seventeen days because I don't remember anything from that time [of the shooting] until waking up in Timberlawn." Bobby Sessions later claimed this memory loss—a convenient one, because he had threatened to kill Shelley during this period.

The sheriff himself assured Shelley that her father had been taken to Dallas. It was June 13, only eleven days since he had shot himself. The sheriff explained to Shelley that if Bobby escaped, he would be the first to know—and he would be sure to get word to her.

Shelley was finally beginning to let herself believe that it was over. Her jailer and tormentor was out of the picture.

She stepped outside—nothing happened. She drove to town and visited friends—nothing happened. She stayed out late, dated and went to parties—and nothing happened. It was as if a heavy set of chains had been cut off her wrists and ankles.

And Linda was amazingly lenient with Shelley. "As long as you come home and live in my house, you can do what you want," Linda told her daughter.

Shelley thought she had her mother back. Just the two of them, with Michael, again. And that Linda had decided to be rid of Bobby, to finally save her children.

She told me if I moved back home—that that's all she wanted, for me just to be back home.

However, this didn't mean in Shelley's eyes that she had to spend a lot of time with Linda, about whom she still felt some resentment.

I wasn't comfortable with her because I knew it was an ordeal for her to go through and it hurt her. I just didn't feel that, at the time, we needed to spend time—she wasn't helping at the time.

Shelley was always gone—or, when home, was with Ricky, the boy who had so threatened Bobby and precipitated the break.

"She was needing a lot of love," recalled Linda. "She wanted to do her own thing, and she felt like, you know, she had been suffocated. So I let her have a lot of freedom." In fact, Linda indulged Shelley. She fed Ricky when he came over to the house, made him feel welcome and welcomed his family.

"We'd go over there, me and my kids," recalled Cherry Layfield, "and they'd go swimming. I carried my grandkids over there, and Bubba [her eldest son, a minister] would go over and Linda was just as nice as could be. She and Bubba would talk religion."

Linda talked to Shelley about taking over the ranch, since Shelley knew how it operated and Linda knew nothing. She was going to divorce Bobby, she told her daughter. And she tolerated Shelley's sudden wildness. "I just felt like all she needed to hear from me was that I loved her and that I loved her and that I loved her and that I wasn't going to put any restraints on her right then. I handled her with kid gloves."

"Linda had her head screwed on so good," recalled Betty Duvall. "She came to our house right after all this happened and told us she had decided to take the children away for a month or two. She said, 'I'll let you know where I am, but I think we're going to go away and get out of here.' And James said, 'Linda, I think that's the best thing you could do. You need to save your children, get out of here, get away from this place and make a new life for you and your children.' "

She was doing such a good job shutting out her old life that Bobby called Betty and told her to go to Corsicana National and pull out all the cash from the safe-deposit box she had opened on his behalf. Sixty thousand dollars. He didn't think that the money was safe anywhere in the bank.

Betty and James stuffed the money into a briefcase and carried it home. Once there, however, they couldn't decide where to put it. Where would it be safe from a burglar? Finally James decided that an intruder probably wouldn't look in the freezer; and they stuffed the briefcase in next to the chicken and beef.

"When my mom found out about it," remembered Betty, "she called and said that we were trying to steal his money. And she wanted twenty thousand dollars of it, per Bob's request." Then Lottie and Bobby's accountant, Travis Kendall, came by Betty and James's house to ask for the money.

"I wouldn't let them have it," said Betty later. "I didn't know what the deal was. . . . I told my mother that I wasn't letting him have anything because Bob had not called me—he had liberty at Timberlawn to use the phone or do anything else he wanted to. And I had no knowledge of him wanting the money."

But a week later Betty received a letter from Bobby, with instructions to give the money to Lottie. Betty concluded that Bobby hadn't called her for fear that someone at Timberlawn might overhear. Lottie sent her new husband to James and Betty's. They loaded the frozen cash into the trunk of the car and drove away.

Bobby kept working on Linda through Sarah Conn, whom he had met through Linda and her connections—fellow Christians at the Beacon Light Church in Kerens. The two women had taken a course together on the obligation of women to be submissive to their husbands. The co-religionists had become close friends. *Keep the family together. Keep the family together.* The fundamentalists' cry. Sarah eventually became Linda's spiritual counselor and a mainstay in Linda's chaotic life. Now she became

Bobby's counselor as well—and message carrier. Finally, she convinced Linda to visit Bobby, just to give reconciliation a try.

"Linda made a fatal mistake," recalled James Duvall. "She had everything wrapped up and could have literally ended up with the entire ranch, the whole operation. . . . But Bob had these big spiritual counselors flown in from Colorado and New Mexico and then went on putting on saying he's changed his life, been reborn, the whole nine yards. And these spiritual counselors and so forth went up and started talking to Linda on Bob's behalf. They made a request of her to go and visit and just listen to Bobby at Timberlawn because his whole life has changed now. And Linda made the fatal mistake of going."

Linda had also seen Leslie Carter, author of popular psychology texts and a psychotherapist at a clinic in Dallas. And he noticed that "there was a good question about how to handle the family situation, whether it was going to remain together, and how she was going to handle her end as the mother." At the same time Carter observed that Linda "tended to close her eyes to a lot of things that were probably somewhat obvious."

The goal of the counseling was always to keep the family together. Someday Bobby would be out of Timberlawn, and Linda was beginning to believe that a happy family was a possibility.

But, as she began to make amends with Bobby, Linda found herself becoming less tolerant of Shelley. It seemed to be the same quirky, destructive imbalance; even from a distance Bobby insinuated himself into the relationship between Linda and Shelley. Linda began telling her daughter she was worried about her and scolded her for staying out and for drinking.

"She didn't want to stay around," Linda later explained. "And I needed her to be there. She wanted to be off and she was acting real silly."

Suddenly Linda couldn't understand why Shelley wouldn't forgive her father and let the family get on with its life. Shelley laughed at such a thought.

"It's all your fault!" Linda screamed. "You're a bitch and a slut!"

"I'm not either!" screamed Shelley, slapping her mother across the face.

She did not want me there. I felt like she thought it was my fault for the things that she called me and the way she acted and that she didn't want me there to remember what happened. She didn't want any—she considered it like a competition or something. She didn't want me around.

If she had thought of me more as her daughter, she probably would have stuck by me. But she was singing in her head, like I was just another woman in the picture instead of her daughter that was abused or hurt.

Linda protested that she *did* want Shelley around even as she made life impossible for her daughter. Shelley too was confused.

When I first moved home all of the family was there and when I'd walk in the room they would all just stare at me and they would all get real quiet and they would start saying things. They didn't know what to say to me. . . . Everybody acted like nothing happened.

So I just kind of looked at them and walked up to my room. And it was just so awkward that I would just stay gone all the time.

And that's when I started drinking. She said, "As long as you live here, do what you want." So I'd leave. I'd come home whenever I wanted. I'd leave early in the morning, come back about dark, change clothes for the night, go back out.

I was the liquor store for everyone in town. We had a bar. I'd come home and go to the bar and get something, go back to town and give it to everybody.

Shelley didn't want to stay long at home. She all but ignored her mother. They lived in the same house, but led almost separate lives.

Shelley and Ricky would take over the bar at the house and drink freely. Shelley couldn't get enough of her new freedom—but then didn't know what to do with it.

I never got to ride around on the drag. Nothin'. So all of a sudden, I was free! *It was great. So I just went! Went!*

I didn't have no other way of taking out my frustrations on nothing else, so I just went wild.

Shelley also spent a lot of time at the Layfields' house, lounging on the sofa in the tiny living room, watching television. "She got to where she'd stay over here till two or three in the morning," recalled Cherry. "And Linda always called and said, 'Is Shelley there?' And I'd say, 'Yes, she is.' 'Well, that's okay then. I just want to know where she is.' She called every night: 'That's fine if that's where she is.' I'd try to send Shelley home and she'd go back to sleep. Couldn't get rid of her."

Shelley found something in this tiny, paint-chipped home that she never knew at her million-dollar mansion.

I loved Ricky's parents to death! His dad would take me boat hunting, and stuff. We'd eat supper there and stay there and I'd always fall asleep over there. Cherry would wake me up and say, "Shelley, you need to go home." I just hated going home. I didn't want to go home. I didn't like it. It was just weird. My mom treated me weird. Everybody treated me weird.

One night she stumbled into the house with Ricky at her elbow. The way Shelley was doubled over and swaying, Linda thought she was sick. Ricky said he would take care of her and escorted Shelley into the bathroom. She vomited. Linda was concerned.

"Ricky, you just stay here as long as she needs you," Linda told the boy. "You just stay right here."

Ricky stayed, with Linda hovering around, until Shelley finally dropped into bed. Linda didn't understand what had happened until the next morning, when she asked Shelley what had been wrong.

Shelley burst out laughing. "You idiot," she said, "I was drunk."

Linda was still in the midst of some sort of denial. "It was like her mom just looked over it, you know," recalled Ricky. It was a roller coaster—for both mother and daughter.

Then I started having flashbacks and stuff and I would say things that, you know, had happened to me, and my friends would be sitting there just wondering what was happening to me.

What was happening to Shelley?

Linda was asking the same question, but for different reasons. Sarah Conn kept bringing messages from Bobby at Timberlawn. He beseeched her to come visit, Sarah told her. He had accepted the Lord, was sorry for what he did and wanted the family together again.

Linda kept pushing Shelley to go to Timberlawn to see the administrative psychiatrist, Dr. Byron Howard, but Shelley couldn't understand how this would help anything. "She was extremely rageful," Howard remembered about the meeting. "Understandably. But she was obsessed with getting even with Bob. And she stated that she would like to take a shotgun and shoot him. That she would have if the opportunity had arose. That she had tried to get a boyfriend to do that."

To Shelley, Bobby *deserved* to die for what he had done to her—but she was smart enough to know better than to do anything rash. She was content with feeling the rage, without acting on it. And she was glad to be free of Bobby.

But Shelley didn't understand that there were other forces at work, ones that were working to support and foster "mental health," which meant keeping everybody together at any price. Fighting that goal had become, in the eyes of the healing profession, "unhealthy," a sign of "problems." Very quickly Shelley had been pushed by the doctors into the same role she had played for years—that of linchpin in the relationship between Bobby and Linda, a key to "family health."

Shelley seemed to instinctively understand the psychological coercion and refused to go back to Timberlawn. But the die was cast.

With psychotherapist Carter, Linda tried to sort out her growing frustration with Shelley. "She talked about how she and Shelley had experienced a good deal of tension," Carter recalled, "and we discussed her style of communication with Shelley, trying to influence Shelley's own tensions by coming across in a calm nature."

But Linda kept consulting Sarah and others about Shelley, expressing her concern about her daughter's "wild" behavior.

Linda called Teen Challenge, a local counseling group. But they couldn't do anything unless Shelley came in voluntarily. And Shelley wasn't going to do anything willingly.

She kept insisting that I go to counseling because she *was going. Then she started taking my brother. She kept insisting that I go to counseling and I kept telling her, "I'm not going to counseling. I don't want to go. I'm* not going *to counseling!"*

Linda went back to Bobby and her religious friends for advice. She talked to Sarah's sister, who had been to Roloff's home, and another woman from the Beacon Light Church, whose son had been to one of his boys' homes. Sarah's son had also gone to one. And they all recommended that Shelley be sent away. So Sarah carried messages back and forth to Timberlawn, gradually working Bobby's recommendations into her own.

Sarah had already told Linda about Lester Roloff's girls' home. "Roloff had a place where a child who is destroying himself can get hold of himself and get the word of God in them," Linda later explained. "They teach them right from wrong and show them to turn to God for their answers. That is the only place you can take your child."

In the circle of believers Roloff, who had died the year before, could do no wrong with the work of the Lord.

"I was just trying to keep her there in the house," Linda later explained. "She had so much freedom. She had a truck and she was just going all the time." In Linda's eyes Shelley had "gone off the deep end."

But by the time Linda decided to try to bring Shelley back, to exert control over her, it was too late. Shelley had been controlled, exploited and abused for too long. She was now as intoxicated on freedom as on booze. And she wasn't about to trade her liberty in for more of what she had been subjected to for eight years. But she enjoyed less than a month of freedom before Linda gave up on her.

"She was acting real strange," Linda remembered. "And I saw that the freedom that I gave her wasn't going to be the answer. There was nothing that I could do for her."

In early July an argument over how much gasoline Shelley was pumping into her Silverado touched off a fight. When Bobby found out, he told Sarah that Linda had to do something. That was it. Linda knew she had to act.

Linda told Henry Edgington what she was planning. And the young Church of Christ minister tried to set her straight. "I told her what I knew about Roloff and the Rebekah Home for Girls," recalled Edgington, who grew up in Corpus Christi, where the home was located. "I mentioned that it wasn't licensed by the state, and there were frequent newspaper articles about child abuse and beating charges."

But Linda was now under the sway of Conn and the Roloff followers. "This radical group caught her when she was really susceptible," Edgington later explained, "at a time when she was at the height of emotion, searching for truth. I keep thinking that if Linda had ever admitted to herself what her husband Bob really did, she would have had such a low esteem and low picture of herself in life that she couldn't have lived with it. And this is what caused her to go ahead and not believe her daughter. Even after that meeting, when she really appeared to believe Shelley and wanted to help—it convinced me."

"She wouldn't talk to anyone," recalled James Duvall. "Just those spiritual counselors. . . . Sarah Conn could tell Linda, 'God told me to tell you to stand on your head,' and Linda would stand on her head."

Now in her second month of freedom, Shelley was beginning to come down a little. But Michael, who was just seven years old, had not come back down to earth.

My brother completely flipped. He didn't know what was going on. All he knew was that his sister was gone, his dad shot himself, his sister is back and his dad's gone. He just got real mean and destructive.

Shelley tried to spend more time at home, especially for Michael's sake. And when she took him shopping in the Corsicana mall one day, her little brother seemed happier than he had been in months.

Not everything was great, but to Shelley it seemed so much better than before that she was beginning to relax—including with her mother. Linda even took her to Dr. Campbell's office for a birth-control prescription.

But Shelley hadn't paid enough attention to the warning signs. Linda was going to Timberlawn, meaning that things were getting patched up with Bobby. And while in Dallas, Linda was seeing her religious therapist, who was then listening to Linda lay plans.

"Linda says the tension has become strong between herself and Shelley," Dr. Carter wrote in his log notes of July 13. "We discussed how Shelley probably has some hidden resentments against her because of the incestuous relation with Dad—probably assuming that she condoned it. We discussed first Linda's need to talk calmly with Shelley about their need to get along with each other. We also discussed her need for structure to keep her away from troublesome interactions. Linda is considering letting Shelley go to a private home."

Linda asserting herself over Shelley was exactly what the doctor had been ordering—but just as Shelley was beginning to calm down. And the counselor's recommendations about the need for structure in Shelley's life fit perfectly with Linda's budding belief that everything *Shelley* did now was "troublesome." Sending Shelley away had somehow become "letting Shelley go." In the course of the previous few weeks, Linda and her counselor had not only shifted the focus of discussion from Linda's troubles to Shelley's, but they had together reinstituted control over Bobby's daughter.

The therapist would later conclude that "there was a real sense of unity between [Linda and Bobby] and it seemed as though Linda had come to grips with what had happened and was willing to forgive Bob at that time and to take him right back. I thought it was rather extraordinary that she was willing to do so, given all the circumstances. . . . I'd say that you could report some success." The little family was coming together—but as it did, Shelley was again being pushed out.

At the ranch the religious types—Sarah Conn and friends—were coming and going, pushing much the same thing. Family. Control. Discipline.

I had come home one day and my mom told me that a friend of hers was coming down with her son and she wanted me to meet this boy. And I said I don't want to meet him because I have a boyfriend. So later, when I went into the study and said, "Mom, I'm going to Ricky's," she said, "I want you to meet them." I knew the lady because she would come down every once in a while and do something with my mom. She was some sort of Christian counselor. But I never thought nothing about her.

Linda's attempts to introduce Sarah and her son to Shelley, to seduce her into the religious world, were fruitless. Shelley had already had enough of the Bible crowd. Her father was now apparently spouting that lingo, and this merely diminished the credibility of religion rather than increase Bobby's respectability. So she didn't really pay attention when Linda introduced her to Sarah Conn and her son one early July day.

"Hi," said Shelley as she scooted out the door.

She missed all the clues.

The next time Shelley would see Sarah and her son was in the middle of a hot night, July 19, when they shook her awake and entreated her to follow them. Shelley did, thinking Bobby had escaped. But within twelve hours Shelley herself was in "prison."

"I just had them come after she went to bed," recalled Linda. "Just take her. It didn't matter if they had to take her by rope. I needed to get something done for her because she was not willing to get counsel. She wasn't willing to get help. She didn't want to do anything that anyone said to do."

Linda had called the Layfields a number of times that Tuesday night, to see if Shelley was still there, when she was coming home. She even had Michael call once.

As usual, Shelley didn't want to leave. "C'mon, go home, Shelley," Ricky urged. "It'll just cause trouble if you don't." Ricky was sick anyway, with a sore throat.

He eased Shelley out of the house, kissed her goodnight. "I'll talk to you tomorrow." But it was the last he would see of her for almost a year.

XVI

TIMBERLAWN

Bobby Sessions was admitted to the Timberlawn Hospital on Monday, June 13, 1983, at seven P.M. He paid cash and said he would pay for all his treatment that way, $1,700 a week, which included charges for psychiatry and neurology, but not for outside psychologists and medical services such as X rays. Bobby peeled off the money from his sizable roll and asked where he could keep the rest—a $20,000 cashier's check and $10,699 in cash. His watch was taken too: a 14k gold Rolex that Bobby said was worth $14,000.

He was told he was allowed $20 per week to spend at the hospital's canteen.

The newly convicted child molester was neatly dressed in a western shirt, blue jeans and boots.

The Navarro County sheriff's deputies paced back and forth during the admission proceedings. James Duvall watched silently. Sessions was very cooperative—and repentant. Any chance he got, he said he had found God. He had talked to God, God had forgiven him, he was a new man.

Although it was a formality, since he was strictly under the laws of probation, Bobby signed himself in as a voluntary patient. That meant he could sign himself out at any time. The catch was that he had to get the judge's permission before the doctors could release him.

Dr. Louis Gibson, Bobby's family doctor, had called Timberlawn the week before to clear the way for Bobby's entry. He described his patient's condition and told Timberlawn doctors that Bobby had not yet been told, but that the deal was in the works to give him a choice of prison or psychiatric hospital. Gibson told his colleagues at Timberlawn that the patient would be a difficult one.

Finally, Bobby was told he would be assigned to the Witt Building and was brought in to meet the administrative psychiatrist, Dr. Byron Howard, who would be in charge of him and oversee a team of mental-health workers.

During their first meeting Bobby was so repentant he told Howard that he didn't need to be there. He no longer had any problems: "I have asked God's forgiveness. God has heard my plea. I have no problems. I know who my saviour is and I am at peace with myself. God has a purpose for me or the bullet that I shot into my chest would have killed me. I am at peace with myself."

It was one of the fastest self-cures in history.

He told Howard that his biggest concern was for Shelley. But by that he meant "I didn't want her name, my wife's name or our whole family dragged through a trial and the publicity that would be associated with that." He told the doctor that his marriage had been rocky for ten years, mainly because of Shelley.

He had come to Timberlawn, not because he needed or wanted help, he told Howard, but because he had no choice. "This is the only alternative that the DA would give me besides going to trial—and I didn't want all the publicity."

"What do you expect to get out of your stay here?" Howard asked.

"To be perfectly honest," Bobby replied, "I have nothing to get here because I have already worked out all of my problems."

Howard later wrote in his log of the conversation with Sessions: "He states that he knows he had problems. He states that he knows that the incestuous relationship with his stepdaughter was wrong and that he should have been in control, but that she was very stubborn and demanding and that she used the relationship to get things she wanted."

That night, as a routine precaution, Bobby was put on a suicide-prevention watch. The close supervision lasted for three days, during which he was checked every fifteen minutes. Whenever he left his room, he was accompanied by an attendant.

It accomplished another goal of Howard's: to give Bobby some "clear limit-setting." Bobby was quickly frustrated and angered at being locked up, and was showing "hypomanic behavior."

He didn't want to be there. "I have never been locked up in my life," he later explained. "I didn't really understand all the ramifications of what had happened, but I didn't want to be locked up. I was in a small room and I couldn't get out. The first two or three days that I remember, I was strapped in a wheelchair, both hands and feet, wrists. I wasn't allowed to do anything or go anywhere. They fed me my meals. And I wanted out very badly."

It was clear that he would be a difficult case. But hospital staff also had to contend with family members who worried, among other things, that Bobby would go crazy if he didn't get his daily doses of Dr Pepper.

Two days after Bobby arrived, Dr. Howard noted very little change in the patient:

"1. Pt. has massive denial of seriousness of recent behavior & effect associated w/ it.

"2. Anxiety & anger rising because of confinement, grandiosity, and better physical condition."

Dr. Howard would be the most consistent observer of Bobby Sessions during his stay at Timberlawn. He saw the patient on "rounds" every day, and made a point of engaging him in conversation. He quickly got to know Bobby.

Howard suggested "vigorous support" for Sessions' family, including therapy for both Linda and Shelley.

Among the problems that Bobby hadn't worked out was his relationship with his wife and children. His daughter was so angry that she wanted to kill him; his son was so confused by what had happened that he was already qualifying for his own stay at Timberlawn. And his wife was planning to divorce him.

Timberlawn psychiatrist Doyle I. Carson was assigned to conduct psychotherapy with Sessions. "Initial contact with Bob Sessions," he reported two days after Bobby had arrived, "shows him to be a remorseful individual who is also a very aggressive person who wants to be out of the hospital as rapidly as he can. He is a very hard-charging, manipulative, aggressive person who is used to having his own way and yet has been through a great personal tragedy of late and it is difficult to know what directions he will go. He will be quite a therapeutic challenge."

A lengthy Diagnostic Summary and Treatment Plan was prepared at the end of Sessions' first week at Timberlawn. It noted that the patient was "extremely intelligent, highly motivated" and also "manipulative, narcissistic, self-centered and episodically impulsive." He had "settled into hospital routine very quickly," but was "denying and minimizing most of what had occurred" and "has turned very vigorously to fundamentalist religion."

A ten-point treatment plan was outlined that seemed to more than justify the $1,700-per-week cost of his care. It included nursing services, consultations with medical doctors and internists, psychological testing, group therapy meetings, evaluations for possible prescription of antidepressant drugs, individual therapy and marital therapy.

The evaluators foresaw a six-month stay as the minimum time needed to evaluate Sessions' condition.

In fact, Sessions had already tried to take charge of his own therapy. Timberlawn was a highly unintrusive institution, and a patient like Bobby quickly maneuvered to take advantage of his "voluntary" status. The day after he arrived, still under suicide watch, he was allowed to have private visits, as needed, with his attorney.

Three days after he arrived, Bobby was allowed to call Sarah Conn. Whether he intended it as such or not, Sarah was a liaison with Linda, who had dropped Bobby. He was allowed to receive calls and visits from his wife, but none came. Sarah was the link.

She had been one of Bobby's first visitors at the Navarro County hospital. And it was her intensive counseling that had made a true believer of Bobby by the time he got to Timberlawn.

She counseled him about the Lord two and three times a week and Bobby listened. Sarah belonged to the "God is your therapist school," and Bobby quickly ushered her into the Timberlawn world. She was among the names on the Diagnostic Summary and Treatment Plan list of professionals who would be handling Sessions' case—even though Sarah had no formal academic or clinical training in psychiatry or counseling.

"I would cry on her shoulder and make all kinds of excuses for what I had been or what had happened, and Sarah would simply kick me in the teeth and tell me that I had been wrong," Bobby recalled. "I had to turn my life over to the Lord and make a new start irregardless of what happened from that point forward."

Through Sarah, Bobby heard of another Christian counselor, Dr. Charles Solomon, from the Grace Fellowship International in Denver. Solomon claimed to have a doctoral degree in "Spirituotherapy" from the University of Northern Colorado, "a word that I coined," he explained, "where the Holy Spirit is the person who does the therapy. . . . In this approach to counseling, unless a miracle takes place, nothing of real importance happens."

Solomon, formerly an engineer who worked on fuel systems for military jets at the Martin Marietta Corporation, had written five booklets about Spirituotherapy, including *Handbook to Happiness, Ins and Outs of Rejection* and *Counseling with the Mind of Christ,* and parlayed his brand of therapy into an organization with a Denver headquarters staff of twenty and offices in Atlanta; Tampa; Indianapolis; Springfield, Missouri; and Buenos Aires.

After Sarah praised Solomon to Bobby, he flew the spirituotherapist directly to Dallas and made a sizable contribution to the group. Bobby was still confined to his room when Solomon got there and wasn't liking it much. "He was rather frustrated," Solomon recalled, "but mentally, he was very stable. There was nothing that I would classify as mental illness."

They talked for almost an hour the first day. Solomon explained the principles of identifying with Christ, and about death and resurrection, drawing for Bobby the same diagrams, like the "Wheel and Line," that he used in his books. On the wheel was the soul, spirit and body. And the line showed how eternal life ran between heaven and hell.

In this way Bobby could see, as Solomon explained it, "his problem was not the sin that he had committed with his step-daughter, which the state would call a crime . . . , but there was a deeper issue, and it was the fact that self, or Bob, was at the center of his own life, running it his way, doing his thing, which no matter how hard he tried to change himself, he couldn't change himself." Once he realized that his problem was his self-centeredness, Solomon told Bobby, he could accept that "the thing with Shelley was not his problem at all."

That night Bobby read two of Solomon's booklets. *The Wheel & Line: A Guide to Freedom Through the Cross* began, "As you read this, you may be in the midst of turmoil," and Bobby was hooked. He got down on his knees and prayed. He then went beyond the assignment to read all of chapters 6, 7 and 8 from the Bible's Book of Romans. "We know that the old self was crucified with him so that the sinful body might be destroyed," he read. "There is therefore now no condemnation for those who are in Christ Jesus."

When Solomon returned the next day he saw a radical and fundamental transformation. "There was a change of countenance," the preacher recalled. "Bob had a peace about himself and an assurance he was no longer the same person that he had been." Solomon saw all Bobby's bitterness gone, the resentment and rancor washed away.

The Denver preacher claimed to be a witness to Bobby's conversion.

"The devil did it to him," Solomon told Dr. Howard after his first meeting with Bobby. "Have you talked to the *girl*?" he asked. The *girl*, of course, was Shelley.

"What do you mean?" Howard replied, perplexed by Solomon's accusatory tone.

"Well, have you seen her? Bob tells me that she was bribing him—and you know that kind of thing can really rack a guy up."

Howard would later recall that "It was very apparent that Dr. Solomon was kind of buying the culprit as primarily being the daughter."

The Timberlawn administrator viewed Bobby's religious conversion as a mixed blessing. "It was helpful in the sense that he developed renewed faith and dedication to make his marriage work, to get his family back in order, and to ask for forgiveness for what he had done," Howard later explained.

"In a harmful way, it put back some denial as to the impact of what he had done. In the first few weeks of hospitalization his attitude was, 'That was a horrible sin, I have confessed and I've gotten forgiveness. Now, let's forget about it and get on with the business of getting back into the family, getting back to work.' That sort of thing."

For Dr. Solomon, Bobby didn't have a personality problem— "He had a sin problem."

Such quick cures were anathema to the psychological profession—and confounded the court system which relied on it. But unlike a regular prison setting, where it didn't have much effect on the sentence, a jailhouse conversion in this clinical setting could have real impact on the amount of time Bobby served: a religious conversion and a psychological cure looked the same. The apparent results were the same. Only the processes differed.

"At a psychiatric facility," Howard continued, "we were interested in working on the origins of his problem. How could such a terrible thing come to pass? And his conversion at times would get in the way of that."

A religious conversion got in the way of treatment mainly because it was so fast. However, it had occurred, and now the psychiatrists had the problem of explaining Bobby's apparent mental health.

"Within a few days [of his arrival], as his physical vigor returned and his religious conversion strengthened him, he had a flight into health," Howard remembered. "His old personality characteristics of 'I can do anything' came back, and those personality characteristics allowed him, in the past, to be very successful financially, to run large enterprises, and to get himself in serious trouble. . . . So he was eager to tell us how to run the hospital more effectively, eager to get on with the program, highly energetic, chafing at the confinement of being in a hospital."

Because of Timberlawn's reputation as a Taj Mahal of private mental hospitals, Bobby was not the first rich, successful, highly driven patient Howard had seen. "They are often community leaders, highly productive, highly successful people. They may work fifteen, eighteen, twenty hours a day, and as long as that sense of 'I can do anything' does not trip up their vision of reality, as it did with Bob, they are some of our most productive citizens. . . . A number of former patients from the hospital have gone on to distinguish themselves around the State of Texas in that way."

Despite the outward appearances of health, Howard saw Bobby's energy, enthusiasm and religious fervor, after just a week at Timberlawn, as anything but completely healthy.

"It was harmful at times simply because of the denial of the reality of the facts," Howard would later complain. "For instance, the religious conversion made Bob think that he could go back, ask for Shelley's forgiveness and everything would be able to be ideal. When, in fact, the reality was that that's not the situation and it wasn't then."

Howard had met with Shelley the week before Solomon issued his pronouncement about "the girl." And he hadn't brought away a very pleasant feeling.

"She is a young lady of very high risk of a chaotic life-style regardless of the incestuous behavior," he observed to fellow staffers after the session. "She does not like him, does not want to see him again and wished he had died when he shot himself, but on the other hand, says things about the future that imply that she expects to have a good bit of contact with him. She denied using their sexual relationship in any way to manipulate."

In his inimitable fashion, Bobby had heard that Linda and

Shelley were coming. "Very worried about Dr. Howard meeting his wife and stepdaughter today," nurse Barnes noted in the daily log.

The contacts and counseling with Bobby's family were part research, part therapy. Sally Moore, a Timberlawn psychiatric social worker, was assigned to Linda, to counsel her as well as glean information that might be used in treating Bobby. Other doctors met with Bobby's mother and sisters to learn about the patient's childhood and family background. Dr. Howard also made calls to a few of Bobby's business acquaintances back home.

"The first two weeks that he was there they could not get anything out of him at all," recalled Bobby's sister Betty. "So the doctors asked the family to come up to be talked to. So my mom told them nothing and my other sister Pat told them nothing. But I told them what he had done to me."

Shelley was another case. For the Timberlawn physicians, she was an integral part of the dynamic that had contributed to their patient's problem. She was not responsible for it, perhaps; but psychologically at least, according to Bobby's keepers, she was part of his problem. In the doctors' view, not understanding Shelley made treating Bobby more difficult.

After Dr. Howard's first meeting with Shelley, he remarked that she was "almost a carbon copy of the patient and, if anything, a great deal more angry than the patient is. She puts all the blame on him, where the responsibility should lie, but there is no question that she is very manipulative, impulsive young lady who used this relationship as much as possible for her own personal gain."

Howard sensed so much anger in Shelley that he warned Bobby that she was dangerous. "I was very concerned after that interview for her safety and his safety, should they be together," Howard said later.

But at the same time Howard foresaw some of the need for concern about "the patient's obsession with his daughter and the daughter's obsession with her father. . . . Neither one of them can leave each other alone."

After this single encounter, Shelley refused to believe in this psychological lockstep, and she refused to honor it with her presence at Timberlawn. Bobby created the problem all by himself; he would have to solve it without her help.

Dr. Doyle I. Carson, the in-house therapist assigned to Bobby by Timberlawn, had had another patient in the spot oil business. "It is a market where there was opportunity to do a lot of illegal activities," Carson recalled. "I saw another guy one time that was making ten million dollars a month doing the illegal part until he got caught."

He wouldn't conjecture whether Bobby had done the same, but he noticed right away that when Bobby "starts talking, you can see the intense drive, competitive drive, that this guy has to make it work."

At an early meeting of key staffers, a nurse complained that Bobby was "taking the role of the father, lecturer, with a lot of intellectualizing" in group therapy meetings.

Howard sympathized with her, explaining that they were "sort of over a barrel" with Sessions because on the one hand they had to "break through the patient's denial of the seriousness of his own predicament" while at the same time "being very sensitive to how badly he feels. He does have a very disturbed conscience," Howard explained. "Part of it is overly harsh and part of it is sort of nonexistent."

It was already abundantly clear to Howard that the patient had a deep-seated problem. "The way he talked about his daughter, especially in puberty and after, was the obsessive need to control," Howard explained, "and he would describe the behavior of other teenagers in the community and how horrible it was, how terrible, that he had to prevent her because she was a wild young girl, from getting involved in all that kind of nasty behavior. He described it that way to me. . . . The first week that was very, very prominent."

Sessions had been sent a clipping from the Corsicana paper that also bore witness to Bobby's denial mechanisms. Howard found it interesting that the front-page story, with picture, elicited only a mild response from his patient. "They only used my name in the caption," he said. "It's not as bad as it could have been."

"This demonstrates the degree of denial and distortion that is going on with the patient," Howard remarked.

A week after Bobby arrived, Dr. Howard sent him to see Dale Turner, a clinical psychologist at the hospital, who ran a battery of six tests. Turner reported that Bobby had an I.Q. of 126 and "appears to be very intelligent"; but he didn't find much in the way of mental disease. "By default I would probably consider him an atypical personality disorder."

And Sessions hadn't changed his story much. As Turner pointed out, the patient told him that "the only problem in his life was his stepdaughter, who refused to show affection toward him. He felt this was substantially due to the way his wife insisted on raising her."

This was the conundrum of the psychiatric profession: it relied largely on outward behavior to ascertain a patient's degree of interior illness. That was fine when a person *looked* sick—and a history of incest and a suicide attempt seemed sick enough. But since the profession relied so heavily on behavior in making its diagnoses, it was often at a loss when the patient no longer *looked* sick. And that was a portrait of Bobby Sessions within two weeks of arriving at Timberlawn. He appeared quite normal. So Howard described the condition as "a flight into health."

Howard asked Turner to test Sessions again a month later—but there were, according to the psychologist, "very few substantial changes."

The irony was that the "punishment" the state had meted out to Bobby was in reality a prescription for an illness, and the duration of the sentence depended on Bobby's behavior. And he was doing his best to act right; to convince his Timberlawn doctors that he was cured.

Linda remained confused and angry. She kept wavering between divorcing Bobby and standing by him—often that depended on whom she was talking to. In any case, she had asked her attorney to start drawing up divorce papers.

All of June she didn't visit Bobby. "I was just trying to keep things going," she recalled. "Just living. I had a little boy and we were just trying to let some of the shock come off, just some time."

She saw a counselor in Dallas, but didn't visit Bobby until July, when Sarah convinced her to give him a chance.

On a couple of occasions in June and July, she told Dr. Howard that "She was going to forgive him and make it go good," he recalled.

"Bob changed," Linda reported. "He did some dramatic changing. I would go to Timberlawn and we were with the counselor there—they just opened up a lot of stuff for us."

At the same time she was telling psychiatric social worker Sally Moore that she was considering a divorce. "She just wanted some distance from her husband at this point," Moore recounted. "But the patient reports that his wife does not want a divorce and wants to get back together."

"I think she tells Bob the same sort of thing," said Howard, "and just keeps him jumping at the end of a string, which stirs up his obsessive-compulsive need to control everything."

Bobby had enough freedom at the hospital to maintain communications with anyone he needed to contact; enough money to guarantee that those contacts were kept open. So he could work on Linda from a distance, via his newfound religious friends, while protecting his assets from her—Betty and James kept a lot of his cash in their freezer.

"Bob is articulate and logical," noted social worker Moore, "frequently talking Linda out of her feelings."

Eventually Linda changed her attitudes about crime and punishment and Bobby's stay at Timberlawn. "Bob was severely punished," she recalled. "His picture was on the front page. He has no reputation. His pride is broken. You can't break a person more than what he's been broken. He's been through hell and back. He tried to *kill* himself, to *murder* himself. He *blew* himself away. Now, you can't go through more. He's broken by what he's been through. A person just can't go through more."

Linda prayed to God, and God talked back. "God was revealing

that to me," she said later, "that He was not only going to change
Bob, that he had heard my prayers for my family, that He was
going to change Shelley's heart too."

And if Linda wasn't stirring Bobby's still powerful obsessions,
the Christian counselors were. Sarah Conn was convinced that
Bobby had undergone a total religious awakening—and that the
experience had completely changed him. "Bob is a very strong
individual," she recalled. "High energy, a lot of drive. And to see
all of that brought to a halt by the machinery that brought it to
a halt in his life—to be brought to a halt and to see him submit
to the conditions that were being imposed upon him. . . . With
fear and trembling, he learned to trust the Lord, to submit to the
authority in his life."

But it didn't work quite that neatly.

When Sarah told Bobby during one weekend in mid-July that
Shelley and Linda were fighting a lot, Bobby was neither resigned
nor peaceful. Sarah explained further that Shelley had just beaten
Linda up—in a fight over car keys that ended when Shelley put
her mom in a hammerlock on the kitchen floor.

Bobby spent the rest of the day furious, frantically demanding
that the nurses on the floor call Dr. Howard at home or let him
call his wife in Powell.

When Howard found out about it, he was upset. "I let the
counselor know that she should not carry messages like that," he
later recalled.

But Bobby was impossible to stop. He used Sarah and Dr.
Solomon, family members, friends, the telephone, and his still
mighty powers of persuasion to keep in touch—and in control.

The beneficial side-effect of all the religious networking, intended or not, was that Linda was pulled closer and closer to her
husband. If he was finding religion, Linda believed, perhaps there
was hope. She wanted to believe that she could patch things up;
she didn't want to leave the ranch and the money. Bobby even
began having the pastor of Linda's church, Ken Goode of Beacon
Light Christian Center, come to visit him. Every Tuesday. And
to help smooth the way, he gave the preacher a pickup truck to

use and gas-pump privileges at the ranch. He flew Solomon to Dallas again. He paid for Sarah Conn's expenses.

"She was either camped on that hospital door or at Linda's house," said James Duvall of Sarah Conn. "Back and forth, back and forth, back and forth."

In fact, Bobby was able to control his far-flung family better than the dozens of Timberlawn staffers could. And he managed to manipulate Timberlawn staffers as well.

One young occupational therapist said, "I thought he was a staff member when I first met him. He had that quality about him, seeming pretty knowledgeable about what was going on on the unit."

Noted another staffer: "The patient has tried to ingratiate himself with the staff and has been successful in some efforts to perhaps establish some obligation, or beachhead of obligation on some staff members." During one group therapy session Bobby had coaxed one of the summer interns into talking about problems he was having with his girlfriend.

Dr. Howard pointed out that Sessions could probably "outsmart most staff."

As Howard himself discovered the morning of July 19. Shelley didn't appear for an appointment he had scheduled for ten o'clock that Tuesday morning. It was to be his second session with her, an important fact-finding mission, given the complexity of the case. With some difficulty, he had set up the meeting through Linda the week before. But Howard waited in vain that morning. No one called.

The day before, in fact, Linda had talked with social worker Sally Moore and told her that she was still considering divorcing Bobby. But she made no mention of the appointment.

But on Wednesday morning, during one of his routine daily visits with Bobby, Howard found out that he'd been duped. Bobby always seemed to have something up his sleeve, but this morning he had a piece of news that concerned Howard—for more than one reason.

"I was just talking to my mother," Bobby told the doctor. "She tells me that Shelley was put in the Rebekah Home for Girls in Corpus Christi this morning."

It was part of a pattern, Howard saw, "a family system of dishonesty" that was to make this case so difficult.

"She will just run away unless there are legal sanctions that hold her there," said Howard, who guessed that Bobby had set up the move to Rebekah.

His primary concern was not for Shelley—but for his patient's continued obsession with controlling her, even from Timberlawn—the same powerful impulses that had carried him down the slippery slope of incest.

"Oh, no—they have physical restraint and they will be able to seclude her and will tie her down if they need to," Bobby replied blandly.

"Well, that may be true," said Howard, "but what do you think about that?"

"She *needs* to be tied down."

Howard had called a staffing conference for later that day to discuss Bobby's condition and treatment program. Bobby had been at Timberlawn for more than a month now—enough time for doctors and staff to form some impressions of their new "hypomanic" patient.

It was "an unusual and atypical staffing," Howard told the group, because Bobby Sessions was an unusual patient. A blackboard was wheeled into the conference room, and twenty different employees invited—doctors, social workers, registered nurses, mental health workers and a medical student.

The biggest immediate problem was getting accurate information about Sessions' past. Dr. Doyle I. Carson, the psychiatrist who had been assigned to Bobby for one-on-one therapy sessions, offered that the patient had been "accepted into a military academy, which would indicate something rather positive going on for him."

But Howard suggested that this was exactly his point. "I have not heard that from his wife or his mother or his two sisters or from his two brothers-in-law—and you would think . . . that that kind of thing would show up."

Carson added that Bobby had also told him that he had been student-body president at Navarro College.

"Perhaps I am way too skeptical," said Howard, "except that I have been living with this guy long enough that things just keep coming up that do not fit together very well." He summarized the information he had gleaned from Bobby's Corsicana physician, then repeated his concern about "the veracity of his stories."

Howard had already uncovered the storytelling Bobby was doing about the incest. "He initially tried to minimize that a good deal," Howard said, "and talked about it happening a few times in over a year. Then it was a year and a half, then it was two years and then it was three. And the family feels it was somewhere between three and four years."

Howard told the group that they were dealing with "a very charming, very bright, very quick guy who has been helpful on the unit, who wants to assume . . . a leadership role in anything he does and to maintain some control over what is going on."

That was why, Carson said, he couldn't understand why Sessions shot himself in the first place. "I asked him, 'Why did you not just lie about it?' It was his word against a teenager. Who would believe her? He said, 'Well, I do not know.'" When Carson asked Sessions why he just didn't go over to the preacher's residence and try to "keep it among the family, he said he thought his wife might shoot him. . . . So here is a guy who you would think is slippery and manipulative that did not think of a slippery, manipulative way out."

Howard offered one theory. "I think for about two years he expected this to blow and had gotten increasingly guilty about it, and increasingly anxious . . . that he had already decided that when it blows, it is going to be such a disaster, it will all be over. It was sort of like waiting for the other shoe to fall—and it did."

In fact, Howard reported, "During the last two or three years all the family members described their own concern that some-

thing funny was going on, that he was obsessed with Shelley."
Howard brought up Linda's remark that Bobby's sexual demands
on her had decreased substantially.

"There was some question that she maybe all along knew what
was going on?" asked Dr. Conway McDonald, a psychiatrist at
the hospital.

"It is a possibility," Howard replied. "And there is some data
to support that."

Carson added, "Bob says that there were many occasions when
Shelley would say, in the midst of an argument with her mother,
'If you only knew what was really going on around here.' "

Those who had met Bobby were unanimous in their assessment
of his manic, obsessive personality. "Bob describes an obsession
with making it work good with this child, have this child love
him," Howard said of Sessions' early years with Shelley. "All the
restrictions, rule-making, that sort of thing in regard to the daughter, the patient took charge of and, somewhere about puberty,
began to get very obsessed with watching her, controlling her and
then that all got worse."

Still describing Bobby's perceptions of his daughter, Carson
added: "She was also becoming an older teenager and getting
interested in guys, beginning to share her with other people and
began to talk with her. 'Was she doing things with other guys?'
And that she should not; that that was not proper behavior. This
was really bizarre to me [sic]."

"He talked about that in group one day," said Dr. Ruth Mar-
dock.

"He shifts out of that kind of lover role to the father role," said
Carson. "And if you are listening, you are still back there in the
other role and he has made the shift—fathering her and telling
her to be nice."

For over two hours the doctors explored Sessions' dual obsession. "He is still almost doing that in a lover way," said Howard.
"He is taking care of his valued object and is also cautioning her
that no one should dare touch her." Remarking that Linda had
described how Bobby followed Shelley everywhere or sent one of

his hands to follow her, Howard concluded, "There is a powerful, obsessive, compulsive quality to that relationship."

When Howard began to entertain possible diagnoses of Bobby's illness, the conversation drifted to other examples of incest that the doctors knew of or had treated. "I remember growing up in a small east Texas town," he recalled, "and there were some folks in the piney woods in east Texas where it was well known that the incest went on in the families and everybody said that was terrible, but that is just the way those folks are and let it go. I don't think anyone got arrested."

On the subject of arrest, the doctors seemed disappointed that incest cases ended up in the courts.

"Most of these things get into treatment channels," said Carson, "rather than criminal channels. . . . I guess this just happened that way, but I still cannot quite get over how all of this got into the—"

"I think one of the things that set it on that track," Howard broke in, "was that the daughter is so rageful at her father for the control issue. I do not think she is that rageful about the sexual aspect, although that is complicated."

Howard had spent forty-five minutes with Shelley earlier in the month. "She was afraid of him," said Howard, "very fearful of him, wanted to get him, and see him in prison, was sorry he did not kill himself, and would have been very happy if he had succeeded. In fact, if he comes back to town she would like to shoot him. She may get some friends to shoot him."

Shelley was at a clear disadvantage in this group. Most of what the doctors knew about her was based on a couple of brief encounters and, more frequently, through the stories that Bobby told about the relationship. Even now she remained the outsider, as Bobby had predicted. He was getting all the attention; the energy of these twenty-one people focused on his, not her problems. His point of view, despite some caveats, was widely played.

"He just wanted to have a good relationship with her," Dr. Carson reported. "They became involved sexually and . . . she was a willing participant, enjoying it. She was very selfish and was only interested in her own needs and not his."

Even though they gave more space to Bobby and his stories, they weren't swallowed whole. "The part that I really do not have well at all is between him and his wife," said Carson. "I think he has distorted that more than the relationship with Shelley."

"I think he has," Howard agreed, "but to make it even worse, I think his wife is a very noncredible person, because her story changes a lot. What she tells me one time is different the next time."

"Has he mentioned that his wife was going to jump off the second floor of their ranch house in Corsicana and kill herself one time?" asked Carson.

"That doesn't surprise me," Howard said. "She is an aggressive, hysterical-looking lady who is very bright and is a handsome woman who looks younger than her age."

The doctors periodically floated the question of a diagnosis. And, as the discussion progressed, a consensus was forming around "compulsive sexual perversion," which could mean either "pedophilia or a compulsive need to have sexual relations with his daughter." But the fact that the case went into the courts, the doctors thought, added another dimension. "It very quickly got into the criminal justice system," Howard said, "and I appreciated over time the obsessive-compulsive characteristics of this situation where I am not certain the patient nor the daughter can leave this alone. And I am very worried about the outcome of that."

Howard then passed around the poem that Bobby had printed in the newspaper when Shelley ran away. "It is sort of incredible," was his comment.

Dr. Ernest Brownlee jumped in for the first time. He too had met with Sessions, twice the previous week. "He came up with a lot of magical answers that things were all different now," said Brownlee, "that he was changed and these would not happen again. But in the course of the interview there were several things that came out that I was impressed with. One, is that he made a statement that whatever Bob Sessions wants, Bob Sessions gets, and that he will do anything to get it."

"His brother-in-law says one of the ways he always gets what he wants is that he gets people in his debt by giving them gifts or being super nice to them," offered Howard. "Or he gets something on them, he plays detective, and he uses that as a lever. The brother-in-law describes things, that I do not know if they are true or not, but photographing people in compromising situations and getting financial arrangements that he could find out about where he could use that as leverage."

"I think he is beginning to find out things about people around here," said Carson.

"He got one of the summer-student mental-health workers to allow him to become counselor-therapist by getting the young man to share personal information and then played therapist to him," said Howard.

"I asked him, 'Why do you try so hard? Why do you go after things so hard?' " Carson added. "He said, 'Why do you?' "

"I see him manipulating these people to affect his treatment," Brownlee suggested.

"You don't think this is a genuine conversion?" Carson asked.

"I think there are some grains of genuineness about it," Brownlee responded, "but I would say for the most part it represents more of the on-off kind of quality that you would see in a borderline-type person where he is really on fire this week and maybe he will be as long as his hands are slapped. He wants to read the Bible all the time—super enthusiastic."

"He says that he is a different man now than he was six months ago," said Carson.

"When I asked him if he enjoyed having sex with his daughter," said Brownlee, "he balked and kept saying no, that it was very painful. And I said, 'Come on! If she's fifteen, sixteen years old, wouldn't that be kind of nice?' And he couldn't handle that in a mature way, saying, 'Yes, I feel real bad about that. I have all these feelings about her, and I enjoyed it.' But it was like, 'No, that is in the past, that is gone from me.' It has that kind of quality about it: 'It does not exist if I do not want it to exist.' There were times in the past where he would get religion and do these things and for periods of weeks he would be doing the right thing for whatever reason it would best suit him."

Howard spoke up. "What his wife says about that period and that involvement [in counseling] was he didn't buy any of it, that she had to force him to go, and that he really wouldn't go unless she threatened divorce."

During those periods, explained Brownlee, when Linda got Bobby and Shelley to counseling, he fooled only himself. "I asked him, 'How often in these counseling sessions did you talk about the incest?' And he said, 'Well, it never came up.' I said, 'How in the world could you be dealing honestly with things if it was being kept secret?' "

Brownlee didn't say whether Sessions responded. Instead he said, "I am just impressed with the primitive level of his faith." He compared Sessions' so-called faith with a young child's powers of concentration—"the same thing you would expect to see in early object constancy, where the object, when it is there, is one-hundred-percent there; but when it is gone, it is gone."

In probing the meaning of Sessions' instant religious "conversion," the doctors drew parallels with his sexual perversion. Brownlee guessed that the "libidinal charge that first went into alcohol and then to his daughter—that same libidinal drive is now channeled into spiritual gratification and he is going to be the most impulsive spiritual person. I am surprised he is not speaking in tongues and things like that."

Bringing the conversation back to the problem of diagnosis again, Howard tried to form an impression of Sessions' libidinal drive from other sources. "The brother-in-law says that in fact he had a fairly lengthy and troublesome homosexual affair with a person in town there in Corsicana, that he would go to Houston on trips and availed himself of prostitutes there, particularly young ones, and that he would make comments about early teenagers that would be seen in the grocery store and other places around Corsicana, about how sexually exciting they were, that he would photograph and videotape, or invite people to watch from a closet while he had sex with a young girl prostitute or people he could pick up in a bar in Houston. There was an obsessive quality about all of this."

Howard pointed out that Bobby and other members of his family denied such activity and the conversation, but also recounted sister Betty's story of molestation throughout childhood. "The reason that we are talking about this is the diagnostic question as to whether or not this patient has a compulsive sexual perversion involving aggression, involving incest, involving sexual interest in young women."

"I cannot rule that out," said Carson.

Brownlee then recalled the first time he met Sessions. "I interrupted him on a phone conversation to his spiritual therapist. As I listened, as he was getting off the phone, he kept calling her 'Sugar,' 'Sugar-babe,' things like that. I said, 'Bob, were you talking to your wife?'" Sessions explained that it was his spiritual counselor and quickly changed the subject.

"I think this may indicate his . . . I would call it more polymorphous perverse sexual identity and I think the guy could be engaged in all those kinds of things," Brownlee concluded.

Those kinds of things? The doctors had a case on their hands. It hadn't taken long for them to realize that his "polymorphous" personality was more than a sexual chameleon. And finally Howard submitted his diagnosis of "obsessive-compulsive neurosis in a narcissistic personality." Howard read the definition of the latter from the Diagnostic and Statistical Manual, the psychiatric Bible. "Grandiose sense of self-importance or uniqueness, preoccupation with fantasies of unlimited success, power, brilliance, beauty, or ideal love, exhibitionism, constant attention and admiration needed, cool indifference or marked feelings of rage, inferiority, shame, humiliation, emptiness."

"How do you treat narcissistic personality, obsessive-compulsive neurosis?" Howard asked.

"Continued psychotherapy," said Carson.

"Why could he not be discharged today and continue in intensive psychotherapy?" Howard suggested. "Corsicana isn't a long drive from Dallas."

No one thought that was a good idea. "You can't just let this guy go," said Carson. "I'm not sure that someone wouldn't get killed if he left."

"I am very concerned about his daughter," said Howard, who then reported what Bobby had told him about Shelley's transfer to Rebekah.

Howard described their brief conversation, expressing his concerns. "I did not have a good feeling about his response, because it seemed like he is really in there wanting to control it," Howard told his colleagues. "And one of our concerns about the use of the phone with the Christian counselor, with his mother and sister, is that I think that he has engineered this."

The doctors had already decided that Bobby was so good at manipulating people, controlling his environment and denying reality, that treatment would be difficult. "One of the tacks I have taken with him," explained Howard, "is to say, 'Bob, you are so good at conning, at manipulating, at selling refrigerators to Eskimos, that you did it to yourself.' You sold yourself that you could control what you were doing."

Dr. McDonald was worried about the impact of the Christian counselors on Sessions' recovery. "Can we let him get that involved in a system that is really supporting his denial mechanism?" he wondered.

The consensus was that since Bobby seemed to trust the religious counselors more than anyone else, they were valuable to his recovery.

"He is extremely eager to sell us on his situation," said Howard. "He will come in and be charming and tell us whatever we want to hear."

"I think you're right," added Brownlee. "He will tell the religious counselors one thing and us something else."

"One of the things that we have come to appreciate about him," Howard said, "is that this guy really does paint different pictures, that he gives you what you want to hear. That is troublesome."

The meeting ranged everywhere—anywhere the assembled doctors wanted to take it. It was as if they struggled to grasp the hands of a clock, to understand what made Bobby Sessions tick, but were finding him too slippery to hold on to.

"It is almost diagnostic in itself," McDonald concluded, "that this man here is on ten years' probation, facing the problem of raping his daughter, and yet is going to be enraged by the fact that he has to stay in treatment. That tells you a whole lot about who we are dealing with, that he does not take it seriously, that he does not understand our concerns, and, 'What do you mean I'm not okay?' "

Shelley was put away; Bobby could relax again. In the week after his daughter was sent to Rebekah, Bobby gained four pounds. He was safe again. Everything was under control again.

FINAL BETRAYAL

They just at first started telling me the dress code—that I had to wear dresses and skirts. And that I was a new girl for the first month and that I had someone watch me to show me everything. And she started telling me all that and I kept demanding to see my mother and she wouldn't let me. She told me to go and change into these clothes that she gave me. I told her I wasn't changing into anything until she let me see my mom.

Suddenly there were rules all around, a fence all around. It was almost as bad as having Bobby all around. Shelley cried her whole first day there.

A stern-faced woman spelled out the rules that first day, but Shelley barely heard her. "You can write a letter home twice a week. One page long, no more. And we read them. And you get one phone call a month—five minutes only."

This sounded an awful lot like prison.

"When you are in your room, you must stay there unless told to leave."

A woman wanted me to take off my jewelry and I wouldn't take it off. . . . And they gave me a uniform to put on. . . . They explained all the rules. . . . And finally I got to see my mom and I thought I could pretty well talk my mom into anything.

Shelley loved her mother. But Linda had betrayed her. How could she have deserted her this way?

She told me that she would divorce him because I was her daughter. Then she turned around and sent me off and dropped the divorce.

In one quick, dark-of-night move, Shelley was swooped up and carried to an ugly, institutional set of buildings on the grounds of the People's Baptist Church of Corpus Christi, far from home. It was in an old, tattered residential neighborhood, south and west of the town on the way to the old airport at Cuddihy Field—and it was as religious as it could possibly be.

It was an accredited high school, but all the classes were Christian. Christian everything. Christian history, Christian English. Everything. In math, if you had a problem to solve, instead of saying something like two apples and two apples is four apples, it's Moses took two apples and Moses took three apples. It's all the Bible.

But Christian wasn't exactly the part of the Bible that the school most resembled. It was not New Testament love that guided the place, but old-fashioned, Old Testament fire and brimstone.

Not so ironically the place was called Rebekah—after the mother of Jacob and Esau, wife of Isaac, the boy whom Abraham had carried off to the butcher's block. Rebekah's place in biblical history came from the favored treatment she tendered Jacob, the younger child, throughout his life. She became the ultimate symbol of the manipulative and scheming mother when she helped Jacob dupe his blind father into giving him the birthright that was really owed Esau.

Shelley felt as if her birthright had also been sold. Her childhood had been stripped from her by Bobby; her mother had allowed it to happen. Now she was thrust into this life of mental isolation. So much was restricted at Rebekah, it seemed, that almost every act required permission; every event was a privilege. It was the routine and culture of prison. Why? What had she done to deserve this?

A phone call was considered a privilege. One a month—and even then it had to be made in an office and be monitored by a teacher or housemother. One complaint about the school and the call was instantly disrupted.

Everything was on a merit and demerit system. If you talk in line, you get demerits. If you get a certain amount by the end of the week—the girls that were good all week watched films, The Three Stooges *or something, and that was a big thing 'cause you didn't watch TV, you didn't hear radio or nothing. And the girls that didn't make it would have to sit in the front living room and just recite sections from the Bible. Two or three hours.*

Henry Edgington had grown up in Corpus Christi and remembered that Rebekah "looks like a prison . . . and never had a good name." No one knew for sure whether it was to keep people in or out, but Roloff had put a high Cyclone fence around the property that succeeded rather well at both. "You didn't mess around with anything there," recalled Edgington of his childhood near Rebekah. "And you surely didn't try to sneak in," recalled Edgington. "It would be worse than trying to sneak out. And the kids that were in there—it was like a prison, just as simple as that."

There were three other "homes" on the bleak, sterile-looking campus—one for women who needed to "rid their lives of the alcohol, drugs and sin that has [sic] ruined their lives"; one for boys who get "the drugs and alcohol out of their systems while the Lord is putting in the Word of God"; and another for normal schoolboys who simply needed to learn that "Christ is really the answer to their problems and struggles."

Roloff was a fire-and-brimstone evangelist and preacher who had started a daily radio program, "The Family Altar Program," in Corpus Christi in 1944, as well as programs for alcoholics, drug addicts and youths as part of his ministry. His treatment of all problems consisted of isolating the participants and subjecting them to round-the-clock Christian fundamentalism. And they were immediately and continually controversial.

Though Roloff himself had died the year before Shelley arrived at the home, his following was such that his radio show continued without him, carried on nationwide. And his followers also carried on the battle of faith.

Roloff's "Statement of Faith" for his People's Baptist Church and Ministry sounded like a combined call to arms and prescription for daily life.

"We believe in the virgin birth, the sinless life, the atoning death and the glorious resurrection and also the premillennial return of Jesus Christ to this earth."

Roloff and his followers swore to "a perpetual hatred for sin" as well as an unswerving loyalty to Jesus Christ. And they were unstinting in their application of that loyalty to all matters of worldly behavior—very little about the life of People's Baptist wasn't church-related

"We believe in separation, dedication and consecration in diet, discipline and dress," the Statement of Faith continued. "We believe the husband and father ought to be the head of the home and demand discipline on the part of the children. . . ."

Linda discovered the Roloff faith, but it was to be Bobby who benefited most by it. In embracing it, Linda agreed to subservience for herself and victimization for Shelley. It suited Bobby perfectly, so well that he would later say he believed that "God has ordained a special place in the family for certain members. Shelley is my daughter and I am her father. God says that Shelley is to be under my authority. I believe that with all my heart."

Bobby found ample support for his rigid and doctrinaire beliefs in the Roloff faith, which prescribed dresses for girls and ladies and proscribed television, rock-and-roll music, iced tea, coffee, tobacco, carbonated drinks and hog meat.

If you didn't eat your lunch, you got a certain amount of demerits. Talked in line. Demerits. Anything. You'd get a certain amount of licks if you had too many demerits. Licks were given with a board. Whittled down, about eighteen inches long and about a foot wide and an inch thick and it hurt. You had to lean over a table.

The state of Texas was never enthusiastic about preacher Roloff's schools, and even as Shelley arrived at Rebekah, the state was trying to shut the school down for refusing to submit to state regulation. After Roloff's death, his homes suffered their worst crisis ever.

They first came under fire from the Texas Human Services Department because of their rigid discipline. The state agency had started after the schools as early as the late 1970s. But Roloff fought off the agency on the grounds that his was a private and protected church organization. He succeeded in keeping the state at bay, refusing to obtain a license or allow any outside monitoring of his facilities.

He even closed the homes briefly in 1979 rather than allow state inspectors on the grounds.

"They were always up on charges relating to physical abuse while I was growing up in Corpus," recalled Henry Edgington. "And you'd hear stories, like kids who got out of line having to walk around with a clothespin on their ear."

Linda had once mentioned to Edgington that she was thinking about sending Shelley to Rebekah. And she got a lecture. "I told her about the frequent newspaper articles which were being written and that the home was not licensed by the state."

Concluded Edgington: "I'd tell her that and the next thing I know Shelley gets woken up one night and some of these radicals take her off. She's the one being punished. Bob belonged down there; Shelley didn't."

The first week at Rebekah was sheer torture for Shelley. Everything about life there called for adjustment, including learning to live with former drug dealers, drug users and prostitutes—the girls whom Rebekah was built for.

Shelley found herself housed in a small room with two other girls in a large two-story building with two hallways on each floor. The other girls' rooms ran along either side of the hallway— almost 300 girls huddled into the tightly packed quarters, three to a room.

It was wild. All types of people and most of them were hard-core druggies. They had veins sticking out all over their arms, where they had shot up.

Snatched away, cut off completely from her friends, Shelley cried and cried. She couldn't call anyone. She couldn't write anyone. Did anyone even know where she was?

XVIII

RICKY AND CHERRY

Ricky Layfield had gone to work over by Eustis with a fever and what felt like tonsilitis and strep throat and flu all at once. The day was already hot and the dust swirled around his head as he ran the big construction roller back and forth over the new roadbed. He ached all over. When he finally felt he couldn't keep his head on anymore, Ricky scampered down from the machine and went in search of a phone. His dad answered.

Ricky groaned, "Gotta come get me—"

"Boy, I want you to take this now," Joey Ray Layfield interrupted. Ricky waited. Then he thought he heard his dad say something like, "Shelley's gone."

"What!" His head throbbed. He thought he might be delirious.

"They took Shelley off to some home somewhere."

Ricky had heard right. Then he remembered what had happened the night before, realizing now how odd it was for Linda to call two or three times—or for Michael to call. They were waiting for her. And Ricky had sent her home!

He begged his dad to hurry. It was a thirty-mile drive, and the fever made the wait even more painful. Hysterical with anger, he had all that time to contemplate what he would do.

"We just went berserk up here," recalled Cherry Layfield. "The whole family just went crazy, trying to find her.

"Shelley had told us she'd be over here at noon the next day. And when she didn't show up, we called the ranch. We didn't get an answer and then we got out looking. We went over there, but nobody was there, and I called Linda's sister Sandra. She wouldn't tell me nothing, until finally she said that Shelley had gone away to school. I told her she was lying, I said, 'Let me tell you something. Shelley wouldn't leave without telling Ricky good-bye. They have taken her somewhere!'"

"When I got home," Ricky said, "I put on my little ole karate pants—the ones she had bought me—and the little shirt that said 'Shelley and Ricky' on the back and I put that on."

"Then I go over to her Uncle Rick's house. He lived on the road that goes to Cedar Lake, right behind Corsicana Lake, the one they are draining. I go and I knock on the door. I'm with my buddy, Junior. He was in karate too. We got chucks with us, and we got my other buddy because he's in karate too."

Chucks are a martial-arts device—a couple of small sticks attached to each other by a foot-long piece of rope. Twirled just so, rapidly, they make a threatening *whoosh* sound, imparting an unmistakable sensation of being too close to a fan.

Ricky and Junior, a black kid, walked up the drive in their loose-fitting dark outfits, looking as if they'd just been dropped out of a chop-chop movie. But this was not play-acting. Ricky knocked on the door. Shelley's aunt Sandra answered.

Ricky's face revealed his hatred as he stared at her. "Where is she at?" he demanded without fanfare or introduction.

"Well, I can't tell you that," Sandra answered, her head now disappearing slowly behind the door.

Ricky jammed the door with his foot. "Well, I'm going to tell you. I'm going to find her. And whenever I find her, I'm going to come after you and Rick and the first one it's going to be is Rick."

Ricky guessed that Shelley's Uncle Rick was behind the abduction, since Linda seemed to have been getting closer to them lately.

"So I took on off, and I went over to Shelley's house, and her grandmother, grandfather, couple of other relatives, and Rick, he was laying by the pool, back in one of them recliners. I just walked all the way around all of them, they're tripping, OHHH, their mouth hung open and shit, they didn't think I'd show up over there. I walked right over to him."

"Where's she at?"

Uncle Rick started to get up. "What are you talking about?"

"Sit down here!" Ricky ordered.

"I started cussing. 'Forget that.' He says something to me and I told him the same thing I told his wife. I said, 'Well, you're first on my list, when I find her, you'll be—pay for it, 'cause, first place, she doesn't deserve that. Anybody going to be locked up, it ought to be Bobby, you know, she don't deserve—' You know, all this shit. 'Whenever I find out where she's at, that'll be double-trouble, you know.' Boy, that was really tough.

"He was attempting to stand up, and you know, I kinda like jumped at him, I was fixing to nail him. Already, the temper was already gone, if he would of said something right away, I would have hit him. You know, that's all it would of took. But he was eating cheese like a rat. He was trying to calm me down, all the time I was getting madder, you know. I was sick too. But, uh, I made a flinch at him, and he almost fell in the pool."

Ricky stormed away, drove home and collapsed into bed, sicker than a dog.

"Ricky was going to whup that man up one side and down the other," Cherry recalled. "Ricky told me he scared him. He said, 'I meant every word I said, too.' And Ricky would have fought a buzzsaw then, he was that mad. He stayed mad for weeks. I mean, he was mad twenty-four hours a day.

"They kept trying to lie to us," Cherry continued. "Sandra said that she'd gone, but I knew Shelley wouldn't have gone without telling us. 'You don't tell us that she wouldn't leave,' I said. 'You-all have carried her off. You-all have done something with her and you better tell us.' "

When Sandra confessed that "She's gone off to school," it wasn't enough for Cherry or Ricky. "Where is Linda?" Cherry demanded. "On vacation," said Sandra.

The next day Ricky was up early, dragging himself out of the sack to return to the Sessions ranch. On the way, Kim Speakes, Shelley's friend, spotted Ricky and waved him over.

Kim told Ricky that if he ever told how he found out, she'd kill him—her mother told her that she would have *her* put down there, too.

"I used to see Kim all the time, I used to date Kim, you know. Shoot, Kim stopped me and Kim's mom and Linda and them were all in that cult thing, like a religious cult deal and Kim's mom told Kim where Shelley was at. And Kim told me where she was at. Shoot, she knew I was going, you know. I went to the bank, and I think I had $400 or $500, and took it all out, chooosh, tore it down, you know."

Ricky was on automatic pilot now. He raced back home in his old Datsun 210 hatchback and started stuffing it with what he thought he'd need to get Shelley out of the home. "I took a twelve-gauge automatic, a load of buckshot, numb chucks, body stars, suitcase with a tent, rod and reel and tackle box, roll net, kitchen bait, all that stuff. Even wire cutters and bolt cutters, for getting through the fence.

"I was planning on getting her, coming back to the country and chilling out. And let 'em try to come get her, you know. Shoot, I was just going to play it, bandito style, you know. I was just going to walk in the place, and anybody who wanted trouble, I was going to give 'em all I could give 'em."

It was late afternoon when Ricky tore out of his drive, headed south. But at the first stoplight, Kerens' only one, he hit the accelerator harder than he should have. The tires squealed and spit—and a few hundred yards later, a police cruiser pulled the teenager over.

"He gave me a ticket for exhibition accelerating. Then I got out somewhere in between Kerens and Corpus, and I had that little car, it had four cylinders in it, but it got fifty-some miles to a gallon and could run a hundred and ten miles an hour, and I was running a hundred miles an hour, and this truck flashed its lights. I'm shutting her down, you know, but at a hundred miles an hour, you can't shut it down that good. Shoot, boy, and that black-and-white was behind me. Clip, he nailed me.

"He said, 'I clocked you at ninety-something miles an hour.' He said, 'What's your hurry, boy.' I knew I was going to jail, he was going to take me to jail, 'cause my insurance card wasn't valid, it was out of date. My insurance was good, but it was just out of date. But he gave me a ticket for sixty-five and put a check down on my insurance—where if I sent proof of my insurance, they'd knock it off. So I think my ticket was something like fifty dollars, it was no big deal."

Cherry Layfield was now double-panicked. Shelley was gone; now Ricky. "He told me that he was going riding," said Cherry, "and he never came back." She knew that meant he had probably found out where Shelley had been taken. Because wherever Shelley was, that's where Ricky would be.

Based on what she knew about Linda and her friends, Cherry had already guessed that Shelley had been taken to the Roloff home. And she sent her daughters up to the baseball field to pull word out of the kids about Ricky.

"Mary Ann got out of the car," recalled Cherry, "and told them girls, 'Let me tell you something—Ricky's life is in danger. If he's gone where we think he's gone, if he's gone to Corpus Christi, he's gonna get killed. And you kids know where he's at.' Then they started telling. And they said he went with shotguns and everything. They started singing like birds then."

Cherry and Joey Ray now had to make a decision. As much as they were convinced that Shelley had been taken against her will, they knew that it was Linda's doing—and legal. And their son could only come to harm if he tried to bust Shelley out. "We called the sheriff's department and told him we wanted him picked up because he was going to get his head blowed off," Cherry recalled. "People told us they patrol with shotguns down there at Roloff, and they said, 'Your boy's going to get killed if he goes down there.' I said, 'He's down there, he's down there now,' so we called the sheriff's department, and we told him what he had done, and we told them, 'We want him picked up and held until we can come get him.' Well, we had to charge him as a runaway; they wouldn't do nothing unless we filed on him as a runaway. We had to file on him.

"And then we sat up here all night, we never even changed clothes, we was ready to go the minute they called us, 'We got him,' we were going to get in that car and go."

"I went ahead, drove and drove, until I went right up in front of that Roloff home," Ricky said. And there's a brown—like them old cop cars, the old Chrysler cars, four-doors, like the old black-and-whites—it was a brown one sitting out there, in front of the place. I cruised right on by, it's just not even good daylight, you know, I cruised in front of the place, and go way down—I think it was a two-lane road down in front, with kinda wide shoulders on it, and I go down about twenty miles. And I aint lying: there was seven cop cars—*chewk, chewk, chewk*—they passed me the other way and I'm going, 'Golly, what's all these cops doing?' I didn't know they was after me, you know. *Chewk, chewk,* they going by, you know. And when I get back out in front of that place, that big brown car is gone and I saw, Oh, shit!

"Right about the time I made it to that gate, that car was meeting me. Man, he comes out of nowhere and he locks that sucker up and slides sideways right beside me. I mean, he's in the middle of the highway, WHAAAAR, boy, he romps down on it, and the white smoke is just rolling off them tires. I look in my mirror and I go oh, oh, you know. I drug my shirt off, 'cause, well, it looks like I'm fixing to get into a fight now, you know.

"Shoot. I pulled down there, and there's a red light—intersection—and I turn in this gas station. He pulls out in the middle of the red, turns his flashers on, whoops out, comes around, gets in behind me. I say oh, oh. So I pulled into this little ole dirt road and it dead-ends. I had to go in there and come back and he's sitting there on the highway.

"When I pull out around him, he yells at me, he says, 'They got a warrant for your arrest and they're going to getcha.' I said, 'Who?' He said, 'The law, and I'm going to follow you until they find you.'

"So I pull in and stop, and he pulls around behind me, and I put that little Datsun in reverse, he puts his in reverse. I get out and walk back there. What I was going to do, I was just going to grab him, jerk him out of that car, you know. I walk back there all cocked up and shit, and I looked and he had one of them old-time double-barrels, a barrel on it about that long, two hammers on it, and he had both of them cocked, pointing at me.

"And he said, 'Son,' he said, 'I'm not playing games.' Ohhfow, I tripped out, I fell on the hood, I said, 'Yessir, I can see *that.*'

"He said, 'You're armed and dangerous.' You know, I had completely forgotten about that twelve-gauge I had in my car. I'd already forgot about all that mess. Shoot, armed and dangerous, what are you talking about? And then I thought about it, oh, I got that gun in there, you know, so I told him, 'Yeah, I got an automatic 1100 Remington in there, I got a tent, sleeping bag, rod and reel.' I said, 'I got all that stuff. We're going camping down here.'

"He said, 'No, son, I know about you. The law'll be here shortly. I said, 'Well, I'll tell you what, I'll just wait on them.' Shoot, what I do that for, man? Not thirty seconds later, boy, there was seven, at least seven, cops, *erererer.* I'm talking about black-and-whites, sliding in from every way. I was tripping, I was going, God. One cop jumps out, *cooosh,* he unbuttons his belt. First one, unbuttons that gun, and I said, 'Wait a minute, you can button that back. There ain't going to be no problem.'

"He walked away, I didn't have no shirt on, no shoes either. They start asking me questions and stuff. You know, what the deal was. 'You got any weapons on you?' I said, 'No, sir.' He said, 'Well that's good, I didn't want to have to search you noway; I didn't want to put no cuffs on you. They over there?' You know, looking at the car. And I said, 'You want to look through that?' I had the chucks and stars hid where nobody could find them—a little ole place up underneath the car, under the bottom of the body.

"I mean, there was more cops pulling up all the time. I bet there was twelve, fourteen cops there, and it was just right down the street from Shelley. I mean, I could see the Roloff home, right there.

"There was girls out there, and I said, 'Well shit, didn't see Shelley,' and that cop said, 'You don't mind?' I said, 'No.' He gets my gun out, you know, and I think I had something in the magazine, didn't have one in the barrel, and when you cock an automatic back it breeches open. That cop, he was looking down the barrel, you know, and all up in there, and I said, 'Wait a minute, fella, that gun is loaded.' He said, 'Well, you need to unload it,' and I flicked the shells out. And he leaned it up next to the traffic, and I said, 'Okay,' I said, 'you all may be arresting me,' I said, 'but that's my gun, and if it gets tore up somebody's going to pay for it.'

"Like I said, I was on a hunting trip, and I had that tent and all that other stuff, so I had valid cause, you know. They took me to jail, and when we got to jail, then they found out that I wasn't old enough to go to jail, so they sent me back across town, to one of those juvenile holding cells.

"When she asked, 'Where you from?' I said, 'Kerens.' And she said, 'Kerens! The founder of this place, my ex-boss, is from Kerens. That juvenile detention center, shoot, it was my schoolteacher's husband who founded that place.'

"And they took me in there, this big old black guy gave me some pants that was about this big around, you know, legs all about this big around you know, but they're about this short, and I said, 'I can't wear them.'

" 'You sure are picky.'

" 'No, I ain't picky, I just couldn't wear them. You know, I ain't walking around with a hole in my pants.' He gives me a pair, I ain't lying—I was small, but these pants were small. Soon as I get 'em up, and we walk to the room, then he says, 'You gotta take the pants and everything off 'sides your underwear. That's all you can have on when you go in your cell. Man, why didn't I just walk through here in my underwear, you know? Struggle to get these things while he tells me all these rules and I tell him, 'Wait a minute, I don't need to know all these rules. You can keep this piece of paper,' and all that. He said, 'Why?' I said, 'My daddy'll be down here before the sun goes down.' It was about nine o'clock in the morning by that time. He said, 'No, son, you'll be here for a while.' I said, 'I sure won't.' "

After staying up most of the night waiting for word, Cherry and Joey Ray and daughter Shawna drove all day, 380 miles, arriving in Corpus Christi in the evening. They were happy just to know that Ricky had been picked up and was all right. "They told us he was in the jail, so we went to the Corpus Christi jail to get him," recalled Cherry. "And I've never seen—whooh! that's a scary place. And we got there and they said we never heard of Ricky Layfield. I had the teletype from the Navarro County sheriff saying we could pick him up, but they said, 'We never heard of him.' "

The Layfields looked at each other with dread, as though their joy had been misplaced. Not until a policeman asked Ricky's age was the mystery sorted out.

"I hadn't talked to nobody," Ricky later explained, "but I guessed that they was the ones that called down here, so I knew that they'd be down. And sure enough, about—I guess it was about dark. They come down there, boy, and I was never so glad."

"We found him at juvenile hall," explained Cherry, "and said first thing, 'I was going to give you-all to sundown, then I was busting out.' And he'd already figured out how he was going to do it."

"My dad never said nothing to me. I'd do it again, if I had to do it all over, I'd do it again, but change it up a little bit.

"Shoot, I got back, I was exhausted, I kind of rested there for about three days and gathered my thoughts. Finally, you know, boy, I tripped out, I was crying over it. All that stuff. I was a guy and I was crying over it, you know. I had to admit it.

"Then Shelley's mom and all them started throwing bad vibes at me, you know, telling me that 'Shelley don't want you' and all that stuff. I'm going, dang, just before she left, you know, it was totally different, you know, I said, 'I don't believe you.'

"I went over there one day, you know, not too long after this happened, and Bobby was supposed to be up there. So I went over there with karate stars in my back pockets, and I wore a pair of baggies—chucks up my pants. If Bobby was there, you know, for sure I was going to try to do him over. That was my full intention.

"But Linda started talking to me, and boy, she just started telling me all this stuff about how well Shelley was doing, how much she liked it down there. She started telling me things that Shelley had said, that I knew was wrong, they was wrong, but boy, tears got to running out of my eyes and I got mad, you know, shoot.

"And Bobby was upstairs the whole time, but she never did let me know it. Michael come downstairs once, to see me. And something made a noise, you know, and she sent him back upstairs, saying something about a cat. Hell, they don't have a damn cat. It was Bobby up there! I know it was. And boy, I was tripping, sitting down there, any minute this dude's going to, *keeeuuu*, bust cap on me.

"Shoot, so I just slammed those stars down on the counter, and I just held them in my hand. She backed up and went to tripping, 'What are you going to do? What? What?' She thought I was fixing to hurt her, and I said, 'No, I'm not going to touch you,' I said, 'But I know Bobby's out,' and I said, 'He's around here somewhere,' and I said, 'You know, if there's going to be a confrontation I'm going to have with him, I am at least going to be equal.'

" 'He's not out,' she starts telling me all this. And I just left."

XIX

FLIGHT TO HEALTH

He got out of Timberlawn in six months, but he was supposed to be there two years. He must have paid somebody off.

He was bringing that preacher from Denver and that other preacher he gave the Mercedes to drive. Just conning everybody. Just getting them all on his side. Do whatever you have to do to get out of there. Anyone who gets convicted of anything always proclaims Jesus Christ. That's the oldest crock in the world.

But no matter what he said they believed it, worshiped him. Whatever you say, Bob. He's just very manipulative. He knows what he's doing. And he just knows how to get what he wants.

At Timberlawn in August, Bobby Sessions' biggest problem seemed to be the sprained wrist he suffered during a volleyball game. He was instructed to wear a splint for a week, which meant he couldn't work on his tennis game or play softball. That bothered him. A staff note said: "He was really pushing Dr. Howard pretty hard last week and over the weekend to let him play softball in it."

In the warm Dallas summer, Bobby relaxed. He played tennis and racquetball and volleyball. He swam in the hospital's pool, took piano lessons and sunbathed. The splint would put a crimp in his new regimen: "recreational therapy."

Two days before Shelley was carried off to her Corpus Christi prison, Bobby was signing in his AMF tennis racquet and case at Timberlawn. Confined to the Witt building for his first month at the psychiatric hospital, Bobby was quickly allowed to spread his wings. Within a month of his guilty plea, he was allowed unsupervised visits and phone calls. He was given back his Rolex. By August Bobby was going to dances on-grounds and taking tennis lessons off-grounds.

Bobby was offering gifts to staffers and advice to the doctors on how to run the unit; he even asked Dr. Howard if he could be an assistant therapist.

He was still exaggerating the facts, stretching the rules and pushing pushing pushing for privileges. A weekend visit with his attorney in late July to discuss business turned into a family party when the lawyer showed up with six of his relatives. Bobby had turned most of his businesses in Powell over to Travis Kendall to run while he was in the hospital.

In early August he was allowed an off-grounds visit with his family. "Dr. Howard had essentially told him no," a staff report noted, "but the patient continued to push until Dr. Howard found himself trying to find ways to get the patient off-grounds when in fact he did not need to be off-grounds. This had to do with buying a birthday present for his son, which was not an essential item and there were many other ways he could get a present for his son."

Manipulating and denying—Bobby seemed to have abilities in spades. And Timberlawn staff were quick to make the connections with Bobby's past: "It was like if he could get Dr. Howard to say it was okay, then it would be all right no matter what," a staffer noted. "This is a little like what he did with his daughter at home—that if he could get someone to say it was okay, then it was all right—and he gets people to say yes by pushing on them."

A battery of psychological tests administered on July 23 showed Bobby with "a general absence of depression, major reliance on denial, rationalization and minimization, considerable character pathology consistent with narcissistic personality."

This meant he was normal. "I think he has already noticed a number of young ladies around the campus, and I suspect we will see action of all sorts," predicted Dr. Howard.

There had been hints of that. Another patient had complained that Bobby had been leading some late-night discussions with some of the younger male patients about sexual matters—specifically about prostitutes.

A progress report dated August 2, 1983, less than two months after arriving, observed that "The staff has identified areas where in a subtle way the patient encouraged sexual talk on the unit. In a subtle way he talks about female patients and staff in those terms. In a subtle way he makes references that this is a very bad environment for him, because of the 'filthy way these kids talk.' "

It was the same talk Shelley would hear as he molested her. Considering what he had done to his daughter, the report noted, "there is something very hypocritical about that.

"Yet, it is reported that this man involved himself at times, on the outside of the hospital, with prostitutes and with some exhibitionistic behavior and the clearly documented incest with his daughter. Yet, he refers to this as being a non-Christian environment, so there is something very hypocritical about that."

With Bobby, as always, each situation had a second meaning. The patient was an expert at spin control.

Had he changed?

He told Dr. Solomon about sexual discussions he was having with other patients—but when Bobby told it, he was just "sharing with some people in the hospital that were homosexual and he was showing them that there was a way of freedom and victory," recalled Solomon. "And he had begun to not only have the freedom within himself, but he was also sharing with other people, which he had never done before. Because now he knew he had an answer. . . . He had never done that kind of witnessing and telling other people about the Lord before. This just wasn't part of his nature in life."

But Bobby continued to sell refrigerators to the Eskimos.

Younger patients were drawn to him, a self-made man, million-aire, rancher, entrepreneur. "He comes on like a counselor with them," noted one staffer. "They pretty much seek advice from him."

He had surrendered none of his bravura to come to Timber-lawn. Younger women patients were attracted—and he encouraged their interest.

There was even talk, the report noted, "that an adolescent teenage female patient and he were getting something going. . . . The staff is concerned about this. Also, one of the young adult female patients repeatedly was spreading suntan lotion on the patient's back. Again, this may be straining a small thing, but for a patient who is supposed to be extremely careful about that sort of thing, the subject keeps coming up."

"The patient's personality scales of manipulativeness and ego-centricity were more obvious," said one report.

Bobby insinuated himself into all facets of hospital life. "Many staff members see him as being quite manipulative and wanting to take over as the therapist for many of the other patients," observed Carson as late as October 28. "He has been confronted about it and feels quite angry at his administrative psychiatrist."

On the tennis court he played hard, and always played to win. He didn't have much tolerance for those who weren't learning as quickly as he did. It was the same in piano lessons. But at the same time Bobby brought an excitement to his play: he sang with gusto at jam sessions, and the young players on the volleyball team liked his enthusiasm.

So good was Bob at manipulation that hospital reports began to turn up rumors about his various schemes. One noted that "Sally Moore heard that there was a rumor that the patient was working with the judge in his hometown to change the court order—that he will be home within a month's time."

Bobby's reputation for getting his way earned him a certain credibility, and even rumors added to the belief in his powers. When Linda met for the first time with Sally Moore, she told Moore that some people in Kerens believed that Bobby and Linda had "dumped Shelley in a 'home' and left for the Bahamas."

Bobby was like a dashing bank robber—criticized for stealing but admired for his turnkey prowess. His bravado seemed to heighten his ability to get away with dubious acts. When a staffer confronted Bobby with the fact that he'd overheard him promising Sarah Conn $500 during a phone call—against the specific directives of the hospital—Bobby blithely said it was for her expenses.

There was considerable skepticism about Bobby's Christian counseling. "He felt he had a bona fide salvation, received forgiveness for his behavior and therefore there was little to work on," was the summary of the hospital report. People said that Sessions was using religion as an excuse and engineering his transfer to a Christian counseling center—another form of denial avoidance. But he kept up his religious counseling, as did Linda, who even flew to Denver to spend a week at Solomon's Grace Fellowship International.

"It is Dr. Brownlee's opinion that he is using [religion] to avoid any guilt and using it to deny the seriousness of what occurred," noted an August 22 progress report. "There is strong evidence to support this."

By the end of September a progress report suggested that Sessions had made no progress: "Dr. Howard continues to hear from other patients that are loath to confront the patient, that he at times is inappropriate with female patients on the hospital grounds. This is nothing gross or easy to get a hold of but just relating to them in generally sexual ways. It is difficult to confront the patient with this, but this is part of why he is in the hospital."

It sounded like Linda—not wanting to raise the issue, unwilling to confront him. A psychological fox, an emotional chameleon, Bobby Sessions perplexed people, including his doctors at Timberlawn. "He was always able to come up with eight or nine reasons why his description is better than your description—people don't like to argue with him because he wins," Howard concluded.

Dr. Carson concluded that Sessions was "one of the most difficult patients I have worked with."

Sessions got himself into Timberlawn with fast talk; he was

getting himself out the same way. It was like a game—being cured; convincing doctors they couldn't do anything more for you often resulted in the same thing. Bobby Sessions managed to combine the disease and the cure with a sophistication rarely seen at Timberlawn.

When his sister Pat Davidson visited him, she was shocked by the change in her brother. "Before, I could look at my brother and we would talk—if you've ever seen somebody who could not tell the truth," she explained, "their eyes dart constantly. There is a nervousness about them. They shake. They are always having to be better. There is a wildness and an instability in their spirit that you cannot see.

"You just know it; you just feel it. If you've ever had feelings about someone, you know they are not right and they are not right with their Lord. When my brother entered my home, for the first time in my life I saw him at peace. His soul and his spirit was at peace and that is beautiful to see—to see a man in torment for forty-two years come to total peace and love for his family. I've never felt so much love for my brother and I craved it for years, for my brother to love me and he did and it was beautiful and I thank God for it."

He had soon enlisted Linda in his struggle for freedom. She visited occasionally, and they were able to get Bobby a pass so they could steal off to a hotel off-grounds. During September and October the couple had what one doctor called "a rather dramatic flight into marital accord." And soon after that, Linda was lobbying intensely for his release, even threatening hospital officials with court action.

Howard responded that Bobby could leave whenever he wanted to—but he risked violating the terms of his probation in not getting permission from the judge in Corsicana who had sentenced him. That reminder seemed to cool Linda off. But the incident also served to remind Howard that Linda was trying to blame the hospital for Bobby's predicament and the harm being caused him, his wife and his son. "One of the things in this family that always goes on," he recalled, "is guilt. Guilt is a pretty good manipulative tool and Bob uses it. Linda uses it and it was used that way toward the hospital."

Linda was not wholly in Bobby's camp. And Bobby never did tell his wife what had happened between him and Shelley. "I had to write up a very detailed report for one of the counselors," Bobby recalled. "They went through it with Linda step by step." But there were never any sit-down discussions about the nitty-gritty.

"A rather symbiotic relationship existed between the patient and his spouse," concluded Dr. Howard, "and while the patient remained superficially aloof from these interactions, his wife was proceeding as he hoped."

Translated, that meant that Bobby had no need to give formal orders to send his daughter to the "home." In his talks with Linda, he inquired about Shelley and reminded Linda that her own happiness was important to him. He also was careful to make her feel guilty if her decisions didn't coincide with his wishes.

"This past week, he was very manipulative in attempting to work out a weekend visit with his wife and using his small son as the excuse," a doctor noted at a team meeting in late September.

"Both Bob and his wife continue to put a great deal of pressure on the administrative psychiatrist to discharge Bob," Doyle Carson remarked.

"Bob seems to play a very passive role in all of this pressure . . . but there is some reason to believe that he says things to encourage her to put pressure on the hospital staff to discharge him."

At the same time that Linda was calling to ask for more visiting privileges, she began to complain about the drive from Corsicana to Dallas—an hour and a half—and the toll it was taking on her and her son.

And Bobby was saying the same things. "The patient very effectively tries to make one feel guilty about having to visit with his spouse here in the hospital," a mid-October report noted, "that it is too long for them to drive, that it is very harmful for their son, etc. Most recently, he stated to Dr. Howard that it was not nice to go to a motel with one's wife, because it does not feel right."

Bobby had been pushing for his release from the moment he had arrived in June—and he reminded staff and patients alike that he always got what he wanted. "As far as he is concerned," said Carson, "he has worked out his problems and the main solution has been a religious one. He says that his life is totally turned around since he has undergone a religious conversion in recent months and that this is the salvation that he has needed."

A September 12 progress note spelled it out bluntly: "The patient has been difficult to confront. . . . He is testy and staff does not trust him. He gets himself in a position of being very manipulative, especially when it comes to the opposite sex."

Two weeks later "he was fairly demanding . . . wanting to go home to Corsicana to go to church, to be with his wife and a number of other things, and unrealistic about the fact that he was sent here to the hospital after being convicted of felony charges."

Gradually, his entreaties had their impact. He was allowed to go home on a Thursday in September, have some stitches in his stomach removed and spend Friday, Saturday and Sunday resting at the ranch. He got passes to visit his sister Pat at her house in Dallas. There was a standing order that Bobby could leave the grounds for "family therapy" meetings at a Dallas clinic. He got to go to the State Fair two days in a row. And in November he was allowed to bring his own car to Timberlawn.

As soon as he got back to Timberlawn, the release chorus began again. "The wife was adamant that the patient be discharged soon," Sally Moore reported in early October. At the same time a progress note said that "Dr. Howard had a good long thirty- or forty-minute rounds with the patient in which the patient demonstrated a lot of introspection, a lot of understanding of his psychodynamics and then promptly began to push pretty hard to go home to Corsicana to be with his wife."

He was soon allowed regular off-grounds visits with friends and family and then home visits on October and November weekends, including Thanksgiving. Knowing that he couldn't keep him forever—or even for the recommended time of one year—Howard wanted to prepare Bobby for his release by gradual re-immersion in the domestic environment. "To reestablish contact with his church, with business associates in the community as a way of facing what I was concerned about, and that was his denial of the social impact of this behavior." Howard anticipated that some of Bobby's old friends would welcome him back and some would not.

Dr. Howard was somewhat relieved to know that Shelley was not at home when Bobby took his leaves. Not that Howard wanted her in Rebekah. "On visits to Corsicana," the Timberlawn administrator remarked, "I cautioned Bobby very vigorously about leaving the house, being around Shelley, because I was concerned that her obsession and his obsession posed serious danger to both of them."

If for any reason Shelley were to show up on Bobby's doorstep while he was home, Howard cautioned the patient that his plan of action had to include getting away from her.

But the cautions didn't seem to be taken seriously. Bobby denied the danger, Howard believed, "because he wanted to make it right again with her." Pastor Goode, despite Howard's reservations, kept counseling that the family be put back together.

Both Bobby and Linda became increasingly exasperated by Timberlawn and Dr. Howard's concern about Bobby's life. Howard noted that Linda "took exception to my continued concern regarding the incestuous relationship with the patient's daughter."

At the same time, Bobby showed no change in his attitude toward the act. "It is his belief, and he will not change from it," Carson noted at the end of September, "that his sexual involvement with her was based upon her continuing rejection of him throughout her childhood years."

He told a new counselor the same thing in October. "His going into the sexual relations with [Shelley] was an offshoot of his deep craving to be loved," reported Leslie Carter, the Dallas psychotherapist. Carter thought that particular observation was "pretty insightful on his part."

Linda had been seeing Carter, a counselor at a private clinic, since the end of June. She arranged for Bobby to see Carter to help bolster the case for an early release from Timberlawn. In fact, Bobby visited Carter five more times in the next two weeks—more frequently than he saw his Timberlawn counselor. And it was Carter's conclusion at the end of those two weeks that "Bob should move to reestablish his permanent position in his own home."

During this time Dr. Carson revealed how Bobby was succeeding in curing himself: "He is so convinced that he has no other problems to work on within a hospital setting that the productivity of psychotherapy sessions has become somewhat diminished. . . . He has become extremely defensive and basically has all of the answers now. These answers are provided for him through religious approaches to life. For example, Bob simply says he will wait until God provides answers and direction for him to everything. He does not need to seek solutions, he does not need to do any active work. If he simply waits, the proper answers to every problem will come to him if he prays. In my opinion, this approach is working very well for Bob Sessions and it should be encouraged and not discouraged."

The final team-member meeting had many fewer people than attended the marathon meeting in July. But the consensus was blunt: "It is felt that this patient has a manipulative character disorder and staff has not altered the basic character structure in the least. . . . The patient talks about his errant daughter now in terms of her problems."

The same meeting questioned Linda's progress as well: "This lady's judgment and reality testing are very much impaired by her emotional responses to the patient. Over the last month she has placed the hospital in the villain role, saying that staff has done things harmful to her husband, probably to her son, by insisting on the patient being in the hospital and that staff really does not know what they are doing. . . . This is a discouraging prospect to Dr. Howard, because it means that she is such a fragile and malleable person, that things at home will probably not change too much."

Finally, the decision was made. Bobby had gained the judge's permission to leave. On the progress note/treatment plan update for November 21, Timberlawn staff stated matter-of-factly: "The patient will be discharged December 5th, at his request. Dr. Howard feels he could benefit from a more substantial stay in the hospital, but at this point in time with the patient being un-motivated to change basic character structure, felt that that is a reasonable discharge time."

Howard had recommended at least an additional two to three months of hospitalization for Bobby.

So Bobby was officially home by Christmas—even though he was really home by Thanksgiving. Not a bad sentence for a convicted felon. It was certainly a more temperate one than the sentence Shelley was serving out.

Bobby had gone home the weekend before Thanksgiving, had a minor surgical repair of a stainless-steel suture in his abdominal wound—staying three days in the hospital—then relaxed around the ranch pool for another six days.

He returned to Timberlawn bubbling with enthusiasm over the leave. Everyone in the family was delighted with his progress; everyone he met in town had welcomed him back; and his wife was again deeply in love with him.

"In fact," he told Dr. Howard, "we are going to get remarried in a special ceremony to rededicate the marital vows."

Bobby really believed he was cured. He believed in miracles and so accepted that his personality had been turned inside out in less than six months of heavy breathing in the sun: "I didn't have the same personality when I left."

His religious fervor had turned the tide for him.

Doyle Carson reported that Bobby had tried to convert him during their last therapy session. "I think he attempted to do this out of a genuine concern for me and a liking for me," he con-cluded.

Pastor Solomon, after all, believed that "the Holy Spirit does the changing of the lives. He is the counselor. We're just a human instrument to teach the individual what they [sic] need to know about themselves and the Scriptures."

But Timberlawn officials remained unconvinced that these religious outbursts represented evidence of a deep or permanent change in Bobby. There was, in the end, a fundamental difference of opinion about whether or not he had changed—or what exactly fundamental change *was*.

Dr. Howard noted the week before Bobby's discharge that the soon-to-be-released patient had "much more insight . . . but he is still so narcissistic and self-centered that all of these other things are just an extension of himself and he has that same need to control everything. He is symptomatically a great deal better, but it is not felt that staff has effected any fundamental personality change in the patient."

The discharge report summed up: "minimized and consciously was dishonest in regarding his incestuous relationship with his daughter, stating that it had occurred once and then later on several occasions during a one year period of time. As it turned out, these events did occur over approximately a four-year period of time and were a frequent and ongoing source of conflict between the patient and his stepdaughter."

When Bobby promised to continue seeing counselors on the outside, the doctors had a way out.

He went home for a weekend leave on Saturday, December 3, and returned on Monday, his official discharge date, just long enough to pick up his belongings and say good-bye. He was gone, officially, less than six months after arriving—with "maximum hospital benefit" and "by mutual agreement"—not a bad way to leave. Any convicted felon would welcome an opportunity to leave prison "by mutual agreement."

SHELLEY GETS OUT

Shelley never found out about Ricky's failed rescue attempt.

And instead of finding Christ in this home, she encountered a mix of the devil and stern discipline.

Each room had an intercom speaker, out of which blared announcements, Bible readings, sermons and orders. The girls gathered regularly in one of two large living rooms—one upstairs and one down—to recite Bible verses.

They brainwash you. You go to sleep with the Bible being read through the intercom. They play a tape over and over, someone saying a sermon. And when you get up you hear it.

Or, everyone would be trying to go to sleep and they'd call everyone out in the hall. "You filthy no-good girls," they'd talk like that. Somebody stole something from so and so and we'll give you ten minutes to bring it back. And nobody stole, she probably misplaced it.

But we'd have to get out in the hall and kneel. And we'd kneel for hours. You'd lose circulation in your legs, you couldn't move. You'd just start wobbling and if you started wobbling, they'd get on you and make you stand up. And then you couldn't relax, like on one leg or something. You had to stand completely flat-footed.

*People would faint and fall down. And they would grab them and
make them stand up again.*

The daily schedule was almost as wearing—predictable, broken
up by infractions, demerits, licks and stints in solitary. Every
morning, at six o'clock, when the intercom voice began blabbing
the Bible verse, Shelley got up and retrieved her cleaning soap and
sponge. Every day she had to wipe down her walls with ammonia;
wipe down her bed frame, the pipes under the cabinet, the tables.

*A friend of mine kept saving cleaning soap—and then she
swallowed a bunch of it. They had to pump her stomach, then she
came back and she did it again and they took her back again.*

*People tried all kinds of things to get out of there. I saw a girl
just throw her arm through a window and take a piece of glass and
just start cuttin' herself all up, so they would take her to the
hospital. She thought she could escape once she got to the hospital.
But she didn't.*

So it was mindless dullness punctuated by attempted escape or
suicide.

*You get your cleaning supplies, you clean, they call you for
breakfast, you line up in the hall—you can never step out of your
room without permission—and you march over for breakfast. And
you line up and whether you like it or not, or whether it makes you
throw up or not, you eat it. You have to eat everything they give
you. And you get fat—because all you do is eat. It's like they want
you to be ugly because they don't let you get fixed up.*

*To them makeup and fixing your hair is primping and it's wrong.
So it's like there are no pretty girls there. It's like they just want
you to be ugly. The kind of food they fed us was all fattening. No
fruit, everything was just water weight gain. There were girls that
came in perfectly model size and went out whoooo, blimp.*

*Then you go back to the dorm and get ready for school and they
call you for school. You line up again and you walk across the
blacktop to the school. Everyone meets in one room and they have
a Bible thing. Then you go to your classes. . . .*

*You go to breakfast, you pray. You go to school and pray. You
have Bible studies at school. When you get out of school, you read
the Bible for one hour, two hours.*

You meet in the living room and you recite certain chapters out of the Bible over and over and over again. It's like a seance or something. One time I stopped reading and listened to everyone. It was like a chant. Brainwashing. If you stop and listened, you know, it's like drilling in your head.

You read certain chapters out of the Bible. And after you go through them once, you go through them again. And you go through them again, and again, until the time is up. You just read them over and over and over and over.

Lights-out at night meant lights-out. There were alarms on all the doors to the outside of the building and alarms on all the windows and a hallwalker who patrolled all night.

If you accidentally bumped a window and the alarm went off, everyone automatically has to sit on the end of their bed and they come by and check, count everybody, count who's not in their rooms. That happened all the time. There was always someone trying to get out.

There weren't many successful breakouts.

It's kind of hard to be running down the road in this uniform, since everyone knows what the uniform is for.

Friday night was the preferred time for trying to make a break. That was when the cafeteria became the site of the "film" showings for the girls who had been good. The kitchen was thrown open for the girls to make, under supervision, junk food like donuts, to eat during the movies. It was the only time during the entire week that the girls—the good ones—could even begin to let their hair down.

It was a big thing because you never got any sugar or sweets or junk food. So you got to eat as much as you wanted and watch those stupid cartoons or some stupid show like Lassie. *At first you thought it was pretty dumb. But after a while, you couldn't wait for Friday night and to be able to watch these stupid shows because it was a big thing to run around and act stupid and be yourself, without worrying, tippy-toeing and getting a demerit or getting in trouble.*

Fridays, even the guards relaxed—or so the girls believed.

Everyone wasn't paying attention and you were having fun.

You'd hide in a closet or something and wait for everyone to leave and then just take off.

I think that's how this one girl always got out—she could always get out, but she always got caught. One time she got caught at the airport. They brought her back and she'd get her licks and stay in lockup—she was there almost the whole time. I'll never forget her. She was bruised and bleeding and everything. But one time she got out and made it—she never came back.

Shelley discovered firsthand the risks of failing an escape attempt after one that she helped orchestrate was foiled.

We had stolen the key to the back door off of one of the guard's key rings—about six or seven of us were in on it—and were going to run down the road to where the uncle of one of the girls lived. But one of the girls freaked out. She got so afraid of what would happen if we got caught that she went down and told.

We didn't know that until after lights-out that night. One by one we heard each girl that was involved called down to the office. I was just sitting there in bed, knowing, Oh, God! they're going to call my name. You knew you were in trouble when you got called down.

Her name soon blared through the sleepy hall. Shelley got up, put on her robe and padded downstairs to the dorm mother's office. Mrs. Barrett waited sternly behind her desk, barrel-chested, long lick board in hand. Shelley saw the other girls, her co-conspirators, looking sheepish and standing stone straight against one wall of the bare-walled room. But on the other side of the office Shelley saw something she immediately thought was weird.

There were these guards, these men in the office. They worked at the place. And they were just sitting there watching us.

They watched as each girl was bent over Mrs. Barrett's desk and hit with the board.

We were beaten. I got eighteen licks while these men were laughing. They were laughing at us while we were crying and getting licked.

Then Shelley learned about lockup as she was led to a special room with no windows and no furniture except a toilet bowl and sink.

It's just a room with bright white walls, shiny white. Like a place to make you crazy. A mattress on the floor. You have no water, you don't get to bathe. People could be in there for seven days, fourteen days, no bathing, no brushing your teeth, nothing. You go to the bathroom and you can't flush it. You don't have any toilet paper. I mean, you are just there.

You'd be going by in the hall and everyone would be sticking their fingers out and screaming, laying there moaning. You could hear them at night crying and screaming, "Let me out of here! I'm going crazy!" and they bang on the walls. It would make you crazy to listen, especially if your room was next to lockup. And it stunk real bad in there because they didn't get to bathe either.

The person who worked there would open the door and slide the food tray in and shut it. And when you got out of there, you could hardly see because you had been in darkness for all this time. God! It's terrible.

Shelley had to stay only one day and a night in the white but black room. That was enough. She was smarter than some of the other girls. Afterward she thought about escaping plenty of times; even plotted it from time to time. But there was never an opportunity tempting enough to risk lockup again.

And after letting her out of lockup, they taught Shelley about confinement, a secondary stage of solitary.

You had to stay in your room. You couldn't speak until you were spoken to. You had to keep your head down, never look up, never look at anybody. And you had to memorize chapters of the Bible and recite them to get out. You had to recite it to someone who worked in the office and if they didn't think you should get off, then they'd give you more to memorize. You have to stand against the wall when everyone goes to eat. You have to wait until everyone else is finished eating and you are still standing. You could be in confinement for weeks.

Shelley remained ostracized for twenty teeth-gritting days. Added to the numbing daily routine was silence.

Shelley dressed for school without saying a word, donning the red and white checkered shirt and red skirt that was the Rebekah school uniform. She ate breakfast in the cafeteria with the other girls, but she wasn't permitted to speak. She then marched across the blacktop to the school building, in silence. Lunch in the school building was silent. She began to chafe at the isolation brought on by the failed escape attempt.

Shelley was cut off from the rest of the world. Instantly disconnected from friends. Part of her cried hard at the injustice of it. Part of her became hard and cold. This was prison, without warning, without excuse.

After nearly six months of captivity she had almost resigned herself to Rebekah when the letter from Michael arrived. She didn't often hear from her little brother—but was never sure that it wasn't because of the censor. Everything was fine, wrote Michael, who had celebrated his seventh birthday in August and thanked Shelley for sending a greeting card. Shelley smiled. But then quickly stopped. She couldn't believe it. Michael signed off, "Daddy misses you."

Shelley held the piece of paper in front of her for an instant, then crumpled it and hurled it against the wall of her room.

I went hysterical. I told the dorm parents. I wanted to know what was going on. I screamed at them. I started writing my mom letters and telling her I wanted to know what's going on. I had a right to know because, you know, I'm going to be coming back home to that and, you know, you're keeping things from me that I should know.

Shelley had no idea that all the adults working on her father and with her mother were also working toward that day when Bobby and Shelley would be reunited. Shelley was the only one who hadn't planned on living with her father again.

Not that anyone had told her. She had simply been left out of the picture, still barely able to contain her fury at being kidnapped and thrown unceremoniously into a prison, let alone understand approaches like "Daddy misses you." Shelley fully expected that Bobby would be out of her life until she was eighteen; that she would *never* live with him again.

The news was devastating. Those first weeks at the "home," she had begged to use the phone but of course got no more than the one monitored call a month. When she tried pleading with her mother to get her out, the phone simply went dead. *Buzzzzz.*

Shelley wrote Linda desperate letters describing the torments to which she had been condemned, but Linda never got them. It wouldn't have mattered anyway. From Linda, Shelley got back only the same tired missives about her religious experiences, her miraculous conversion and sunsets at the ranch.

"It seems like almost every home we've ever had always had a good view of the sunset," recalled Linda, "and we would run to the window every evening—it would be around dinnertime—and we'd just marvel at the sunset and talk about how different they were every evening.

"And I knew Shelley was feeling very alone and I could imagine the devastation she was feeling and it was just so that she would know that—just so I could touch her—I told her, 'Shelley, at night don't forget about the sunset because if you're looking at the sunset, you know that I'm at the window looking at that sunset and that's how close I am to you.' "

I would like write five letters asking the same questions. She would never answer anything that was important. She only wrote things that I could really care less about. When I'm in a place like that, I don't care about the sunset because, for one thing, I don't even see them and that's all she was trying, you know, she was trying to change the subject. She didn't want to answer anything that was important.

There were 300 girls packed into the home. A section for boys was located at the other end of the grounds, but there was no contact. Three girls to a room; in each, an intercom system. Ostensibly, the "speakers" were designed so that administrators could bark messages and orders to each girl in her room, but they were also listening devices; at any time, staff could tune in on conversations in any room.

The "school" was little more than a jail for young female juvenile delinquents, drug addicts, alcoholics, prostitutes and the suicide prone. Shelley didn't fit any of those categories, but there were a few girls there like her: unfortunates whose parents simply didn't want them around the house.

The regimented life-style was steeped in repetition and submission. Every day was the same. A bell rang at dawn. While the girls put on their uniforms, passages from the Bible were read over the intercom. In school, at study hall, each girl sat at a desk surrounded by six-foot-high wooden panels.

If a girl had a question for a teacher, she would wave a colored stick in the air and then place it in a hole on her desk. If the blue end was up, you needed to ask the teacher a question. If red was up, it meant you had a paper to be graded.

Their classes sounded like those at most high schools, but almost all instruction had a religious slant. History, for example, wasn't that of the founding fathers. Instead, biblical fathers like Abraham and Isaac were studied. Even math incorporated Christian themes and examples. Shelley had to attend a Bible class for an hour each day. Back in the dorm after school, she had to recite scripture for another hour. Then there was dinner, more Bible study, then church. By ten, it was lights-out.

The place might have been called a Bed & Bible.

Older, "good" girls were made "trustees" of the newer, younger, or "badder" girls. Trustees could—and were encouraged to—hand out demerits for violations of any of the countless rules. Not eating all your food earned a demerit. Talking in line warranted demerits. Ten demerits earned you ten licks, administered by the house parent, Mrs. Barrett. Hands on the table. Bend over. Mrs. Barrett brought her big wooden paddle snapping across the offender's bottom. If the paddle broke—over someone's backside—she replaced it with a rubber stick. Indestructible. Shelley was frequently at the receiving end of the paddle or the stick. And the licks were followed by four hours of solitary Bible reading while the other girls got to go watch a Three Stooges movie.

Everything I thought would happen, happened. My mom didn't stand behind me and I felt that I was paying for what he did.

Shelley kept hoping she would be rescued; if not by Ricky, at least by her mother, who had put her in. For months Shelley told herself that Linda simply didn't understand what this hell was really like, and if she found out, she'd be down quickly to take her away.

She tried everything to get word to the outside world—meaning her mother.

"Mom!" Shelley would yell into the phone those first few precious calls she had. "They are beating us—" Click. Buzzzzzz. "Get me out of here—" Click. *Buzzzzz.*

I mean, these parents were thinking, "Oh, this is a Christian place, dah, dah, dah." They didn't know.

When a friend was about to be released, Shelley sat her down and had her memorize her mom's phone number. "Call her," Shelley pleaded. "And tell her everything. Tell her what they do to us down here." Shelley knew the spin put on the school to people like her mother: "religious school for girls."

I was hoping she would realize it was just a front and it really wasn't like you hear it is and that she would come and get me.

It didn't work. And Shelley languished, disobeying, earning demerits, getting licks and dreaming of rescue—until one day Mrs. Barrett's husband, Brother Barrett, told her sternly, "Until you accept the fact that your dad will be back at your house, you won't get out of here."

Something clicked. Not an acceptance of the fact that she would have to live in the same house as Bobby, but the realization that, even here, she had some control over her destiny.

I started watching all the girls that never got in trouble. And I started having regular talks with Brother Barrett, trying to figure him out and what I needed to do to get home.

Shelley decided the way out was to fake it. Almost overnight she became a good girl. She changed the tone of her letters home. She even gathered together a group of girls who met every day to help her compose her letters.

Every day at school, usually in p.e. class, me and some friends would sit around and think of the perfect letter home. We got to write one letter a week. So we made this letter just so good—quotes from the Bible and everything. And the six or seven of us would think up bits and pieces all week, then all write home the same letter.

Shelley soon became a trustee.

I acted so Christ-like. It was what they wanted to hear, so I told them. I made up my mind, no matter what, I knew I was going to get out.

And Linda believed Shelley was finally getting religion: she missed home and was learning a lot at Rebekah; she appreciated the Bible study classes and even the discipline.

"Oh, Shelley," came the replies, "you're doing so good."

Then at Thanksgiving dinner the dorm parent called me up in front of the cafeteria and told the girls to thank me because my dad had sent all the money for our Thanksgiving dinner and I just went crazy.

To Shelley, there could be nothing more despicable than this—the man who had abused her being praised to her face. She was not making the fine distinctions that others on the outside apparently were. Somehow, because he was her father, she was expected to forgive him, forget what he'd done to her, then move back in with him.

She screamed at Brother Barrett: "What do you mean, he provided this? He can't do that! He's supposed to be locked up. No phone. He can't do anything. He can't maneuver from where he's at." Shelley knew immediately what was up.

Emotionally, she could hold none of those pseudo-religious tenets about the sanctity of the family at all costs. Michael's "Daddy misses you" letter had been the icing on the cake.

Intellectually, however, she recognized what had to be done to escape. And she again steeled herself to the task of pretending to forgive and forget. She wrote her mother, politely asking that Bobby write her—she had to verify what she suspected: that he had been released from Timberlawn.

They told me he would be there for two years and that he would not be out until I was eighteen and then if he got out before then, that he would be sent to another place, so I would be away from him totally.

Shelley was away from him, all right. This isn't what she had in mind, however. She now realized how completely the tables had been turned. But she also realized that there were only two ways out of Rebekah: turn eighteen or turn good. Linda never answered Shelley's question about Bobby. She never wrote about *anything* that Shelley really cared about—only what she cared about.

Finally I wrote my mom and said I forgave him and wanted everything to be like a regular family again; and just have him write me.

Shelley gritted her teeth and wrote, "Dear Dad. . . ." She gushed all over the letter, welcoming him home.

It worked. Bobby replied. And to make sure that he was actually home, she wrote to ask that Bobby get on the phone during the next month's phone call. A week later, the intercom order squawked through the speaker box. "Shelley, phone call!"

She ran to the office and leaped at the receiver. Linda was on the line, more syrupy than usual. "Someone wants to talk to you," she finally blurted. Shelley gripped the phone hard as she heard the familiar voice. It shook her, but she held her composure.

I talked and was just as sweet and lovely as could be. I love y'all and I'm sorry about everything and I forgive you. Everything's going to be just fine when I get home.

And within a few weeks, Shelley had a new pen pal. She grimaced every time she read one of his letters, hearing him talk about building trust and starting a new family.

I started writing him and trying to play the game that he'd played with me. I decided that if that's the only way I'm going to get out, then I'm going to tell them whatever they want to hear. So I just made it up. And I got good at it.

Since Bobby believed in his own miraculous change of heart, he believed in Shelley's as well.

"She wrote and said that things had changed," he recalled. "She had got her life right with the Lord. She loved me. Several letters like that."

It was wonderful news.

Bobby had been out of Timberlawn barely a month when James Duvall leveled the charge. After what he had seen of Bobby during those last months of deception the previous May and June, James wasn't going to stay silent again.

"The rumor has it that you're trying to put the make on

Michelle," said James. "You need to come talk to me, Bob." Shelley's nineteen-year-old cousin, Michelle, had complained.

When confronted with the charges, Bobby denied them. No such thing, he told James. "She was working for me in the office. She told me that she was real tight and her shoulders hurt. She was real tense."

And she was, according to Bobby, completely wrong about what had happened. Returning to the ranch, Bobby found Michelle getting in her car to leave.

"Do we have a problem?" he asked her.

"No, we don't."

"I understand that you think I'm trying to put the make on you."

"I don't know where that came from," Michelle said evasively.

"It came from your mother," Bobby said, so sure of himself.

He marched Michelle straight in to the office where her mother, Sandra, was waiting.

Bobby went over everything for Sandra—the charge by James, his surprise and Michelle's denial. It had all seemed so simple and straightforward. And Sandra was confused. Bobby seemed to have completely unraveled Michelle's story. "Michelle, that's what you've been saying," Sandra almost pleaded with her daughter. Michelle just looked away.

"Look. If there's been a misunderstanding," Bobby continued, "I'm sorry. It was a gross mistake in judgment on my part."

"Forget it," said Michelle.

Bobby did forget it. And he gradually covered over most of what had happened as he reintegrated himself into the community and went back to his ranch work.

He tried to get Richard Ruiz, whom he had fired in a fit of pique in the months leading up to his unveiling as a sex abuser, to be ranch manager again.

"Every time he called he would offer a little bit more money," Ruiz recalled. "He had once loaned me $12,000 and I was paying him back. Every time I would go and make a payment to him he'd offer me something to come back."

And Bobby also talked about what had happened. "He confessed it all," said Ruiz. "But he always left the impression that it wasn't all his fault. And that's what I told him. I said I don't give a flying hoot what the circumstances were. What you done was wrong. But he always left that impression—like it wasn't all his fault."

Just after Christmas, more than six months after being taken away, Shelley saw her new strategy pay off—she was allowed her first visit from home. Bobby, Linda and Michael drove to Corpus Christi. And they were so excited about Shelley's change of heart that they brought Sarah Conn along with them. Bobby rented three hotel rooms for two days and two nights.

They arrived on a Thursday evening and went right to church at Rebekah. After the service Bobby hung back among the other worshipers as Linda rushed up to Shelley and hugged her. It had been a long time: the last time mother and daughter had seen each other was the day Linda had turned her back on Shelley the day she was admitted to Rebekah. Shelley held back her feelings as she gurgled her cajolery. When she noticed Bobby standing off to the side, she seemed not to hesitate in running up and hugging him as well. Bobby wept.

"Forgive me, Shelley, forgive me," he bawled.

The next morning the family picked up Shelley at the home and took her to the hotel: she had been given a three-day pass for their visit. But they hadn't been in the room for more than minutes before an argument between Shelley and Linda broke out when Linda told her daughter she wouldn't be going home on this visit.

Shelley had miscalculated the effectiveness of her *nice* campaign. And when Bobby tried to intercede for Linda, Shelley turned on him as well. She couldn't hide it any longer: "How dare you come down here after what you did to me!"

"You're right, Shelley," Bobby answered. "You're right. All the things that you can think about me and all the things you can say are absolutely true. I have been all those things and worse. But God can forgive. And God can change our lives."

Shelley rejected this. How dare he visit her when he was supposed to be locked up? How dare he tell her *she* had to stay locked up?

But he could and he did. Bobby and Linda promptly returned Shelley to Rebekah. Her three days of freedom had been reduced to one.

"I repeatedly cautioned him that his neurotic obsessive interest in making everything right with Shelley, getting her forgiveness, helping a very disturbed young lady straighten her life out could be harmful to him," recalled Byron Howard. "My concern was that he could pursue a helpful relationship with her and get himself hurt. I did not think that was good for her or for him."

In Kerens, the months had dragged slowly on for Cherry Layfield, who was waging a lone and lonely battle to get Shelley out of Rebekah. She found herself all but hog-tied, but knew what Rebekah was like. "I just cried—I cried more than I ever had in my life," she recalled.

She asked Melanie Hyder at the juvenile probation office to find out if there was anything that could be done. "She told me I was worrying about something I didn't need to worry about," recalled Cherry. "She said, 'Shelley is a survivor. She did survive and she will.' "

Hyder was right. Shelley had figured out something about Rebekah—that it responded to her behavior, not to her being. She began to write again. She and Bobby again corresponded frequently, at least every week. And now Linda was writing Shelley.

After the outburst at the six-month visit, Shelley immediately calmed down and determined to make things work.

Once again her letters were filled with flummery. And on the ranch Bobby and Linda soaked it up. "Linda and I were praying that the Lord's will be done in Shelley's life and our lives," recalled Bobby.

I was in a prison. I did not understand why I was there. I hadn't done anything wrong. And I wanted out.

When the family went back in April for another visit, they found Shelley perfect. "It was really funny," Bobby remembered, "because Linda and I had been praying. I had been wanting to get Shelley home and get her into one-on-one counseling and, of course, we knew that Shelley wanted to come home. All of her letters said she wanted to come home."

Why he didn't, as her father and still legal guardian, just remove her, he explained this way: "I just wasn't in a position to say, 'bring Shelley home,' because I really felt it was Linda's decision. She had put her down there." Bobby, so powerful and manipulative in all other things, now claimed impotence, yet another masking of true motives.

But Shelley too had learned a lesson about the dynamic of mental illness. And at the nine-month visit, she confused everyone: she didn't even ask to come home.

I was just as happy and content as could be. I didn't ask to come home. Acted like I was in lala land and loved it here. Everything was just fine. And they were freaking out. I didn't beg and they thought I was perfect and wonderful.

She wasn't coming home. She didn't want to come home. And it worked.

"We really just seemed to be doing super," Bobby recalled. "So Linda and I had been praying, and we finally went to our pastor and said, 'We feel the time is right. We need to bring Shelley home. . . .' So we called Roloff's and they said no. 'It's not the time. You need to leave her another month and a half or so.' We just said no. 'We feel like the time is right to bring Shelley home.' So we went down June 14 to get her and bring her back home."

Shelley's conforming strategy had worked. It took eleven months, but finally the word came over the intercom in her bedroom. "Shelley," the voice crackled, "you will be going home. Your parents will be here to pick you up on Saturday."

BACK HOME

The big ranch house felt different to Shelley now. Not that she had so many agreeable memories of living there. But *she* was different. One year is a long time—especially when spent with strangers, under duress. She had brand-new memories of old and ragged scars.

She was home because above all else she had wanted to escape Rebekah. But now that she was out, she wanted nothing to do with the home of Bobby Sessions. She knew that from the first day of her freedom. On June 14, 1984, she had walked out of Rebekah—no tears—and climbed into the family Winnebago. Her mom, her brother and her dad were inside it. They drove off. Freedom. It felt almost like bliss. Until she remembered the pain.

Saturday, over the intercom I heard, "Shelley Sessions, you have a phone call," and I went running. I knew what it was. So I picked up the phone and my mom said, "We're leaving Corsicana," and I just went screaming. I couldn't wait for them to get there. I mean, it was the best day of my life getting out of this place.

Despite Bobby at the wheel, only a minor inconvenience at this point, Shelley reveled in seeing the pavement and the white roadlines roll by once again.

And that reminded her of her pickup. She asked Linda how it was. "I can't wait to get back in that. I bet it sure has missed me."

Linda glanced furtively toward Bobby, then back to Shelley. "There won't be any pickup, Shelley. Luther has your truck."

Shelley threw a brief fit, then changed the subject and asked about her friends. "I sure missed all of them."

"Well, Shelley, you're not going to have those friends anymore," said Linda. "We have new friends for you. You will like them. They are Christians."

That almost started it again. Shelley didn't want a new set of friends, especially so-called Christian ones. It was under the influence of Christians that she'd been sent to the Rebekah Home. Then Linda announced that Shelley would be going to a private boarding school, not back to Kerens High. If Shelley had learned anything at Rebekah, it was to withhold her feelings. She climbed into the rear of the Winnebago, lay down on the cot.

The next thing she knew, the RV was slowing down and Bobby was wheeling it off the side of the road. "Let's pray," he said. Shelley knew that her mom had been in the Christians' thrall, but never her dad. This turn of events was news to her.

Bobby and Linda had been cultivating their church ties, especially with the Beacon Light Christian Center in Corsicana, where the two went at least once a week. This was a church where special congregants spoke in tongues, a sign of salvation, and God healed cancers and other diseases through the laying on of hands.

Bobby was healed there. Now Shelley needed healing. In the back of the Winnebago, on the side of the interstate, Bobby, Linda and Michael put their hands out over Shelley. At first she resisted, but then thought better of it; they were still too close to Corpus Christi and the Rebekah Home for Girls.

I was laying there with my head pointing backwards. And they kneeled down, laid their hands on my head and prayed that the devil would come out of me and all this stupid stuff.

I just lay there and didn't say nothing. I was mad. I thought, I cannot believe this. *And a little later my mom started telling me how it's going to be different when I come home. I wouldn't be allowed to wear shorts anymore—I mean, like I was making him do this because I wore shorts! There would be no more bathing—if I wanted to go swimming I had to wear a one piece. And I had to wear a T-shirt over it.*

It was like they wanted me to wear a paper bag. She just didn't understand that it wasn't what I wore—it wasn't what I had on that made him sick. That didn't matter. But to hear her, it was my fault because I wore shorts. I just thought, "Oh, my God, I'm not believing this."

There was no such thing as freedom, Shelley thought. Out of Rebekah less than two hours and she was already being given the rules.

That night at the ranch, Bobby invited the relatives over to welcome Shelley back. At first Shelley bristled, but at the same time she didn't mind seeing her family. The next day her mother took her shopping for new clothes in Corsicana—and a girl from Kerens saw Shelley, welcomed her back. And the phone didn't stop ringing. Linda and Bobby reminded Shelley that she would have new friends now; that she was going to a new school; that she wouldn't be seeing her old friends. The crackdown, now in the name of Jesus, had begun.

Shelley noticed that her dad had repainted his construction company trucks. The eighteen-wheelers and giant gravel trailers had large, bold letters on their sides: PRAISE THE LORD!

He just wanted everyone to know that he was changed. It would have been fine if he was real about it. I wouldn't knock it, but when you know the person doesn't even believe what he's saying—It was phony. Anyone could see that. A child of God is supposed to be Christ-like. Well, he's not Christ-like.

It was the second night that set Shelley off. Bobby and Linda still wouldn't let her see Ricky or any of her friends. Instead, she walked into a houseful of strangers welcoming her home.

"All the youths in our church had asked if they could throw a welcome-home party for Shelley," Bobby remembered. "We thought that was really super because I know how I felt when I came home. I thought, 'Well, nobody is going to speak to me. Everybody is going to shun me, and it's going to be pretty lonely for a while.' "

But Shelley didn't feel the same guilt and shame that Bobby did, for Bobby no longer controlled her feelings about herself. She didn't worry about her friends adjusting to her—she just wanted to see them as soon as possible. But Bobby and Linda didn't grasp that fact.

"Of course, she didn't know any of them," Bobby later admitted, "but we thought it was awfully nice."

It was control time again.

I walk in and all their church friends are in our swimming pool, acting like it's a resort. And I was just going, "What are these people doing here?" I didn't know any of them I just got back from being locked up for a year and all these people are here and I don't even know them. I just wanted to be with my friends and my family and not with the whole world.

I watched these girls go up to my room. And they said, "Hello, I am so and so and I am just going up to your room." You know, I just got back from being locked up and they say, "How was that school that you went to? I heard that it was really nice." And then they start to ask me all about it.

And I said, "I didn't ask to be sent to this private school. It wasn't a private school—it was a prison." And then me and these girls got into a scrap and I kicked them out of my room.

A few hours later, the whole family was in bed and the lights off when Ricky Layfield came trotting quickly and quietly up the dark driveway. "They wasn't going to let me find out she was back," Ricky said later. "So me and my black buddy, he's real fast and I'm pretty fast too. He's crazy, he'll do anything. So I had another buddy drop us off out there by the railroad tracks and we jogged up there to see if we can talk to her, see her. I think her light was the only one that was on in the house."

Ricky's plan was to reach the corner of the house and shimmy up a drainpipe on the brick wall and reach Shelley's window. But the two teens didn't make it.

"We run right in the gate and we're running the concrete driveway—it's real long. We're running together when all of a sudden the front door opens. Whoop. We hit the deck. And I'm real close to the house. It's Bobby. He steps out in his little old shorts. And he has a gun in his hand. I wasn't no piece from him. And he turns on the light goes around the house. And my buddy—all you can hear is his footsteps. Tickatickatickatick. Going the other way. Shoot, I'm running too. We hit that cotton-field and it's just tearing us up. We didn't wait around for noth-ing, boy. We knew he was crazy."

But the word was spreading that Shelley was home; the Sessions phone was suddenly ringing constantly. Shelley was allowed to talk to her old friends only by phone—not see them. She told them how creepy it was—back in the same bedroom, unable to sleep, knowing he was just down the hall. Ricky offered her a place to stay if she needed one.

And the day after the welcome-home party given by the church youth, Shelley was at the pool with her mom, asking if she could go visit friends. She had had enough. Three days back; she should be able to see her friends. When Bobby arrived, Linda turned to him. "Bob, Shelley would like to go visit some friends. Is that okay?"

Even as she heard the question, Shelley flinched. It seemed absurd now for her to ask him for permission to do *anything*. It was only *as if* Bobby had authority. Shelley *felt* he had forfeited all rights over her.

"I don't think so, Shelley," Bobby began. "You have to build up your trust again. And I have to learn how to trust you." He had written Shelley the same kinds of things while she was in Rebekah. The smug assumption was always there: Shelley would come home, take her place there as an obedient child. That that possibility had been forever shattered—and by his own nefarious acts—did not occur to Bobby. "I had explained to her that I had understood there was going to be some time needed for a recon-ciliation and for trust to be earned," Bobby recalled later. "I knew not only would I have to earn her trust, but she would have to earn ours. There wouldn't be a lot of privileges, and that we were trying to walk one road. With God's help we could make it."

Shelley had laughed bitterly when she read those letters—why should there be "one road"? Now she knew what it meant. And she almost reeled with anger as Bobby tried to reassert his authority. She looked at Linda, who was watching, not comprehending.

Bobby pushed on. "What would you do if I was to come down to your bedroom? You have to learn to trust me."

Shelley gave Bobby a look that could have knocked him into the pool. "I'm leaving! Before it happens all over again!" Eight years of sexual assault could not be erased by a simple lecture, especially one that sounded like a veiled threat that he would do it again. As far as Shelley was concerned, Bobby had forfeited his parental rights.

But Bobby didn't see it that way. "I tried to tell her that she couldn't leave without my blessings," he later asserted, "and as her father I was telling her that she couldn't leave. If she did leave, she was not only leaving from under my authority but from under God's. Because that's what the Bible tells us. She needed to stay home. . . . I knew I couldn't physically force her to stay home because I was still on probation. I knew that if I used force it was very possible that it could be used against me and I might have to go to jail."

Shelley stormed back into the house and called Ricky. "Come and get me. I'll be ready in a few hours."

But Ricky by now had become as wary as Shelley. "No," he said. "I'll come right now. Before they get it in their heads to send you somewhere else."

Shelley threw some clothes in a bag, called another friend, then went to the front door. In less than twenty minutes a car pulled up. Inside were two of Ricky's high school friends—but no Ricky. Shelley started for the car, but before she reached it, she heard one of the boys scream to the other, "No way, man!" The car lurched forward.

"Hey, come back!" Shelley screamed. The car stopped again. But then she saw what had frightened them.

Bobby was sitting in the front seat of his pickup truck, cleaning a shotgun. "You realize that you are taking a minor away from her home without her parents' consent?" he shouted at the boys in the car.

Bobby had called his pastor while Shelley packed, and the

pastor had told him to "run your bluff." That meant, in Bobby's mind, that he should forbid Shelley to leave. "Just let Shelley know very certainly that you know that this is wrong and that she can't leave and that there's consequences that she will have to pay if she does leave," the pastor urged. Bobby added his own twist to the "bluff": the shotgun.

Shelley called the bluff. "Don't worry," she laughed. "He won't do anything." One of the boys threw open the door and motioned frantically for Shelley to hurry.

"You're going to pay for this!" Bobby screamed at them. "You're helping a minor run away from home!"

Shelley threw her bag into the car and jumped in. The tires spat rubber and gravel for fifty feet as the teenagers sped away, the boys expecting a shotgun blast to end their adventure at any moment.

As the car whirled around the first bend, Shelley saw a figure crawling out from behind a shrub, waving. The driver slammed on the brakes and skidded almost past the youth. But he was already lying flat across the backseat before it had stopped. "Yeeee-haaaah!" they all hooted, speeding off in a cloud of dust.

Ricky directed his friends toward Trinidad, ten straight miles east on Route 31. He explained to Shelley that his parents had a small trailer house on the lake there and that she could hide out in it for a while. But when the group arrived, Cherry and Joey Ray Layfield were already there.

Cherry looked somber. She had taken off from work and driven to Trinidad, meeting Shelley and the boys at the trailer. And she was shaking her head dubiously even as Shelley got out of the car—"This isn't gonna work. Bobby and Linda know about this place. They'll be down here soon as you can blink and have it surrounded." Cherry had already heard from the mother of one of the boys in the car. The outraged woman quickly reminded Cherry that not everyone in town sympathized with Shelley Sessions. "She said, 'You go over there and get that girl and take her back home,'" recalled Cherry. "Boy, was she mad."

"Ricky, you get Shelley out of here," the woman told her son.

"Take her up to Mary's right now. Take the back roads. There ain't no telling what Bobby's going to do."

That was the lesson learned by the Layfields during the last hideaway battle with Bobby. Mary was Cherry's eldest daughter, and Midlothian was, even on good roads, an eighty-mile drive north and west.

Shelley hid out with Mary, rarely leaving the house, until she found out that she had relatives in the town—and that they knew about her. So she fled to another Layfield household—to preacher Bubba's house at the Missionary Baptist Seminary in Jacksonville, a hundred miles back east.

A week later, after everyone at Bubba's had gone to bed, Ricky appeared at the door. "You're leaving," he said.

"Where to?" asked Shelley.

"To my house."

"Is it okay with your parents?"

"Don't worry about it."

So Shelley was on the lam again. She arrived in the dark of night at Layfield headquarters. And in this tiny two-bedroom house Shelley spent the next six months.

"She almost never went out," recalled Cherry. "And when she did, we had her wear a hat and scarf over her head and lay down on the floorboard, covered with a blanket."

And she carried a pistol. Ricky had borrowed it from a friend and shown her how to use it and it went everywhere with Shelley, even in the house.

If I went to take a bath, I took it and laid it on the side of the tub. If I was watching TV, I carried it. If I went in to fix a sandwich, I took it with me. And I knew how to shoot. I was ready.

I asked a neighbor what would happen if Bobby came over here and I shot him. And he said he had to be inside the house. And I said, "What if he wasn't?" He said, "If I were you, I'd drag him in."

Most of the time Shelley stayed indoors, in the living room. During the day she was there by herself. Since the Circle S had a construction job not far away, the Layfields worried that Bobby might use it as a cover to come over. Joey Ray Layfield carried a loaded shotgun to work with him every day—just in case.

"You cannot know what insane people will do," reasoned Cherry Layfield. "When he shot himself—that's the stunt of somebody whose mind's not right. And Joe Ray told us that if he'll shoot himself, he'll shoot anybody."

The Layfields were one of the few families in town who weren't afraid of Bobby. They were as poor as he was rich, but it didn't mean the same to them. "We knew we were never going to have anything," Cherry explained later. "There wasn't any way that Bobby could buy us off. He probably would have tried if he thought he could have. But he grew up knowing Joey Ray and he knew he won't do nothing dishonest. And you don't push him."

Joey Ray was a big, ruddy-faced man with hands the size of a steer and the strength of rawhide. But his voice was soft as spring—he had the air of a wise and kind man who could melt the muzzle of a gun with his stare.

He was just like a dad to me. If I did something in the house he didn't like, he'd sit me down there at the table and say, "Now, Shelley—" and say whatever he had to say. I mean, for the first time in my life somebody was telling me what to do that was saying it right, without screaming and whipping me and grounding me.

Joey Ray took Shelley fishing and hunting and taught her how to cook dove and quail. Cherry taught Shelley how to shop without a credit card.

In the house, Shelley was constantly vigilant. Scared to death.

I carried that gun at all times. I just knew that a hit man was after me.

Any noise, a car moving up the driveway, and she and her pistol would be in the closet in the back bedroom. She wouldn't answer the door. They developed a phone code so Shelley would know when to answer. Even when the Layfields had friends over, Shelley stayed out of sight, sitting for hours on the bench Ricky made for her in the back closet. No one knew she was there. All of her belongings were stored in the closet, so that no one wandering through the house would see any sign of her. Ricky and the

Layfields even spread rumors about Shelley's whereabouts. One week it was a story about her running off to California. Another time, Shelley had gone to live with a girl she met at Rebekah.

No one really knew where I was. I had rumors spread around that I was living in the Panhandle. I was in El Paso. I was in Houston. So nobody knew exactly where I was.

Bobby never tried anything, but Shelley and the Layfields never stopped worrying about him. No one believed for a moment that he had been cured at Timberlawn in just six months. And no one doubted that he would come looking for Shelley.

"Whenever it got dark, I was conscious of my surroundings," remembered Ricky. "I was scared of that man the whole time."

One of the advantages of Shelley's enforced domesticity was that the Layfields got their house cleaned and Shelley learned how to cook.

"She was very industrious," said Cherry. "She cleaned house, washed dishes, cooked—and burned her hands."

That was a big joke around here because I would always grab the hot pot or pan.

Shelley loved her stay at the Layfields'. And fell in love with Ricky at the same time. But by September everyone was getting cabin fever. Ricky was starting school. Shelley was becoming stir crazy. She wanted to get out; anything.

So Ricky would pull up the family car almost onto the porch of the house, Shelley would dash in, duck down, and they would go for a drive.

Shelley went to her first football game of the season disguised. She sat in the stands, close to the Layfields, not moving far.

In the meantime, Cherry desperately sought a way to keep Shelley out of Bobby's clutches. "We called everybody," she said later. "Oh God, we called everybody in the state of Texas trying to get custody of her, legal custody. And we were told that because she was seventeen years old he could come get her anytime he wanted to—even after what he did. He had the laws in his pocket."

He had the people of Kerens back in his pocket as well.

Bobby had resumed his life in Kerens and Powell as if he had never left. And people would still say, "Well, maybe she deserved it."

"A lot of people were saying, you know, that she might have been wanting it," Ricky later stated. "But I don't think so. Because, you know, why would she want something like Bobby when she could have anybody, her pick? I don't know, but I think she was just terrified. That's my guess. He just had her brainwashed, terrified."

Bobby didn't hear from Shelley until a little after Thanksgiving that year—five months after she had left home. She called Linda to ask for money for the dentist, to get a cap for her tooth. Shelley was evasive about why she needed a cap. And Linda put Bobby on another phone so he could listen in on the conversation. But it didn't go far.

"We were more concerned with Shelley's spiritual well-being and the fact that she could lead a normal life," Bobby recounted later, "than we were about whether or not she got a cap put back on her teeth so she could look pretty."

Bobby couldn't let go. Saying he only wanted to help Shelley, his aid came with more strings than a foreign-aid package to Israel.

"I should have known better than to call you," said Shelley in disgust, and hung up.

A couple of weeks later Shelley came to the ranch with a deputy sheriff and a court order. Bobby had seen a police cruiser and a van moving up the front drive from his office. By the time he got to his house, a deputy sheriff, George Scott, was already coming out the front door.

"Sorry, Bobby," said Scott, "I've got some bad news."

At the same time Cherry Layfield came through the door carrying a cardboard box.

"What's going on here?" Bobby demanded angrily.

"We're here with a court order," said Scott, "to get some clothes for Shelley." The document ordered Bobby to allow Shelley to pick up her clothes.

"That's okay," Bobby murmured. "But to tell you the truth,

I'd really rather Shelley get what she wants and nobody else be in the house."

Scott asked Cherry to wait outside, then followed Bobby into the house. They climbed the wide steps and found Shelley in her bedroom, throwing clothes, lots of them, into more boxes.

"Why did you have to do it this way?" Bobby asked.

"I didn't think you'd give 'em to me any other way." She didn't admit out loud to Bobby that she was afraid he would hurt her if she didn't bring along police protection.

Bobby would later claim that, coincidentally, he had "just got through talking with our pastor about what to do if Shelley called us needing clothes or anything else. He had counseled us that if Shelley called us and wanted clothes, to give her the clothes that were at the house. You know, we can't wear Shelley's clothes. We have no need for them and to give them to her. But Shelley didn't ask us. She came with a court order."

"Let us help you," Bobby said to her.

She looked directly at her father and stopped what she was doing. "I don't want any help and I don't need any help, especially not from y'all."

One of the unexpected results of life on the lam for Shelley was the considerable change in life-style it demanded. The Layfields were such a refreshing breath of kindness that Shelley didn't mind her tiny quarters. Even the hours hidden in the small closet off the kitchen, pistol cocked and readied, were bearable. It was much better than the lockup at Rebekah.

It didn't matter, because I was free. It was my choice to go in the closet.

And the most interesting change came with the absence of money. Accustomed to having whatever she wanted, Shelley now had to get used to price-shopping—or not shopping at all. "She didn't know how to shop," recalled Cherry. "She just went in and jerked stuff down. I want this and this and she never looked at prices."

Cherry and Joey Ray split their expenditures in thirds; for Ricky, his sister Shawna and Shelley.

But Shelley realized that she didn't even have money for a Christmas present for her brother. She went pecan picking, rounding up dollars by the day. Not many of them: a tall sack would sell for $25 and take a day to pick; enough to buy her brother a nice present.

When Shelley called the ranch the day before Christmas to ask Michael if he'd received the present yet, he said no. Shelley hadn't seen her eight-year-old brother very often since she left the house. When she had come back under a protective custody order of the court to pick up her clothes, Bobby had told her she would never be allowed to see Michael again. But Shelley sneaked over to the house on several occasions to visit her brother.

"Maybe it got held up in the mail," Michael now offered about Shelley's present.

"No," said Shelley. "I gave it to Grandma. Why don't you ask Mom where it's at?"

A few moments later Linda came on the line. "I'm not going to give him the present, Shelley," she said, "because anything that has anything to do with you he clings to. I don't want him upset."

At the Layfields', meanwhile, Shelley was made part of the family for Christmas. The three children got the same things.

But Shelley's life didn't seem to get any easier. And in so many ways the threats of her father were always coming true, causing her more pain.

I have nightmares that come, just him—I can just see him, and I'm running from him and he's following me and having people following me. I had them in Corpus Christi. I can't watch things on TV or things on the news about anything similar. And just certain things that somebody might say that I have heard him say or just anything. I have flashbacks of things that happened or if somebody mentions something, I can see him doing something to me. Or if I see someone wearing something that he used to wear, certain boots—or just someone's attitude.

Shelley's friends were pressing her to do something to take this load off her. How much longer could she run from her father?

One of Ricky's relatives offered to take care of Bobby permanently.

*He came up to me one day and said, "You know, if you want
me to, I'll go over there and kill him for you." He was serious. I
mean, I had some people who were against me; but other people
said we ought to hang him by his you know what.*

Shelley had too clear a head for that. She had been trying to figure
out a strategy ever since learning, while at Rebekah, that Bobby
had gotten out of Timberlawn. Now she was finding she had the
support of other clear heads as well. Cherry Layfield, especially,
urged Shelley to take legal action.

"What should I do?" Shelley asked.

"I don't know, Shelley," Cherry told her, "but you should go
talk to some attorney and find out if there is anything you can do
to get that Bobby put behind bars."

Shelley went to the district attorney's office and spoke with an
assistant DA.

*When he was convicted, I wasn't even present. I didn't get to
testify or nothing. They all did it without my even knowing it. I had
no say. They just did it.*

Shelley explained her frustration: she was sent away while the
man who had committed the crime was free and living just the
way he had lived before. It wasn't fair. But the attorney now said
she couldn't send Bobby to jail because he had already pleaded
guilty to the crime. The only alternative, the prosecutor suggested, was a civil action. She wasn't at all sure that there was any
legal merit to such an action, but she gave Shelley the name of
a law firm in Waco, not too far away.

Rod Squires couldn't believe the story the two women were spool-
ing out for him. The young Waco attorney listened to Cherry
Layfield and Shelley recount the tale of incest, thinking it was the
most bizarre case he'd encountered. Cherry assured Squires that
there was documentation for all of it.

Squires, who had formed his civil-litigation firm with two other
young partners just a few years before, asked Shelley how much
she would like to sue for.

"Ten million!" Cherry blurted out.

"Are you nuts?" Squires asked with a smile.

But at the end of an hour, the attorney promised he'd study it and get back to them. That was the middle of January 1985.

On their return drive, Shelley told Cherry that perhaps it wasn't worth it. She didn't want the money.

"Shelley, you need to do this," Cherry said. "You have to hit him in the pocketbook, because that's the only way you are going to make him pay for what he did. He hasn't paid. He's never spent a night in jail. His wife never said a cross word about what he did."

The pressure of months of close living at the Layfields' and constant worry about Bobby were beginning to take their toll on Ricky and Shelley. The house was so small that Ricky, Shawna and Shelley had all been sleeping in one bedroom—separate beds, the same room. Ricky's temper seemed to be growing shorter.

He couldn't handle all of this. He didn't know how to take it. At the very beginning he was so hurt that I didn't come and tell him what was going on. And that started to come out.

He'd always say, "You told Jackie, why didn't you tell me?" Well, how do you tell your boyfriend, you know? And he couldn't understand why I stayed down at Rebekah for a year. "Didn't you love me?" I mean, there was a lot of hurt and confusion. It was a hard thing for everybody involved.

He began to get very violent with me. I had teeth knocked out.

The Layfield house had gotten too small for that kind of tension. Ricky told Shelley she wasn't taking enough precautions. "This man's a maniac," he said. "He shot himself, and he'd definitely shoot you or me or anybody in my family. You're putting our whole family in jeopardy 'cause you take the notion to go to the store."

Shelley remained very closemouthed about what had happened with Bobby. She still had told no one the details. And she didn't understand why that riled Ricky so much.

It's hard to be out in public because it's a small community and everybody knows everything. But then nobody really knows what I went through. I am all by myself.

Ricky tried to understand, but he couldn't. And Shelley would do careless things like getting out of the car when she was uptown, and "I'd get mad. I'd just go off the hammer."

Ricky and Shelley's fights grew more and more frequent and bitter. Neither teenager knew exactly why; though Cherry guessed that it was too hard living so close. Ricky called her bad names.

"Bobby made you a slut!" he shouted. And another of her dad's predictions became reality. Shelley, exasperated, would storm out of the house. Ricky would go find her, usually at her Aunt Betty's, and apologize. Betty once got on Ricky's case, calling him "white trash," "no good."

"I knew I wasn't no good for what I did," Ricky later explained, "but then she told me, 'You're no better than Bobby Sessions.' Oh, man! That would have been it. Somebody would have got killed because I sprung up."

"If you lay one hand on me or Shelley," Betty said, "James will kill you in the worst way."

"Lady," Ricky glowered, "you call me Bobby Sessions again and that's going to have to happen."

Shelley was watching from a safe distance across the room. "No, Ricky," she finally said. "Just calm down. *Calm down.*"

"I ain't molested nobody," Ricky persisted. "Don't come with that. You know that's wrong."

But Betty, a temper to match her red hair, stood her ground. "She had hate in her eyes," Ricky remembered, "and that just crawled up and down me. And that's one of the reasons I said, 'Forget it.' It's a losing battle. Like what they call pissin' in the wind."

So Shelley went home with Ricky. But the fighting continued. "We got into one fight," Ricky recalled, "and I got ahold of Shelley right around her neck, and my mom picked up my bench-press bar and throwed it at me. I kind of blocked it and sent it into the wall. Knocked a hole in it.

"And Shelley come at me and I put up a front kick and hit her in the chest, flounced her on the bed and then I booked. Then she booked."

That was what convinced Shelley to move out. And in February she packed up and moved. "One day I come in and she was gone and that was it," recalled Ricky. "My dad told me, 'That's it, boy. I don't want to have you throwing them fits no more. That's it now. If it's meant, she'll be back; if it isn't, she won't.' And she didn't come back, so I knew I had done messed up."

Betty, the only member of the immediate family who was friendly to Shelley, offered her a room.

Shelley now tried to settle down. Since she hadn't had a chance to finish high school, she took a correspondence course from Texas Tech, which didn't work. Then she attended classes at Navarro College, took a series of tests and received her high school diploma.

But she didn't seem to have any more friends.

They don't know what to say to me or how to act. And they have questions, but they don't know what to say. They don't want to hurt me and we just—I used to have a lot of close friends and I don't— all I ever do now is have acquaintances that I say hi to. I don't have any friends. I don't have a family life. All I have is my Aunt Bea and my Uncle James. Everybody else has turned to him because of his power.

Shelley didn't really want to leave, but there was no choice. She still loved Cherry and Joey Ray. But Ricky would have killed her had she stayed.

Cherry, meanwhile, kept on Shelley to press the lawsuit forward. She did, and in March the lawyers from Waco told her that they would take the case. No payment was necessary, they said, unless they won the suit. They would take their payment out of the proceeds from a victory; if they lost, that was their problem. It sounded like a reasonable proposition to Shelley.

"I had never seen a case like this," recalled Rod Squires. "I didn't know if there was anything we could really do for her, but her story was incredible—and it had been vouched for by the assistant DA in Corsicana."

Because there was no precedent for an incest victim suing for damages, the Waco attorneys investigated Bobby's businesses and ranch to know how much he was worth and then filed a civil claim against Bobby Sessions for $10 million.

And they learned more when they called Bobby for a pretrial discovery deposition. That meeting, on April 11, 1985, proved to Squires what kind of fish he would be dealing with. "I could tell," the lawyer recalled, "that the man was a master of manipulation. He used the deposition to attempt to reconcile with Shelley, get her to change her mind about the suit."

During that first deposition, Shelley had to confront her dad for the first time in months. Linda accompanied Bobby. She and Shelley, on opposite sides of the room, listened as Rod Squires pressed the questions in a small conference room of Bobby's attorney in Corsicana. And Shelley had to hear what seemed like meaningless, too-little-too-late, lies from Bobby, who kept insisting that all he wanted to do was help Shelley.

"What kind of help were you offering her?" the lawyer asked him.

"Same help I've always offered," Bobby replied. "I have only talked to Shelley once and that was in December when she came with the court order to get some clothes. I asked her then couldn't we please—wouldn't she please—let us get her some help." Bobby looked hurt as he described Shelley's rejection, then turned to Shelley, who sat on the other side of the small room, a few feet away, her back to Squires. "I've told you and I'll tell Shelley again: what's happened has been wrong. I'm sorry. I love you. You need some help. You need some counseling. Spend every dime I've got to get you the help you need."

Rod Squires wasn't at all sure that this suit was going to be the best thing for Shelley when he went into the deposition. And he was even less sure of it after he came out of the two-hour session.

"If you met Bobby Sessions, you'd like him," explained Squires. "He has got charisma, he has got good bullshit, he's a good talker.

"I was very mixed up about the case after taking his deposition because he almost convinced me that it was in Shelley's best interest not to proceed," Squires remembered.

Even before he had agreed to take the case, Squires had been worried enough about the effect of a trial on Shelley to have her see a psychologist. Dr. John Wise, a child psychologist from Waco, met Shelley twice in January and once in April. His conclusions were strong but inconclusive. Shelley had suffered a "very traumatic" experience, Wise said, but "was not amenable to working on her problems. She was suffering from a type of delusion of omnipotence. She thought she had everything under control."

Of course, at the same time, Wise pointed out, such delusions are typical of teenagers, and it would depend on how Shelley was "going to come crashing down" when she finally confronted the real world. Untreated, said Wise, Shelley at that point would end up in a hospital for six or eight months suffering from severe depression. In fact, Wise terminated *his* treatment of Shelley after the April session.

In the end, Wise told Squires, a trial would be "not harmful nor helpful." That conclusion at least gave Squires the confidence that if Shelley wanted to proceed with the trial, she wouldn't be doing herself any great harm by it.

And Shelley had become more and more sure of her goal: she wanted the money from Bobby—to get her own help her own way and to be free from him forever. Bobby's deposition didn't move her one bit, and she told Squires what she thought.

"It was like talking to a rock," recalled Squires. "In talking with her afterwards, I threw out the idea of other options, of not proceeding or trying to reconcile on some basis, or exploring some sort of settlement. And she rejected all of that outright. To her this idea of the newfound religion, of reconciling, of wanting to get the family back together, was just part of an attempt to manipulate her and keep what he had."

Even after deciding to continue the case, Squires didn't believe it would ever get to trial. He was sure that Bobby would settle. "He was the master of negotiation, what his whole success was built upon—I couldn't imagine him risking it all by going in front of a jury."

But that's what Sessions was willing to do. And Shelley was more than happy to take him on.

XXII

TRIAL

*I really didn't know until the very end which side they [the jury]
were—you know, who they believed. Because I couldn't tell by their
expressions. They didn't really show any emotion or anything, until
the end. You could see some disgust now and again, but you
couldn't really tell one way or another who they were for.*

Robert Krienke, the foreman of the jury that deliberated over
Shelley's claim, stood talking to a reporter from the *Waco Tribune Herald.* Rod Squires and his partner Dale Williams stopped
to shake Krienke's hand. The foreman made his way toward the
door of the courtroom, passing Shelley, who had stayed to talk
with other jury members after the verdict.

"Just by chance, we all ended up by the elevator," Krienke
recalled. Shelley and he, among others, got on to ride down from
the third floor.

They descended one floor, the elevator opened and there were
Bobby and Linda and their attorneys. They didn't get on the
elevator and the doors closed again.

Just before it touched ground on the first floor, Shelley turned to Krienke. "All I wanted," she said, "all I wanted was my mother to believe me."

Four days before, on Monday, August 26, 1985, Judge Derwood Johnson of the District Court of McLennan County, Texas, the 74th Judicial District, brought Cause Number 85-542-3 to order. An eighteen-year-old Navarro County woman was before him to sue her forty-three-year-old father for repeated sexual abuse over a three-year period of her childhood.

The judge was a big man, over six feet, with thinning hair, who seemed to be in his early fifties. He had a reputation as a fair judge, who expected that the lawyers who practiced in his courtroom be well prepared. Attorneys who had pressed cases before Johnson knew that his judicial style was not intrusive; he preferred to referee the opposing counsels rather than direct them.

Before him were two young, well-established Waco lawyers, Rod Squires and Dale Williams, representing Shelley. The defendant's attorneys included one familiar face, Fred Horner of Waco, and two from Corsicana, Jack Smith and Savannah Robinson. The case had landed in Johnson's courtroom because the defendant had allegedly molested his daughter in Waco while they attended a livestock show.

That much the judge knew.

Shelley was somewhat hopeful that her father's influence didn't reach all the way to McLennan County, but she wasn't counting on anything.

As late as a week before the trial, her father's lawyers had tried to have the trial postponed. Jack Smith asked to be excused from the trial. He argued that he had done work for an insurance company that his client had bought a policy from and therefore he had a conflict of interest. Judge Johnson dismissed that contention.

Then Smith argued that the new lawyer, Fred Horner of Waco, who would have taken over for him, was still in the process of joining the defense team. Horner needed time to prepare. Again, Judge Johnson said no.

Squires and Williams decided that Bobby was looking for a delay, possibly to "sock his money away." But they also figured it was likely that Bobby would take a settlement. They didn't think he wanted to suffer a long, highly publicized trial.

"Our lowest demand was $500,000," recalled Williams. "We wanted to make sure her college was taken care of. And [that] she had some financial stability to start her own life. I really think his own lawyers thought, 'Well, surely he will put up $500,000 to take care of this girl.'" But Bobby Sessions had other ideas, maybe because he felt God would take care of it. Or maybe he had the cockiness that Dale Williams saw in him. "I think he felt he was invincible," Williams remarked later. "He is such a manipulator, and one on one, eye to eye, he can convince you that he's a prince. There are a lot of people you can say that about, but he's one of the best I have ever seen."

Officially titled *Shelley Sessions, by Next Friend, vs. Bobby Rowe Sessions* (because she was a minor her attorneys acted as guardians, or "next friend," as well), the case was in reality *Dallas* in Waco—and a scandal.

Bobby did not want to settle the lawsuit and was now facing a $10 million claim from his daughter. No one knew of any precedents. But Shelley cared little for either money or precedent. She entered the third-floor courtroom for one thing: justice. Her father was given a vacation for his crime against her. She wanted to set the record straight.

By coming to civil court, Shelley and her lawyers were notifying the legal establishment that the sanctions applied to child abusers were sorely inadequate. "Bobby Sessions had not paid the full price for what he had done," Rod Squires explained. "The criminal justice system was another aspect of society this man was able to manipulate to his best interest."

The case had its domestic repercussions. Shelley had hauled her own father to court and brought disgrace on the family. That, at least, was one version of the events. From the looks of the courtroom seating, it was a popular version: Bobby Rowe Sessions, defendant, was surrounded by his kin. Shelley Rene Sessions, plaintiff, sat alone. From afar the town of Corsicana was on edge. The entire county was watching.

Rod Squires felt as if he'd stepped on a landmine: he had agreed to take Shelley's case, but where were the precedents to be found?

"I did a little research and we couldn't find another case in the nation like it," he recalled. "Normally we have what you call parental immunity, but we couldn't find any legal impediment in Texas that would prevent us from filing it."

Dale Williams had been practicing law for over ten years. Much of that time he had taught personal-injury law at Baylor University Law School in Waco. His firm, which included Squires, co-counsel for Shelley, and Spike Pattillo, specialized in wrongful-death suits or accidents involving paralysis or loss of limbs.

When Shelley had first interviewed with Squires about what legal amends she could demand from her father, he and Williams had known immediately that this case wasn't in their usual line, but they had found the challenge irresistible.

In the courtroom, a jury of nine men and three women—chosen by the opposing attorneys from a random pool of Waco residents the day before—watched closely as Dale Williams stood up and walked over to them. "You've got a little bit of an idea of what this case is about," he said quietly, gently, "and we're fixin' to start the evidence phase of the trial.

"You know that something very horrible happened," Williams continued, "and they are not going to deny that." Not exactly deny; but "they"—Bobby Sessions and his defense team—would, Williams knew, try to "mitigate."

This was a civil trial. Shelley Sessions was suing her father for actual and punitive damages—$5 million to compensate her for what he had done and $5 million to punish him as an example to others. "And after hearing all the evidence, you will decide how much this girl has been damaged," said Williams, "not just in the past, but how much she will be damaged in the future. How much it will be worth every time she thinks about her junior high and high school years, every time she thinks about cattle shows, every time somebody asks her about her parents and every time somebody asks her about her dad. Every time she is in an interpersonal relationship with a man."

How much was all that suffering worth? To Shelley it could not be measured in dollars, though that is what the jurors would be asked to determine: give the horror a number. Worse, this was not a horror past; like Scrooge, on a voyage to Christmas future, the jurors were asked to attach a number to *future* horror.

"It would be real nice if, in a situation like this," Williams said, "somebody could come back to court every year or every five years or even every ten years and say 'Okay, here's what my damages have been in the past ten years,' and let the jury decide. But our system doesn't work that way.

"You're allowed to come to court just once."

Williams spoke softly—but frankly. "He had an office on the ranch," Williams told the jury about Bobby, "and he could watch when his wife would leave. And when she'd leave, he'd hightail it back to the house and sexually assault his daughter.

"I didn't want to run the risk of offending anybody by the frankness of the testimony," recalled Williams.

He tried to prepare the jury for the explicitness.

"No matter what happens in this trial, from beginning to end," Williams said, pointing to Shelley, "that little girl right there is a brave little girl. She is scared to death of that man over there— sexually and physically scared of that man." And the point was, Williams continued, that "the reason, throughout our nation, that this is swept under the rug is because of that fear."

Anticipating a defense that would try to complicate the affair, Williams reminded the jury that "There is black and there is white and there is right and there is wrong. And if she is right, he is wrong."

Could it be that simple?

In what was perhaps a hint of things to come, Bobby's lawyer Jack Smith asked to delay his opening statement until the defense began its case. And Williams called as the plaintiff's first witness Bobby Rowe Sessions.

Jack Smith, a tall man with a mustache, sat facing the jury intently. "You could see he was trying to read our various reactions," Robert Krienke said. "It almost got to be a game where he was trying to count the votes. If he saw a little crack of a smile or a nod or something he was making notes."

Bobby Sessions was proof that nothing was as simple as it seemed. In an objective, sensible world, perhaps, there was a right and wrong, black and white, and a logic that said if Shelley was right, then Bobby was wrong.

But in Waco, Texas, that Monday afternoon, the jury was quickly introduced to the gray areas.

When Dale Williams began questioning Sessions, the lawyer knew right away that he was not going to be able to lead him down any paths. "He had a knack of whatever your question is of trying to change it and twist it," Williams recalled. "I just let him do it."

At first Bobby seemed reluctant to answer. He kept his head down, not making eye contact, and answered in a monotone: yes, no.

Asked by Williams what happened in the motel room on the trip back from New Jersey in 1978, Bobby said, "There really wasn't much of anything that happened." He explained that Shelley and Michael usually slept in one bed and he and Linda in another. But that night the two children wouldn't settle down, so they were split up.

"Michael had a real problem sleeping with me," said Bobby in his low drawl, "so I simply put him over in the bed with Linda and crawled in bed with Shelley." As Bobby described it, he simply went to sleep until "the next thing I knew, Shelley is yelling, everybody gets up, she and Linda go in the bathroom, she comes out. I said, 'What happened?' Shelley said, 'You put your hand on my pants.' I started crying, Shelley was crying. I apologized. I didn't know anything about it, I was asleep. Shelley said, 'That's okay.' We hugged each other, loved on each other and that's all there was to it."

They "loved on each other"? What kind of thing was that between a father and daughter?

That's all there was to it—except what happened over the next eight years.

When Williams asked Bobby about Shelley's thirteenth-birthday present, the defendant grew quieter. The judge had to ask him to speak up.

If Bobby thought his quiet demeanor suggested repentance, he was badly misjudging his audience. "It was hard for us to hear him. He wouldn't speak up, and I found that real annoying," recalled juror Sharon Storrs, a typographer for an advertising agency and the mother of two girls.

Bobby was not repentant: he thought that sexually abusing his daughter was a way of showing and getting "some attention, some affection."

And what was Shelley's reaction to his fondling her and putting his fingers into her vagina? "Shelley seemed to enjoy it very much."

Even Dale Williams didn't expect such boldness. "She *didn't* seem to enjoy it very much?" he asked incredulously.

But Bobby willingly corrected him and repeated: "She seemed to enjoy it very much."

"You'd think somebody who had abused his daughter as much as this man had, had been through criminal proceedings, had pleaded guilty to a criminal act, had shot himself, had been through what he had been through, that you could put somebody like that up on the stand and just murder him," Williams said.

Williams wondered what Bobby expected to gain by such tactics: "I didn't expect him to admit some things."

When Williams asked Bobby about the first time he performed oral sex on Shelley, he said that it was his daughter who initiated it: "She was laying on the couch and she didn't have any clothes on."

Bobby Sessions was revealing the secret of his success: the big lie. In this case, the big lie was that Shelley was a partner. He was a master salesman because he seemed to know instinctively where the fundamental need was. And now, whether deluded or merely deft, he managed to hit on the only possible weakness in the plaintiff's case: that Shelley *enjoyed* what was done to her.

And when he was recalling for the jury his memories of sex with his teenage daughter, he claimed that "most of the time Shelley would ask me to perform oral sex on her."

In fact, said Bobby, "it seemed to really be kind of a one-way street. And one night I asked her if she would do that to me."

It sounded so simple, logical—except that Sessions was talking about his young daughter, a girl too frightened even to move when he performed his various sexual acts on her. It all made sense except that he was lying; except that he was speaking about a thirteen-year-old girl who was also his daughter.

Sharron Storrs watched incredulously. "I thought: 'You must be out of your mind. What are you trying to put over on me? This is no "affair"—it's molestation!' "

Storrs watched Shelley as her father testified. She imagined what Shelley might have in common with her own two daughters. "At the time, she was eighteen," Storrs recalled. "She looked more to me like a little girl."

Shelley remained in the courtroom throughout her father's testimony. Her mother did not. Linda did not want to hear the details. But Bobby Sessions was as bold on the stand as he was at a hotel check-in counter. "Shelley and I had discussed having sex after the oral sex, and Shelley asked me if we could go ahead and do that."

How deep the deception ran!

"So, by the time that this girl is thirteen years and four months old, you sexually assaulted her by putting your finger in her, by performing oral sex on her, and by intercourse, is that correct?" asked Williams.

"Yes, sir."

"Did you realize at the time, Mr. Sessions, that you were violating that little girl's rights?"

"I didn't think about it that way, no, sir."

"You didn't realize that a little girl had a right not to be violated?"

"It never crossed my mind."

As Williams explored the factual terrain with Sessions, he made the big lie more and more apparent. Williams would not let the jury forget that Bobby Sessions was not talking about some sexual liaison with a paramour—the person he had created in his mind to justify his actions—but with his daughter.

"Did you think of your daughter as your daughter when you were performing these sex acts on her?"

"Not while we were having sex, no, sir."

"Did you want her to think of you as her father when you were performing these sex acts on her?" Williams continued.

"Not while we were having sex, no, sir."

As Sessions had tried for the logical jugular with his lie, so Williams quickly brought him to that logic's fundamental flaw. Bobby Sessions claimed to have been driven to have sex with his daughter to gain her filial affection; moments later, he described her as if she were an adult partner. Gradually, Sessions exposed his perversions to the jury—with the same flare for drama as he had used when he exposed his private parts to his daughter.

He admitted to sexual assault after sexual assault. "We had sex when my wife was in the house, yes, sir." But when Williams asked why he wanted naked pictures of his daughter, Bobby said, "I really don't know."

All he seemed to know was that "It happened lots of times, in lots of different ways, for lots of different reasons."

But Bobby, whenever he could, tried to bring the jury into his delusion: "I enjoyed what we had together. Shelley seemed to enjoy what we had together. And whenever an opportunity presented itself, we would have sex."

Unfortunately, for Bobby, he was then a defendant in a suit brought by the girl he said enjoyed his sexual kinks. He would have to prove some wild twists of attitude by his daughter to prove that assertion. Did she suddenly cease to become the difficult child he had asserted she was? And if she had, what made her change again, and bring this suit? He wanted it both ways. Williams was confident that the jury wouldn't let him have it.

He questioned Bobby from his seat, speaking directly to him, not worrying about the jury. "I let my partner detail the reactions." But in this instance, Williams couldn't help but notice jurors in the front row. "Several rolled their eyes and shook their heads. And I actually saw just a little bit of pure anger, that they'd like to strangle this guy," he said.

Almost forty minutes into the examination, Williams hit a soft spot. He was pressing Sessions about his habit of punishing and rewarding his daughter by demanding or excusing her from "turns."

"It's very hard to sit up here and answer these questions and everything sounds so this way, that way, without knowing what it was," protested the defendant. "When you're in a position you can't get out of and you have no control, and that's one of your problems—you want control."

Bobby broke into sobs. Williams waited quietly until he regained his composure.

So even Bobby recognized he was a control freak. Nothing escaped his need to know, his need to be in charge. His adoptive daughter had violated his rules of order—a little meteor with her very own voice and temperament. "When Shelley misbehaved or did things she wasn't supposed to do, or broke the rules or did things to bring about mistrust," Bobby said, almost pleadingly, "how do you discipline somebody when you don't have any control? And you've also got a complete and utter fear of being totally done in."

Who was afraid of whom? At first it seemed that Bobby meant he was frightened of a little girl's transgressions—as if his inability to control her would annihilate him. But soon he seemed to be saying something different.

"I was in a box I couldn't get out of. I couldn't say no and put my foot down and tear her butt up if that's what it took—for fear of being turned in to the police or telling her mother."

What most terrified Bobby Sessions was his daughter turning him into the cops. "The only way I had out," he explained, "was to say, 'I can let you do what you want to do, if this will happen.'"

Williams prompted him: "When you say, 'If this will happen,' what did you require to happen before you would give in?"

"The only avenue I had was the sexual approach."

Sessions was right about one thing: he was indeed in a box. He had somehow convinced himself, he tried to say, that if *he* demanded sex from Shelley, *she* wouldn't turn him in for sexually abusing her!

In fact, he was working up to accusing his daughter of soliciting sexual favors from him—just as he had promised Shelley would happen. "I'm not here to paint my daughter black," he told Williams disingenuously. "I love Shelley with all my heart. And I'm very sorry for what's taken place. If I could undo it, I would. I can't. I want to help Shelley. I don't want to sit up here and have you play games with words that I say to make Shelley look like something she's not or to make me look like something I'm not."

Williams took up the challenge. "All right," he said, "let's ask you what your words are."

Sessions said there had been "several events." He first described Shelley's wanting to go to parties. "She was only fourteen, fifteen years old," he said, "and we told her she couldn't date until she was sixteen. I couldn't hold a hard line on anything. It was too hard. And finally I told Shelley she could go if she would just back off the boys."

"Back off the *what?*" Williams demanded.

"Back off the boys."

"The boys?"

" 'Just don't kiss the boys,' " Sessions quoted himself, almost innocently re-creating the pathological dynamic he had first made for his daughter. " 'Go dance, do whatever, just don't kiss the boys.' She needed to back off a little bit. Give us some room to trust. I had to let her go. She was being too belligerent not to go. So she went.

"When I picked her up from the party, I asked her, 'Did you do what you were supposed to do?' And she told me flat-out, no, she hadn't.

"I got very angry and very upset and I was yelling and I said, 'I'm going to carry you back to the party. If you want to act that way, you can stay with the people that act that way. I'm going to leave you here.' And Shelley started screaming at me, 'Hey, don't carry me back, I'll do whatever you want to do! I'll add turns, I'll do anything you want me to do—just don't carry me back to the party.' "

Williams knew that Sessions was now the one who was stumbling into the minefield—and he didn't even seem to know that bombs were exploding.

"Let's talk about that for a minute," said the lawyer. "You've got a daughter who is fourteen or fifteen years old at this time, and as far as you are concerned, she is too young to be kissing any boys?"

"That's not what I said!" Sessions protested.

"Did you tell your daughter you didn't want her kissing any boys?"

"For that particular time, yes, sir."

"Why didn't you want her kissing any boys?"

"It was just a vehicle to try to get a point across to her that she had to learn to earn some trust by doing something that we said to do or to not do."

Williams was ready for the kicker. "You're having sex with your daughter and you don't want her to kiss boys to earn trust? Is that what you're saying?"

"Not the way you're putting it, no, sir," Sessions stammered.

Of course Sessions didn't think it was the way Williams put it. It was too simple that way. It made it sound as if there were something strange about protecting your young daughter from a boy's kiss while you are screwing her. It was the same box. And Sessions still didn't know the way to the exit.

When Williams brought up the subject of Ricky Layfield, Sessions found himself once again caught in a logic that made for a good story but ultimately made no sense. He told the courtroom that on his return from Switzerland in the spring of 1983, Shelley had run up to him to say that Ricky had come to the house and was a perfect gentleman. "She was going to have him back," Sessions explained, "and I said, 'That's fine.' "

So how did it come to pass that Bobby went to the high school and created a scene? Williams asked.

The agriculture teacher. Joe Dan Kilcrease. "He is a good friend of mine and he loves Shelley very much," Bobby said. One of Bobby's spies. The teacher called him, said Bobby, "and he said, 'Shelley and Ricky are going together and she's just about disowning all the other kids at school and it's going to cause her some problems. It's not going to be good for Shelley and you need to do something about it.' "

"Did he know that you were molesting Shelley?" Williams's quick question was like blast from a claymore mine. Bobby's tale was believable—but only in a believable context. Williams's job was to remind the jury that these were not in any ways normal circumstances. He broke the spell of Bobby's narrative.

Sessions just couldn't hold the line; his mainstream premise couldn't support, or justify, what happened next. Bobby wanted the jury to believe that he went to Shelley's school just to talk to her—why couldn't he wait until she got home?

A few minutes later Bobby described his suicide attempt in the language of psychotherapy. "I had a very selfish thought," he told Williams, "that the best way to keep the situation out of the news and keep everything at home was to take myself out of the picture."

But then Bobby had a sudden loss of memory: "I have absolutely no recollection from the time I shot myself until the third or fourth day I was in Timberlawn Hospital."

He didn't remember calling Shelley to say he was going to kill her.

What Bobby Sessions wanted the jury to believe was that he hadn't thought much about what he was doing to his daughter; that he realized now that he made a mistake.

"I'm learning every day," he told Williams during some harsh questions about his massaging his niece after he had been released from Timberlawn. "One of the things that I'm having to learn about myself and everybody else is the fact that I can never be positively sure about what you think or what somebody else thinks. The only person I can be absolutely, totally sure of is what I think."

"Tell the jury," Williams immediately said, "why you were

massaging your nineteen-year-old niece's neck?" Sessions again retreated to his position of feigned naiveté. "I didn't think anything about it." But he was also on the horns of the same dilemma—his amoral blindness, even if real, might have been an explanation, but it didn't sound much like an excuse for a grown man. "She asked me to," was Sessions's answer to Williams.

This was what he had tried to insinuate about Shelley. *She* had asked *him* to make love to her. Now it was cousin Michelle's turn to be the perpetrator: she had asked Bobby for a massage. "She said she was very tight in the shoulders and her back," Sessions told the jury. "Michelle and I had talked. She's a very levelheaded young lady. She is my niece. She is my godchild. I didn't think anything about it."

Bobby was preaching now. "I was going on one premise in my life and that's where it tells me in Romans that 'old things are passed away and all things become new.' I had talked to Michelle about that. Michelle said she absolutely had no problem with me being different than I was. She could see that, so forth and so on. I believed her. I had no reason to think in my mind that Michelle would think anything other than I was massaging her shoulders."

And if she had thought otherwise? So far it was the same explanation he had given for his sexual molestation of his daughter.

"The mere fact that it caused a problem says to me that my judgment was very much in error. I have no problem with that at all. I apologized to Michelle, to her mother, and that's all there was to it. There was absolutely no intent on my part for anything other than massaging Michelle's shoulders."

Williams didn't linger over the massage episode. He quickly changed the subject on Bobby, saying, "Mr. Sessions, you know your daughter has undergone some pretty substantial psychological damage as a result of what you did to her, do you not?"

"If you ask me for a personal opinion," Sessions stammered, "I've got to tell you that I've got to believe Shelley needs counseling."

Williams had him in a tight corner. Bobby had already contended that Shelley was a "difficult" child, implying that she had a problem. Ergo . . .

"And in your opinion," Williams continued, "you are aware that this has caused her humiliation and embarrassment, are you not?"

"I would have thought that; and I would think just on the surface that that might be true. There are lots of things right now that I don't understand and I don't know where they're coming from and I don't know why."

Williams would gladly help him out, since Sessions was now in the process of admitting Shelley's case against him. "Do you agree, in your opinion, that she has suffered emotional injuries?"

"I would think," Sessions said, rushing headlong into unwitting submission, "she has to be emotionally upset by not just that, but lots of other things."

Williams pulled out a sheet of paper. "Mr. Sessions, last week your attorneys filed an answer to our lawsuit on your behalf. And they stated that Shelley Sessions has—'that Defendant denies that Shelley Sessions has suffered emotional injuries or mental anguish as a result of the relationship.' Is that your opinion?"

"No—"

"Your Honor"—Jack Smith was now on his feet—"we would object to that type of question. Mr. Sessions is not an attorney. He did not prepare the pleadings and I don't believe he's qualified to answer and get into those particular matters."

This was the first dispute in the courtroom—but it was over the heart of the case. "Your Honor," Williams continued, "this is the specific denial that they have made that the girl has not suffered mental anguish or emotional injuries, and I want to know if that came from this man." He pointed to Sessions, on the stand.

Smith protested that Williams had taken the written answer out of context. He asked that Williams read more.

"I'll be glad to read the paragraph, Your Honor," said Williams. " 'Defendant denies that Shelley Sessions has suffered physical injuries or pain although Plaintiff should have emotional turmoil concerning the relationship, Plaintiff has refused numerous offers of aid from her family and refused medical attention. Thus, Defendant denies that Shelley Sessions has suffered emotional injuries or mental anguish as a result of the relationship. Thus, Defendant denies that Shelley Sessions requires medical care and attention.' "

Williams paused only briefly. "Now, do you deny that your daughter needs medical care and attention?" he asked again.

"What that pleading is based on is very—"

"All right, I'm going to ask you that question again," Williams interrupted. "Do you deny that your daughter needs medical care and attention?"

"Objection!" Ms. Savannah Robinson was now on her feet on Sessions' behalf. "He's entitled to explain his answer," she told Judge Johnson. "If the answer is more than a simple yes or no, he is entitled to give the jury a full answer so that they are not misled."

The judge agreed and told Sessions that "if a simple yes or no is not a truthful answer, you have the right to qualify your answer with an explanation."

"Well, a yes-or-no answer is not sufficient," said Sessions. "In my opinion, which has been my opinion from day one, we have tried to get Shelley counseling and medical help. My doctors at Timberlawn said Shelley is going to need help to get through this thing. Everybody said that. Every counselor said, 'Shelley is going to need medical help.' "

Sessions was in a difficult position. On the one hand he wanted to show that he was a caring father, so he expressed his desire to help Shelley. On the other hand, Shelley was suing him for damages, so his opinion that she needed counseling seemed to be an admission of guilt.

But when Williams asked if "she's had psychological or emotional injuries over what you have done," Sessions balked.

"I can't say that," he shot back. "I think she needs counseling."

Was there a distinction? Was it possible that Shelley needed counseling—but hadn't been damaged?

"You can't deny that she's had psychological or emotional injuries, can you?" pressed Williams.

"I can't deny it and I can't confirm it," Sessions responded, again showing his prowess for obfuscation.

Williams changed the subject slightly again, asking Sessions now about the period of time when he was "using [sexual relations] as a method of control over her."

"The sex was not a method of control," Sessions protested.

"I thought you told us earlier that that was your only method of controlling her, that when she said that she wanted to do something, you had to give in by telling her that it was going to cost her ten more turns—that was your way of controlling her?"

"That was in one instance that you asked me about, sir," Bobby shot back.

"And in that instance you were using it to control her?"

"Not to control. Defining words is real hard when you get into that kind of situation. We were in a real bad situation."

"Uh-huh."

"Real bad situation."

"Uh-huh."

"At times, for other reasons," Sessions continued. But he had dug himself in. "At times it was used as a control on me."

That might have been an interesting avenue to pursue—how Sessions perceived Shelley's control over *him*. For, at some lower level of unconscious thought, and on some level of their relationship, that was exactly what happened. He had let his daughter control him.

"You admit that what you did with your daughter was very wrong, do you not?" asked Williams.

"Yes, sir, I do."

"Did you know at the time that it was against the law?"

"Yes, sir."

"Why did you just disregard the law?"

"After a point in time, it didn't seem to make any difference."

"Did you ever feel dirty about what you were doing?"

"Yes, sir."

"Did you ever realize that you were hurting your daughter?"

"Yes, sir."

"We will pass the witness at this time, Your Honor." Williams looked up from his notes on the table. He felt he had scored well. He thought he did.

It was the end of the first day of the trial.

At nine o'clock the next morning Shelley was sworn in. She was nervous. The previous day had been the first time she had ever been in a courtroom; today, she mounted a witness stand for the first time.

Rod Squires had been preparing Shelley for three days prior to this Tuesday morning. "She could hardly talk. I was extremely concerned about putting her on the stand. I mean, there was no choice, but I did not have that good an expectation of what was going to happen," he recalled. "If she didn't open up, then it was just going to be a situation of keeping her on there the minimum time necessary to cover the subjects that needed to be covered for evidence purposes."

Squires and Shelley had met at his office for several hours each day. He believed that Bobby would be a formidable witness, articulate and persuasive. Shelley, he thought, wanted to confront her father, but she feared that he would manage to look like the victim. "I mean, you had to literally squeeze it out of her," Squires recounted. "She didn't want to talk, she didn't know how to talk, it was just something that she had buried in her psyche."

Squires and Williams had been concerned since first meeting Shelley almost eight months before that the psychological risk she was taking might be too great. The two lawyers had sent her to Dr. John Wise, a scheduled witness, to find out what they might expect. The answer they got was, "Who knows?"

"I told her that this was her one chance to tell her story," Squires said. "She had to speak from her heart and soul. That she had to bare her soul to the jury and let them see the hell that she had lived through."

In spite of the months of preparation, Squires found he was still hearing some of the atrocious details of Bobby's assaults for the first time. "I didn't know until the day before why she didn't just close her door and lock it," Squires said. But then Shelley told him how Bobby took her bedroom door off its hinges when they first moved to the ranch.

"Do you solemnly swear to tell the whole truth and nothing but the truth, so help you God?"

"I do," Shelley said meekly.

As the trial approached, Shelley had found a new life opening up for her. Her trio of brash young Waco attorneys, who specialized in civil damage cases, became her confidants, friends and guardians. They helped her get into Baylor University, their alma mater, and advised her on everything from counseling to boyfriends.

"From the first moment that I met Shelley," Rod Squires recalled, "it was very difficult for her to express any emotion, and what worried me the most was you had this very charismatic, dynamic person, the defendant, and on our side we had Shelley, who was very unemotional, very rote, the way she described what she had been through. We couldn't crack her. She was hard as a rock. Obviously part of her coping mechanism for what she had gone through."

Shelley stood up well under Squires's gentle, direct questioning, but defense attorney Robinson was another matter. The strategy of Bobby's attorneys was to picture their client as just a caring dad who had loved his daughter too much, had repented, and now wanted to make amends. Shelley, on the other hand, was pictured as an ungrateful, unmanageable young delinquent whose rebelliousness was directly responsible for the excesses into which the father-daughter relationship had fallen.

Shelley was hardly prepared for such a sophisticated attack, but her defense was in her honesty.

"Did you ever love your father?" Robinson asked.

"No, ma'am."

"You didn't love him when you were a baby?"

"I don't know when I was a baby."

Shelley kept her head. Not because she was especially well prepped for the trial but because she had had years to form opinions about her feelings toward her father and so could answer without hesitation or ambiguity.

"Did you like your Christmas gifts?" the defense counsel asked.

"Yes, ma'am."

"But you didn't like your dad?"

"No, ma'am."

"Did you thank your dad for birthday presents?"

"Yes, ma'am."

"Did you like your birthday presents?"

"Yes, ma'am."

"But you didn't like your dad?"

"No, ma'am."

Robinson next tried to poke holes in Shelley's testimony by suggesting that touching can have meanings other than the sexual. "Isn't your whole family sort of 'huggy'?" she asked. "You walk into their kitchen, they grab you and give you a hug?"

"His side of the family is," Shelley said matter-of-factly.

Robinson was trying to lay the groundwork for refuting Shelley's charge about the first instances of molestation in New Jersey.

"Is it possible that your daddy was trying to help?" she pushed. "That you had muscle cramps?"

Shelley was unflappable.

"No, ma'am," she said without hesitation. "Because when you are that young, you are energetic and you don't have cramps."

"You don't think your daddy might have had some other motivation and that motivation might have been to help you?"

"No, ma'am," she said quietly.

Robinson continued on that tack, constantly suggesting to Shelley that she had misunderstood her father's concern for her. But Shelley proved herself to be well aware of the cunning distinctions the defense attorney was trying to make; the traps she was preparing.

"You didn't realize that having sex at the age of thirteen was wrong?" Robinson asked at one point, hitting another defense theme: that Shelley was a willing participant in the "affair."

"I don't know."

"I think you've testified previously that you only realized it was wrong later."

"I realized it was wrong for a father to do it to his daughter."

"Do you think if you had told your mother it would have stopped it right then?"

"No, ma'am."

"Why wouldn't it have?"

"Because even though I did tell her now," Shelley said, "she's not sitting over there behind me. She's behind *him.* " Shelley had just cut to the quick of her predicament: she had been exploited by both parents. As she pointed out, her mother was now revealing to the entire courtroom the loyalties that had guided her through the years that her daughter was being abused by her husband. We know Linda stood behind him then, said Shelley, because she is behind him now.

"You don't think your mother has been through a very great deal of turmoil and it has taken her a long time for her to decide where her place is?" Robinson asked.

"She might have," Shelley agreed. "But not like I have."

Robinson tried to suggest that the bickering between Shelley's parents proved that Linda was on her daughter's side. "Hasn't she stood up for you when it came to going to the pool or going to watch the horses at the circus?"

But Shelley understood the meaning of those fights. "She would in little spats, but whenever it came to anything big, my mother is very weak and she won't even stand up for me."

Shelley instinctively reminded the jurors that this case was not about circuses and swimming pools, but about "big" things—like eight years of sexual abuse. And she evinced a logic that continually confounded her adult examiners.

"Would you be surprised if your mother testified later in this trial that she thought that you were wild and that you needed to have some restrictions?" asked Robinson.

"Yes, ma'am," said Shelley, "because I was not—there was no way for me to be wild when I was not allowed to be anywhere but home."

Where was the line to be drawn between legitimate parental concern and exploitation and abuse? Shelley's point of vulnerability on the witness stand was her youth—she was a teenager who, like all teens, was rebellious and believed her parents were crazy, uncaring and overprotective. Her strength as a witness was her searing honesty.

"Were your mom and dad concerned about your school activities?" Robinson asked.

"*He* was very concerned."

Robinson kept pushing the theme of parental concern and Shelley pushed right back.

"What were the rules?" the lawyer asked. "Did [your parents] have a curfew when you had to be in the house?"

"I never had a curfew," said Shelley, "because I never went out at night."

Robinson followed up: "Was there an age that you would be allowed to date?"

"No, ma'am, because I wasn't allowed to date." Shelley's anger toward Bobby was unreserved. It was an emotion at trial that betrayed Shelley's illogic even as it proved her sense of shame and hurt.

"Do you think Bob has gotten help?"

"He's gotten help," Shelley responded, "but I think he's still sick. He'll always be sick."

"What makes you think that he will always be sick?"

"Because of his will and his mind. He knows how to handle any situation, any person. He can handle anything at any time. He can do anything he wants and he can put on a show for anybody. I've never seen anything like it." But again, the burning angst over her father's infinite powers seemed to drive Shelley to a finely focused perception of reality. Since she hadn't talked to Bobby or seen him interacting with people for almost a year, Robinson wanted to know, "Do you have any real experience that you can relate to me that will explain to me why you think your father has not changed?"

Shelley did. "The lying and the hiding. If you've changed and you're a Christian, you're not going to hide and you're not going to lie about the facts."

"And you think your father is lying?"

"Yes, ma'am, I do."

"How good is your memory, Shelley?"

"For the things that happened to me, I remember the pain and what I went through."

"But you don't remember the good things that have ever happened to you, do you?"

"There weren't too many good things in my life that I could say were good."

"You don't remember winning trophies or good recognition or being put in the newspaper?"

"But at the same time, my life was being destroyed, so it didn't matter."

Shelley could not be budged, could not be tricked.

When she couldn't remember the date that she first had intercourse with her father, the lawyer immediately jumped on her: "If you can't remember, why do you think your father is lying?"

Shelley's voice shook with emotion. "Everything shows he's lying. That's him. He is a liar."

"You don't like your father, do you?" Robinson asked, still trying to shake from Shelley some kind of guilt about her feelings for her father or the suit.

"No, ma'am, I don't."

"You hate your father, don't you?"

"Yes, ma'am."

"You're bringing this lawsuit to punish your father, aren't you?"

Shelley had already had too many accusatory fingers wagged in her direction to be daunted by this combative attorney.

"To punish him," she said clearly, "and to show everybody what really happened—and I think he should compensate me for what I'm going to go through, what I have gone through, and what I'm going through now."

"Okay. Did you ever tell somebody you wanted to take a shotgun and kill him?"

"Probably have."

"Did you tell another doctor that you were willing to see him die?"

Shelley said she couldn't remember saying that, but then offered, "If he would have died when he shot himself, my life would have been a lot better."

"If your father had died, would it have solved your problems?" the lawyer shot back.

"No."

"If your father dies, are you going to like your mother better?"

"No, ma'am."

"If your father dies, are you going to like yourself better?"

"No, ma'am." Shelley sighed. "But I wouldn't have to see him in town and have a reminder of what happened to me."

The word "father" was gradually losing its aura of authority. Shelley wouldn't be daunted by it, wouldn't let the attorney cow her into a subservient, "daughterly" stand.

"You genuinely do not believe that your father could have gone through a deep religious conversion and be on the road, if not fully recovered?"

"He could have," Shelley replied, "but that doesn't change what he did to me or how I'm going to feel about it."

"Does it change whether or not you can love him?"

"I will never love him."

"Does it change whether or not he can be interested in reestablishing the family and including you in that family unit?"

"There is no family to be established."

As far as Shelley was concerned, Bobby Sessions had forfeited his fatherly rights. She owed him no filial loyalty or affection.

Shelley told Robinson that Bobby needed additional punishment, that "he only spent a short time at really a country club and got on probation and I'm the one that's suffering everything, not him. . . . What he took away from me, I can't get back."

"And for all the years that you hated him and wouldn't love him, even as a child, how is he going to get that back?"

"He can't," Shelley said bluntly.

"How is he going to get back a loving daughter, Shelley?"

"He never had one."

Robinson kept trying to make Shelley into an ungrateful daughter. And Shelley kept accepting the label.

"Did your father ever hate you, Shelley?"

For the first time all afternoon, Dale Williams interjected. "Your Honor, we're—" But he stopped, shaking his head. "Never mind," he said. Shelley was doing just fine; why bother the momentum now?

"Did your father ever hate you, Shelley?"

"Like I said earlier," Shelley replied, "he loved me more than he should."

Robinson tried to suggest that Bobby's offer of help to Shelley should prove his goodwill toward his daughter.

But Shelley would have nothing of it. "If I can get help, I will get it," she said, "but I will not get help from him. From him saying, 'I will pay for it.' I don't want anything that has to do with him. He can't help me. I can try to help myself and try to find someone that I think can help me."

Shelley wouldn't accept a counselor selected by Bobby, even if there were no strings attached because, she said, "he could care less, really."

"You think your father could care less about your continued well-being?" asked Robinson innocently.

"If he cared about me," Shelley shot back, "he wouldn't have done what he did to me."

Shelley was becoming more forceful—and emotional—as Robinson pushed on: "Is there any reason for you to make this any worse than it was?"

"I want the truth out and I'm tired of him trying to cover up what happened to me."

"And ten million dollars is going to cure that?"

"No," said Shelley. "But this right here is curing it. Everybody knows." That was important to her. For all these years she had to suffer the abuse; then she had to watch as he twisted even that to his advantage.

"When he shot himself, everybody didn't know?"

"He did that for sympathy!" shouted Shelley, "to get every-body back under his thumb. . . . If he was going to kill himself, he would have shot himself in the head. He knew what he was doing."

Shelley was a refutation of everything that the new "psycholog-ical" society represented: she judged her father by his acts, not his motives. She didn't care what he said, only what he did. And she judged her mother and other relatives in the same matter-of-fact manner.

"Is there no way that this family can demonstrate to you that they love you?" Robinson asked, pointing toward the rows of seats behind the defense table. "That they want you back in the fam-ily?"

"They all turned on me. They can't show me that they love me. Every one of them has turned on me." Shelley looked out at the courtroom. Her family was arranged behind the defense table, on Bobby's side of the courtroom.

"And your Aunt Pat," Robinson said. "She's turned on you?"

"Yes, she has," said Shelley forlornly. "You see her sitting out there with him."

"Just because she's sitting with him, that means she's turned on you, Shelley?"

Shelley was failing now. After the many months of being strong, she was beginning to let herself feel. "It depends on a person's morals," she whispered. "A person has morals." A tear rolled down her cheek as she looked out at all the people who had abandoned her. It was the first tear that Dale Williams had seen Shelley shed.

"You think any relative of yours that stands by Bob has no morals?" Robinson asked.

"Yes, I do."

Robinson handed Shelley a tissue. She left the stand.

My family and everything tried to really make sure how rebellious I was. And I always thought, "Well, what do you expect! You expect me to be happy, happy-go-lucky and everything's great!" So that was a joke because in court for the whole week they just tried to make me look so bad—"Oh, she was so rebellious, she's a terrible, terrible child."

But I got along and was disciplined by everybody and never got in trouble in school or nothing. It just takes common sense to figure it out.

Shelley did not stay in the courtroom, as she had for Bobby's testimony, when her lawyers and the opposition called their expert witnesses.

"She really didn't express a burning desire to be there or to not be there," recalled Rod Squires. Squires and Williams urged her to stay out while the doctors testified.

Shelley had been to psychologists with her family, of course, long before the lawsuit required their judgments. Squires had urged her to enter therapy, for her own good. He had insisted that she see Waco psychologist John Wise, to get his opinion if the lawsuit could cause her greater stress and turmoil.

Shelley's opinion was that she had already been through the worst.

Wise followed Shelley to the witness stand. The fifty-five-year-old clinical psychologist, who had a Ph.D. from Baylor, had seen Shelley a total of four times.

The lawsuit was "a tearing apart of Shelley, not only from her father, but from her mother, her brother and from the rest of her blood relatives who had certain allegiances to her father," Squires began. "And you know it was pretty much drawing a line in the dirt saying, 'You're being cut off from everything that you have grown up with.' " Wise was blunt. "Not harmful, not helpful." Squires and Williams were trying to establish that Shelley would be suffering emotional damage throughout her adult life, and that the doctors here in the courtroom could anticipate this.

The defense strategy was to argue that true health lay within the family—and that to continue this trial would damage that health-giving bond even further.

So they brought in Dr. Leslie Carter, who had said that Shelley could be helped. He wanted to unite the family.

*   *   *

Dale Williams' analysis of the defense suggested that Carter would not help Bobby:

"Most of the research that you will find on a national basis is pretty consistent with the type of damage and the problems that are experienced by children who have been sexually abused. And I really did not expect Dr. Carter to vary from that. And when we took his deposition that's pretty much what we found. So we were not concerned about his testimony. We thought that [the defense] would recognize that he was going to do them more damage than good.

"For example, when they called Sarah Conn to the stand. Well, Sarah was there to show that with forgiveness and with the love of God you can work through these problems and you could lead a normal life. Well, the national experience is that that's not true. In my opinion, Dr. Carter just re-emphasized that Shelley is going to have problems the rest of her life. That she is a candidate for a complete psychological breakdown, a candidate for suicide, for drug abuse. That she's a candidate for relationships that will be abusive throughout her life. And Dr. Carter really supported all of that. I mean, he obviously knows that his time is being paid for by the lawyers from the other side, and he doesn't want to go overboard. There are ways to try to mask some of that a little bit, but he really is very much a straight shooter. And, in my opinion, he was just as favorable for us as was Dr. Wise."

Dr. Wise told the jury that Shelley could look forward to a life of "severe depression. Severe anxiety. Possible suicidal attempts. Leaning on substance abuse, drugs or alcohol, to survive the pain that she feels, psychologically."

As it turned out, Shelley was not the only incest victim in the courtroom. Sarah Conn, the Texas housewife and member of Dr. Charles Solomon's Grace Fellowship International, revealed that she had been abused as a child.

The revelation came as a surprise to Shelley's lawyers—and as Dale Williams recalled, was an unexpected and welcome gift from Bobby's lawyers.

"Sarah Conn was there to show that with forgiveness and with the love of God you can work through these problems and you could lead a normal life," recalled Williams, but if there was one thing Doctors Wise and Carter agreed on, it was that the prognosis of an incest victim is likely to be a tormented one. Both doctors agreed that the problems weren't insurmountable, but that depression, illness and unsuccessful relationships with the opposite sex were likely.

From Williams' view, Sarah Conn was a case in point.

Mrs. Conn's departing words from her direct examination by Savannah Robinson were made between sobs.

Robinson handed her a tissue. "You were at one time yourself a victim?

"Yes, I was," answered the housewife turned counselor.

Dale Williams recalled the look on Sarah Conn's face as she answered these last questions, and decided to drop his initial line of questions about her qualifications to judge a person's ability to recover from psychological trauma. "Most of the time, on cross-examination you don't want to take chances." Squires would later explain. "You don't want to explore unexplored areas for the first time on cross. But Dale kind of broke the golden rule with Sarah Conn. And that, I guess, is maybe why it was so dramatic. Because it was totally unexpected, and no one was prepared for what she ultimately testified and the manner that she testified."

Williams decided to take the chance—he hoped it wouldn't hurt too much. . . .

"I'm sorry, Mrs. Conn," he began. "I didn't hear about the problem you had—did you say four different times?

"Yes."

"How were you molested?"

"When I was about four there was a teenage neighbor boy—do you want me to be specific?"

"As much as you feel comfortable with."

"There was a teenage boy when I was four who asked me to hold his sex organs and I don't remember how, whatever, but that happened or, you know, but was probably the—it wasn't anything a whole lot more than that. At four.

"And at six, there was an older man, ah, that my parents took to church, who molested me two or three times."

"In particular, what way?"

"Well, just putting his hands on me. And then when I was ten my brother—there was never any penetration, but everything but penetration."

"What do you mean by that?"

"Do you know what I'm talking about when I say 'penetration'?"

"Yeah, I understand that, but what do you mean by 'everything but' that?"

"Everything—well, he satisfied himself, using my body."

"How old was your brother?"

"Fourteen—thirteen, fourteen."

"Did it—you've told us these three occasions—"

"And when I was fourteen, I was—there was a deacon in a church that I was going to go home with and stay with him and his wife and my parents took me to where he worked, and he lived outside of town, and he was going to take me home, you know, to spend several days with them, and he started to try to feel me in the elevator—got me by myself in the elevator—and whenever I could get free from him, I ran and—this was downtown Fort Worth—and I ran from him, leaving all my belongings and called somebody to come get me. So, other than just being in that elevator—you know, didn't go beyond just, you know—"

"Have you ever been penetrated . . . I mean as a child?"

"No."

"Were you ever asked to perform oral sex on anybody, as a child."

"No."

"Anybody ever perform oral sex on you as a child?"

"Not as a child."

"Not as a child?"

"No."

"Does that—those four occasions of sexual abuse that you've described bother you?"

"Did it bother me?"

"Yes."

"It bothers me that they happened, yes."

"You'll never forget them, will you?"

"No."

"No more questions, Your Honor."

Robert Krienke was moved by this exchange. Sarah Conn was crying.

Rod Squires summed it up later: "I think it demonstrated very graphically that these scars just do not heal up and the scab falls off and you're well. That thirty, forty, fifty years afterwards that it's going to be there and it's going to be very intense pain and very intense sorrow."

Dale Williams believed that it "turned out to be wonderful testimony."

Linda Sessions was the last witness to testify in her daughter's lawsuit. She came to the stand carrying a large Bible, a book that the state of Texas does not require when swearing in witnesses. She had sat through the proceedings selectively, leaving the courtroom when her husband's and daughter's testimony turned explicit. She had been called to the stand Tuesday, but her testimony was cut short by Dr. Carter, who had traveled to Waco from Dallas.

Linda, recalled Storrs, was a pretty woman, well-dressed, not overdone. "Still being a mother, that was the only reference that I had in this case," said Storrs, who has two daughters. "I just couldn't understand her." Linda's allegiance to Bobby, exiling her daughter to Rebekah—both were acts of a woman apparently indifferent to her own daughter.

For juror Storrs, Linda Sessions was the most "bizarre piece in the puzzle."

"Linda was called to convince the jurors that Bob had experienced a true conversion and that he was a different man and that he did not need to be punished," Williams recalled. But the recurring question became, *Where was Linda while her husband assaulted her daughter numerous times over such a long period?*

It was a question that Jack Smith raised while he was trying to

lead Linda gently back over the years when the fights she witnessed were so violent. It strained credibility that Linda could
have missed Bobby's sneaking around and Shelley's hurt.

"Now, I believe you testified yesterday that during the time
that the relationship was going on between Shelley and Bob that
you were not aware of that," said Smith.

"That's right," answered Linda.

Dale Williams sat directly in front of her. The Bible was held
conspicuously in her hands. "Linda's a religious person, but that
doesn't mean she's totally honest," he later said. "Do you feel like
that there was a subconscious knowledge of it that you suppressed?" asked Smith. "Or, if not a knowledge of it, that's why
you would question once in a while, maybe you would suspect the
situation that you kept suppressed the whole time, Linda?"

Smith was asking for a psychological insight from Linda, and
at first he got agreement. "Yes," she answered innocently. But
then she found religion.

"Last night the Lord showed me I was suppressing that. I did
suspect it and I—you know, I couldn't admit it because it just
seemed like—you know, I—well, like last night I really felt it, I
failed her."

Linda was sitting not ten feet from Shelley. And during the
course of her testimony she tried to talk directly to her daughter,
telling her that she needed to forgive Bobby so that she could
become a whole person again and they could be a family again.
And in her hand, clutched tight, was her Bible, for everybody to
see.

But when her attorney asked her, "What is your concern for
Shelley, Linda?" Linda lost all composure.

"Shelley has not come to the place where she forgives her
mother, and Shelley has not come to the place where she forgives
her father," Linda said, her voice rising. She even leaned forward
in the witness stand and pointed at Shelley. "If Shelley does not
come to God and ask Him to forgive her, she's going to go to hell,
and that's the most important thing to me."

* * *

While the jury deliberated, Rod Squires, Dale Williams and Spike Pattillo went to lunch.

"We always go eat barbecue. That's kind of a tradition that we've got. We feel like it is kind of good luck to go eat barbecue when the jury starts deliberating," said Rod Squires. "We talk about how long, and we'll make predictions sometimes on what we think will happen. I don't remember doing it on this case, though."

Williams says he wanted a white-collar jury. "They were intelligent and I didn't want people that I thought would be swayed by the simple emotionalism of [Bobby's] religious conversion. I wanted people that I thought were smart enough to be able to see through that."

The jury got the case at eleven in the morning. By two that afternoon, including a lunch break, the twelve men and women had finished their business. Most of the time was spent on formalities such as picking a jury foreman and reading the list of rules by which juries in the State of Texas were governed.

"We were cautious and wanted to do everything by the book," recalled Storrs. "We didn't want this thing to get messed up and Shelley's chances get blown or the trial to have to be redone."

After procedural questions, the biggest part of the jurors' deliberations concerned whether they could award Shelley *more* than the ten million dollars she had requested. "Somebody in the group wanted to give her five million more," recalled Storrs.

No one bought Bobby Sessions' religious conversion as a meaningful one. Nor did anyone believe that Shelley was in any way a willing party to "the affair." In fact, some jurors were offended by the suggestion that it was an affair.

Linda Sessions came under some scrutiny. "How could a mother allow this to happen and not intervene?" asked one man rhetorically.

"The money," said someone else, summarizing the feeling of the jurors toward Shelley's parents. "She chose sides. She made the choice and her choice was with Bobby Sessions and not with her daughter."

And it bothered the jurors that Bobby Sessions, who had been convicted of a crime, was sent to "a country-club detention center," as Krienke described it, "and Shelley was sent to the Lester Roloff home in Corpus Christi. It was pretty explicit who was having the fun and who wasn't."

When the nine men and three women walked slowly back into the courtroom that afternoon, Shelley could barely contain herself.

Krienke looked directly at Shelley when he stood to read the verdict. "We find for the plaintiff," he said. Shelley broke out in a big grin. When Judge Johnson asked about damages, Krienke responded, "Five million dollars." When he asked about compensation, Krienke said, "Five million dollars."

Jack Smith wanted the jurors individually polled. Sharon Storrs didn't like the idea. "I was scared to death," she recalled. "I was scared of Sessions. Because several times Shelley had painted a picture that he was extremely manipulative and he had a lot of influence in a lot of places and I almost had him pictured as a member of the Mafia. He was just, to me, sinister, evil."

And Storrs didn't stay around after the verdict. "I was too shaken up and I felt like I'd better get on out. I was getting ready to break down. I just passed her and gave her a quick hug and told her good luck and walked out as quickly as I could. There were TV cameras and I certainly did not want to be on TV. I was in no condition to talk to anybody and I just wanted to get my car and go home."

Shelley was standing at the box, crying. She had won. After all these years of secrecy and shame, she had stood up to her father, her family and her community to deliver a message. He was wrong. She was right. She smiled.

Bobby Sessions was wrong. Shelley Sessions was right.

EPILOGUE

After the verdict finding her father liable for $10 million, Shelley was ecstatic. She hugged jurors, her attorneys and Betty and James Duvall—the only members of the family who had stood by her. When she and the Duvalls arrived back at the Hilton, where they had stayed during the week of the trial, porters and clerks congratulated her. The trio packed up, got into James' van, and sailed back to Corsicana in high spirits.

Shelley and her attorneys had achieved something extraordinary. In Utah, several years previously, there had been a case in which an incest victim had sued and won, but the reward had been nominal. Never before in the history of American jurisprudence had an incest victim received substantial compensation for her sufferings. Shelley's steadfastness in facing the publicity of a trial, and in confronting her wealthy and socially prominent father and family, had won her many admirers. "You were one hundred percent right to take the action you did," wrote a woman from Dallas, "and I respect the courage it took to bring all of your pain into the open."

Shelley would also need considerable courage to face what still awaited her.

Within a few months of the verdict, Shelley married a boy she had gone to school with—and within a few months she regretted it. Her husband quickly revealed his true nature and became an abuser.

At the same time Bobby filed for bankruptcy. The $10 million judgment suddenly seemed in jeopardy. The filing also proved beyond doubt to Shelley that Bobby's tears at the trial were fake. If he were sorry for what he did, he wouldn't try an end-run around his legal obligation. And the bankruptcy claim set in motion yet another legal process, one that took almost two years to resolve. Bobby held his ground, making a settlement the only feasible way for Shelley to get any of the court-awarded judgment.

Shelley's husband was also escalating his attacks on her. His anger bore no relation to what Shelley did. If he didn't like his dinner, or the channel that the TV was tuned to, or the tone in which Shelley asked him how his day went, his fists flew. One day Shelley was doing the dishes when she saw him in the backyard throwing rocks at the dog. She tapped on the window, motioning for him to stop—instead, he turned and heaved a rock through the kitchen window, spraying his young wife with splintered glass.

Then came a day, after work, when he announced that he still had a girlfriend in Houston. Then he disappeared. When he came back, two days later, Shelley was on the phone with Williams and Squires partner, Spike Pattillo, the attorney with the firm that was handling her post-verdict affairs, telling him she wanted a divorce.

"I just married you for the money, anyway," Shelley's husband sneered. Since Shelley wasn't going to get any, he said, there wasn't any reason to keep up pretenses.

That was another low point in Shelley's strained life, one that added to the burden of isolation that her father had forced on her. Whom could she trust?

Fortunately, her attorneys doggedly pursued her case. Finally, in her scrapbook, Shelley noted: "June 16, 1987, settled lawsuit. Thank God it's over!"

She had to settle for property that was worth barely a tenth of the amount awarded her by the Waco jury—"But it was still worth it."

In the settlement Shelley, then twenty years old, took control of her father's construction business and the ranch. The cattle— including her prized Brahman—and farm equipment were sold at auction, and the mansion and acreage put up for sale (asking price: $1.87 million). All the equipment from the Circle S Construction Company was auctioned off on a hot Saturday in a vacant lot across the street from McDonald's in Corsicana. Shelley had to attend, writing each sale down, to make sure that her dad didn't try anything sneaky. He didn't.

In fact, the agreement with Bobby even seemed to bring about the possibility of reconciliation. He had asked for, and Shelley had acquiesed in, the right to live in the ranch house until the property was sold. He would pay for the utilities, but would have free rent in return for keeping up the property. Shelley and her new boyfriend, Robbie Shelton, even visited on occasion.

I was beginning to think that maybe we could work it out, and sort of be together again. Despite her anger Shelley wanted to relate to her father. The trial had given her a means to vent her rage as well as reach out.

Linda and Bobby, meanwhile, maintained their religious connections in town, and members of the church seemed friendly to Shelley when she ran into them there. *Maybe he had changed.*

Gradually, Shelley's life reached another plateau. She and Shelton fell in love and decided to get married. She had first met him through her boss at Cato's clothing store in Corsicana, where Shelley worked for $3.75 per hour as a cashier. Her boss's boyfriend was Robbie's roommate. And although they had talked a couple of times, it wasn't until March 22, 1986, that they really met. "She scared me to death," was how Robbie remembers that night. She was bruised and bleeding—the result of her husband's fists.

After the divorce, Shelley and Robbie hooked up again. Soon it was for good. They were married on September 26, 1987, only a few months after the settlement with her father. "I knew that he wasn't after my money," she says of Robbie, a softspoken young man who has worked at the K Mart distribution center for seven years.

The newlyweds used some of the auction proceeds to buy a new three-bedroom house on the western edge of Corsicana. And it wasn't long before Shelley became pregnant. On December 17, 1988, at 9:32 P.M., Brandon Shelton weighed into the world, a month early, at 7 pounds 10 ounces. It wasn't an easy birth. Because Shelley's blood pressure had jumped up during the eighth month of her pregnancy, doctors had decided to induce labor. Then, when dilation stopped at 9 (on a scale of 10), they had to bring Brandon out by cesarean. It was an ordeal. *Robbie was with me the whole time. He even took pictures in the delivery room.*

But Brandon didn't come out of the woods immediately. Later that night he had to be rushed to Baylor Medical Center in Dallas because his lungs were collapsing. Corsicana had no ventilator. Robbie went along, but Shelley was still too weak to move. She waited two days before her doctors would let her travel to see her baby. *Even then, I was in a wheelchair. And I had these terrible headaches, which were from getting up too soon.* By the end of the week, little Brandon was off the ventilator and on his way home. "I love him," says Shelley. "He's got his dad's blue eyes and his ears; he has my mouth and chin."

Today Shelley, Robbie and Brandon are living a quiet life in Corsicana. Robbie still works at K Mart. Shelley teaches aerobics at the local YMCA two times a week and the rest of the time minds her house and baby. Both she and Robbie love vehicles. And, although they traded in their motorcycle, they still have a Corvette, a four-wheel-drive Chevy pickup (with forty-one-inch tires!), a Blazer ("for Brandon") and a boat for waterskiing.

It was while riding in the boat on Cedar Lake one afternoon that Shelley was to begin a reassessment. She spotted her mother on a large cabin cruiser. When the two boats joined, Shelley was given a tour by the owners. Refrigerator, stove, bed, full bath. A beauty. But the shocker came when Linda Sessions told her daughter that Bobby—who was not aboard—was buying the boat. *It was just another one of those things that made me believe that he had money stashed in Switzerland. For someone who didn't have a job, he seemed to have plenty of money.* And drove another wedge in the already splintering reconciliation.

Shelley and Robbie still visited her dad and mom from time to time, and the family still got together on family occasions. It was not a big happy family, however; it never had been. But at least the air had seemed clearer. For a time. But true clarity proved elusive. *I really wanted to believe that my dad had changed.*

But he hadn't. His obsession with control kept surfacing. Sessions constantly pulled Robbie aside at family gatherings and apologized for what he had done, as if trying to test Shelley's husband and ingratiate himself into their lives. And he would call Shelley on the phone to tell her he hoped that the family would get back together like before. *He even sang a song to me on the phone.* Even Shelley's mother was beginning to notice how Bobby would stare at his daughter. *My mom even remarked on how he was looking at me. And I said, "Doesn't it ever bother you to be sleeping with someone who has done that to your own daughter?" And she said, "I don't sleep with him. But God told me to stay." Now, isn't that a little weird! What a way to make a marriage.*

At one point Linda convinced Bobby to go to a religious counselor in Oklahoma for two days. *When they got back, my mom said, "God made him fine." It's all just crazy.*

One of the continuing sources of sorrow for Shelley is her younger brother, who still seems confused by what has happened to his family. *I asked my mom if she ever told him what happened. She said, "Yes." But when I asked her what she said to him, she said, "I told him that his father had done something wrong to Shelley, and that he had been forgiven and everything is okay."*

There were times when Michael lashed out at Shelley for causing all the family's problems and for taking all the family's money. At other times he seemed overwhelmed by the rigid discipline Bobby submitted him to. He asked Shelley if he could move in with her.

My mom and dad think that this can all be forgotten and we can just be one big happy family. But he hasn't changed. And it can never be the way they want it.

As Shelley gains more control over her own life, and more insight into it, she may at least be able to have things the way *she* wants them. She has settled into life in Corsicana, and in many ways it is completely different from what preceded it. Around town she notices many of the people who figured so prominently in her life, but she isn't close to any of them except James and Betty Duvall, who talk with her almost every day. Cherry Layfield calls Shelley from time to time just to find out how she's doing. Ricky Layfield still works in construction. He and Shelley will wave if they pass each other, but they make no point of getting in touch. Henry Edgington has moved to another Texas parish and hasn't spoken with Shelley since the trial.

Gradually, Shelley is making a family. And she sees nothing odd about trying to do that in the same county that her father and former abuser still lives in. She sees no reason to move because of what he did. It is as much her home as his. Shelley has never lost sight of the fact that he was wrong and she was right. And for Shelley Sessions, it's been worth the fight.

There are many people who had a hand in ensuring that this book became a reality. I am most grateful to my wife, Janet, for her constant support and patience. Dorothy Gilbert lit all the early fires, lending the enthusiasm, confidence and sensitivity that this kind of project dearly needs—without her there would be no book. Kelli Pryor offered invaluable research assistance in the early stages. John Drape was there again, in the middle and at the end, a vigilant, expert and invaluable practitioner of the four Rs—reporting, researching, reading and remembering. And Stacy Creamer, our editor, kept the faith.

Thanks to all of you.

—Peter Meyer